The critics love

2019 Ringo Award nominee for best writer (Richard Dent), best artist (Ronilson Freire), and best letterer (Taylor Esposito).

"This story is written by Richard Dent much like Jack Kirby drew his art: incredibly detailed and sophisticated, yet not cluttered or confusing at all. The story is very complex, yet it unfolds naturally and clearly, and I never once felt lost. Myopia #1 is indeed a complex pattern of events, with intriguing players being set in place to reveal a full story of incredible scale."

— SPECULATIVE 66

"Myopia is fascinating to follow. Dent leads us along with a Lost-like quality, generating plenty of interest by continuing to develop the story with layers of mysteries. This chapter continues to set the stage for a world that has plenty of story left to give, and the fact that it ends with a suspenseful — (enter sound effect from the end of each Lost episode) MYOPIA."

— S.T. LAKATA, FANBASE PRESS

"As a work of science fiction, there's plenty about Myopia: The Rise of the Domes to recommend. It's commentary on social media dependency and global climate change are clear without being preachy or distracting from the larger narrative. The mysteries it sets up are compelling, and the setting feels fully realized."

— MIKE MCNULTY, BAMSMACKPOW.COM

"Myopia: Rise of the Domes is a solid read for those who like their sci-fi hard and wordy. The story is interesting, the characters are well formed, and the art is absolutely gorgeous. I can recommend this to anyone up for this kind of heavy reading. Feel free to check it out."

— JOSHUA DAVISON, BLEEDING COOL

"Myopia – The Rise of the Domes #1 remains an enjoyable and original experience. The character of Chase is a compelling central figure, and his relationship with Matthew is interesting and well-drawn. The supporting characters have personality and well-defined motivations, and the threat of the domes and the already-sinister machinations of Formula Media are intriguing. I don't want to spoil the story, but the reader can feel it building momentum throughout, and the shape of the issue serves to accentuate an increasing sense of foreboding."

— JEREMY RADICK, CAPELESSCRUSADER.ORG

Nick Barrucci — CEO / Publisher
Juan Collado — President / COO
Brandon Dante Primavera — V.P. of IT and Operations

Joe Rybandt — Executive Editor
Matt Idelson — Senior Editor

Alexis Persson — Creative Director
Cathleen Heard — Senior Graphic Designer
Nick Pentz — Graphic Designer

Alan Payne — V.P. of Sales and Marketing
Vince Letterio — Director of Direct Market Sales
Rex Wang — Director of Sales and Branding
Vincent Faust — Marketing Coordinator

Jim Kuhoric — Vice President of Product Development
Jay Spence — Director of Product Development
Mariano Nicieza — Director of Research & Development

KICKSTARTER
DYNAMITE

Online at www.DYNAMITE.com
On Facebook /Dynamitecomics
Instagram /Dynamitecomics
On Twitter @dynamitecomics

ISBN: 978-1-5241-1943-0   Second Pinting 10 9 8 7 6 5 4 3 2

Myopia™ Volume 1. Myopia copyright 2022 Richard Dent. All Rights Reserved. "Dynamite" and "Dynamite Entertainment" are ®, and the "DE Logo" is ™ and ©, Dynamite Entertainment. All Rights Reserved. All names, characters, events, and locales in this publication are entirely fictional. Any resemblance to actual persons (living or dead), events or places, without satiric intent, is coincidental. No portion of this book may be reproduced by any means (digital or print) without the written permission of Dynamite Entertainment except for review purposes. **Printed in Hong Kong**

For information regarding press, media rights, foreign rights, licensing, promotions, and advertising e-mail: marketing@dynamite.com

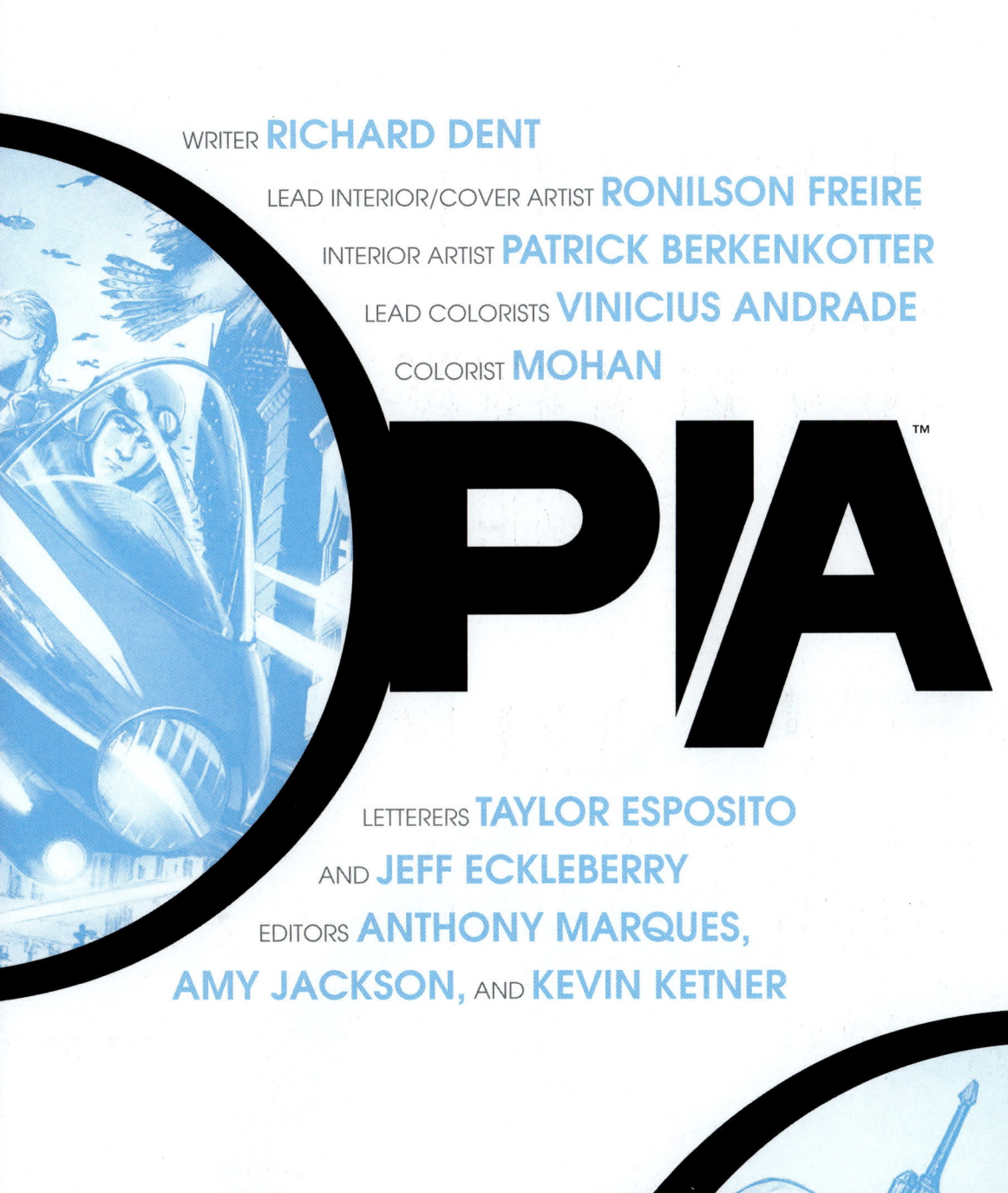

WRITER **RICHARD DENT**
LEAD INTERIOR/COVER ARTIST **RONILSON FREIRE**
INTERIOR ARTIST **PATRICK BERKENKOTTER**
LEAD COLORISTS **VINICIUS ANDRADE**
COLORIST **MOHAN**

LETTERERS **TAYLOR ESPOSITO**
AND **JEFF ECKLEBERRY**
EDITORS **ANTHONY MARQUES,**
AMY JACKSON, AND **KEVIN KETNER**

Special thanks to Victor Serrano, April Glatzel, Daniel Lambert, and Robyn Kaufman for their proofreading help; Nick, Juan and the Dynamite team as well as everyone else who supported this project on Kickstarter™, including Dean Koontz, Jim Butcher, Margaret Atwood, Aimee Bender, Ruth Connell, Mark Sheppard, Scott Koblish, Bruce McAllister, Neil Gaiman, and George R.R. Martin.

I would also like to thank my mother and everyone else who lent their emotional support along this journey.

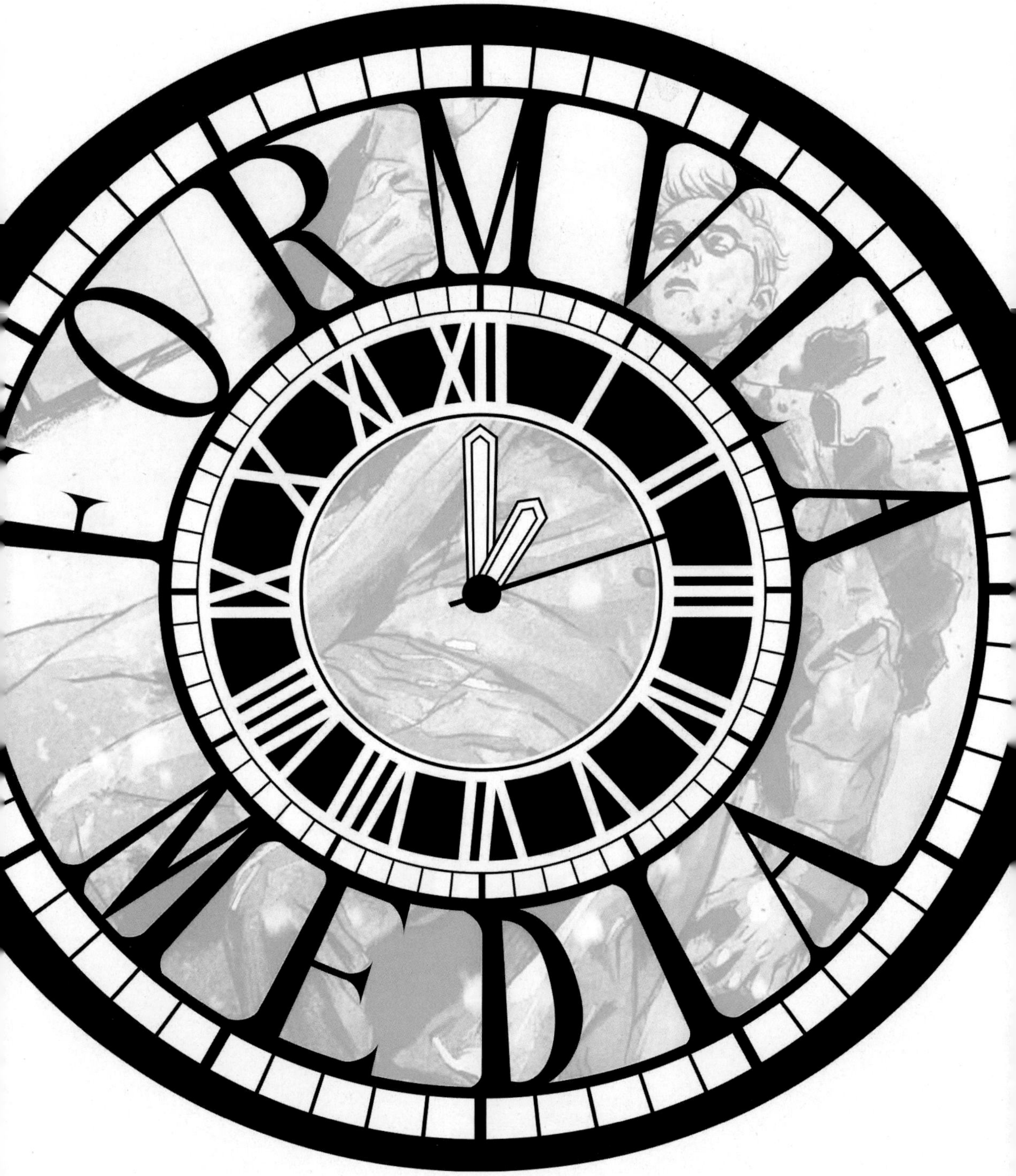

CHAPTER 01

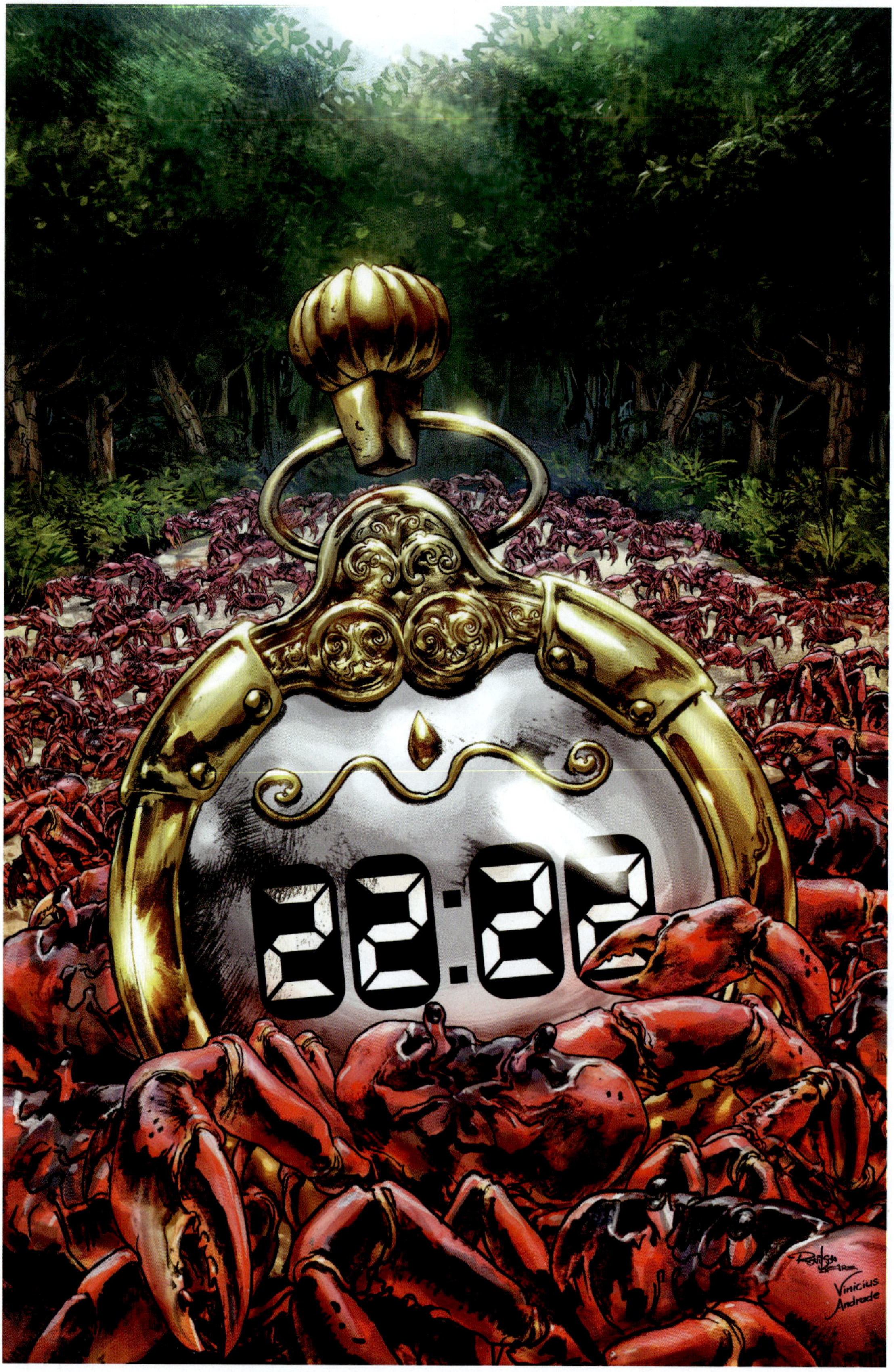
22:22
Vinicius Andrade

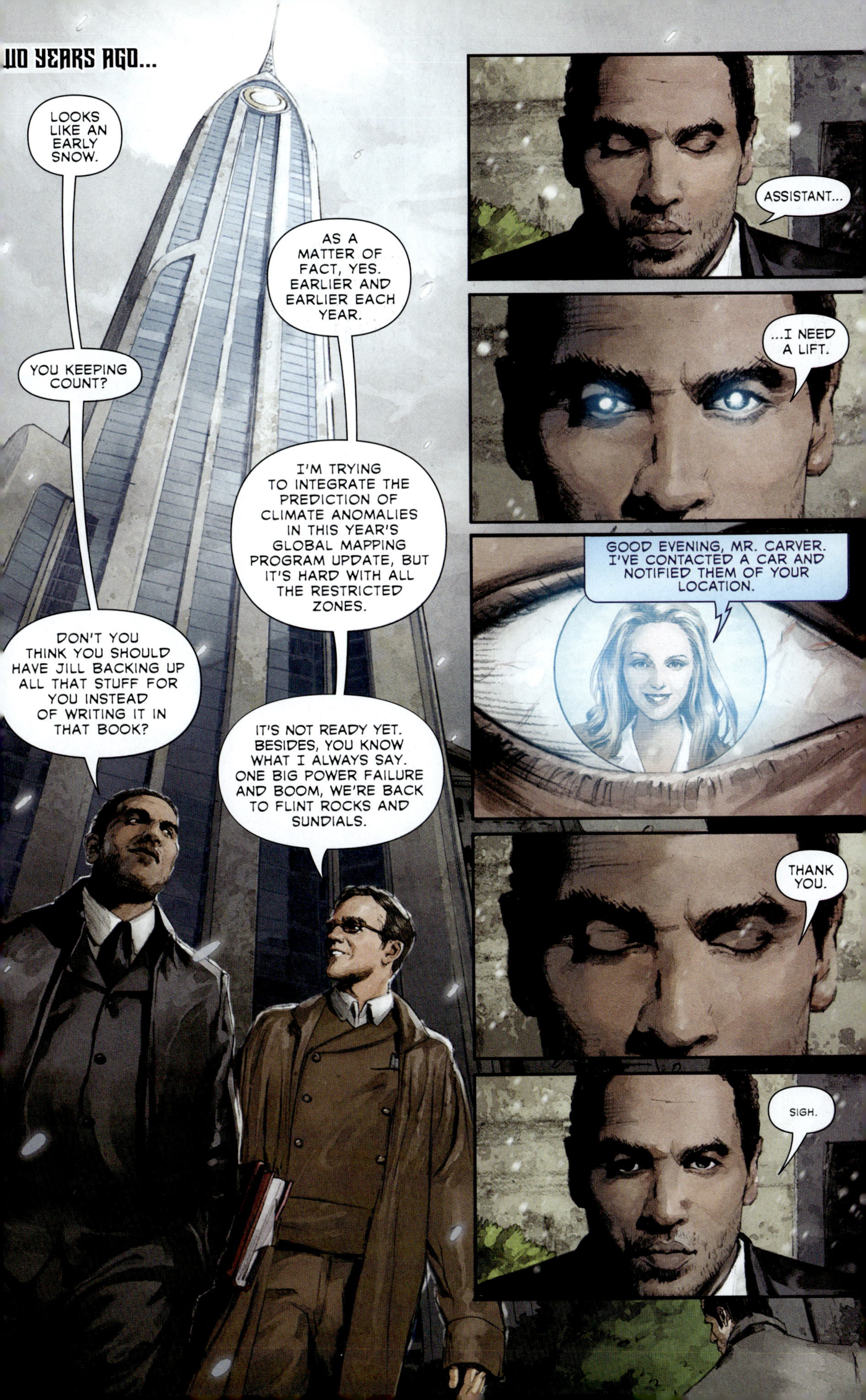
10 YEARS AGO...
LOOKS LIKE AN EARLY SNOW.
AS A MATTER OF FACT, YES. EARLIER AND EARLIER EACH YEAR.
YOU KEEPING COUNT?
I'M TRYING TO INTEGRATE THE PREDICTION OF CLIMATE ANOMALIES IN THIS YEAR'S GLOBAL MAPPING PROGRAM UPDATE, BUT IT'S HARD WITH ALL THE RESTRICTED ZONES.
DON'T YOU THINK YOU SHOULD HAVE JILL BACKING UP ALL THAT STUFF FOR YOU INSTEAD OF WRITING IT IN THAT BOOK?
IT'S NOT READY YET. BESIDES, YOU KNOW WHAT I ALWAYS SAY. ONE BIG POWER FAILURE AND BOOM, WE'RE BACK TO FLINT ROCKS AND SUNDIALS.
ASSISTANT...
...I NEED A LIFT.
GOOD EVENING, MR. CARVER. I'VE CONTACTED A CAR AND NOTIFIED THEM OF YOUR LOCATION.
THANK YOU.
SIGH.

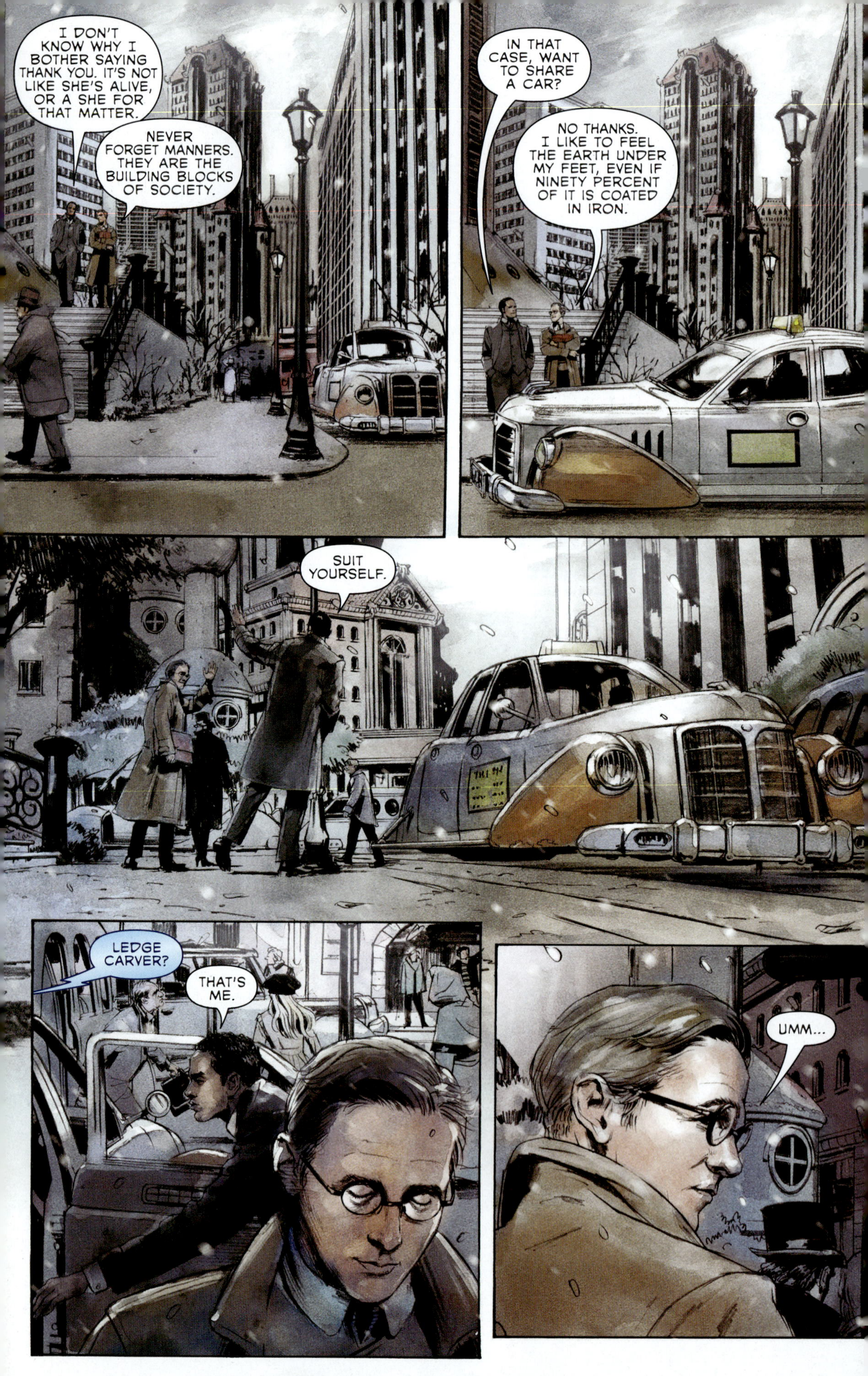
I DON'T KNOW WHY I BOTHER SAYING THANK YOU. IT'S NOT LIKE SHE'S ALIVE, OR A SHE FOR THAT MATTER.
NEVER FORGET MANNERS. THEY ARE THE BUILDING BLOCKS OF SOCIETY.
IN THAT CASE, WANT TO SHARE A CAR?
NO THANKS. I LIKE TO FEEL THE EARTH UNDER MY FEET, EVEN IF NINETY PERCENT OF IT IS COATED IN IRON.
SUIT YOURSELF.
LEDGE CARVER?
THAT'S ME.
UMM...

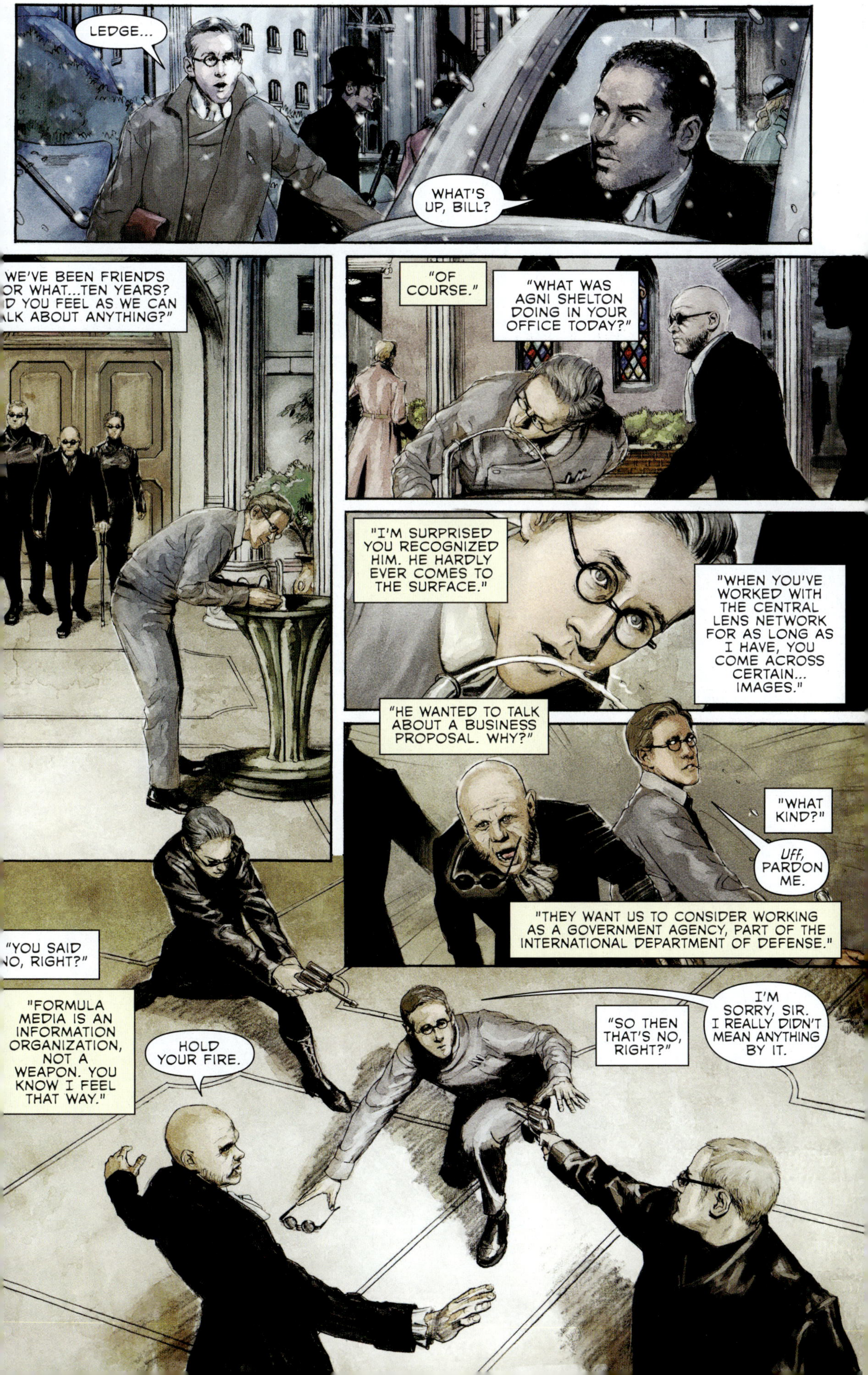
LEDGE...
WHAT'S UP, BILL?
WE'VE BEEN FRIENDS OR WHAT...TEN YEARS? D YOU FEEL AS WE CAN LK ABOUT ANYTHING?"
"OF COURSE."
"WHAT WAS AGNI SHELTON DOING IN YOUR OFFICE TODAY?"
"I'M SURPRISED YOU RECOGNIZED HIM. HE HARDLY EVER COMES TO THE SURFACE."
"WHEN YOU'VE WORKED WITH THE CENTRAL LENS NETWORK FOR AS LONG AS I HAVE, YOU COME ACROSS CERTAIN... IMAGES."
"HE WANTED TO TALK ABOUT A BUSINESS PROPOSAL. WHY?"
"WHAT KIND?"
UFF, PARDON ME.
"THEY WANT US TO CONSIDER WORKING AS A GOVERNMENT AGENCY, PART OF THE INTERNATIONAL DEPARTMENT OF DEFENSE."
"YOU SAID NO, RIGHT?"
"FORMULA MEDIA IS AN INFORMATION ORGANIZATION, NOT A WEAPON. YOU KNOW I FEEL THAT WAY."
HOLD YOUR FIRE.
"SO THEN THAT'S NO, RIGHT?"
I'M SORRY, SIR. I REALLY DIDN'T MEAN ANYTHING BY IT.

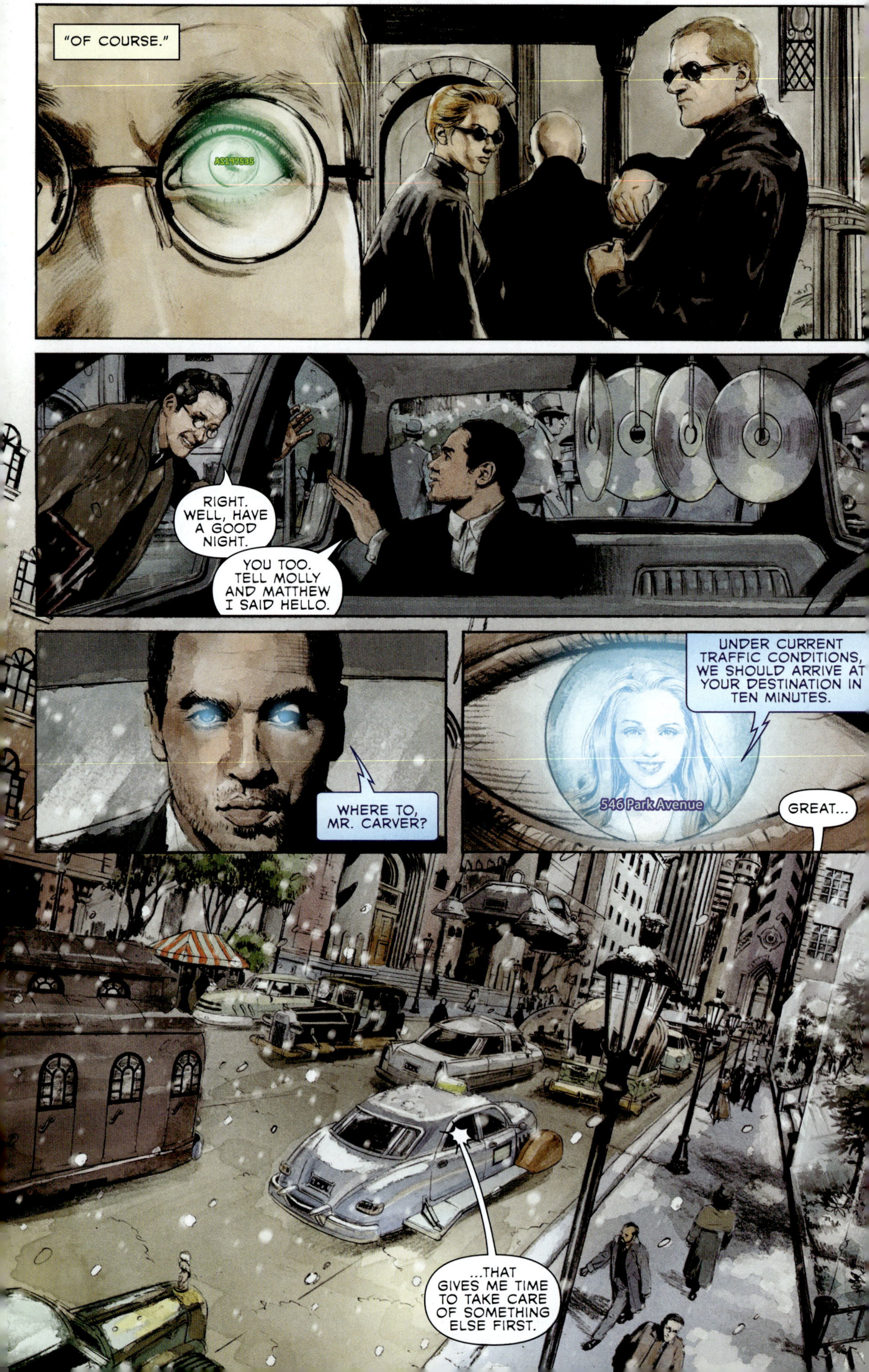
"OF COURSE."
RIGHT. WELL, HAVE A GOOD NIGHT.
YOU TOO. TELL MOLLY AND MATTHEW I SAID HELLO.
WHERE TO, MR. CARVER?
546 Park Avenue
UNDER CURRENT TRAFFIC CONDITIONS, WE SHOULD ARRIVE AT YOUR DESTINATION IN TEN MINUTES.
GREAT...
...THAT GIVES ME TIME TO TAKE CARE OF SOMETHING ELSE FIRST.

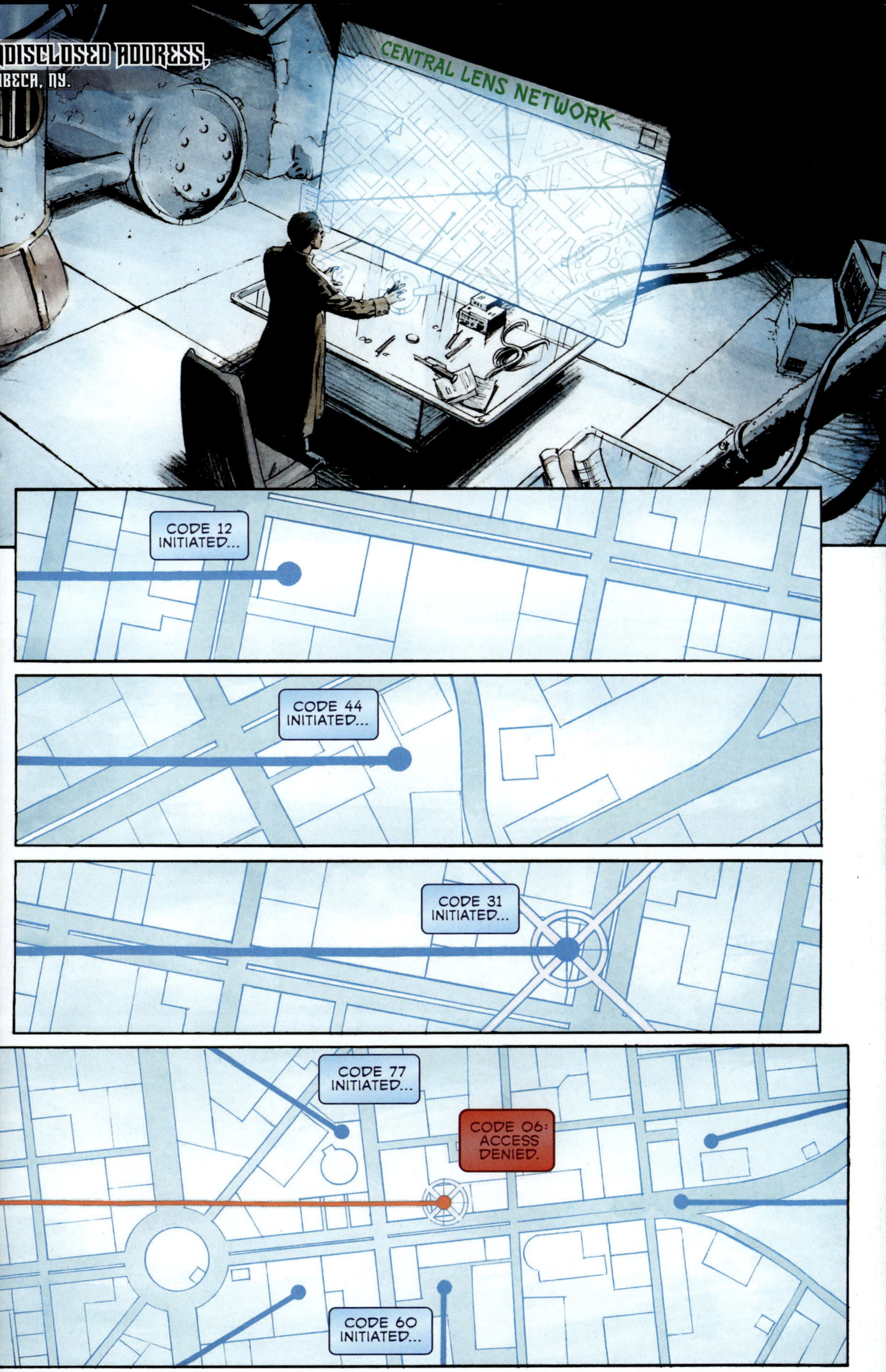

DISCLOSED ADDRESS,
BECA, NY.
CENTRAL LENS NETWORK
CODE 12 INITIATED...
CODE 44 INITIATED...
CODE 31 INITIATED...
CODE 77 INITIATED...
CODE 06: ACCESS DENIED.
CODE 60 INITIATED...

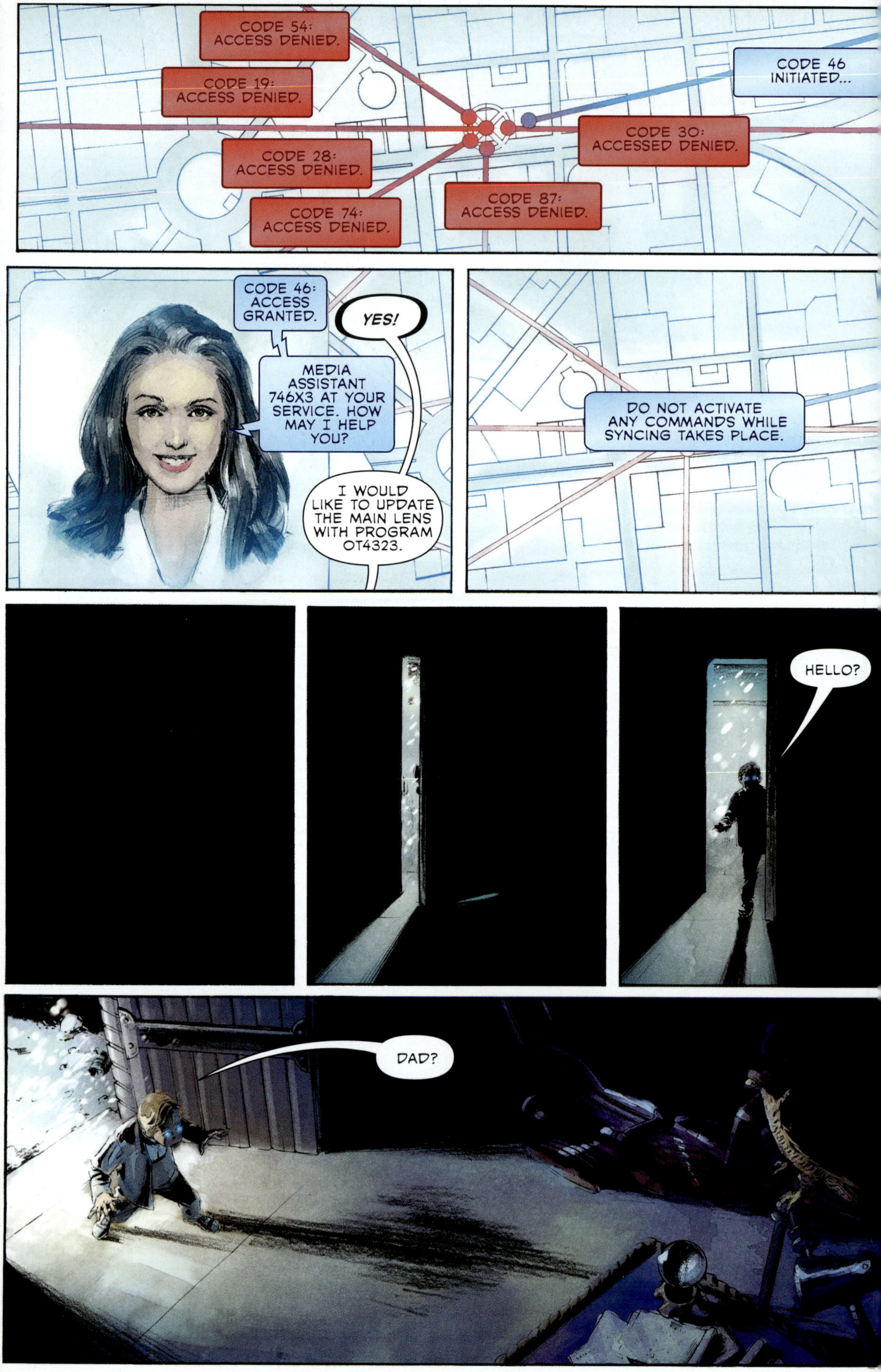
CODE 54: ACCESS DENIED.
CODE 19: ACCESS DENIED.
CODE 28: ACCESS DENIED.
CODE 74: ACCESS DENIED.
CODE 87: ACCESS DENIED.
CODE 30: ACCESSED DENIED.
CODE 46 INITIATED...
CODE 46: ACCESS GRANTED.
MEDIA ASSISTANT 746X3 AT YOUR SERVICE. HOW MAY I HELP YOU?
YES!
I WOULD LIKE TO UPDATE THE MAIN LENS WITH PROGRAM OT4323.
DO NOT ACTIVATE ANY COMMANDS WHILE SYNCING TAKES PLACE.
HELLO?
DAD?

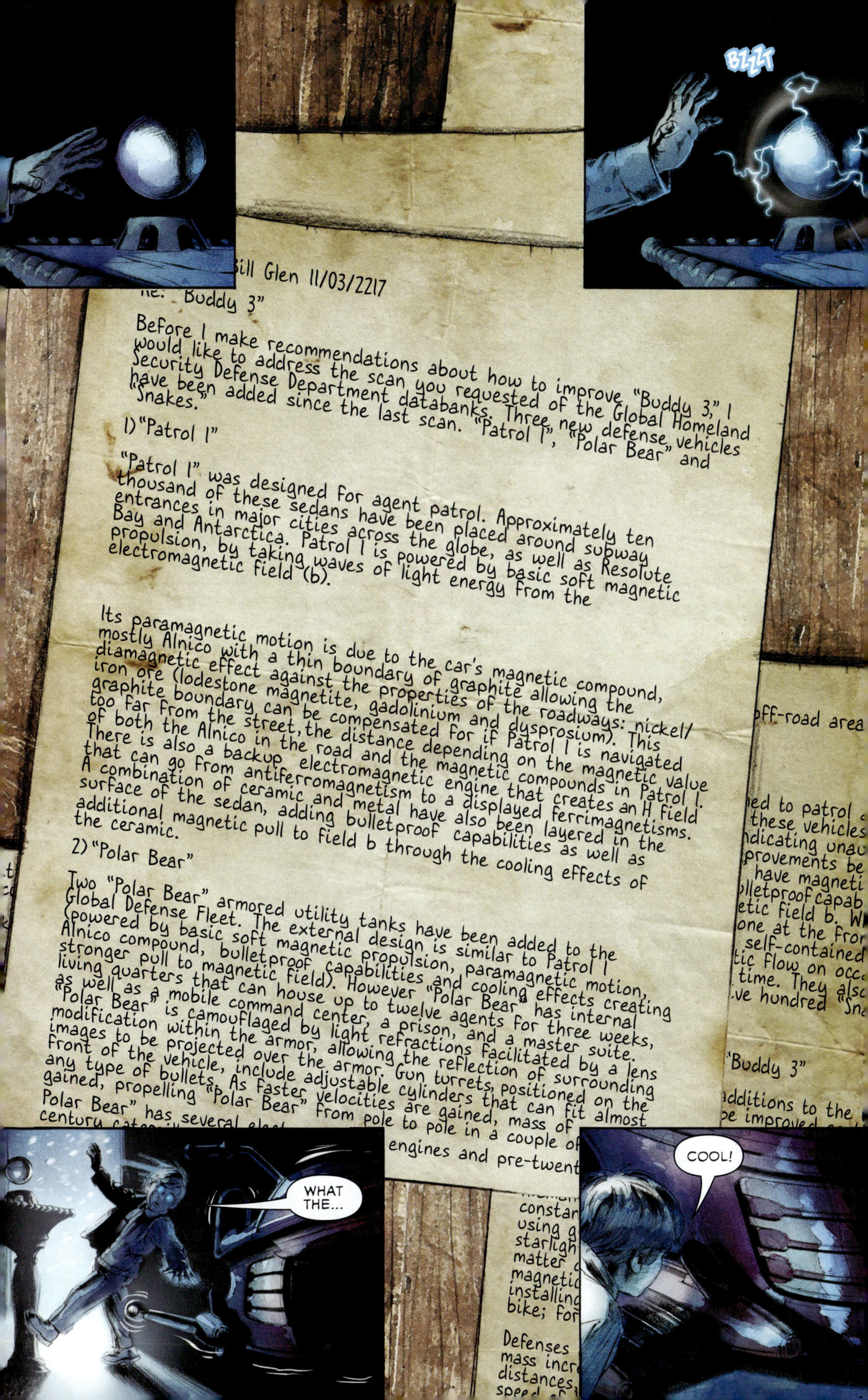
Bill Glen 11/03/2217
Re: "Buddy 3"

Before I make recommendations about how to improve "Buddy 3," I would like to address the scan you requested of the Global Homeland Security Defense Department databanks. Three new defense vehicles have been added since the last scan. "Patrol 1", "Polar Bear" and "Snakes."

1) "Patrol 1"

"Patrol 1" was designed for agent patrol. Approximately ten thousand of these sedans have been placed around subway entrances in major cities across the globe, as well as Resolute Bay and Antarctica. Patrol 1 is powered by basic soft magnetic propulsion, by taking waves of light energy from the electromagnetic field (b).

Its paramagnetic motion is due to the car's magnetic compound, mostly Alnico with a thin boundary of graphite allowing the diamagnetic effect against the properties of the roadways: nickel/iron ore (lodestone magnetite, gadolinium and dysprosium). This graphite boundary can be compensated for if Patrol 1 is navigated too far from the street, the distance depending on the magnetic value of both the Alnico in the road and the magnetic compounds in Patrol 1. There is also a backup electromagnetic engine that creates an H field that can go from antiferromagnetism to a displayed ferrimagnetisms. A combination of ceramic and metal have also been layered in the surface of the sedan, adding bulletproof capabilities as well as additional magnetic pull to field b through the cooling effects of the ceramic.

2) "Polar Bear"

Two "Polar Bear" armored utility tanks have been added to the Global Defense Fleet. The external design is similar to Patrol 1 (powered by basic soft magnetic propulsion, paramagnetic motion, Alnico compound, bulletproof capabilities and cooling effects creating stronger pull to magnetic field). However "Polar Bear" has internal living quarters that can house up to twelve agents for three weeks, as well as a mobile command center, a prison, and a master suite. "Polar Bear" is camouflaged by light refractions facilitated by a lens modification within the armor, allowing the reflection of surrounding images to be projected over the armor. Gun turrets, positioned on the front of the vehicle, include adjustable cylinders that can fit almost any type of bullets. As faster velocities are gained, mass of gained, propelling "Polar Bear" from pole to pole in a couple of

Polar Bear" has several ele ... engines and pre-twent

century
BZZZT
WHAT THE...
COOL!

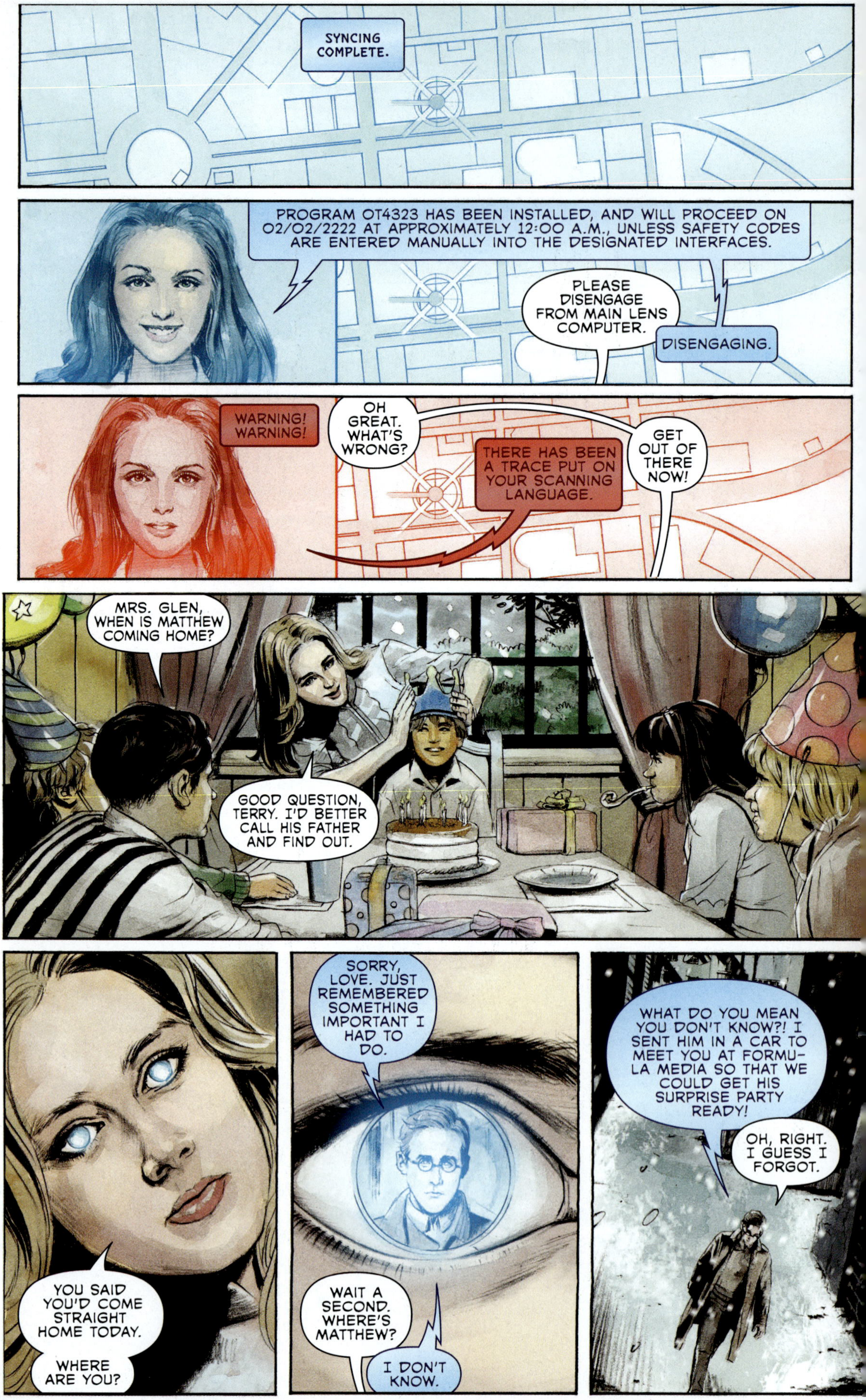

SYNCING COMPLETE.
PROGRAM OT4323 HAS BEEN INSTALLED, AND WILL PROCEED ON 02/02/2222 AT APPROXIMATELY 12:00 A.M., UNLESS SAFETY CODES ARE ENTERED MANUALLY INTO THE DESIGNATED INTERFACES.
PLEASE DISENGAGE FROM MAIN LENS COMPUTER.
DISENGAGING.
WARNING! WARNING!
OH GREAT. WHAT'S WRONG?
THERE HAS BEEN A TRACE PUT ON YOUR SCANNING LANGUAGE.
GET OUT OF THERE NOW!
MRS. GLEN, WHEN IS MATTHEW COMING HOME?
GOOD QUESTION, TERRY. I'D BETTER CALL HIS FATHER AND FIND OUT.
YOU SAID YOU'D COME STRAIGHT HOME TODAY.
WHERE ARE YOU?
SORRY, LOVE. JUST REMEMBERED SOMETHING IMPORTANT I HAD TO DO.
WAIT A SECOND. WHERE'S MATTHEW?
I DON'T KNOW.
WHAT DO YOU MEAN YOU DON'T KNOW?! I SENT HIM IN A CAR TO MEET YOU AT FORMULA MEDIA SO THAT WE COULD GET HIS SURPRISE PARTY READY!
OH, RIGHT. I GUESS I FORGOT.

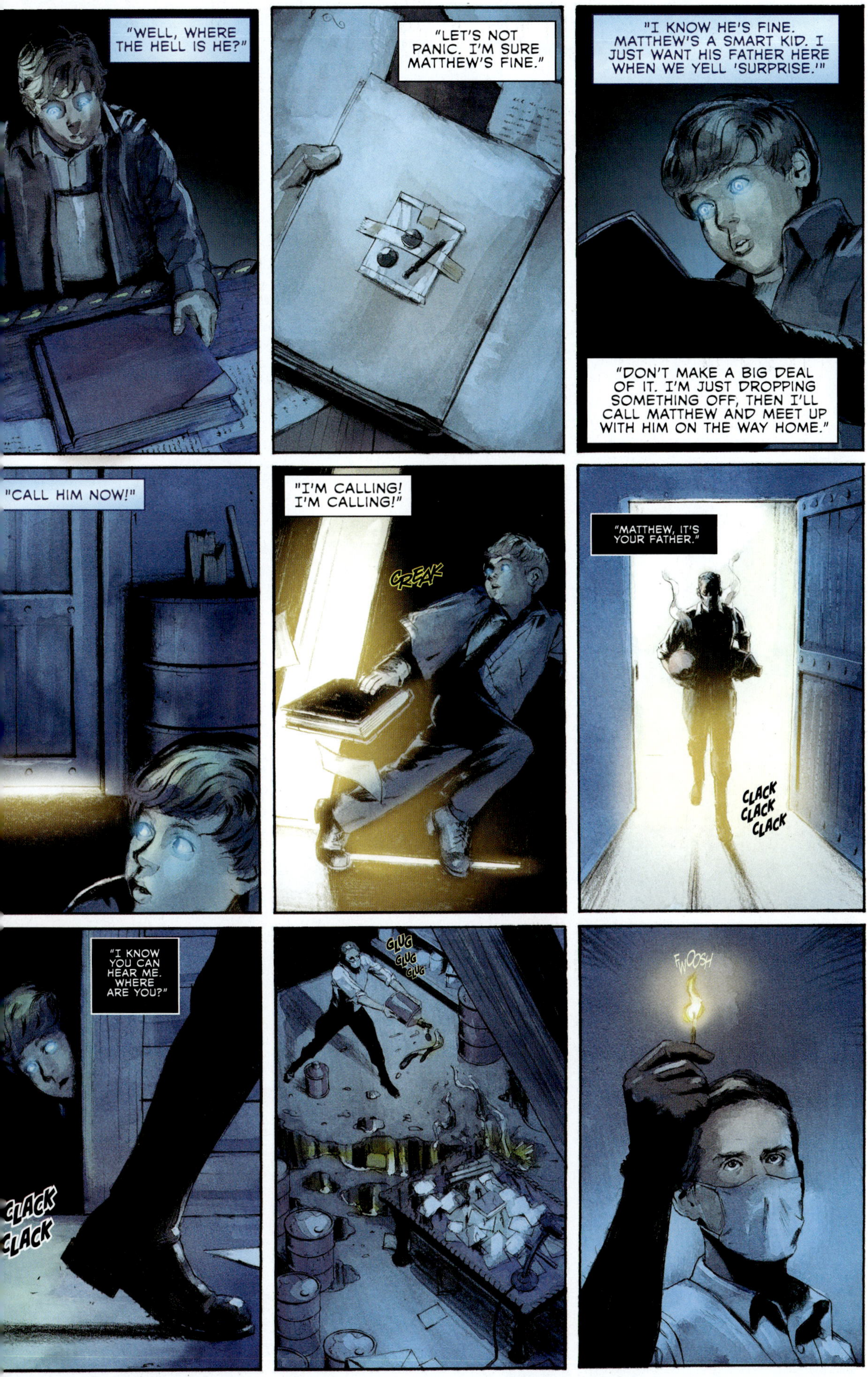
"WELL, WHERE THE HELL IS HE?"
"LET'S NOT PANIC. I'M SURE MATTHEW'S FINE."
"I KNOW HE'S FINE. MATTHEW'S A SMART KID. I JUST WANT HIS FATHER HERE WHEN WE YELL 'SURPRISE.'"
"DON'T MAKE A BIG DEAL OF IT. I'M JUST DROPPING SOMETHING OFF, THEN I'LL CALL MATTHEW AND MEET UP WITH HIM ON THE WAY HOME."
"CALL HIM NOW!"
"I'M CALLING! I'M CALLING!"
CREAK
"MATTHEW, IT'S YOUR FATHER."
CLACK CLACK CLACK
"I KNOW YOU CAN HEAR ME. WHERE ARE YOU?"
CLACK CLACK
GLUG GLUG GLUG
FWOOSH

SHRIEK!

Amous
President of Shelton
Mining Corporation
1467 Shelton Drive
Houston, Texas 77001
United Americas

September 5th, 2212

...er Armand
...tionale
...e De ...ersite
...Paris 07 SP
...tates of Europe

...rime Minister:

We have received your latest report about the fallen satellites, and I can assure you that the temporary flickers in the magnetic field are nothing more than an adjustment period to our new mining schedule. If you have noticed, since the magnetic flow was transferred into the nickel foundations laid in London, Paris, and Madrid, energy prices are at an all-time low, even compared to when oil was abundan... however, as with any new technology, there are sure to be "bugs" that need to be worked out.

When addressing the United Nations about these satellites, please keep this in mind, and remind the delegates how magnetic energy is powering the world.

Amou...

Amous Shelto...
President of Shelton
Mining Corporation
1467 Shelton Drive
Houston, Texas 77001
United Americas

June 12th, 2214

President Kamau
Kapital Street
Garki Area 11, P.m.B. 25
Garki, Abuja
Nigeria
United Continent of Africa

Dear President Kamau:

First I would like to congratulate you on your recent victory. Nigeria is an exciting location for a new federal government, and ... am sure that you will go far in helping Africa realize its place in ... world of magnetic energy. On that note I do want to express my sympathies on the slow pace it has taken for Shelton Mining Operations to help Africa expand its infrastructure and energy supply. At the present time we are unable to fund any nickel upgrades without first receiving payment in full for the last installment of roadways.

In regards to your concern about the scorching of the Serengeti... the extinction of several game animals--please understand tha... the magnetic field is going through an adjustment period and certain parts of the planet will inevitable feel the scorch of sola... storms more than others. We take all data into consideration before moving ahead with mining developments and none of ou... staff scientists predicted a "mass extinction." To that end we would like to donate infrastructure to your city of Garki, not o... show our confidence that you will find the means to bring Afr... into the future with the rest of the world, but also as a token o... recognition for the price your continent has paid in the name ... progress.

...resident Kamau, I went to the Serengeti to hunt the elephan... ...st a couple years ago. I can't believe they are gone. I am tru...

...s Shelton
...Shelto...

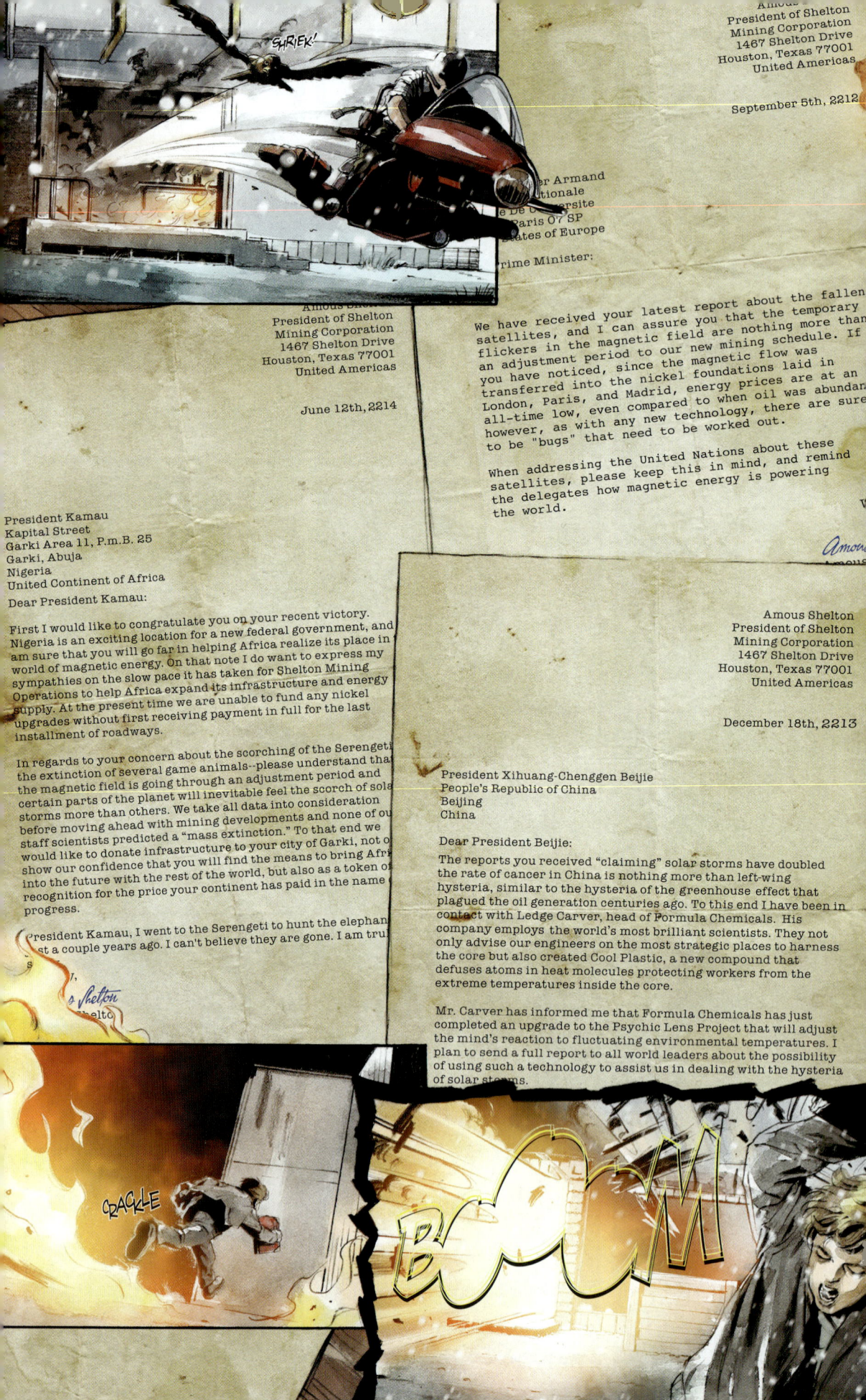

Amous Shelton
President of Shelton
Mining Corporation
1467 Shelton Drive
Houston, Texas 77001
United Americas

December 18th, 2213

President Xihuang-Chenggen Beijie
People's Republic of China
Beijing
China

Dear President Beijie:

The reports you received "claiming" solar storms have doubled the rate of cancer in China is nothing more than left-wing hysteria, similar to the hysteria of the greenhouse effect that plagued the oil generation centuries ago. To this end I have been in contact with Ledge Carver, head of Formula Chemicals. His company employs the world's most brilliant scientists. They not only advise our engineers on the most strategic places to harness the core but also created Cool Plastic, a new compound that defuses atoms in heat molecules protecting workers from the extreme temperatures inside the core.

Mr. Carver has informed me that Formula Chemicals has just completed an upgrade to the Psychic Lens Project that will adjust the mind's reaction to fluctuating environmental temperatures. I plan to send a full report to all world leaders about the possibility of using such a technology to assist us in dealing with the hysteria of solar st...s.

CRACKLE

BOOM

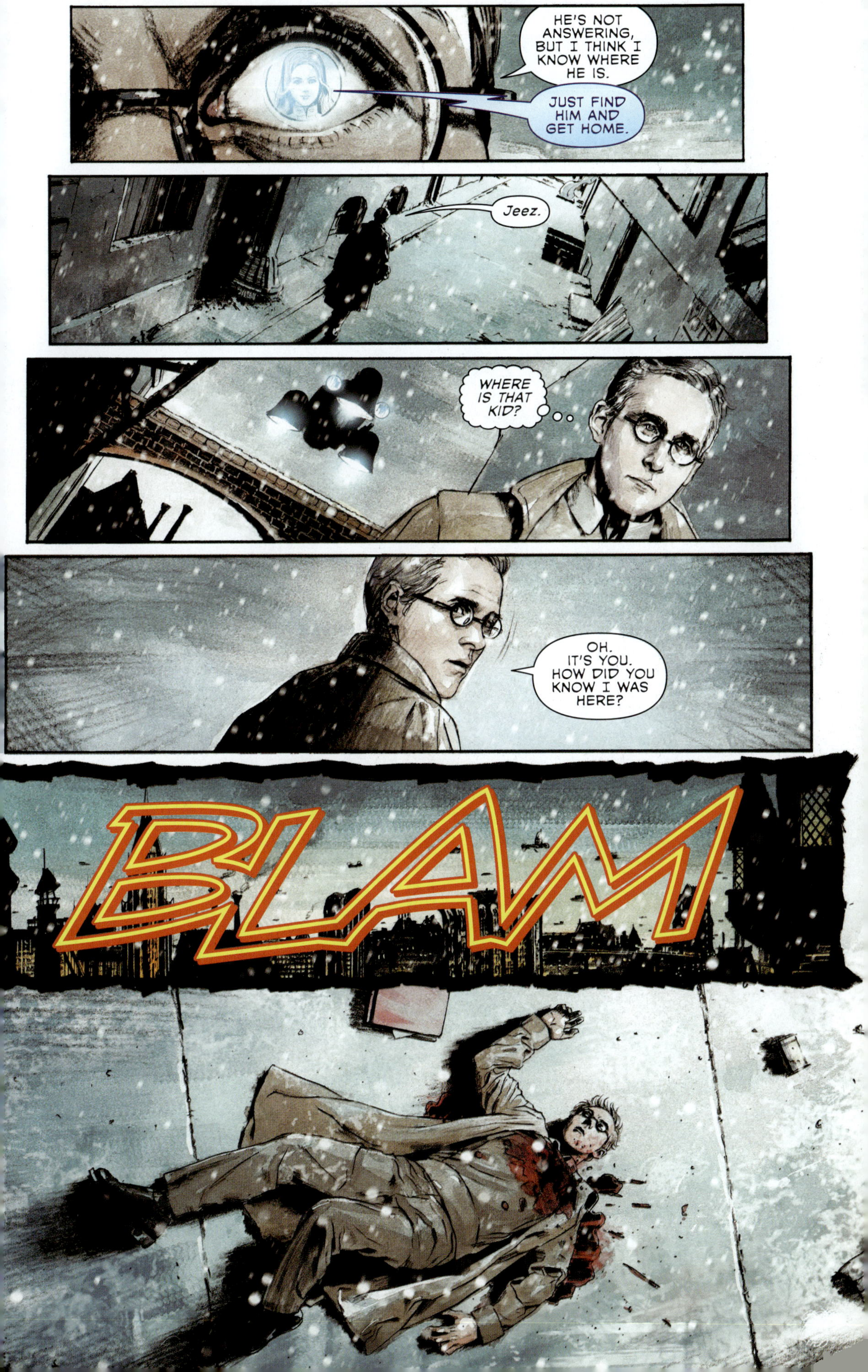
HE'S NOT ANSWERING, BUT I THINK I KNOW WHERE HE IS.
JUST FIND HIM AND GET HOME.
Jeez.
WHERE IS THAT KID?
OH. IT'S YOU. HOW DID YOU KNOW I WAS HERE?
BLAM

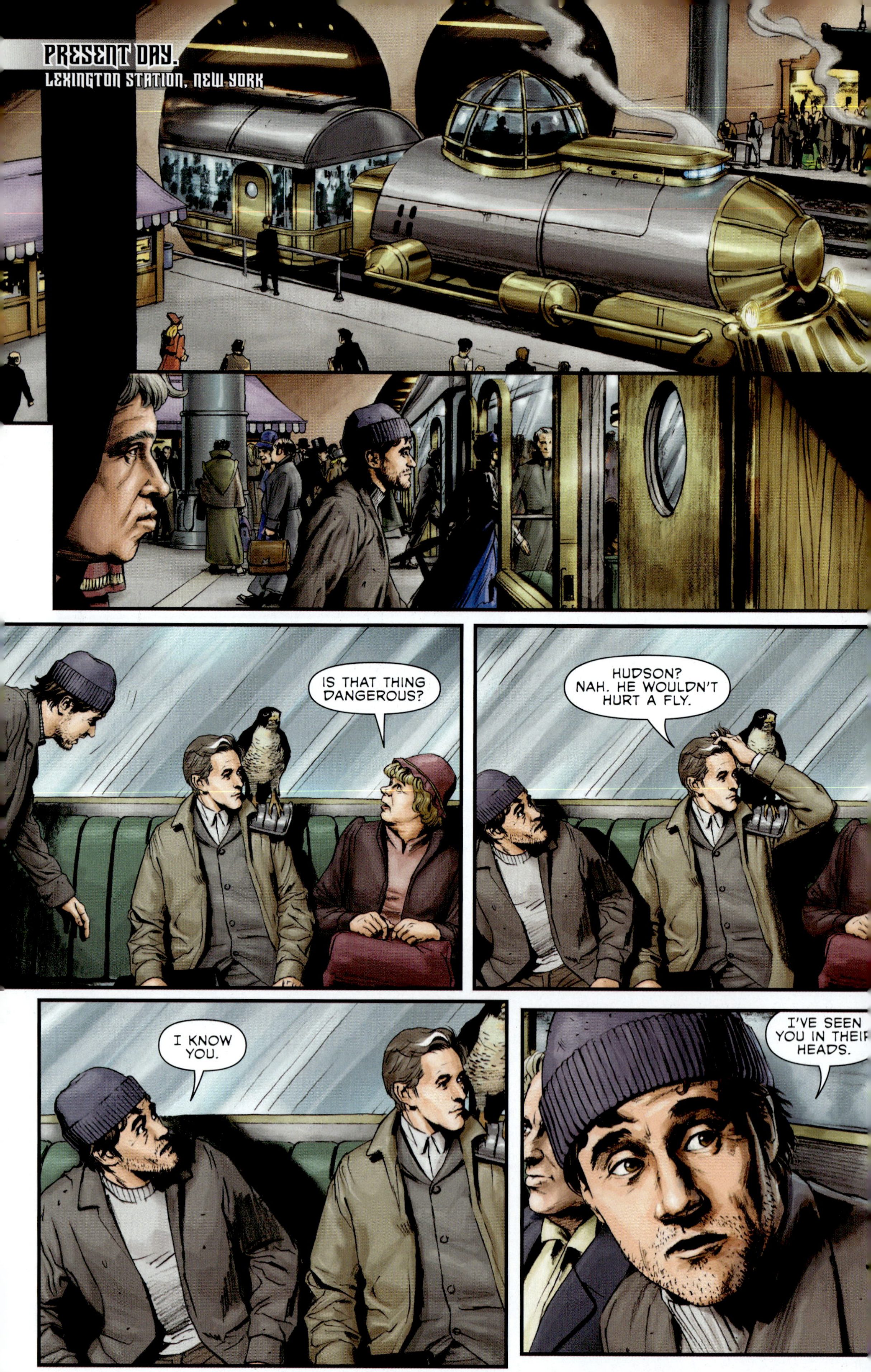
PRESENT DAY.
LEXINGTON STATION, NEW YORK
IS THAT THING DANGEROUS?
HUDSON? NAH. HE WOULDN'T HURT A FLY.
I KNOW YOU.
I'VE SEEN YOU IN THEIR HEADS.

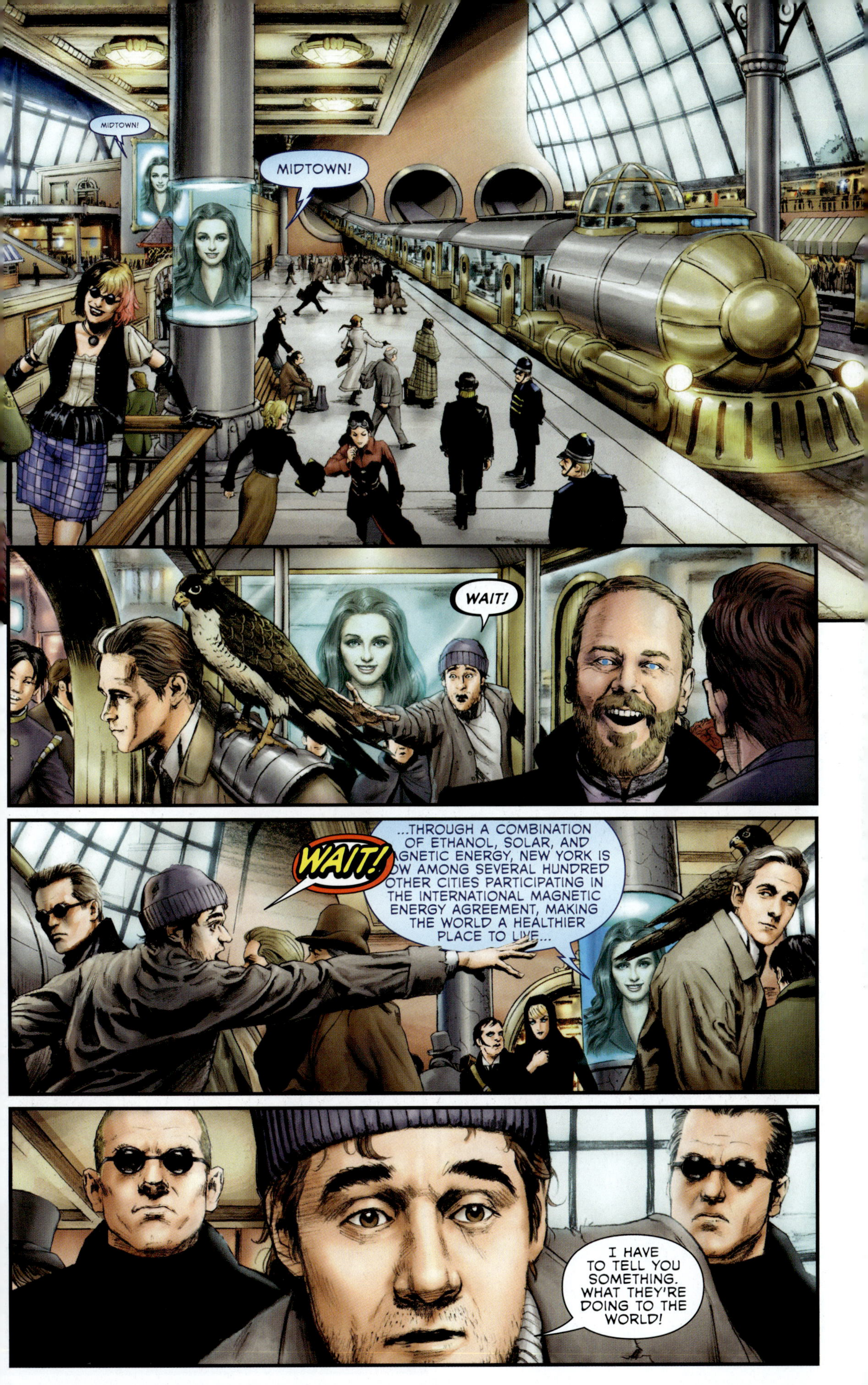
MIDTOWN!
MIDTOWN!
WAIT!
WAIT!
...THROUGH A COMBINATION OF ETHANOL, SOLAR, AND MAGNETIC ENERGY, NEW YORK IS NOW AMONG SEVERAL HUNDRED OTHER CITIES PARTICIPATING IN THE INTERNATIONAL MAGNETIC ENERGY AGREEMENT, MAKING THE WORLD A HEALTHIER PLACE TO LIVE...
I HAVE TO TELL YOU SOMETHING. WHAT THEY'RE DOING TO THE WORLD!

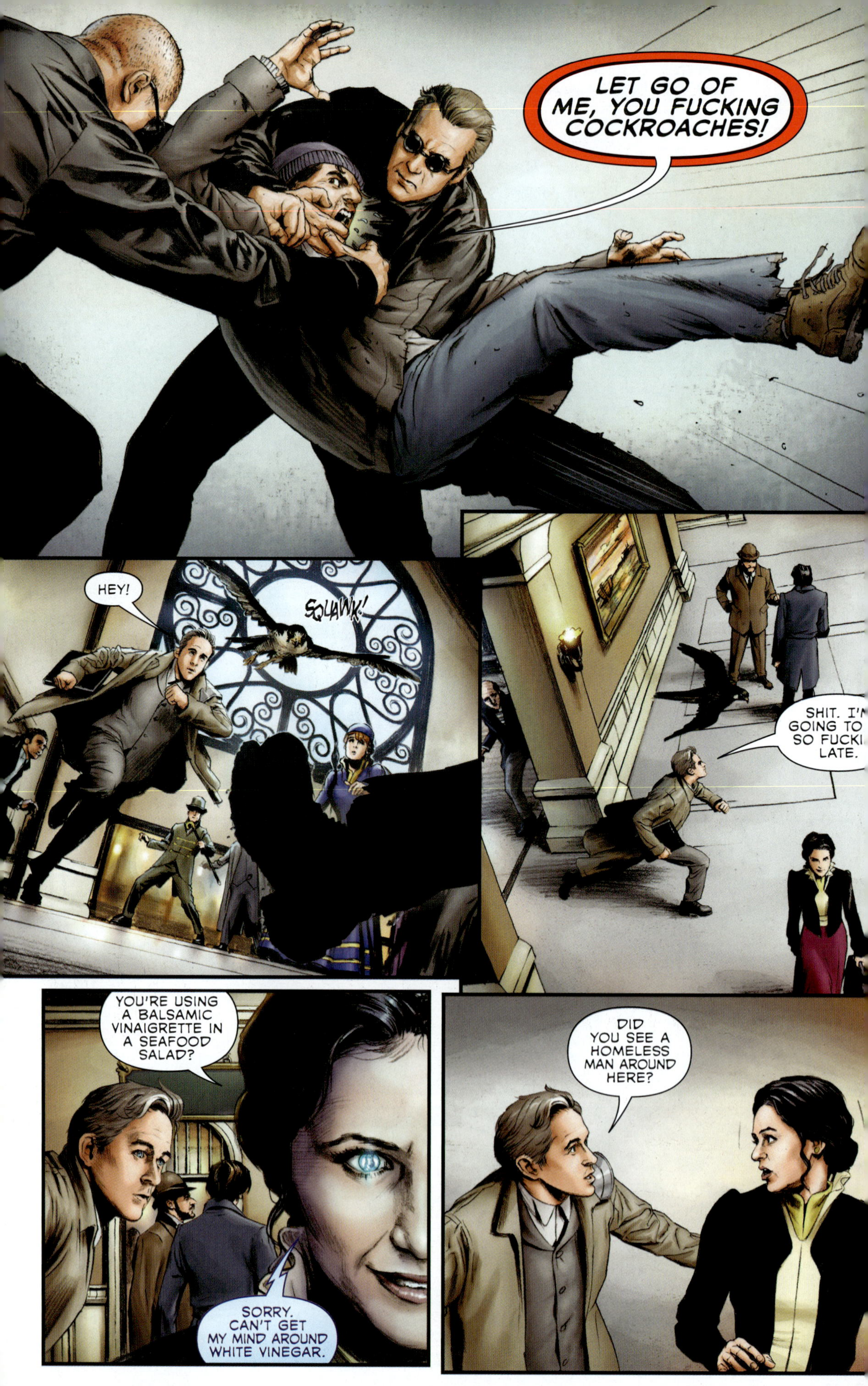
LET GO OF ME, YOU FUCKING COCKROACHES!
HEY!
SQUAWK!
SHIT. I'M GOING TO SO FUCKI LATE.
YOU'RE USING A BALSAMIC VINAIGRETTE IN A SEAFOOD SALAD?
SORRY. CAN'T GET MY MIND AROUND WHITE VINEGAR.
DID YOU SEE A HOMELESS MAN AROUND HERE?

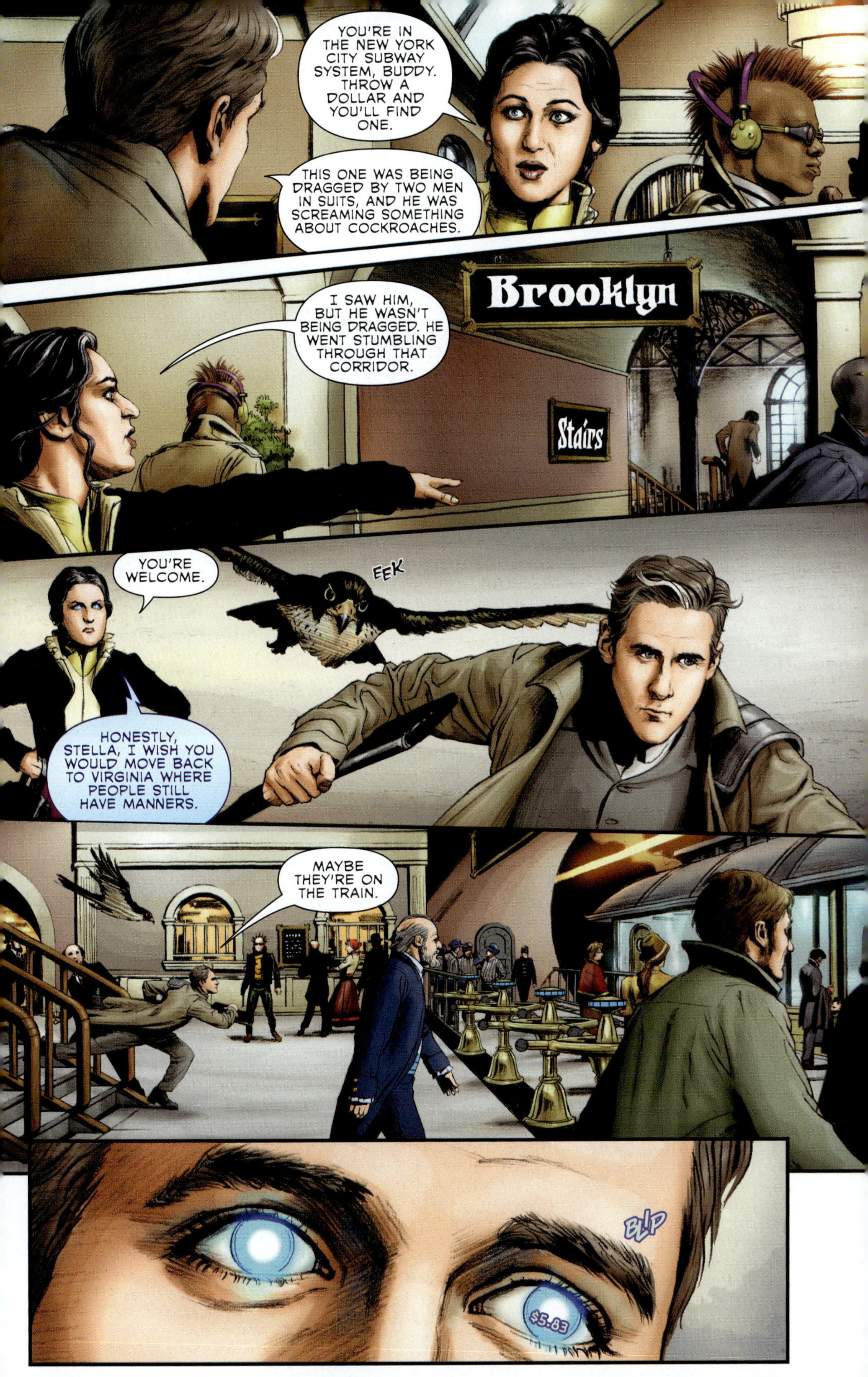
YOU'RE IN THE NEW YORK CITY SUBWAY SYSTEM, BUDDY. THROW A DOLLAR AND YOU'LL FIND ONE.
THIS ONE WAS BEING DRAGGED BY TWO MEN IN SUITS, AND HE WAS SCREAMING SOMETHING ABOUT COCKROACHES.
Brooklyn
I SAW HIM, BUT HE WASN'T BEING DRAGGED. HE WENT STUMBLING THROUGH THAT CORRIDOR.
Stairs
YOU'RE WELCOME.
EEK
HONESTLY, STELLA, I WISH YOU WOULD MOVE BACK TO VIRGINIA WHERE PEOPLE STILL HAVE MANNERS.
MAYBE THEY'RE ON THE TRAIN.
BLIP
$5.83

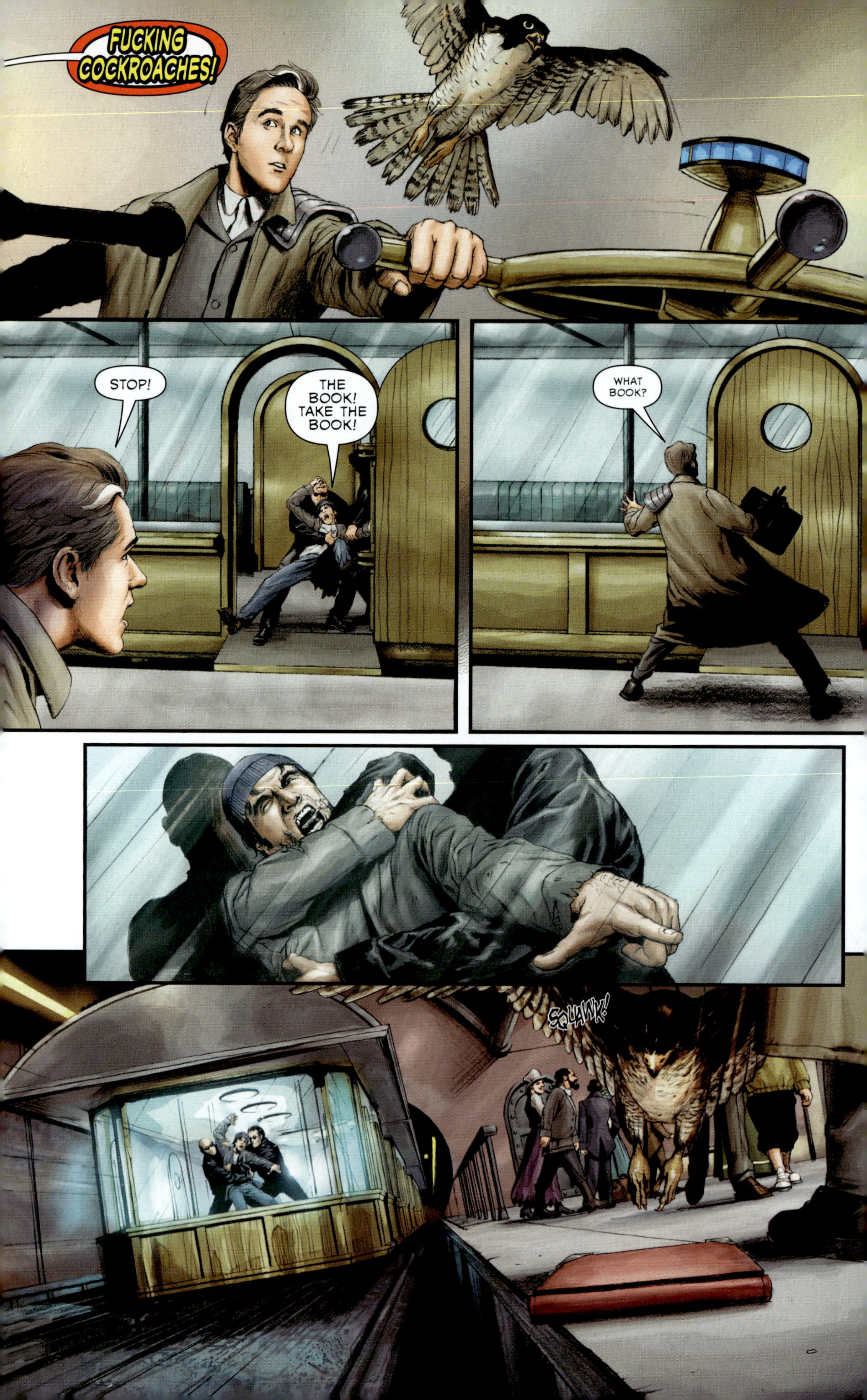
FUCKING COCKROACHES!
STOP!
THE BOOK! TAKE THE BOOK!
WHAT BOOK?
SQUAWK!

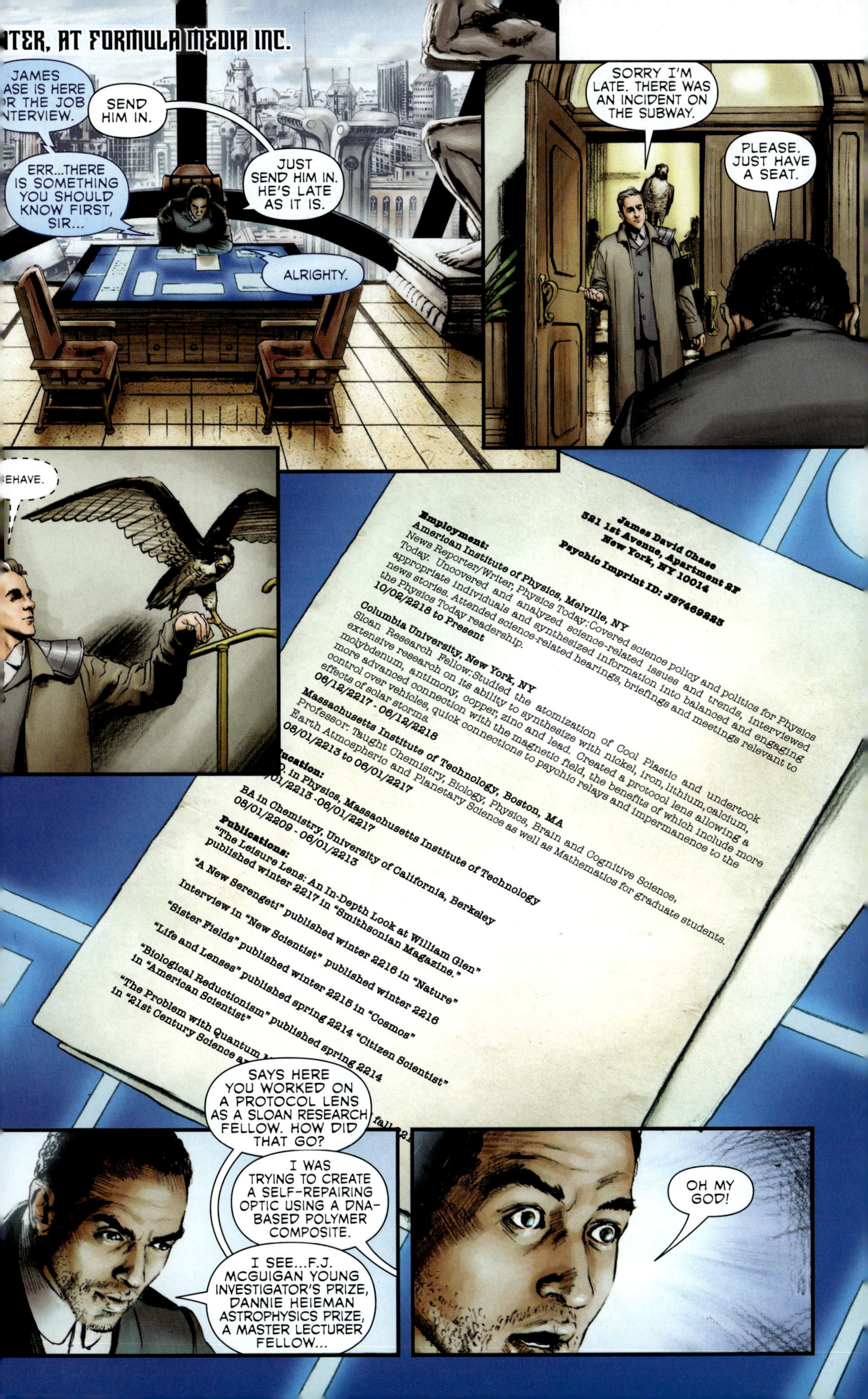

TER, AT FORMULA MEDIA INC.
JAMES
ASE IS HERE
R THE JOB
TERVIEW.
SEND HIM IN.
ERR...THERE IS SOMETHING YOU SHOULD KNOW FIRST, SIR...
JUST SEND HIM IN. HE'S LATE AS IT IS.
ALRIGHTY.
SORRY I'M LATE. THERE WAS AN INCIDENT ON THE SUBWAY.
PLEASE. JUST HAVE A SEAT.
EHAVE.
James David Chase
321 1st Avenue, Apartment 2F
New York, NY 10014
Psychic Imprint ID: JS7469223
Employment:
American Institute of Physics, Melville, NY
News Reporter/Writer, Physics Today: Covered science policy and politics for Physics Today. Uncovered and analyzed science-related issues and trends, interviewed appropriate individuals and synthesized information into balanced and engaging news stories. Attended science-related hearings, briefings and meetings relevant to the Physics Today readership.
10/02/2218 to Present
Columbia University, New York, NY
Sloan Research Fellow: Studied the atomization of Cool Plastic and undertook extensive research on its ability to synthesize with nickel, iron, lithium, calcium, molybdenum, antimony, copper, zinc and lead. Created a protocol lens allowing a more advanced connection with the magnetic field, the benefits of which include more control over vehicles, quick connections to psychic relays and impermanence to the effects of solar storms.
06/12/2217 - 06/12/2218
Massachusetts Institute of Technology, Boston, MA
Professor: Taught Chemistry, Biology, Physics, Brain and Cognitive Science, Earth Atmospheric and Planetary Science as well as Mathematics for graduate students.
08/01/2213 to 06/01/2217
ucation:
. in Physics, Massachusetts Institute of Technology
01/2213 -06/01/2217
BA in Chemistry, University of California, Berkeley
08/01/2209 - 06/01/2213
Publications:
"The Leisure Lens: An In-Depth Look at William Glen" published winter 2217 in "Smithsonian Magazine."
"A New Serengeti" published winter 2216 in "Nature"
Interview in "New Scientist" published winter 2216
"Sister Fields" published winter 2215 in "Cosmos"
"Life and Lenses" published spring 2214 "Citizen Scientist"
"Biological Reductionism" published spring 2214 in "American Scientist"
"The Problem with Quantum
in "21st Century Science a
fall 221
SAYS HERE YOU WORKED ON A PROTOCOL LENS AS A SLOAN RESEARCH FELLOW. HOW DID THAT GO?
I WAS TRYING TO CREATE A SELF-REPAIRING OPTIC USING A DNA-BASED POLYMER COMPOSITE.
I SEE...F.J. MCGUIGAN YOUNG INVESTIGATOR'S PRIZE, DANNIE HEIEMAN ASTROPHYSICS PRIZE, A MASTER LECTURER FELLOW...
OH MY GOD!

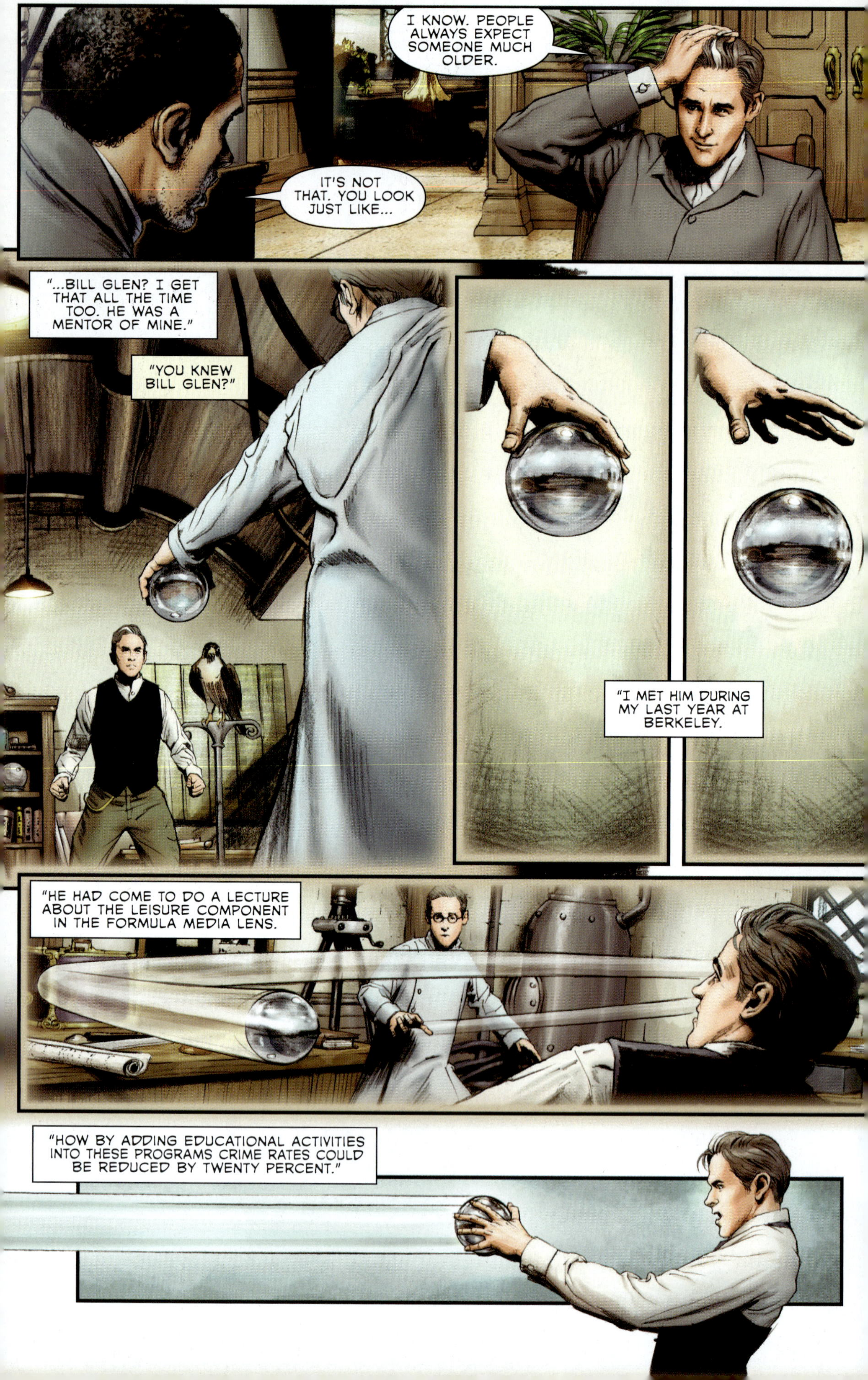

I KNOW. PEOPLE ALWAYS EXPECT SOMEONE MUCH OLDER.
IT'S NOT THAT. YOU LOOK JUST LIKE...
"...BILL GLEN? I GET THAT ALL THE TIME TOO. HE WAS A MENTOR OF MINE."
"YOU KNEW BILL GLEN?"
"I MET HIM DURING MY LAST YEAR AT BERKELEY.
"HE HAD COME TO DO A LECTURE ABOUT THE LEISURE COMPONENT IN THE FORMULA MEDIA LENS.
"HOW BY ADDING EDUCATIONAL ACTIVITIES INTO THESE PROGRAMS CRIME RATES COULD BE REDUCED BY TWENTY PERCENT."

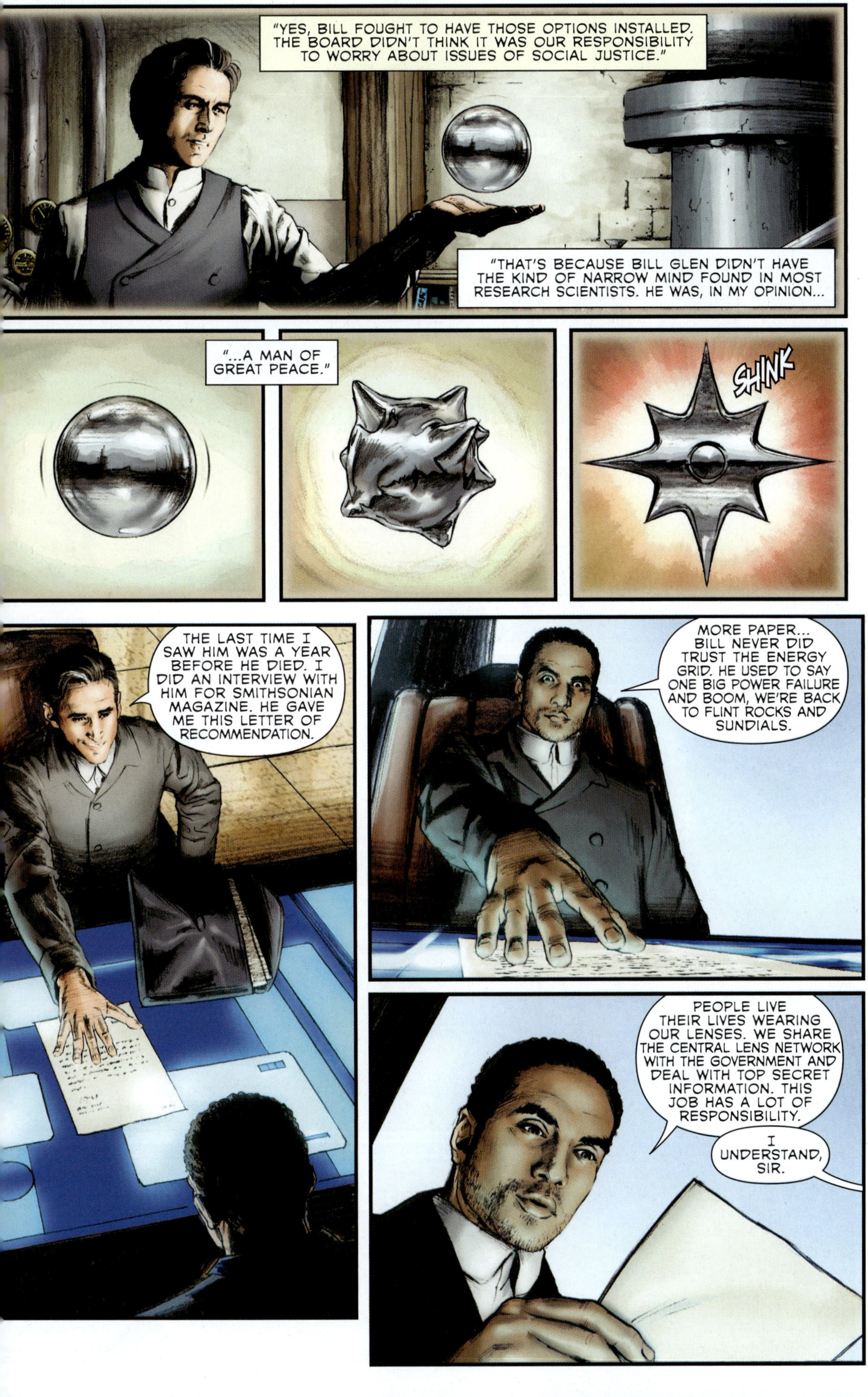
"YES, BILL FOUGHT TO HAVE THOSE OPTIONS INSTALLED. THE BOARD DIDN'T THINK IT WAS OUR RESPONSIBILITY TO WORRY ABOUT ISSUES OF SOCIAL JUSTICE."
"THAT'S BECAUSE BILL GLEN DIDN'T HAVE THE KIND OF NARROW MIND FOUND IN MOST RESEARCH SCIENTISTS. HE WAS, IN MY OPINION...
"...A MAN OF GREAT PEACE."
SHINK
THE LAST TIME I SAW HIM WAS A YEAR BEFORE HE DIED. I DID AN INTERVIEW WITH HIM FOR SMITHSONIAN MAGAZINE. HE GAVE ME THIS LETTER OF RECOMMENDATION.
MORE PAPER... BILL NEVER DID TRUST THE ENERGY GRID. HE USED TO SAY ONE BIG POWER FAILURE AND BOOM, WE'RE BACK TO FLINT ROCKS AND SUNDIALS.
PEOPLE LIVE THEIR LIVES WEARING OUR LENSES. WE SHARE THE CENTRAL LENS NETWORK WITH THE GOVERNMENT AND DEAL WITH TOP SECRET INFORMATION. THIS JOB HAS A LOT OF RESPONSIBILITY.
I UNDERSTAND, SIR.

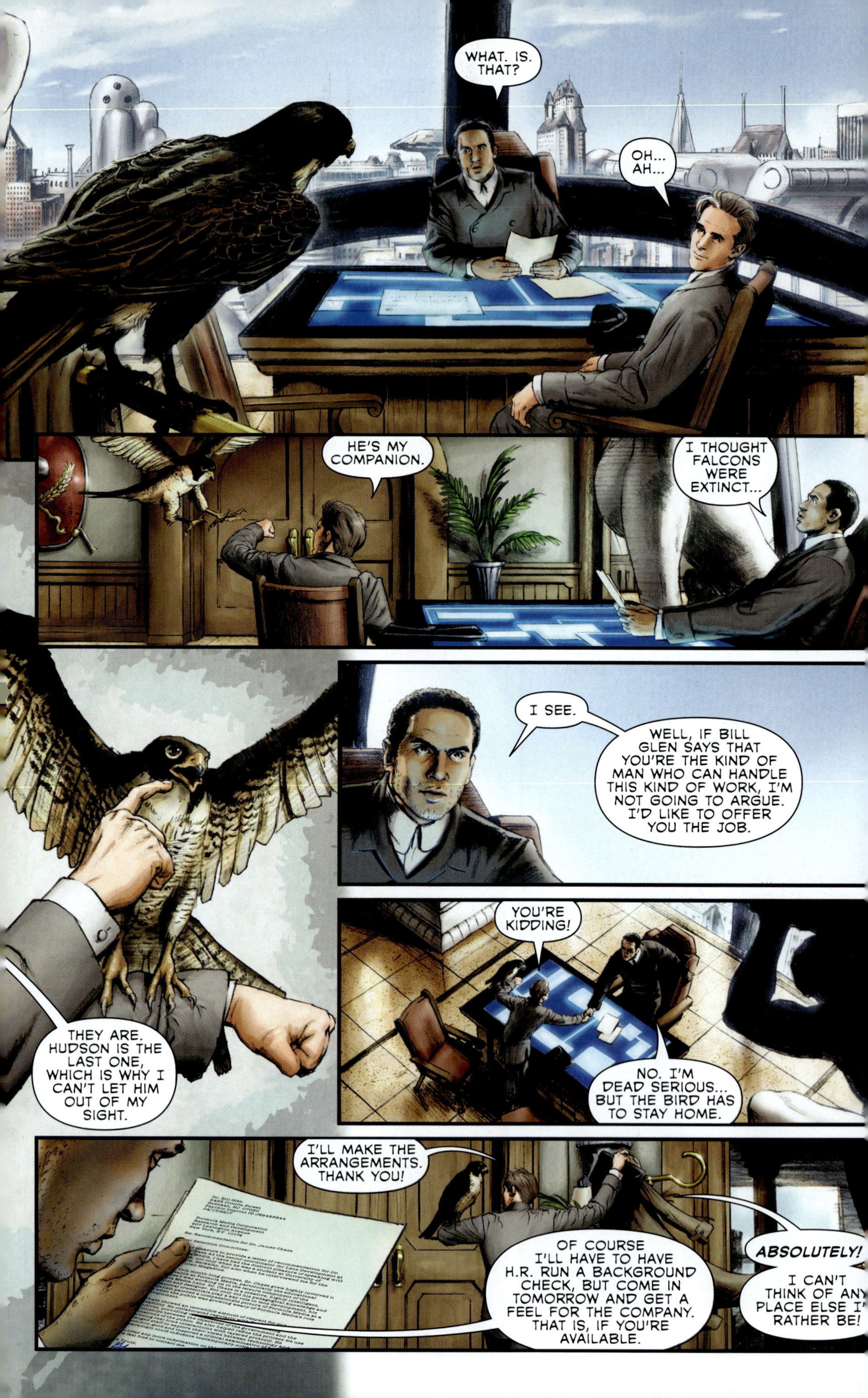
WHAT. IS. THAT?
OH... AH...
HE'S MY COMPANION.
I THOUGHT FALCONS WERE EXTINCT...
THEY ARE. HUDSON IS THE LAST ONE, WHICH IS WHY I CAN'T LET HIM OUT OF MY SIGHT.
I SEE.
WELL, IF BILL GLEN SAYS THAT YOU'RE THE KIND OF MAN WHO CAN HANDLE THIS KIND OF WORK, I'M NOT GOING TO ARGUE. I'D LIKE TO OFFER YOU THE JOB.
YOU'RE KIDDING!
NO. I'M DEAD SERIOUS... BUT THE BIRD HAS TO STAY HOME.
OF COURSE I'LL HAVE TO HAVE H.R. RUN A BACKGROUND CHECK, BUT COME IN TOMORROW AND GET A FEEL FOR THE COMPANY. THAT IS, IF YOU'RE AVAILABLE.
ABSOLUTELY!
I CAN'T THINK OF ANY PLACE ELSE I'D RATHER BE!
I'LL MAKE THE ARRANGEMENTS. THANK YOU!

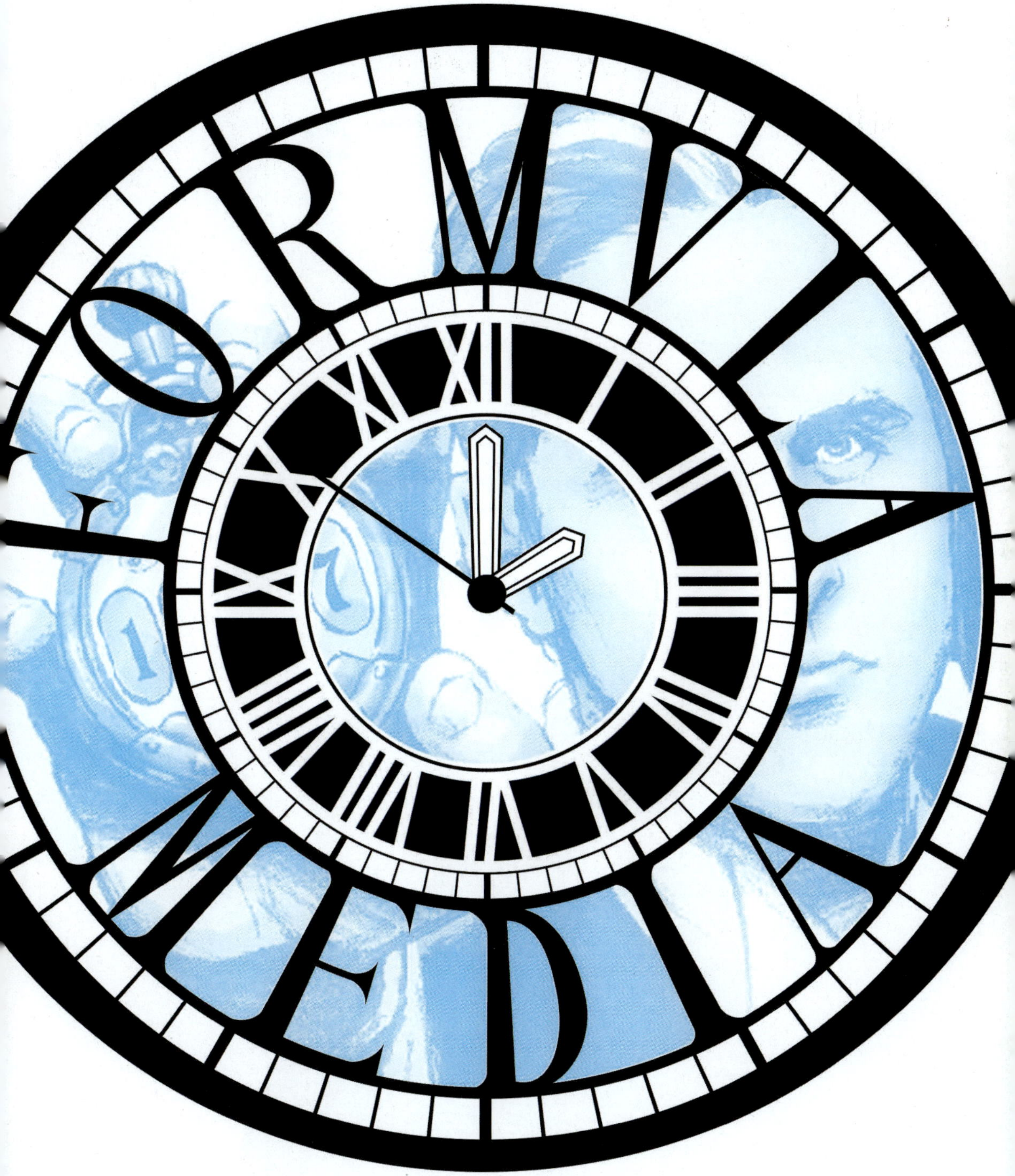

CHAPTER 02

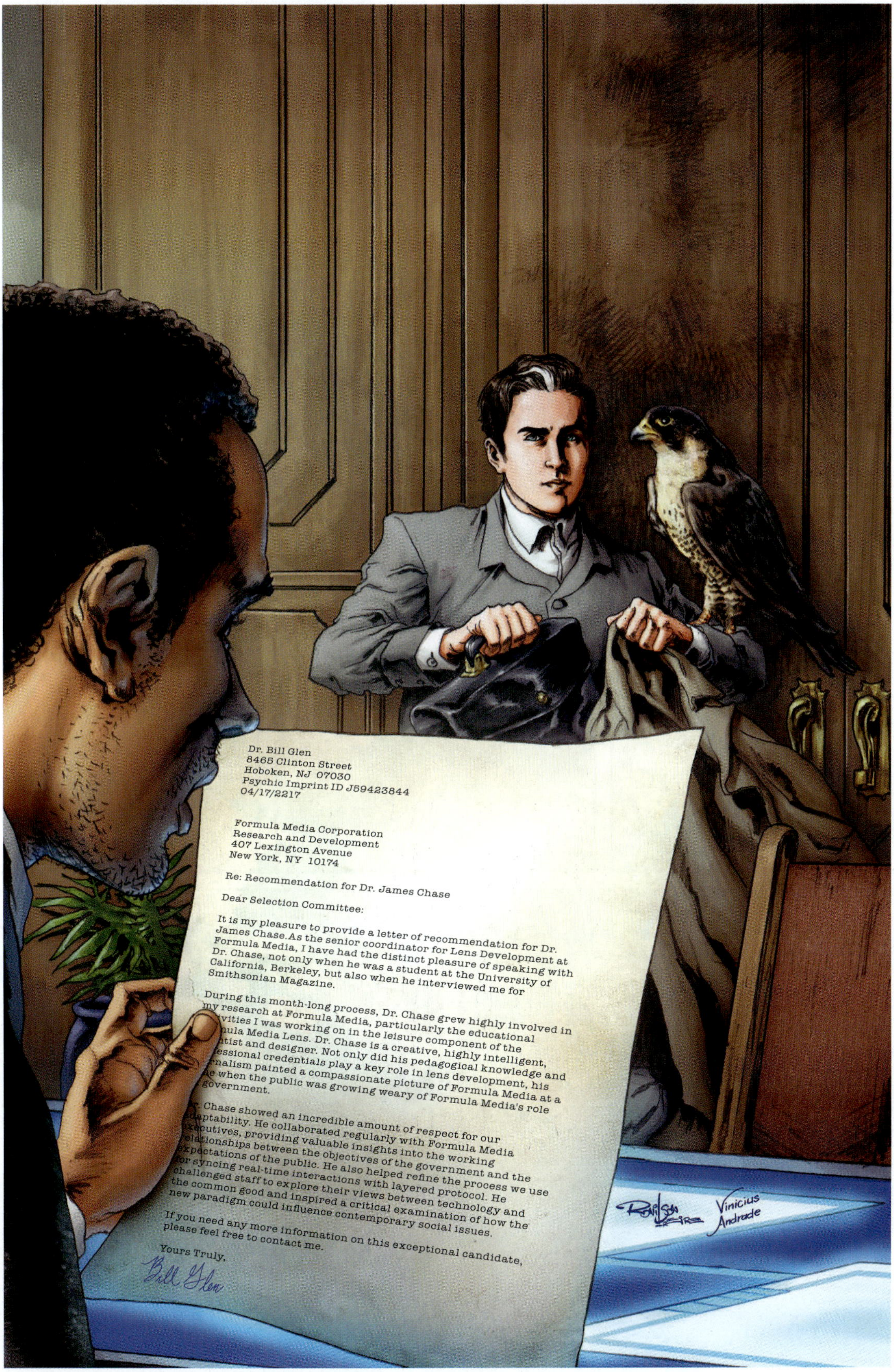
Dr. Bill Glen
8465 Clinton Street
Hoboken, NJ 07030
Psychic Imprint ID J59423844
04/17/2217
Formula Media Corporation
Research and Development
407 Lexington Avenue
New York, NY 10174
Re: Recommendation for Dr. James Chase
Dear Selection Committee:
It is my pleasure to provide a letter of recommendation for Dr.
James Chase.As the senior coordinator for Lens Development at
Formula Media, I have had the distinct pleasure of speaking with
Dr. Chase, not only when he was a student at the University of
California, Berkeley, but also when he interviewed me for
Smithsonian Magazine.
During this month-long process, Dr. Chase grew highly involved in
my research at Formula Media, particularly the educational
vities I was working on in the leisure component of the
ula Media Lens. Dr. Chase is a creative, highly intelligent,
tist and designer. Not only did his pedagogical knowledge and
essional credentials play a key role in lens development, his
nalism painted a compassionate picture of Formula Media at a
e when the public was growing weary of Formula Media's role
government.
. Chase showed an incredible amount of respect for our
daptability. He collaborated regularly with Formula Media
xecutives, providing valuable insights into the working
elationships between the objectives of the government and the
expectations of the public. He also helped refine the process we use
or syncing real-time interactions with layered protocol. He
challenged staff to explore their views between technology and
the common good and inspired a critical examination of how the
new paradigm could influence contemporary social issues.
If you need any more information on this exceptional candidate,
please feel free to contact me.
Yours Truly,
Bill Glen
Vinicius Andrade

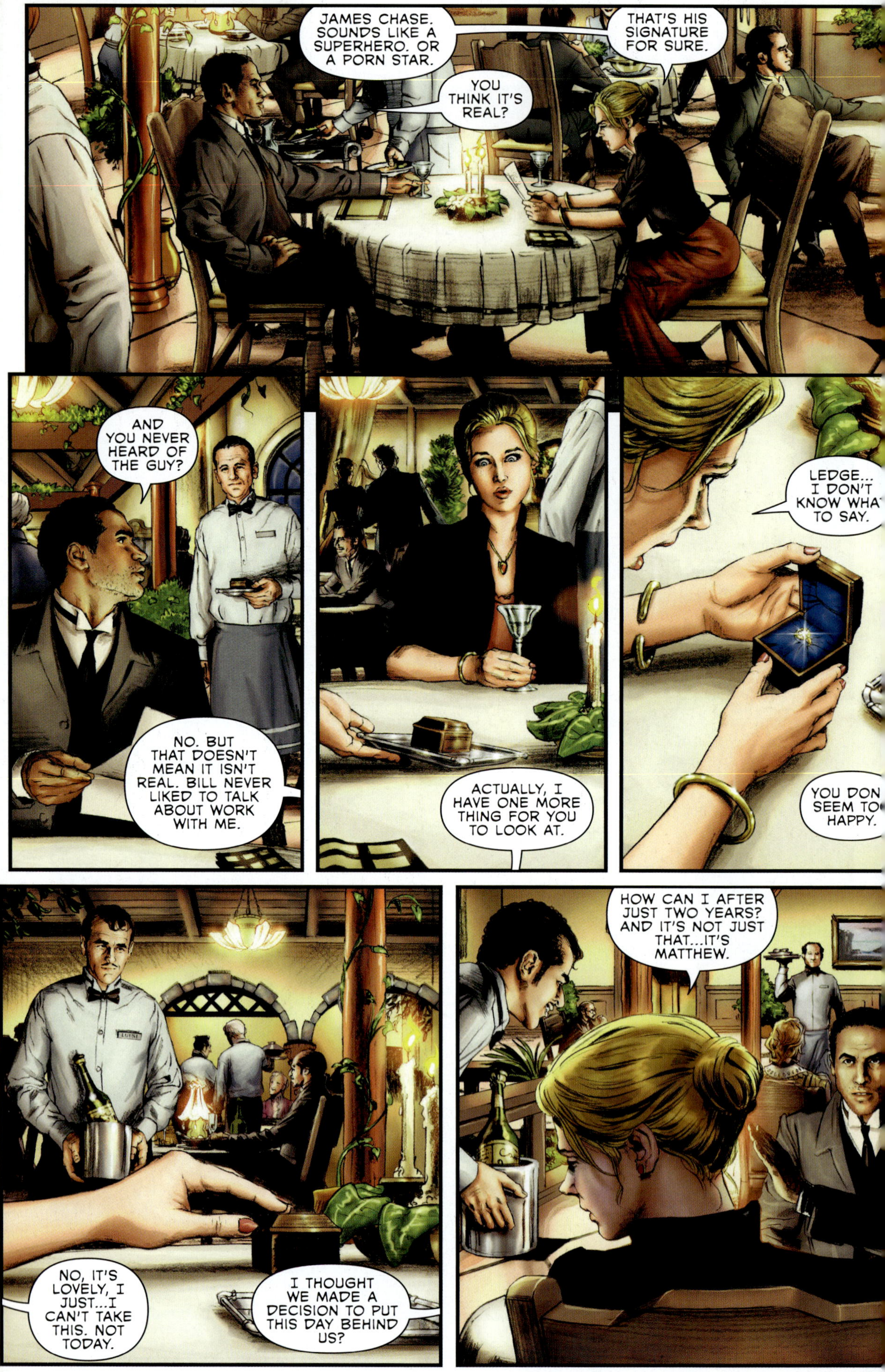
JAMES CHASE. SOUNDS LIKE A SUPERHERO. OR A PORN STAR.
THAT'S HIS SIGNATURE FOR SURE.
YOU THINK IT'S REAL?
AND YOU NEVER HEARD OF THE GUY?
NO. BUT THAT DOESN'T MEAN IT ISN'T REAL. BILL NEVER LIKED TO TALK ABOUT WORK WITH ME.
ACTUALLY, I HAVE ONE MORE THING FOR YOU TO LOOK AT.
LEDGE... I DON'T KNOW WHA
TO SAY.
YOU DON
SEEM TO
HAPPY.
NO, IT'S LOVELY, I JUST...I CAN'T TAKE THIS. NOT TODAY.
I THOUGHT WE MADE A DECISION TO PUT THIS DAY BEHIND US?
HOW CAN I AFTER JUST TWO YEARS? AND IT'S NOT JUST THAT...IT'S MATTHEW.

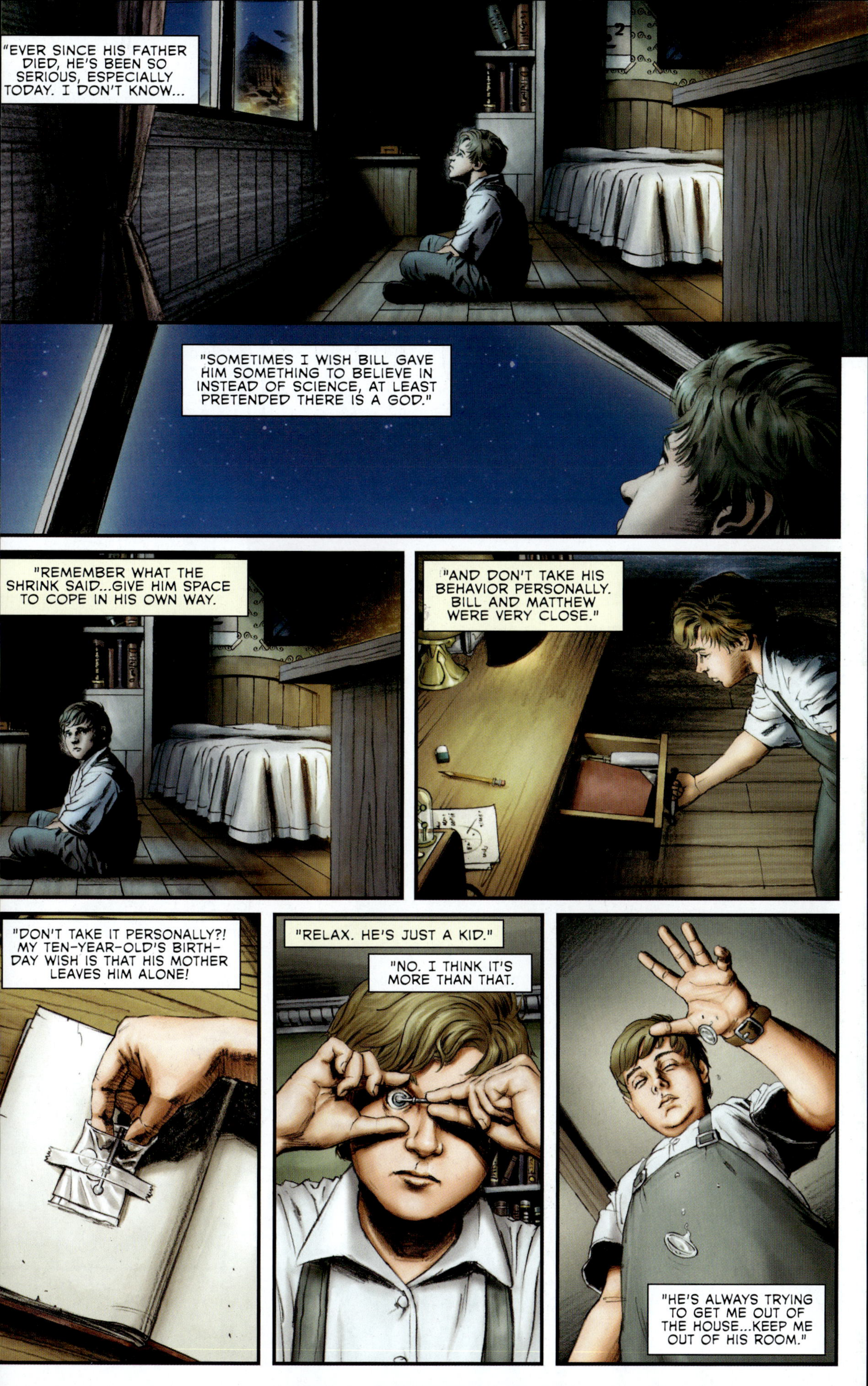
"EVER SINCE HIS FATHER DIED, HE'S BEEN SO SERIOUS, ESPECIALLY TODAY. I DON'T KNOW...
"SOMETIMES I WISH BILL GAVE HIM SOMETHING TO BELIEVE IN INSTEAD OF SCIENCE, AT LEAST PRETENDED THERE IS A GOD."
"REMEMBER WHAT THE SHRINK SAID...GIVE HIM SPACE TO COPE IN HIS OWN WAY.
"AND DON'T TAKE HIS BEHAVIOR PERSONALLY. BILL AND MATTHEW WERE VERY CLOSE."
"DON'T TAKE IT PERSONALLY?! MY TEN-YEAR-OLD'S BIRTH-DAY WISH IS THAT HIS MOTHER LEAVES HIM ALONE!
"RELAX. HE'S JUST A KID."
"NO. I THINK IT'S MORE THAN THAT.
"HE'S ALWAYS TRYING TO GET ME OUT OF THE HOUSE...KEEP ME OUT OF HIS ROOM."

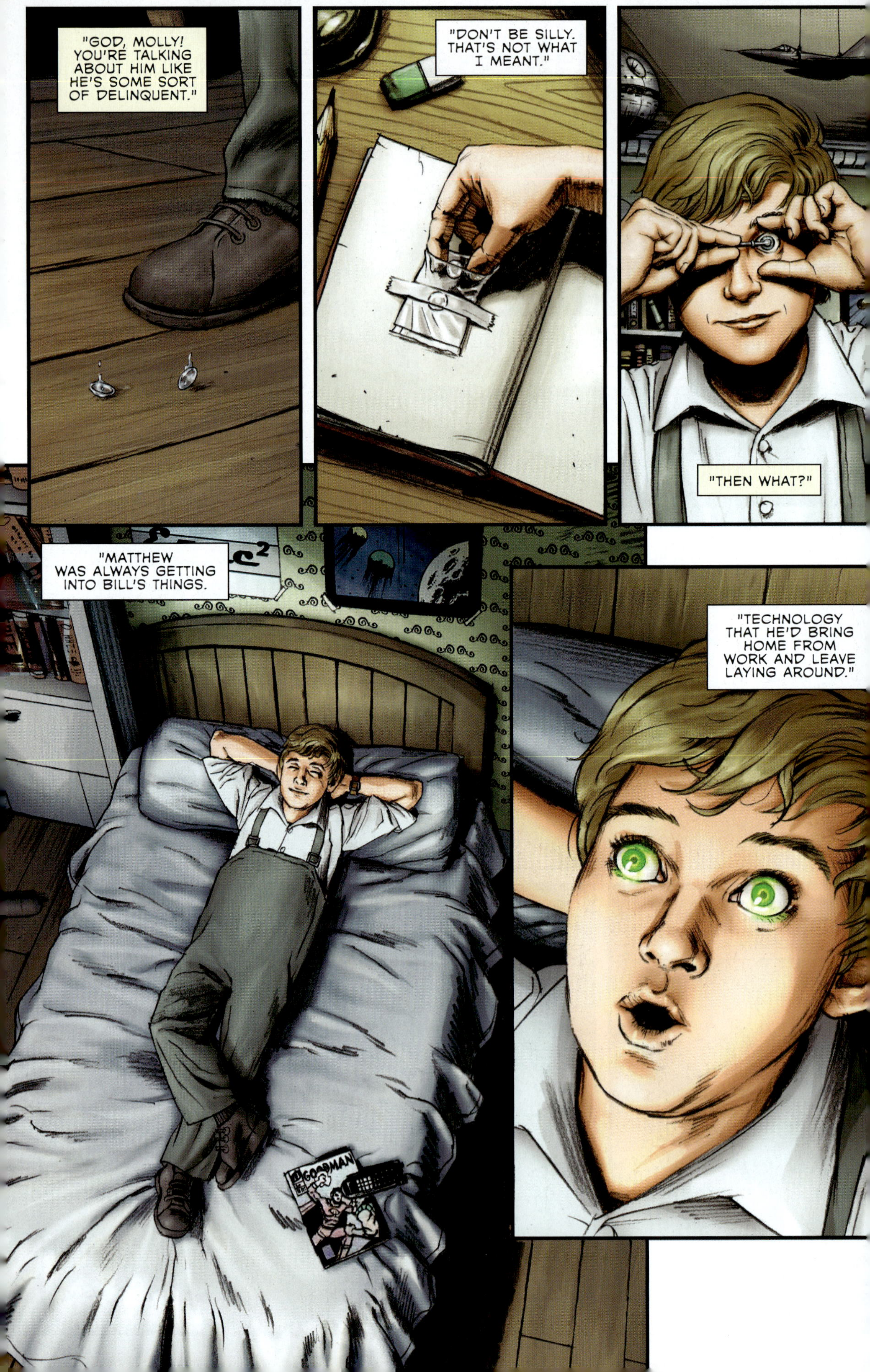
"GOD, MOLLY! YOU'RE TALKING ABOUT HIM LIKE HE'S SOME SORT OF DELINQUENT."
"DON'T BE SILLY. THAT'S NOT WHAT I MEANT."
"THEN WHAT?"
"MATTHEW WAS ALWAYS GETTING INTO BILL'S THINGS.
"TECHNOLOGY THAT HE'D BRING HOME FROM WORK AND LEAVE LAYING AROUND."

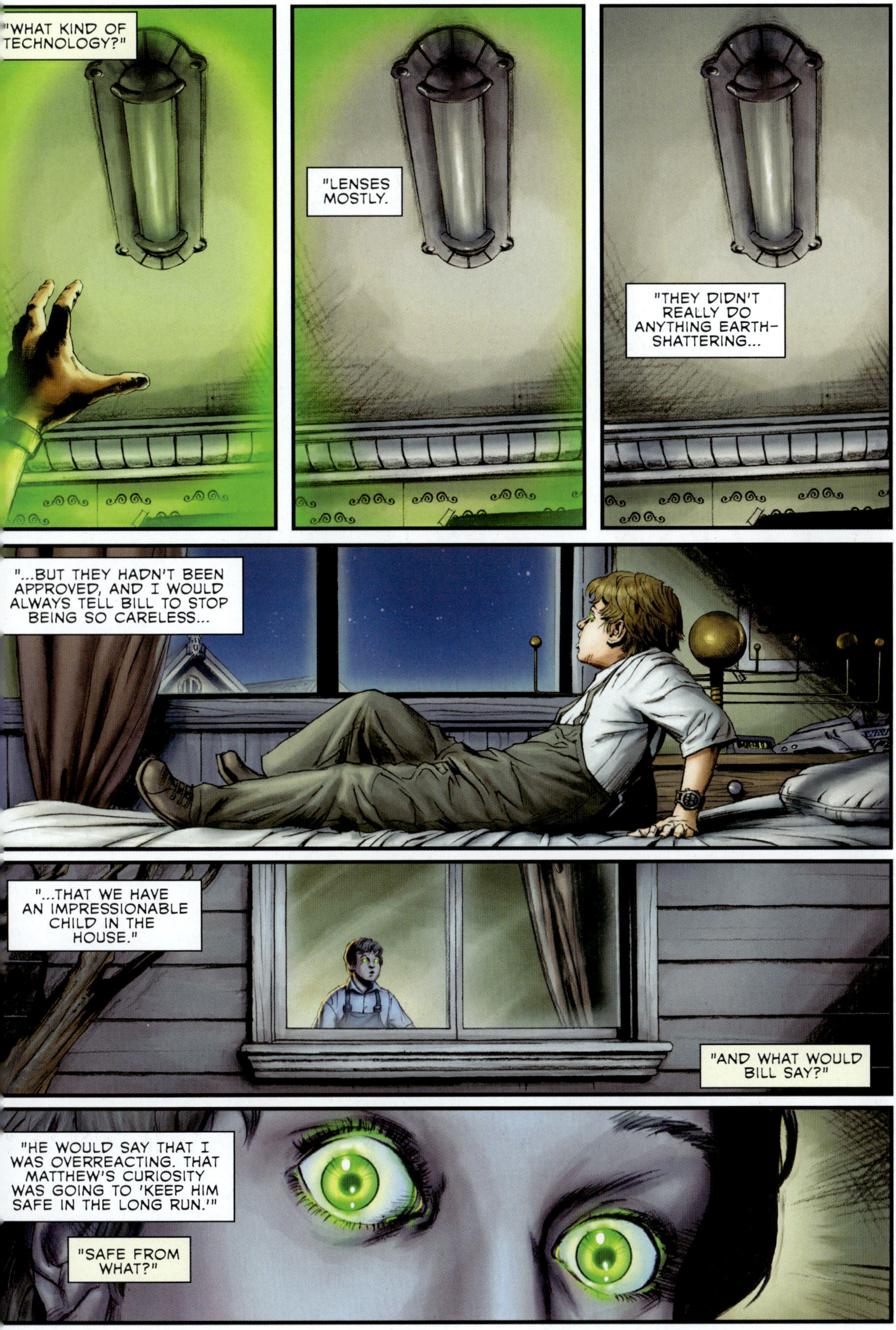
"WHAT KIND OF TECHNOLOGY?"
"LENSES MOSTLY.
"THEY DIDN'T REALLY DO ANYTHING EARTH-SHATTERING...
"...BUT THEY HADN'T BEEN APPROVED, AND I WOULD ALWAYS TELL BILL TO STOP BEING SO CARELESS...
"...THAT WE HAVE AN IMPRESSIONABLE CHILD IN THE HOUSE."
"AND WHAT WOULD BILL SAY?"
"HE WOULD SAY THAT I WAS OVERREACTING. THAT MATTHEW'S CURIOSITY WAS GOING TO 'KEEP HIM SAFE IN THE LONG RUN.'"
"SAFE FROM WHAT?"

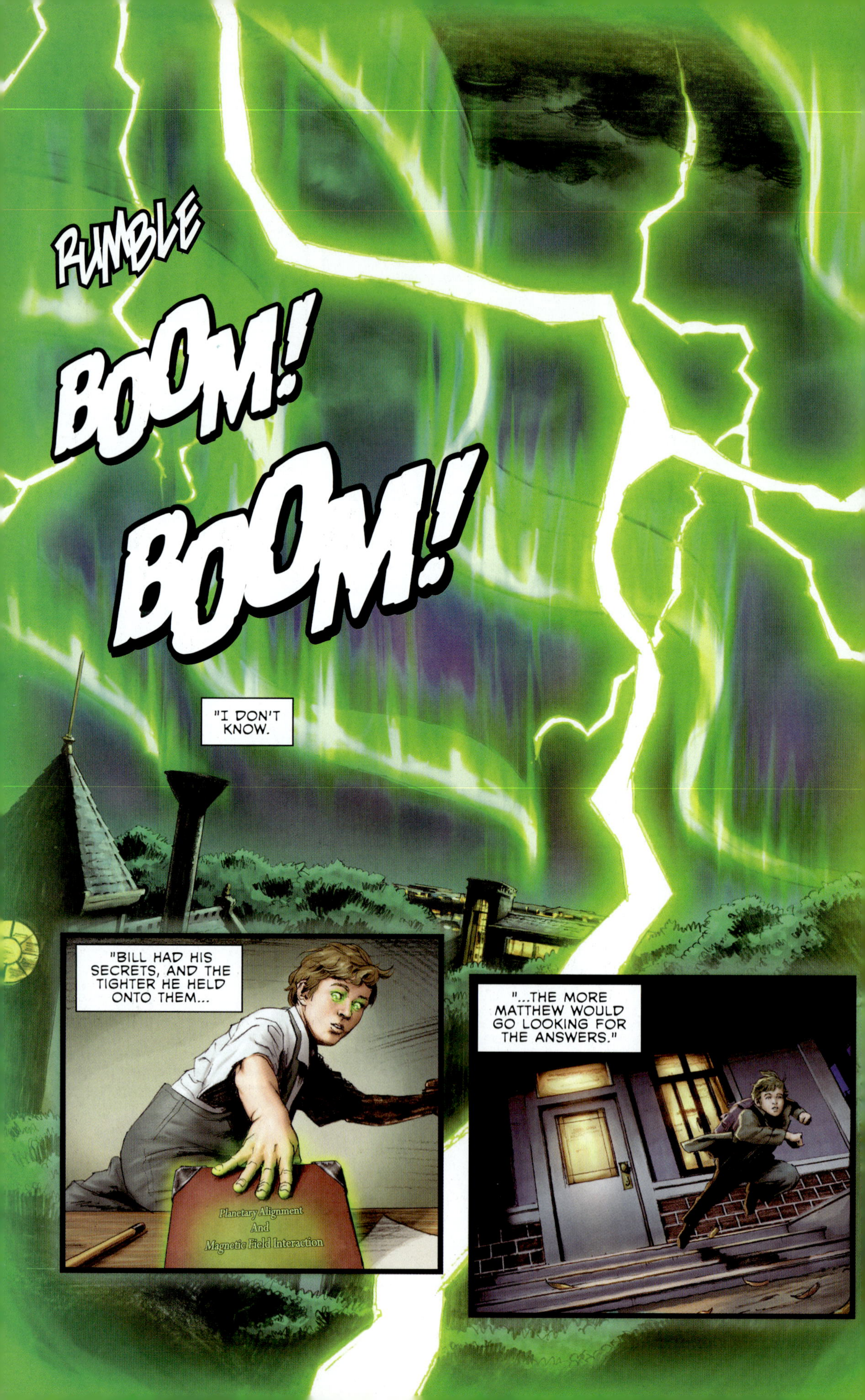
RUMBLE
BOOM!
BOOM!
"I DON'T KNOW.
"BILL HAD HIS SECRETS, AND THE TIGHTER HE HELD ONTO THEM...
Planetary Alignment And Magnetic Field Interaction
"...THE MORE MATTHEW WOULD GO LOOKING FOR THE ANSWERS."

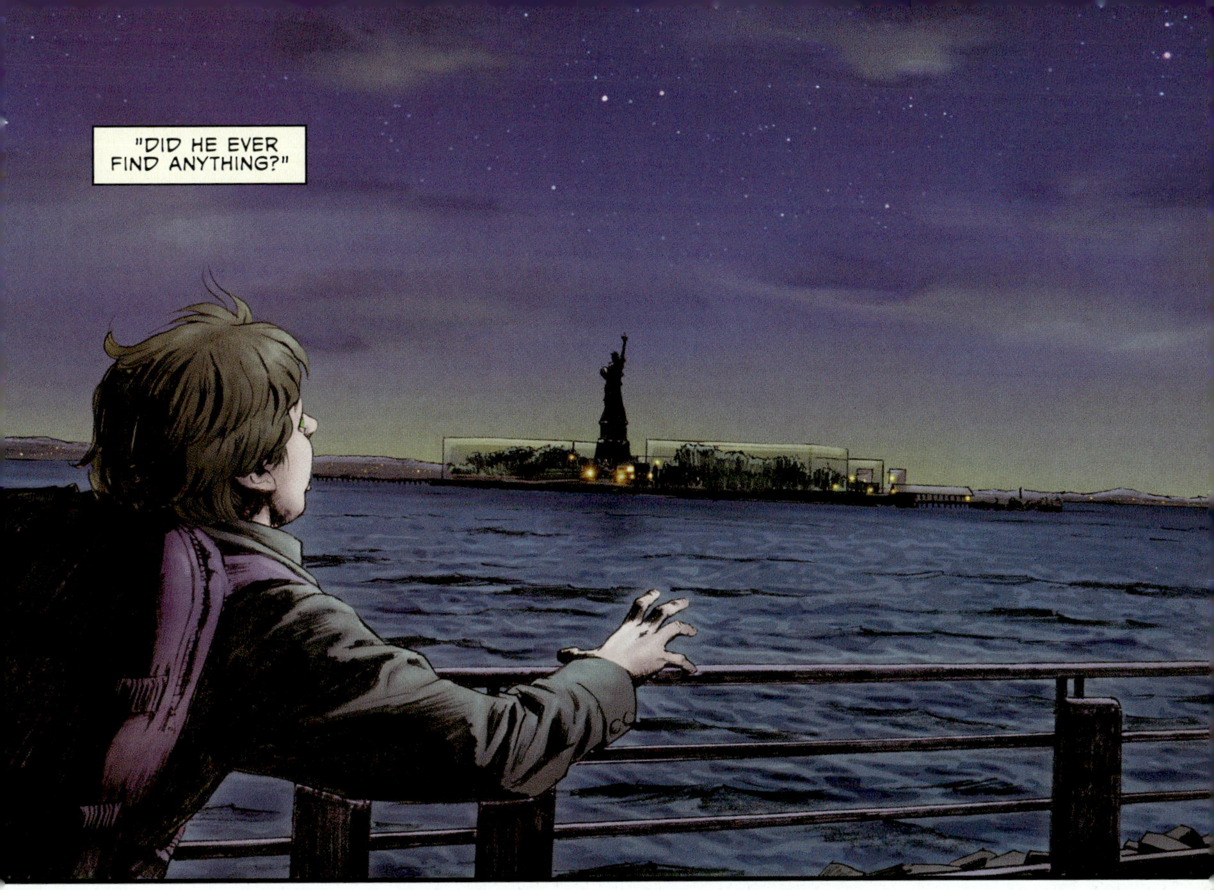
"DID HE EVER FIND ANYTHING?"

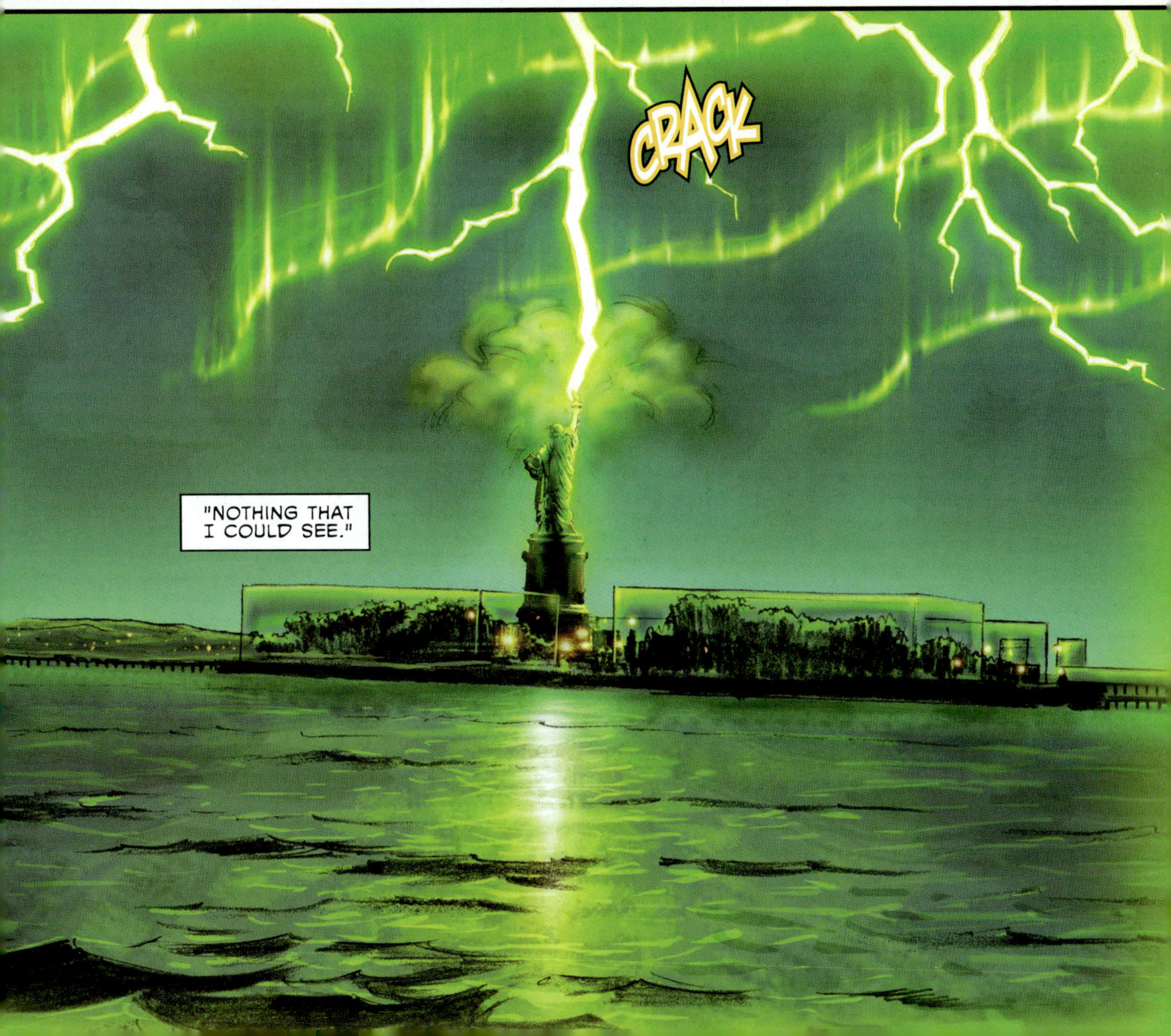
CRACK
"NOTHING THAT I COULD SEE."

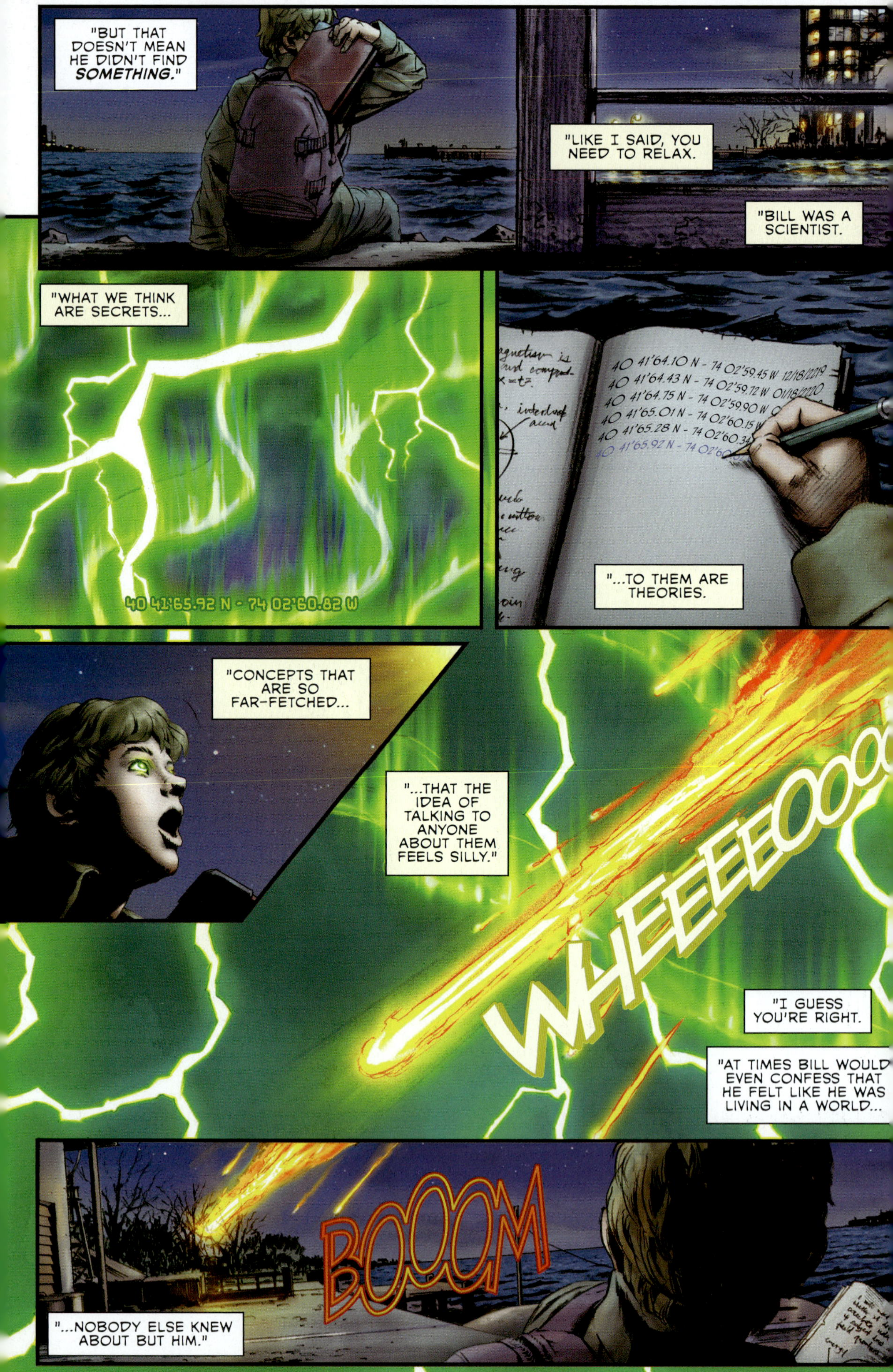
"BUT THAT DOESN'T MEAN HE DIDN'T FIND *SOMETHING*."
"LIKE I SAID, YOU NEED TO RELAX.
"BILL WAS A SCIENTIST.
"WHAT WE THINK ARE SECRETS...
40 41'64.10 N - 74 02'59.45 W 12/18/2019
40 41'64.43 N - 74 02'59.72 W 01/18/2020
40 41'64.75 N - 74 02'59.90 W
40 41'65.01 N - 74 02'60.15 W
40 41'65.28 N - 74 02'60.34
40 41'65.92 N - 74 02'60
"...TO THEM ARE THEORIES.
40 41'65.92 N - 74 02'60.82 W
"CONCEPTS THAT ARE SO FAR-FETCHED...
"...THAT THE IDEA OF TALKING TO ANYONE ABOUT THEM FEELS SILLY."
WHEEEEOOOO
"I GUESS YOU'RE RIGHT.
"AT TIMES BILL WOULD EVEN CONFESS THAT HE FELT LIKE HE WAS LIVING IN A WORLD...
BOOOM
"...NOBODY ELSE KNEW ABOUT BUT HIM."

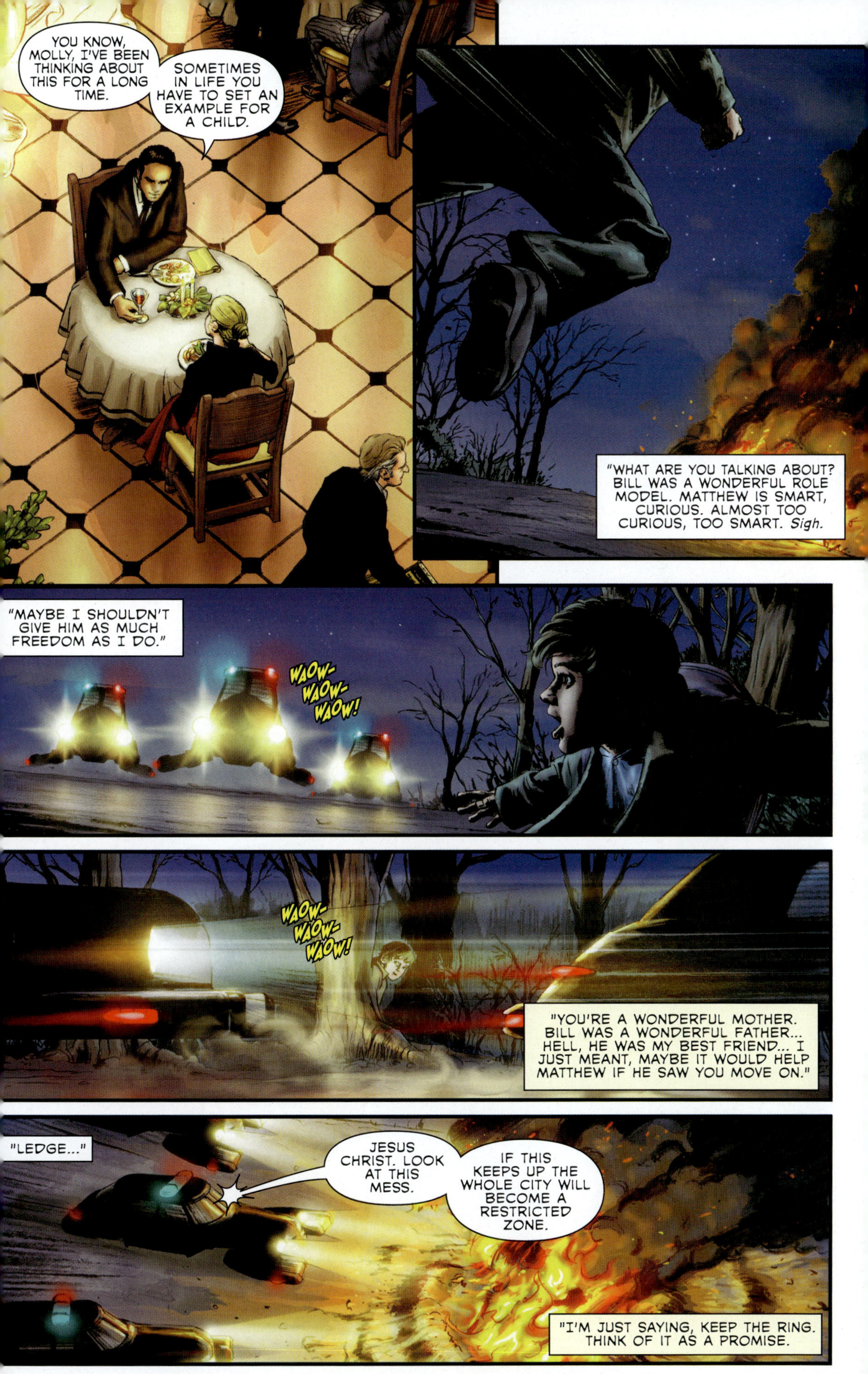
YOU KNOW, MOLLY, I'VE BEEN THINKING ABOUT THIS FOR A LONG TIME.
SOMETIMES IN LIFE YOU HAVE TO SET AN EXAMPLE FOR A CHILD.
"WHAT ARE YOU TALKING ABOUT? BILL WAS A WONDERFUL ROLE MODEL. MATTHEW IS SMART, CURIOUS. ALMOST TOO CURIOUS, TOO SMART. *Sigh.*
"MAYBE I SHOULDN'T GIVE HIM AS MUCH FREEDOM AS I DO."
WAOW-WAOW-WAOW!
WAOW-WAOW-WAOW!
"YOU'RE A WONDERFUL MOTHER. BILL WAS A WONDERFUL FATHER... HELL, HE WAS MY BEST FRIEND... I JUST MEANT, MAYBE IT WOULD HELP MATTHEW IF HE SAW YOU MOVE ON."
"LEDGE..."
JESUS CHRIST. LOOK AT THIS MESS.
IF THIS KEEPS UP THE WHOLE CITY WILL BECOME A RESTRICTED ZONE.
"I'M JUST SAYING, KEEP THE RING. THINK OF IT AS A PROMISE.

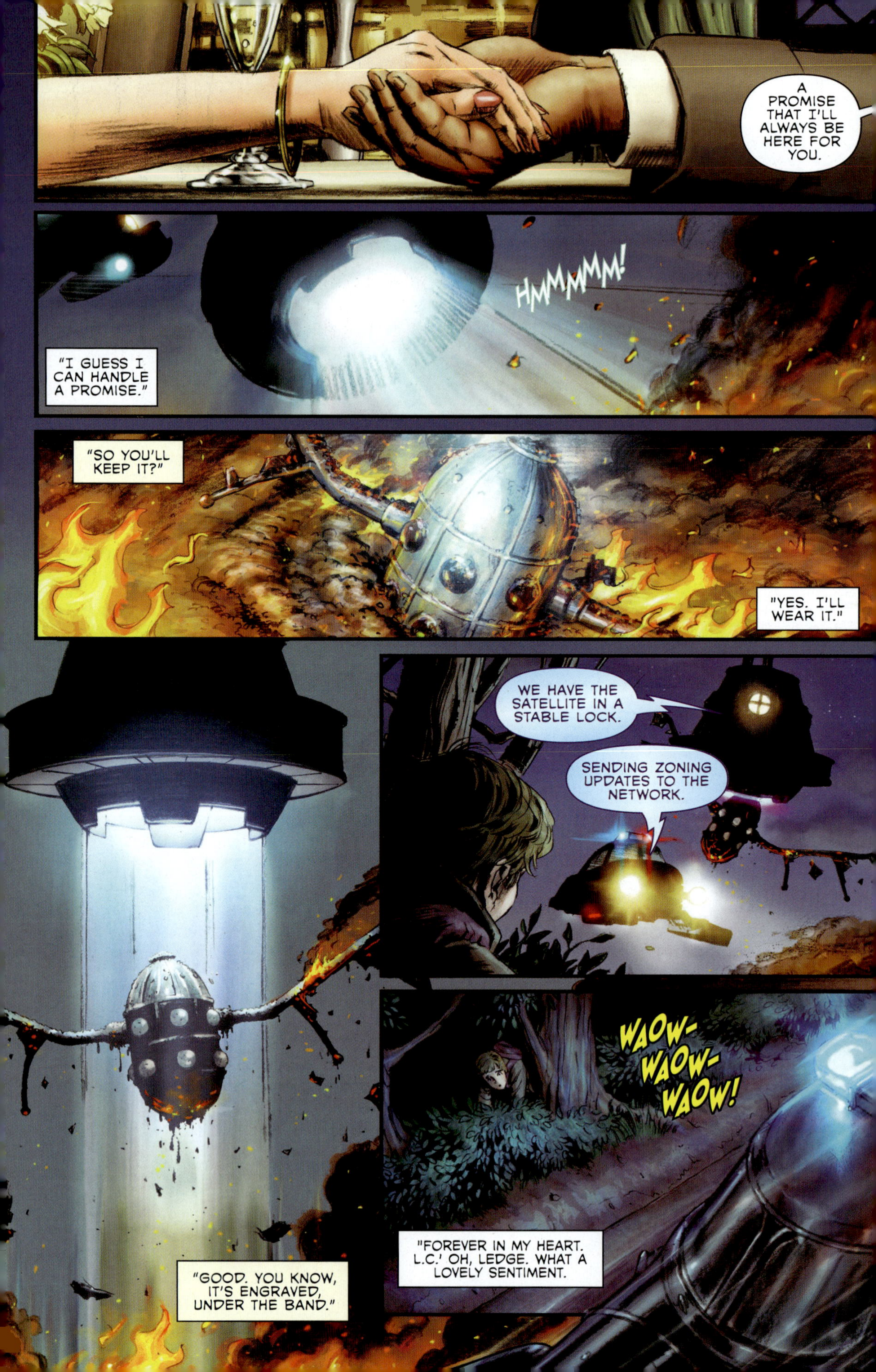

A PROMISE THAT I'LL ALWAYS BE HERE FOR YOU.
HMMMMM!
"I GUESS I CAN HANDLE A PROMISE."
"SO YOU'LL KEEP IT?"
"YES. I'LL WEAR IT."
"GOOD. YOU KNOW, IT'S ENGRAVED, UNDER THE BAND."
WE HAVE THE SATELLITE IN A STABLE LOCK.
SENDING ZONING UPDATES TO THE NETWORK.
WAOW-WAOW-WAOW!
"FOREVER IN MY HEART. L.C.' OH, LEDGE. WHAT A LOVELY SENTIMENT.

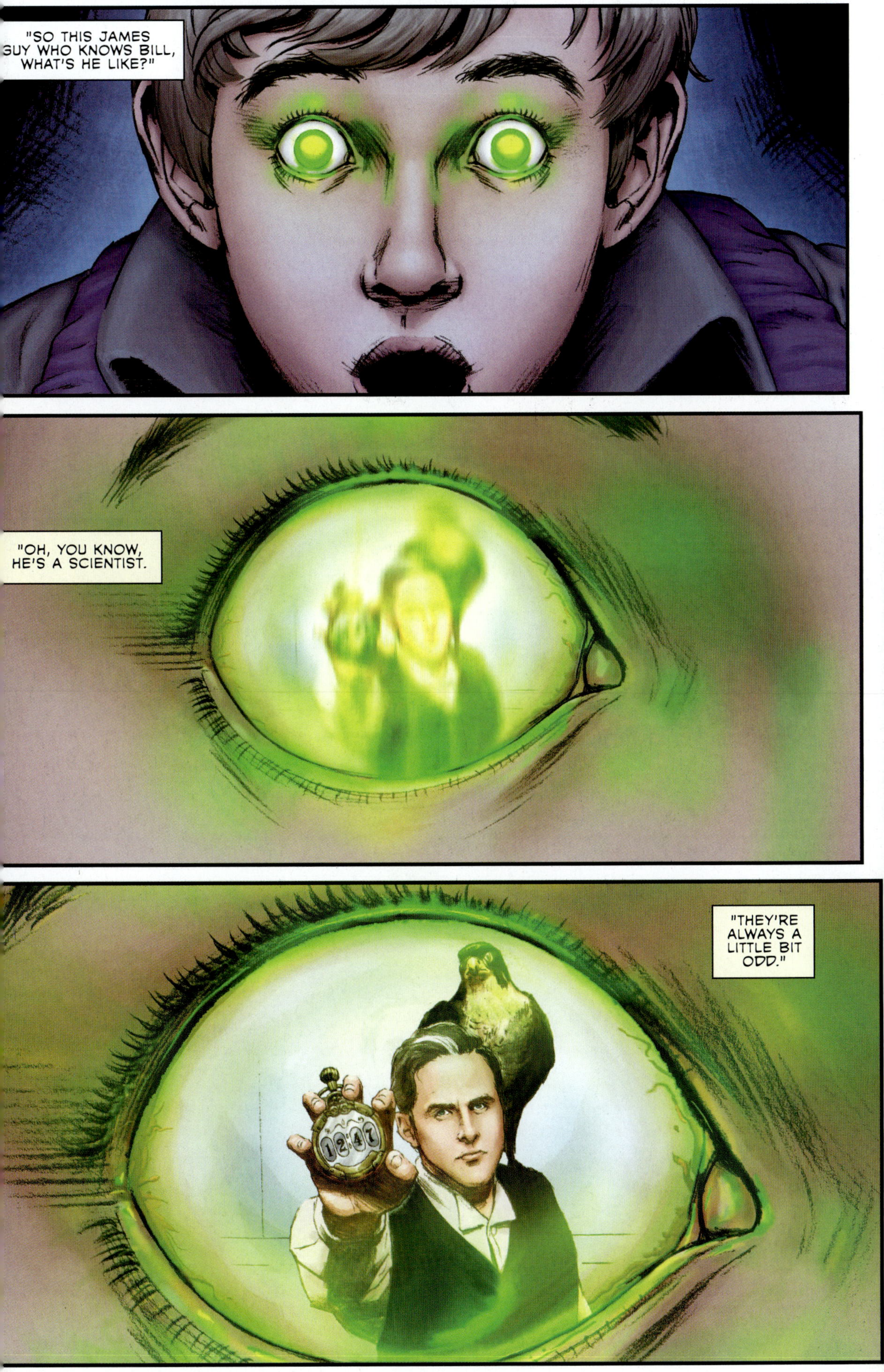
"SO THIS JAMES GUY WHO KNOWS BILL, WHAT'S HE LIKE?"
"OH, YOU KNOW, HE'S A SCIENTIST.
"THEY'RE ALWAYS A LITTLE BIT ODD."

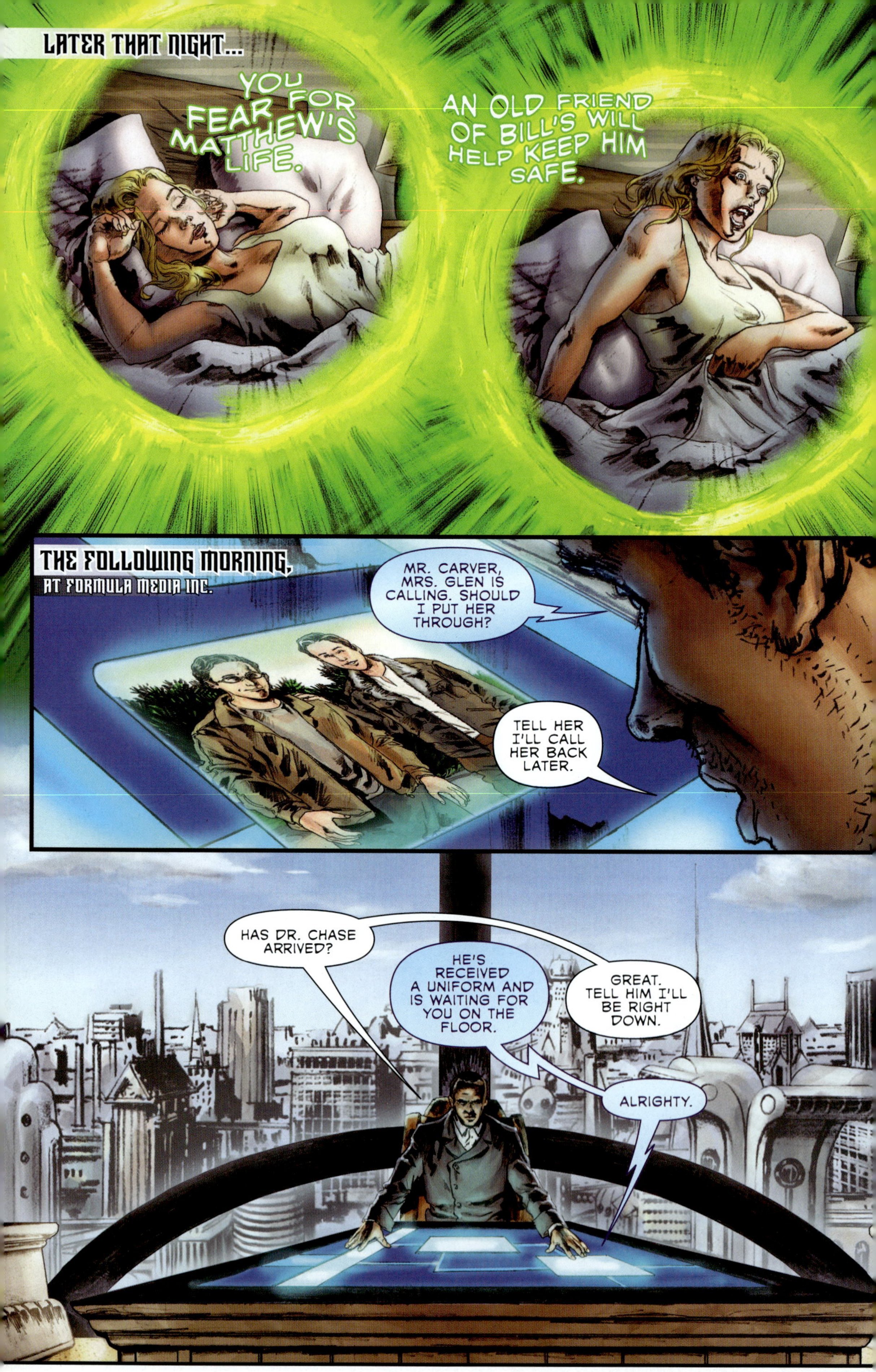
LATER THAT NIGHT...
YOU FEAR FOR MATTHEW'S LIFE.
AN OLD FRIEND OF BILL'S WILL HELP KEEP HIM SAFE.
THE FOLLOWING MORNING, AT FORMULA MEDIA INC.
MR. CARVER, MRS. GLEN IS CALLING. SHOULD I PUT HER THROUGH?
TELL HER I'LL CALL HER BACK LATER.
HAS DR. CHASE ARRIVED?
HE'S RECEIVED A UNIFORM AND IS WAITING FOR YOU ON THE FLOOR.
GREAT. TELL HIM I'LL BE RIGHT DOWN.
ALRIGHTY.

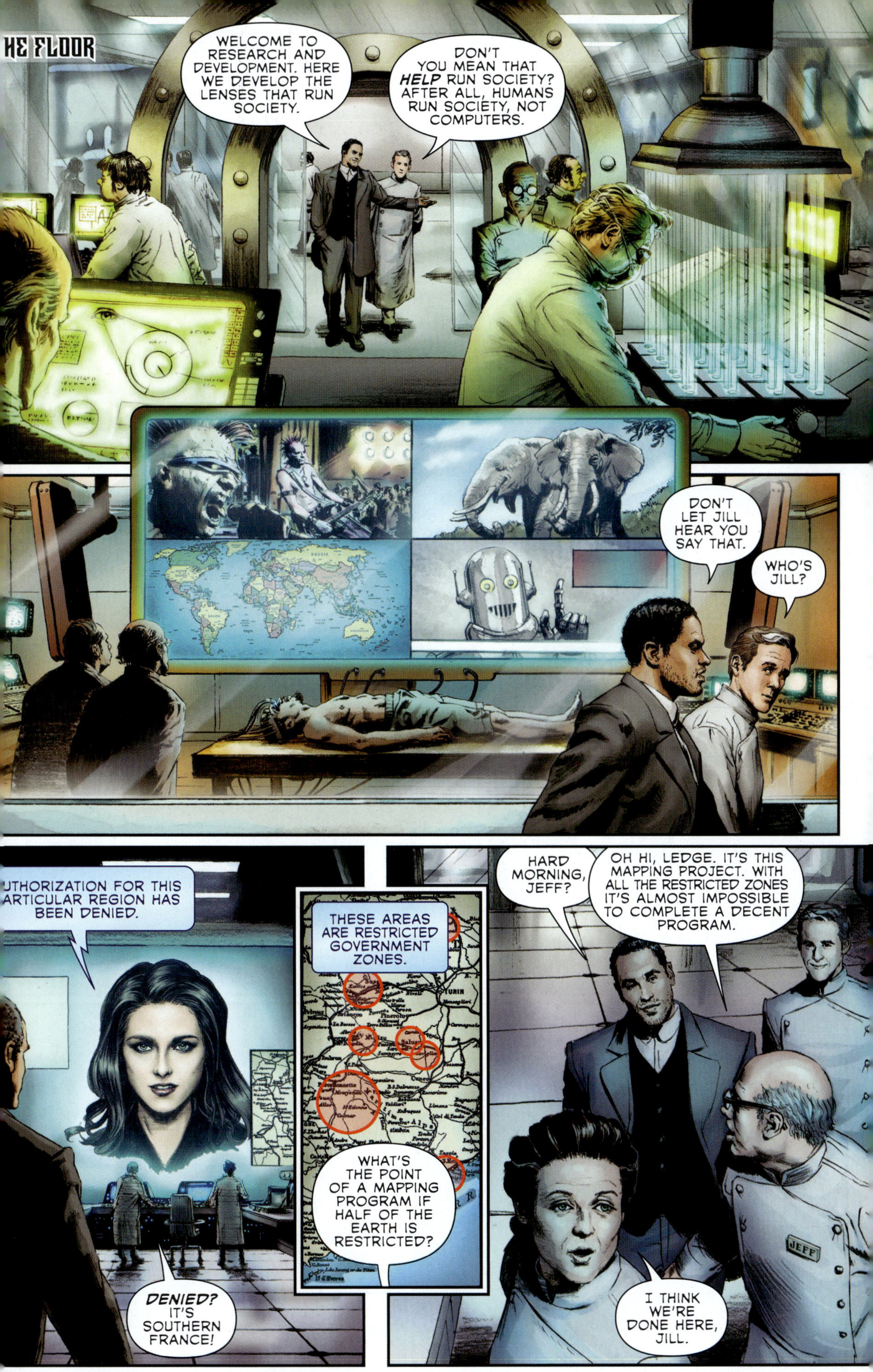
HE FLOOR
WELCOME TO RESEARCH AND DEVELOPMENT. HERE WE DEVELOP THE LENSES THAT RUN SOCIETY.
DON'T YOU MEAN THAT *HELP* RUN SOCIETY? AFTER ALL, HUMANS RUN SOCIETY, NOT COMPUTERS.
DON'T LET JILL HEAR YOU SAY THAT.
WHO'S JILL?
UTHORIZATION FOR THIS ARTICULAR REGION HAS BEEN DENIED.
DENIED? IT'S SOUTHERN FRANCE!
THESE AREAS ARE RESTRICTED GOVERNMENT ZONES.
WHAT'S THE POINT OF A MAPPING PROGRAM IF HALF OF THE EARTH IS RESTRICTED?
HARD MORNING, JEFF?
OH HI, LEDGE. IT'S THIS MAPPING PROJECT. WITH ALL THE RESTRICTED ZONES IT'S ALMOST IMPOSSIBLE TO COMPLETE A DECENT PROGRAM.
I THINK WE'RE DONE HERE, JILL.
JEFF

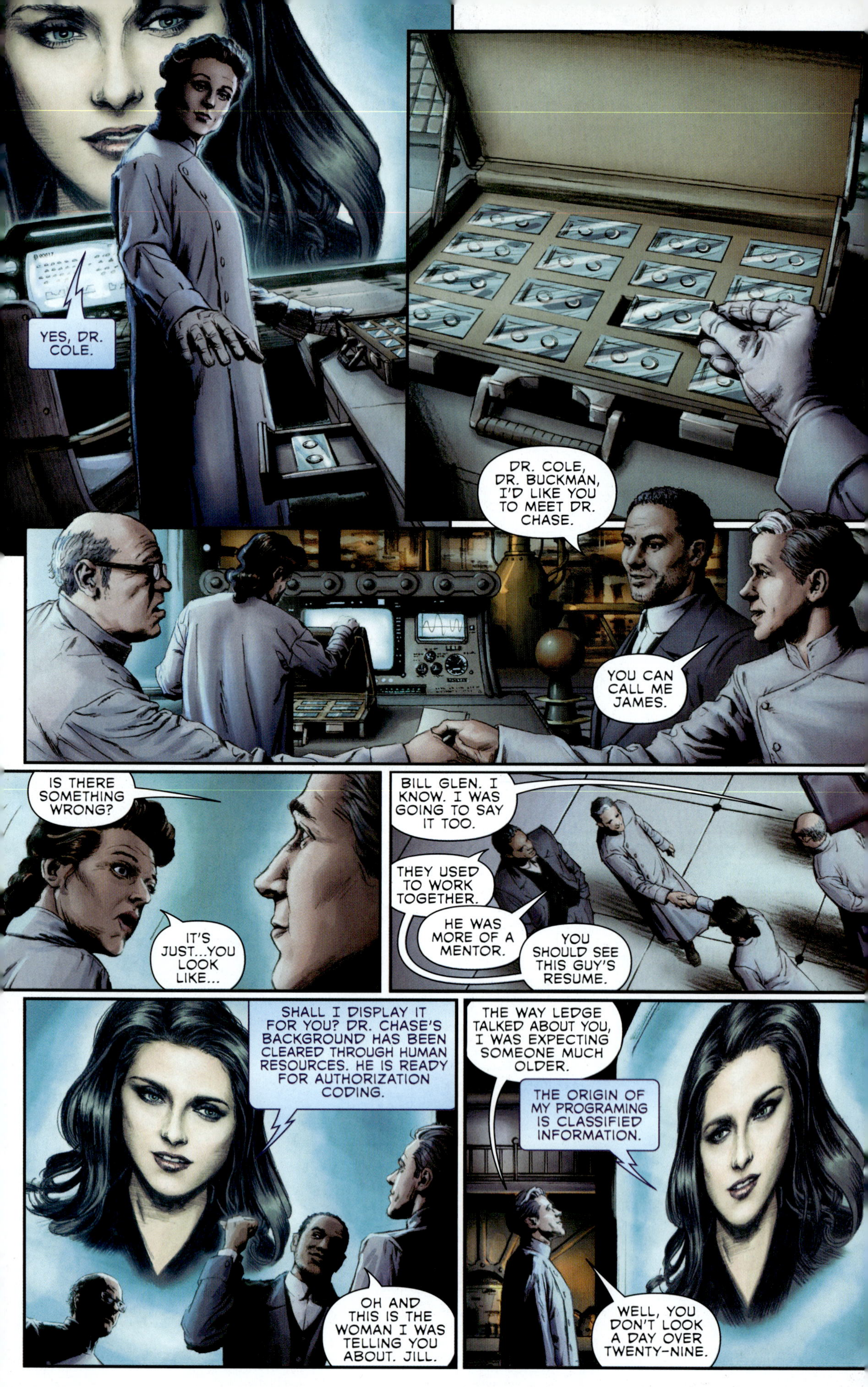
YES, DR. COLE.
DR. COLE, DR. BUCKMAN, I'D LIKE YOU TO MEET DR. CHASE.
YOU CAN CALL ME JAMES.
IS THERE SOMETHING WRONG?
IT'S JUST...YOU LOOK LIKE...
BILL GLEN. I KNOW. I WAS GOING TO SAY IT TOO.
THEY USED TO WORK TOGETHER.
HE WAS MORE OF A MENTOR.
YOU SHOULD SEE THIS GUY'S RESUME.
SHALL I DISPLAY IT FOR YOU? DR. CHASE'S BACKGROUND HAS BEEN CLEARED THROUGH HUMAN RESOURCES. HE IS READY FOR AUTHORIZATION CODING.
OH AND THIS IS THE WOMAN I WAS TELLING YOU ABOUT. JILL.
THE WAY LEDGE TALKED ABOUT YOU, I WAS EXPECTING SOMEONE MUCH OLDER.
THE ORIGIN OF MY PROGRAMING IS CLASSIFIED INFORMATION.
WELL, YOU DON'T LOOK A DAY OVER TWENTY-NINE.

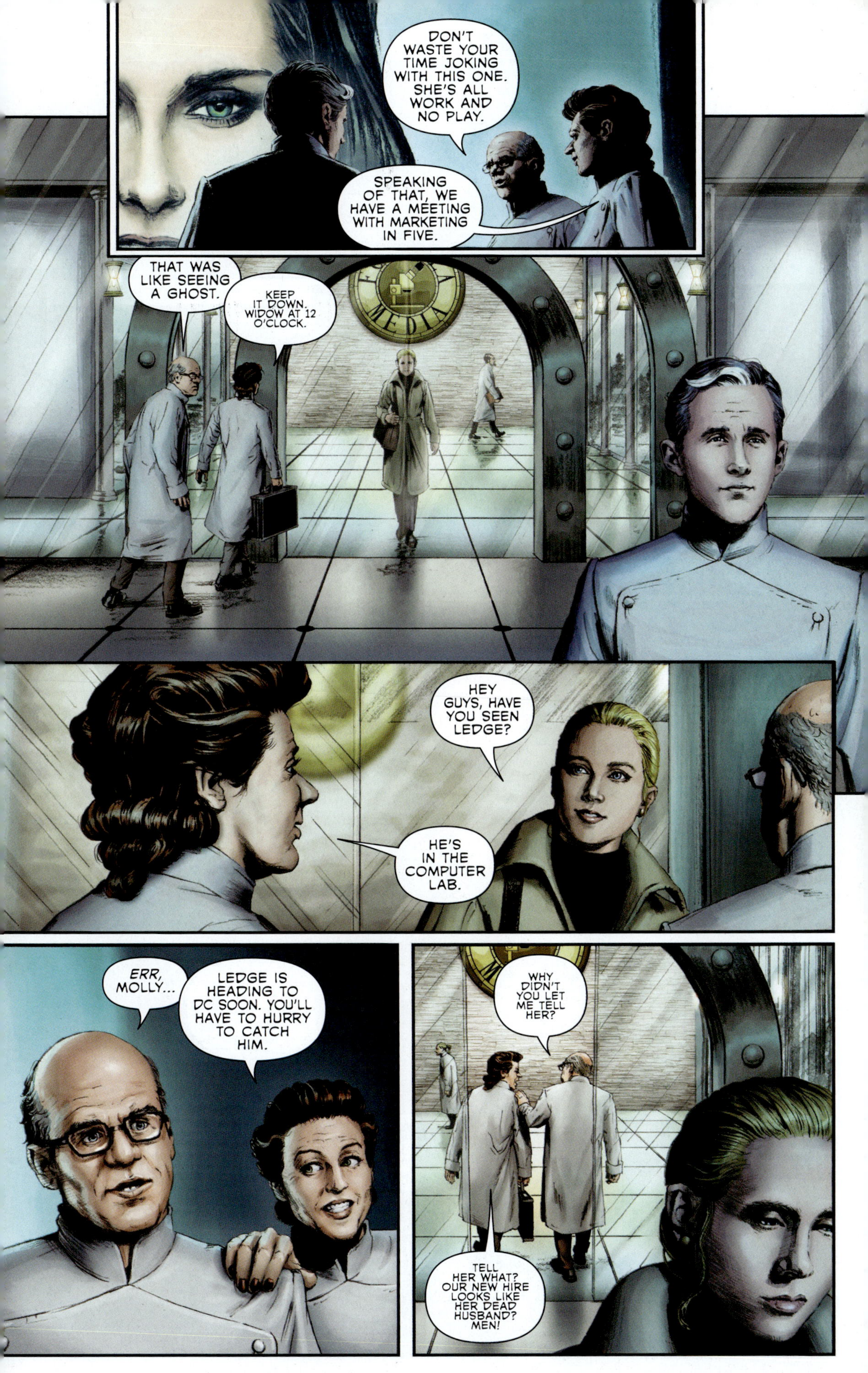
DON'T WASTE YOUR TIME JOKING WITH THIS ONE. SHE'S ALL WORK AND NO PLAY.
SPEAKING OF THAT, WE HAVE A MEETING WITH MARKETING IN FIVE.
THAT WAS LIKE SEEING A GHOST.
KEEP IT DOWN. WIDOW AT 12 O'CLOCK.
HEY GUYS, HAVE YOU SEEN LEDGE?
HE'S IN THE COMPUTER LAB.
ERR, MOLLY...
LEDGE IS HEADING TO DC SOON. YOU'LL HAVE TO HURRY TO CATCH HIM.
WHY DIDN'T YOU LET ME TELL HER?
TELL HER WHAT? OUR NEW HIRE LOOKS LIKE HER DEAD HUSBAND? MEN!

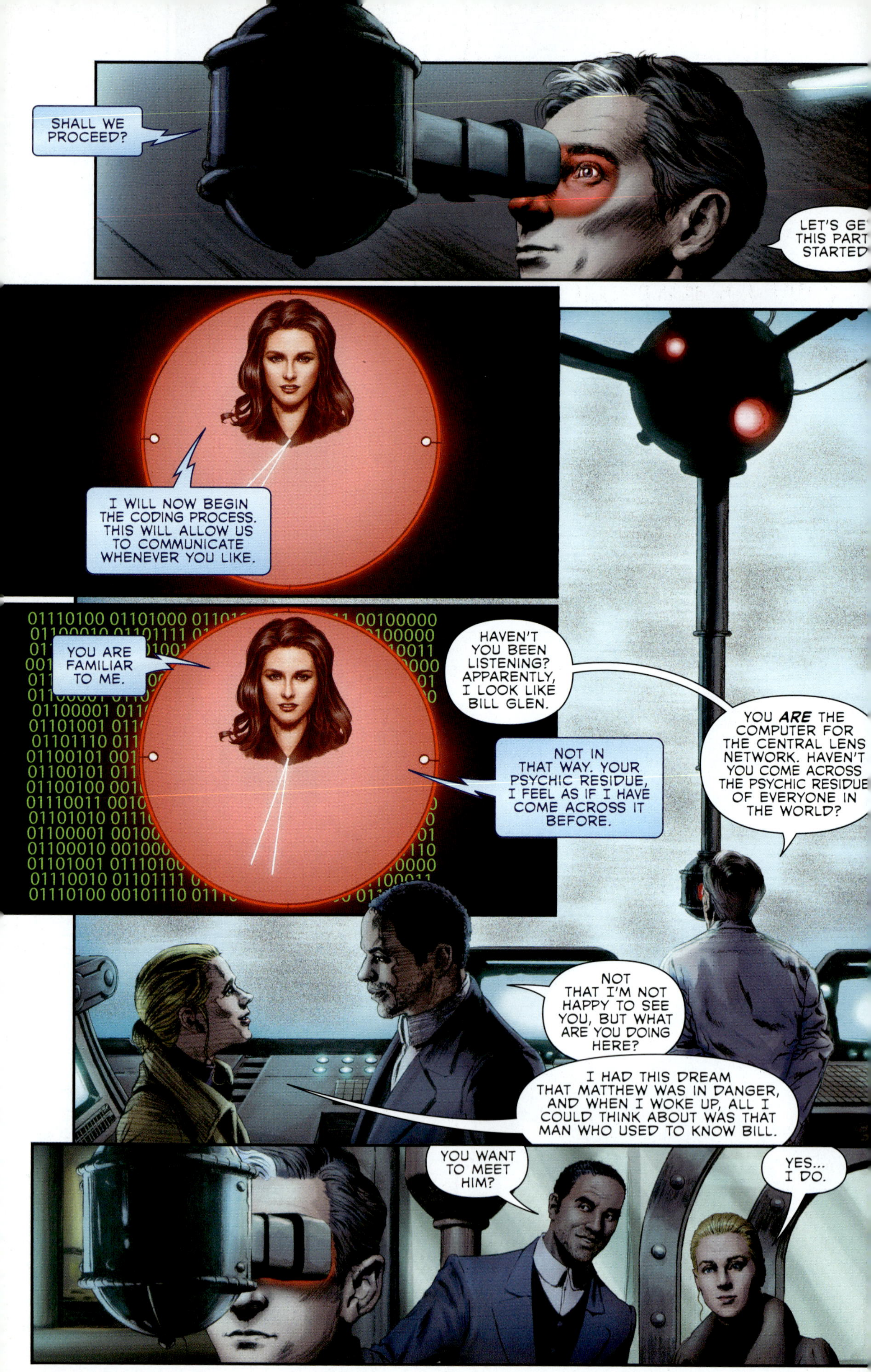
SHALL WE PROCEED?
LET'S GE THIS PART STARTED
I WILL NOW BEGIN THE CODING PROCESS. THIS WILL ALLOW US TO COMMUNICATE WHENEVER YOU LIKE.
YOU ARE FAMILIAR TO ME.
HAVEN'T YOU BEEN LISTENING? APPARENTLY, I LOOK LIKE BILL GLEN.
NOT IN THAT WAY. YOUR PSYCHIC RESIDUE, I FEEL AS IF I HAVE COME ACROSS IT BEFORE.
YOU ARE THE COMPUTER FOR THE CENTRAL LENS NETWORK. HAVEN'T YOU COME ACROSS THE PSYCHIC RESIDUE OF EVERYONE IN THE WORLD?
NOT THAT I'M NOT HAPPY TO SEE YOU, BUT WHAT ARE YOU DOING HERE?
I HAD THIS DREAM THAT MATTHEW WAS IN DANGER, AND WHEN I WOKE UP, ALL I COULD THINK ABOUT WAS THAT MAN WHO USED TO KNOW BILL.
YOU WANT TO MEET HIM?
YES... I DO.

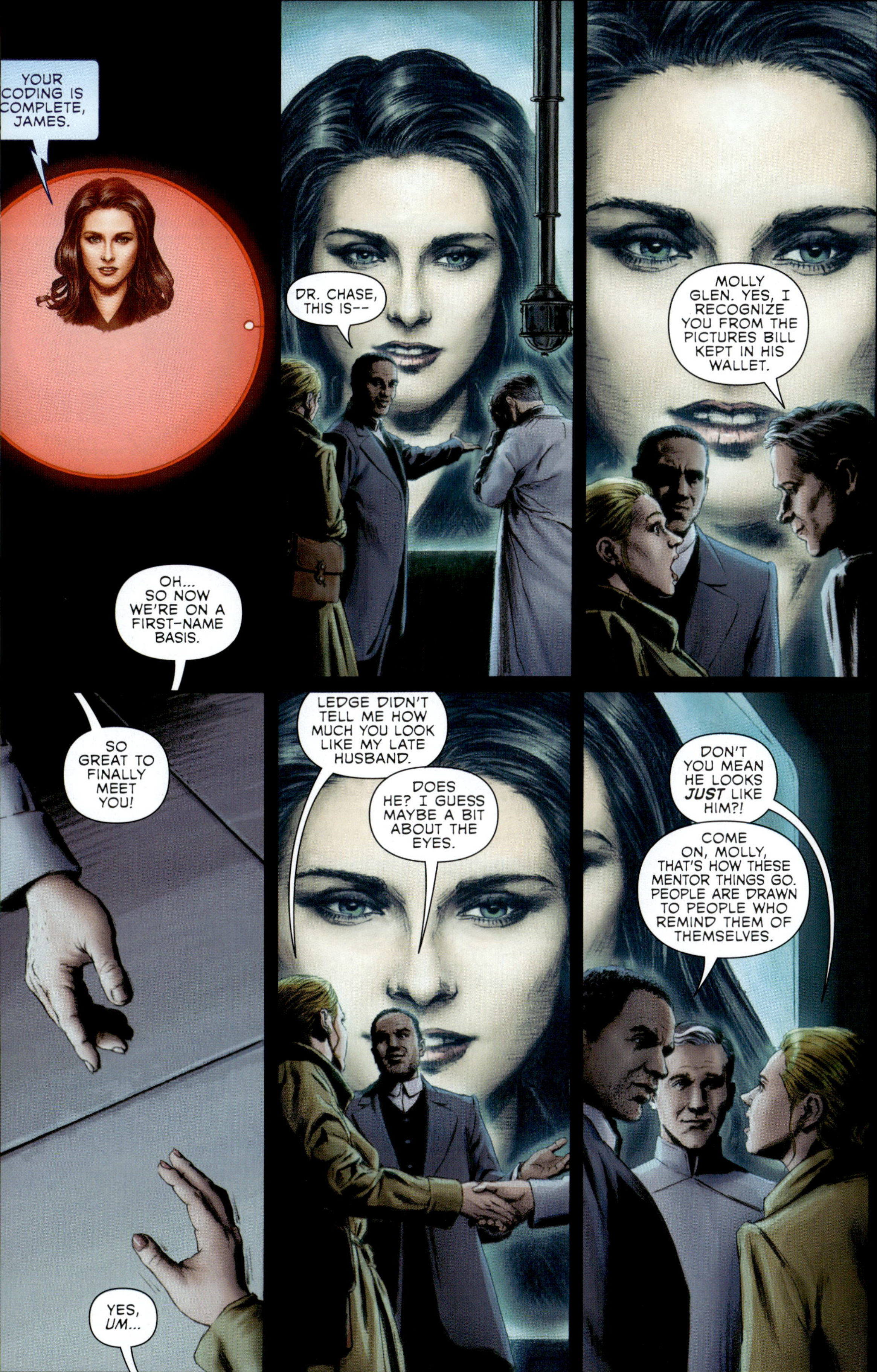
YOUR CODING IS COMPLETE, JAMES.
DR. CHASE, THIS IS--
MOLLY GLEN. YES, I RECOGNIZE YOU FROM THE PICTURES BILL KEPT IN HIS WALLET.
OH... SO NOW WE'RE ON A FIRST-NAME BASIS.
SO GREAT TO FINALLY MEET YOU!
YES, UM...
LEDGE DIDN'T TELL ME HOW MUCH YOU LOOK LIKE MY LATE HUSBAND.
DOES HE? I GUESS MAYBE A BIT ABOUT THE EYES.
DON'T YOU MEAN HE LOOKS JUST LIKE HIM?!
COME ON, MOLLY, THAT'S HOW THESE MENTOR THINGS GO. PEOPLE ARE DRAWN TO PEOPLE WHO REMIND THEM OF THEMSELVES.

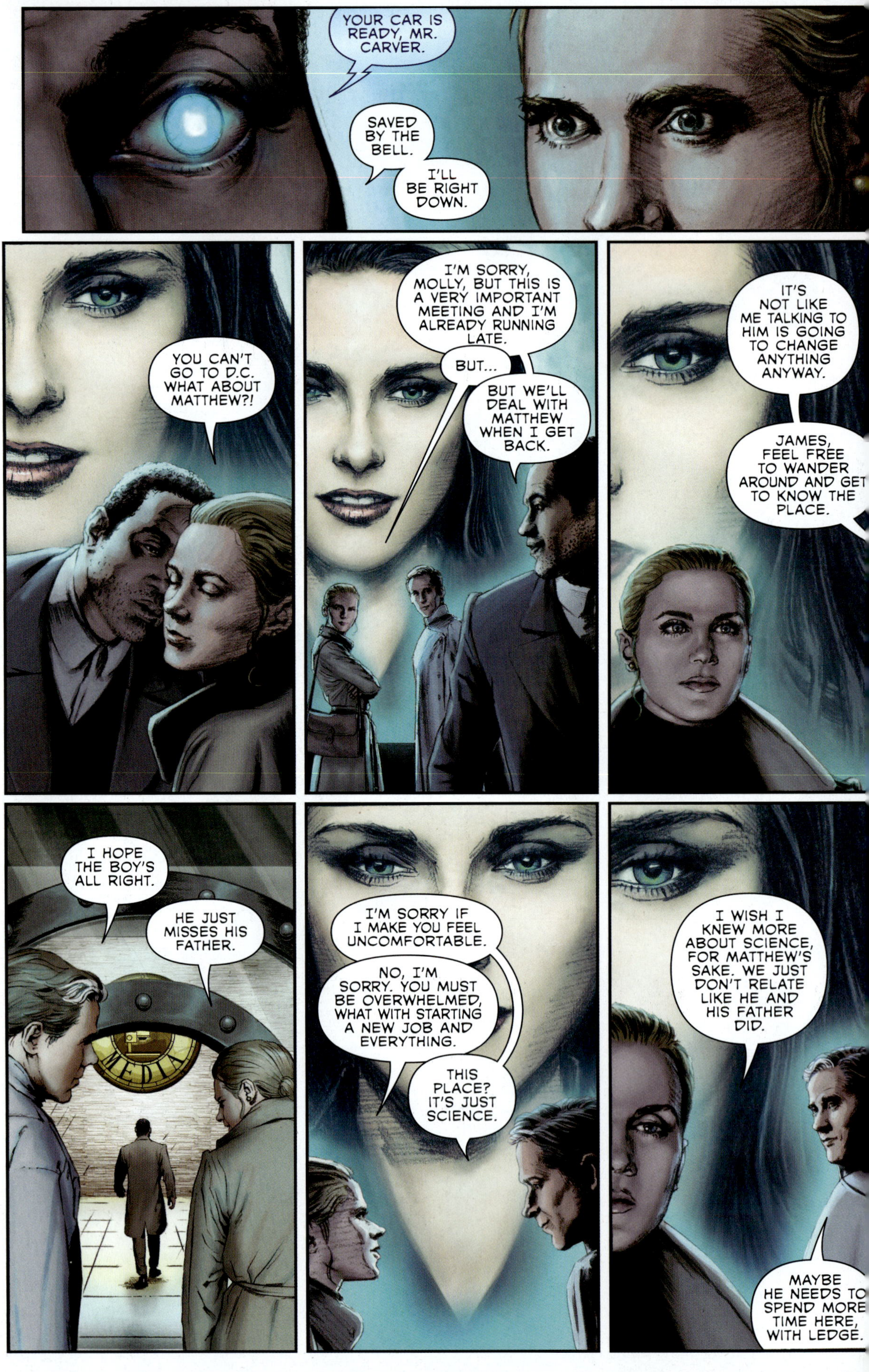

YOUR CAR IS READY, MR. CARVER.
SAVED BY THE BELL.
I'LL BE RIGHT DOWN.
YOU CAN'T GO TO D.C. WHAT ABOUT MATTHEW?!
I'M SORRY, MOLLY, BUT THIS IS A VERY IMPORTANT MEETING AND I'M ALREADY RUNNING LATE.
BUT...
BUT WE'LL DEAL WITH MATTHEW WHEN I GET BACK.
IT'S NOT LIKE ME TALKING TO HIM IS GOING TO CHANGE ANYTHING ANYWAY.
JAMES, FEEL FREE TO WANDER AROUND AND GET TO KNOW THE PLACE.
I HOPE THE BOY'S ALL RIGHT.
HE JUST MISSES HIS FATHER.
MEDIA
I'M SORRY IF I MAKE YOU FEEL UNCOMFORTABLE.
NO, I'M SORRY. YOU MUST BE OVERWHELMED, WHAT WITH STARTING A NEW JOB AND EVERYTHING.
THIS PLACE? IT'S JUST SCIENCE.
I WISH I KNEW MORE ABOUT SCIENCE, FOR MATTHEW'S SAKE. WE JUST DON'T RELATE LIKE HE AND HIS FATHER DID.
MAYBE HE NEEDS TO SPEND MORE TIME HERE, WITH LEDGE.

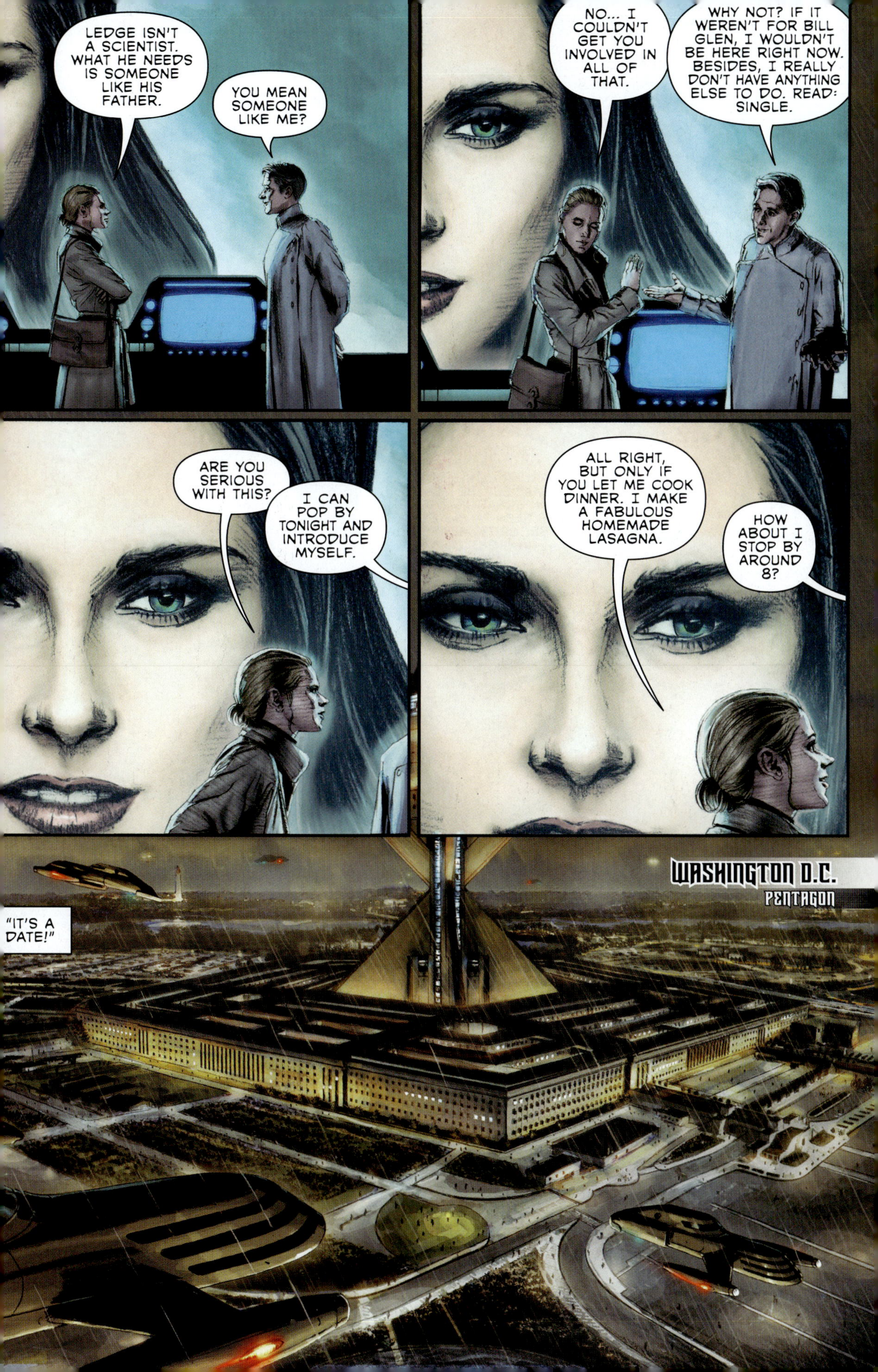

LEDGE ISN'T A SCIENTIST. WHAT HE NEEDS IS SOMEONE LIKE HIS FATHER.
YOU MEAN SOMEONE LIKE ME?
NO... I COULDN'T GET YOU INVOLVED IN ALL OF THAT.
WHY NOT? IF IT WEREN'T FOR BILL GLEN, I WOULDN'T BE HERE RIGHT NOW. BESIDES, I REALLY DON'T HAVE ANYTHING ELSE TO DO. READ: SINGLE.
ARE YOU SERIOUS WITH THIS?
I CAN POP BY TONIGHT AND INTRODUCE MYSELF.
ALL RIGHT, BUT ONLY IF YOU LET ME COOK DINNER. I MAKE A FABULOUS HOMEMADE LASAGNA.
HOW ABOUT I STOP BY AROUND 8?
WASHINGTON D.C.
PENTAGON
"IT'S A DATE!"

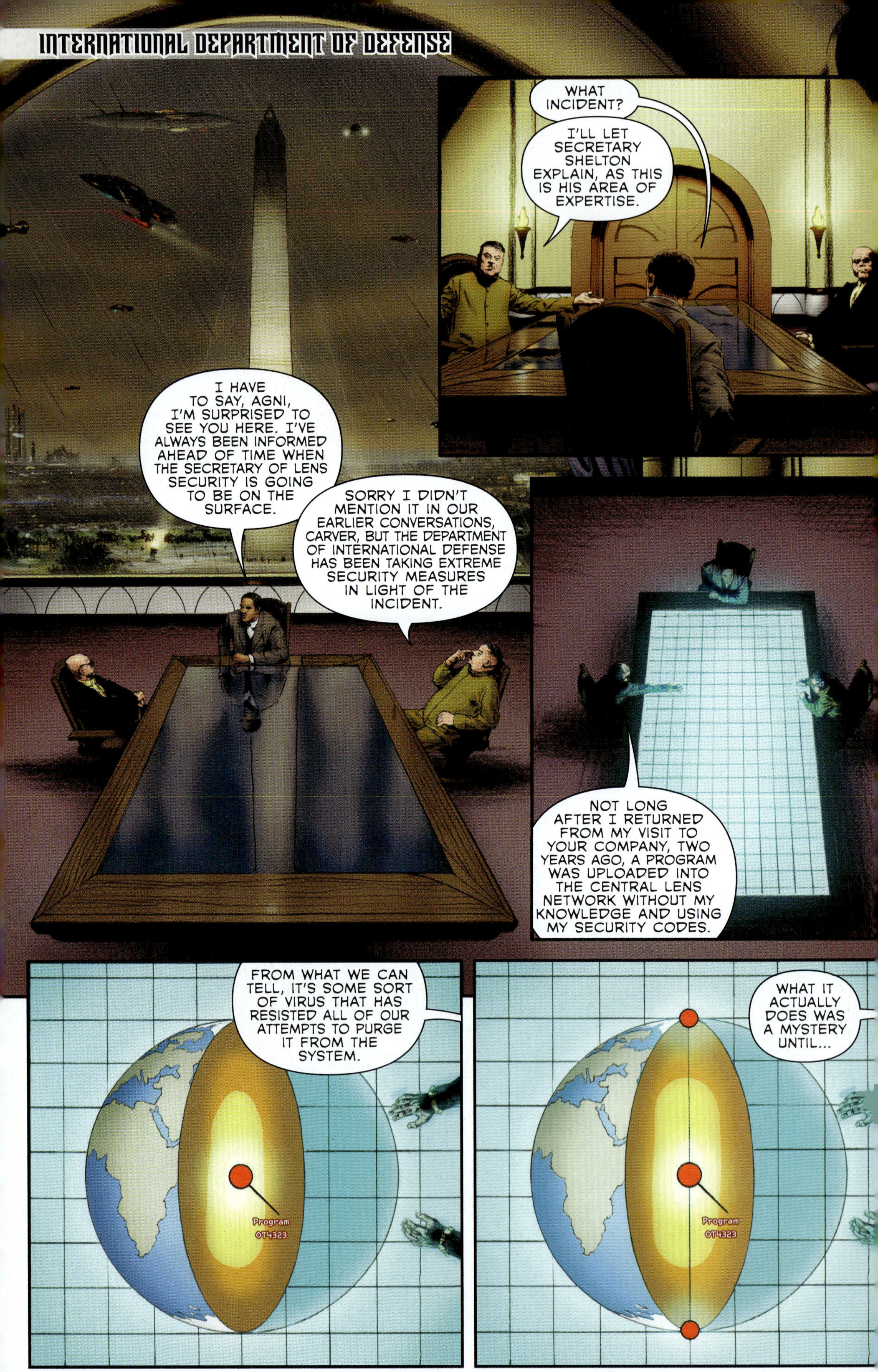
INTERNATIONAL DEPARTMENT OF DEFENSE
I HAVE TO SAY, AGNI, I'M SURPRISED TO SEE YOU HERE. I'VE ALWAYS BEEN INFORMED AHEAD OF TIME WHEN THE SECRETARY OF LENS SECURITY IS GOING TO BE ON THE SURFACE.
SORRY I DIDN'T MENTION IT IN OUR EARLIER CONVERSATIONS, CARVER, BUT THE DEPARTMENT OF INTERNATIONAL DEFENSE HAS BEEN TAKING EXTREME SECURITY MEASURES IN LIGHT OF THE INCIDENT.
WHAT INCIDENT?
I'LL LET SECRETARY SHELTON EXPLAIN, AS THIS IS HIS AREA OF EXPERTISE.
NOT LONG AFTER I RETURNED FROM MY VISIT TO YOUR COMPANY, TWO YEARS AGO, A PROGRAM WAS UPLOADED INTO THE CENTRAL LENS NETWORK WITHOUT MY KNOWLEDGE AND USING MY SECURITY CODES.
FROM WHAT WE CAN TELL, IT'S SOME SORT OF VIRUS THAT HAS RESISTED ALL OF OUR ATTEMPTS TO PURGE IT FROM THE SYSTEM.
Program OT4323
WHAT IT ACTUALLY DOES WAS A MYSTERY UNTIL...
Program OT4323

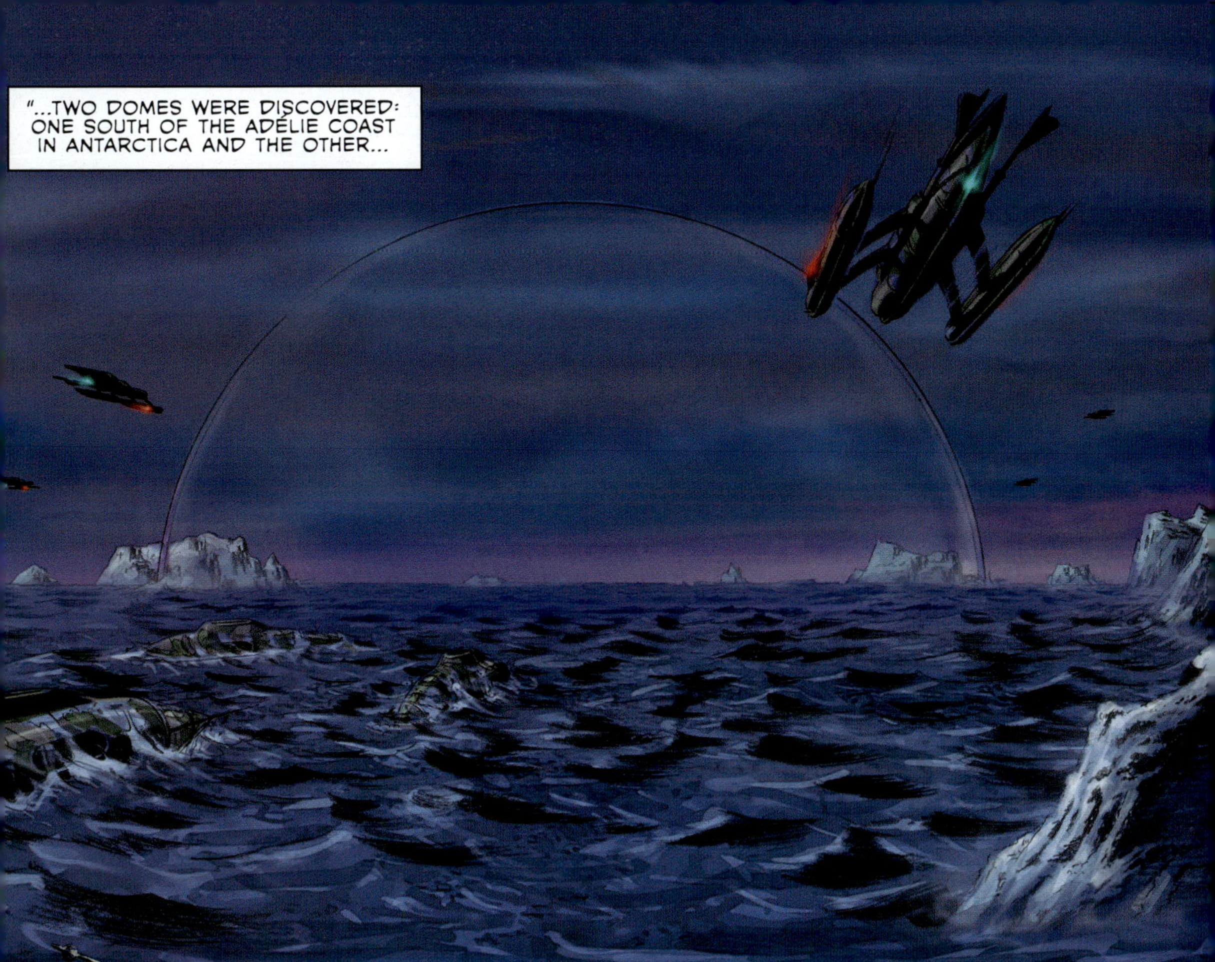
"...TWO DOMES WERE DISCOVERED: ONE SOUTH OF THE ADÉLIE COAST IN ANTARCTICA AND THE OTHER...

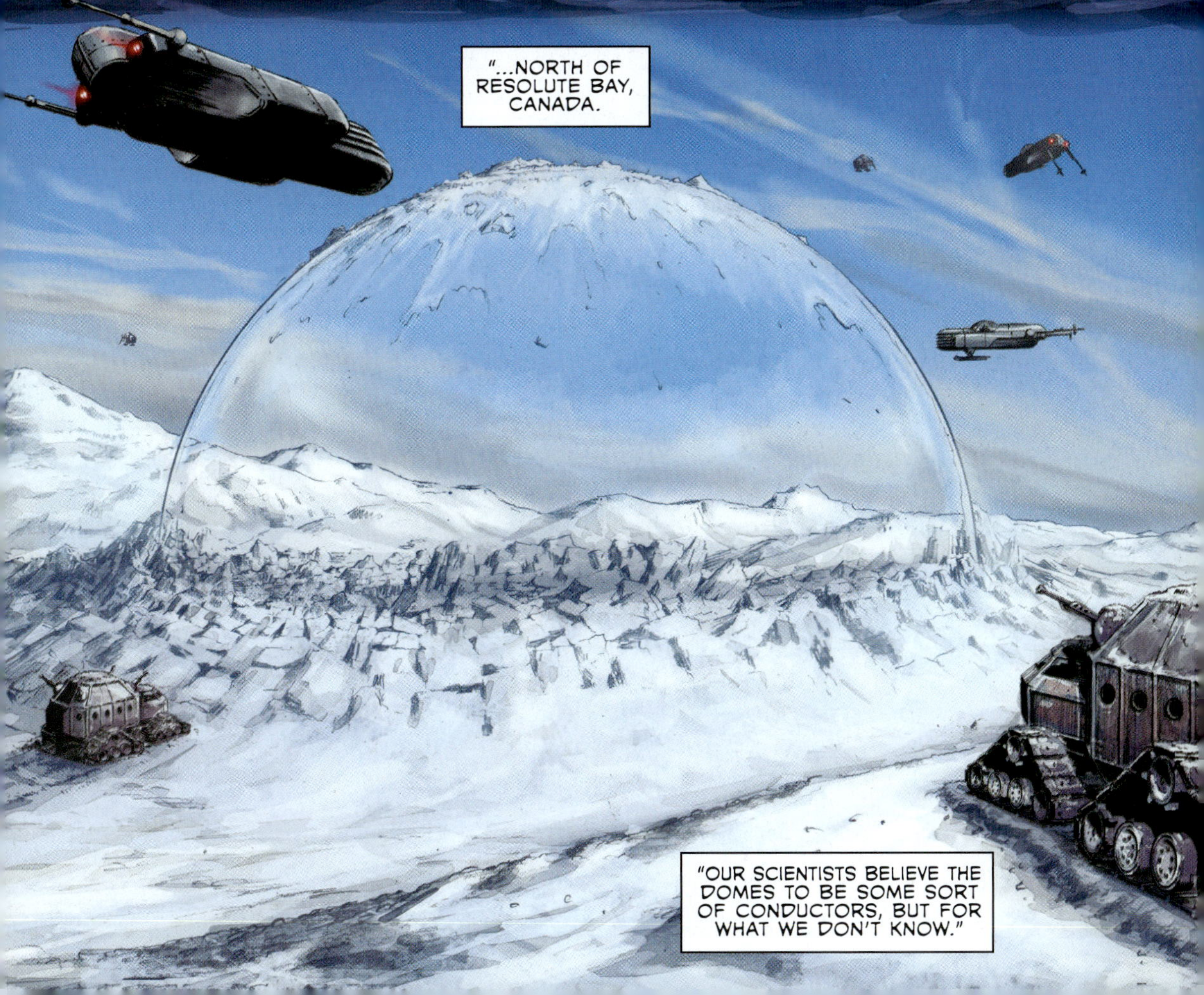
"...NORTH OF RESOLUTE BAY, CANADA.
"OUR SCIENTISTS BELIEVE THE DOMES TO BE SOME SORT OF CONDUCTORS, BUT FOR WHAT WE DON'T KNOW."

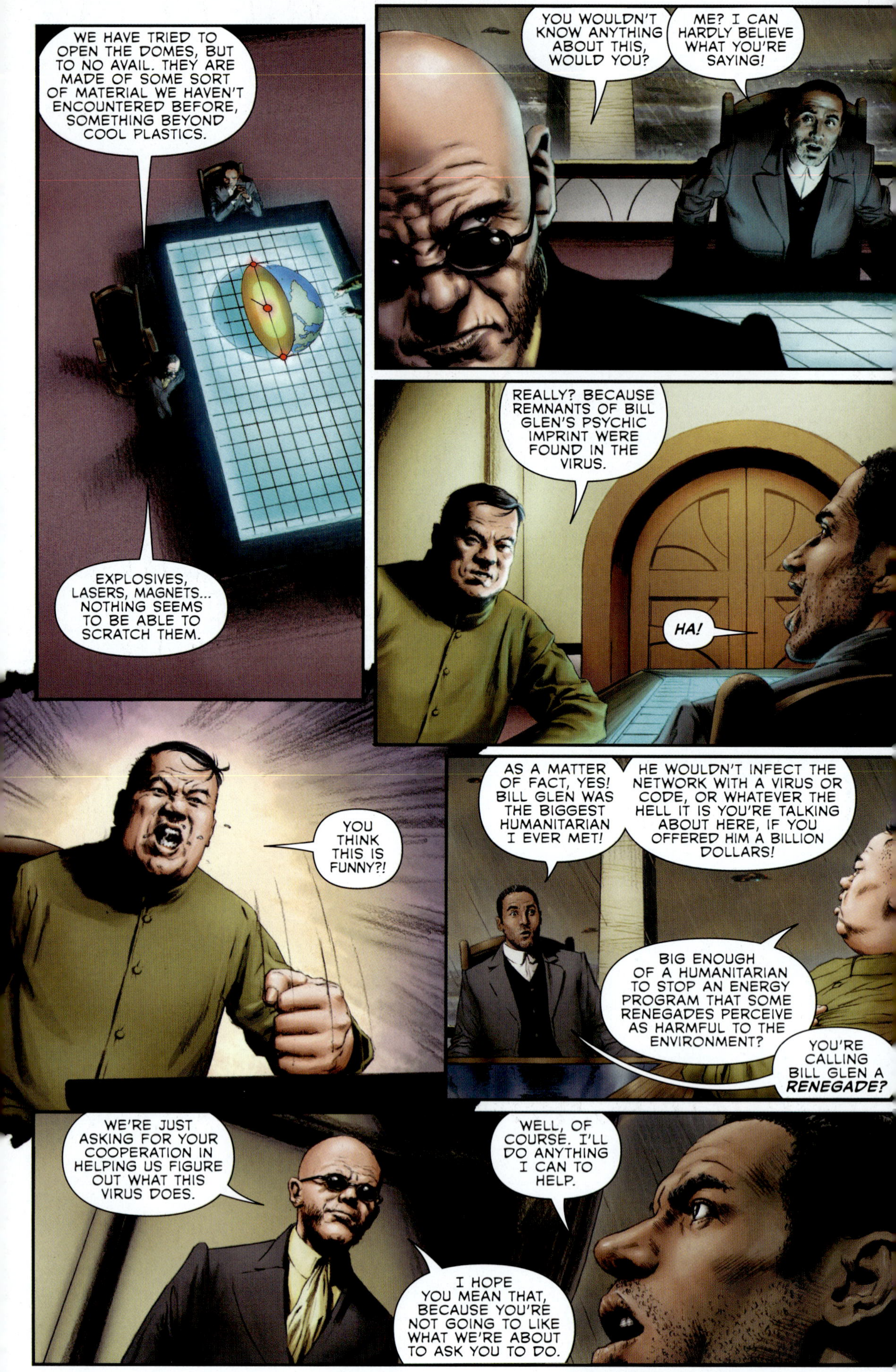
WE HAVE TRIED TO OPEN THE DOMES, BUT TO NO AVAIL. THEY ARE MADE OF SOME SORT OF MATERIAL WE HAVEN'T ENCOUNTERED BEFORE, SOMETHING BEYOND COOL PLASTICS.
EXPLOSIVES, LASERS, MAGNETS... NOTHING SEEMS TO BE ABLE TO SCRATCH THEM.
YOU WOULDN'T KNOW ANYTHING ABOUT THIS, WOULD YOU?
ME? I CAN HARDLY BELIEVE WHAT YOU'RE SAYING!
REALLY? BECAUSE REMNANTS OF BILL GLEN'S PSYCHIC IMPRINT WERE FOUND IN THE VIRUS.
HA!
YOU THINK THIS IS FUNNY?!
AS A MATTER OF FACT, YES! BILL GLEN WAS THE BIGGEST HUMANITARIAN I EVER MET!
HE WOULDN'T INFECT THE NETWORK WITH A VIRUS OR CODE, OR WHATEVER THE HELL IT IS YOU'RE TALKING ABOUT HERE, IF YOU OFFERED HIM A BILLION DOLLARS!
BIG ENOUGH OF A HUMANITARIAN TO STOP AN ENERGY PROGRAM THAT SOME RENEGADES PERCEIVE AS HARMFUL TO THE ENVIRONMENT?
YOU'RE CALLING BILL GLEN A *RENEGADE?*
WE'RE JUST ASKING FOR YOUR COOPERATION IN HELPING US FIGURE OUT WHAT THIS VIRUS DOES.
WELL, OF COURSE. I'LL DO ANYTHING I CAN TO HELP.
I HOPE YOU MEAN THAT, BECAUSE YOU'RE NOT GOING TO LIKE WHAT WE'RE ABOUT TO ASK YOU TO DO.

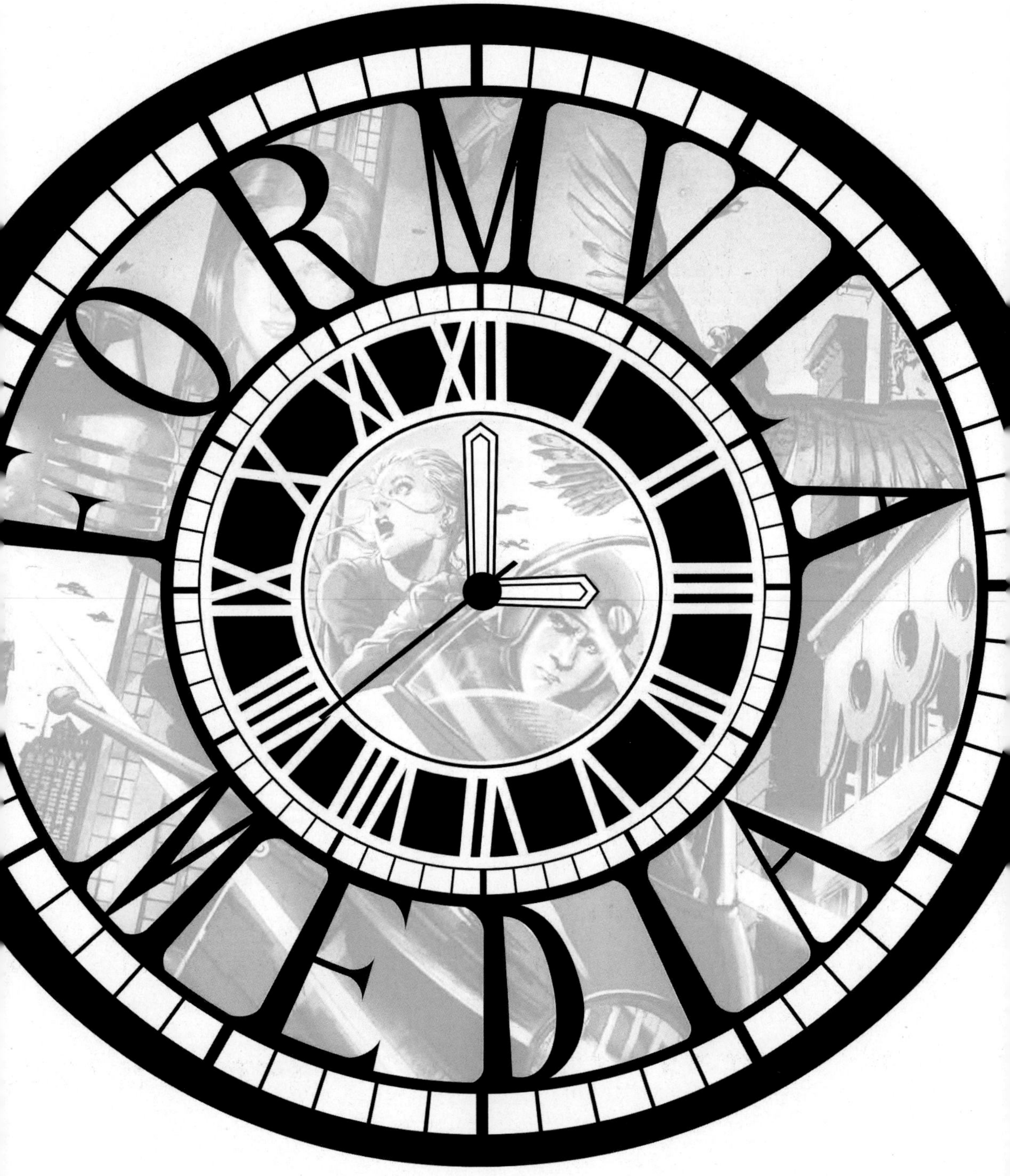

CHAPTER 03

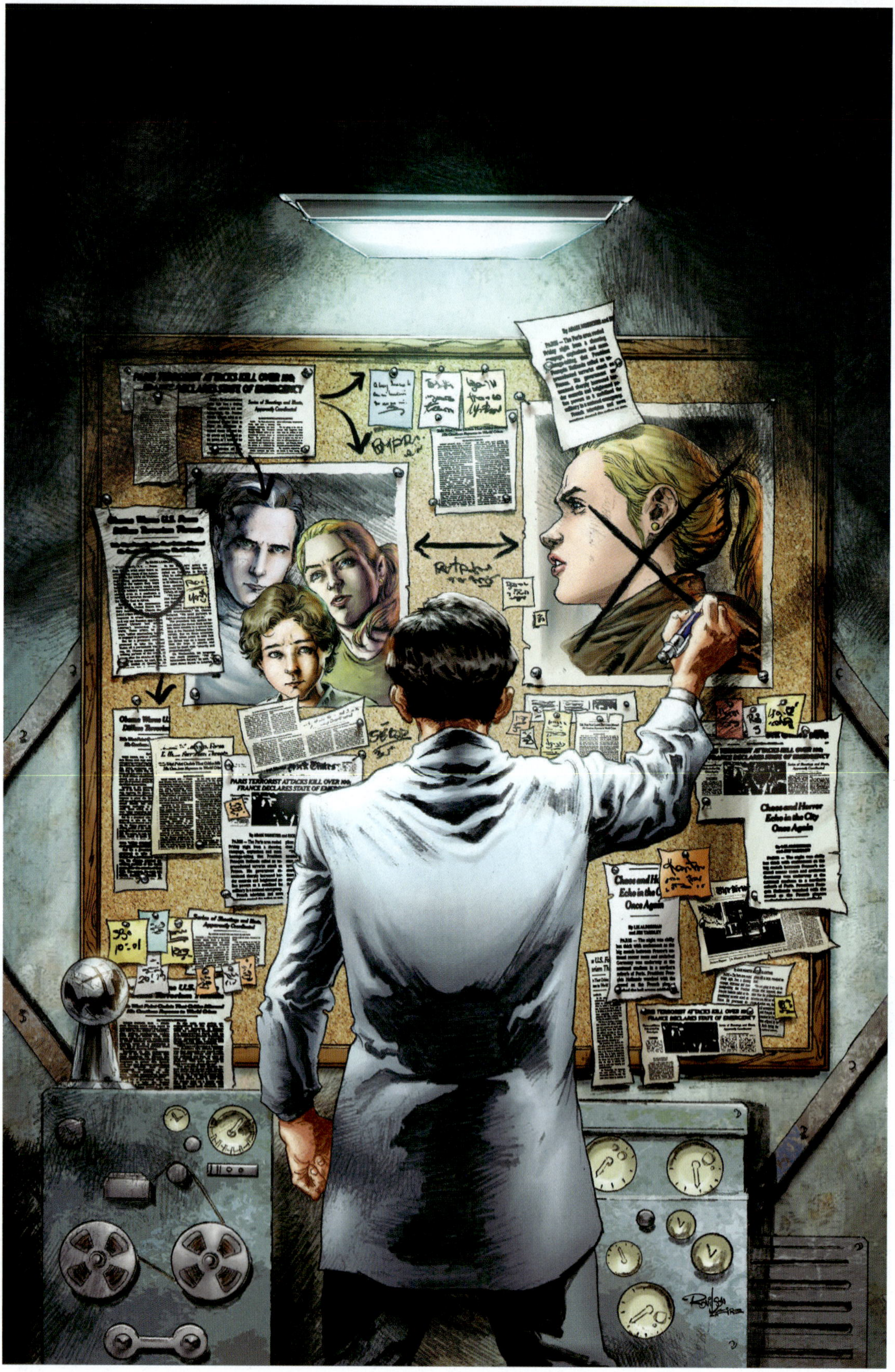
PARIS TERRORIST ATTACKS KILL OVER 100;
FRANCE DECLARES STATE OF EMERGENCY
Chaos and Horror Echo in the City Once Again

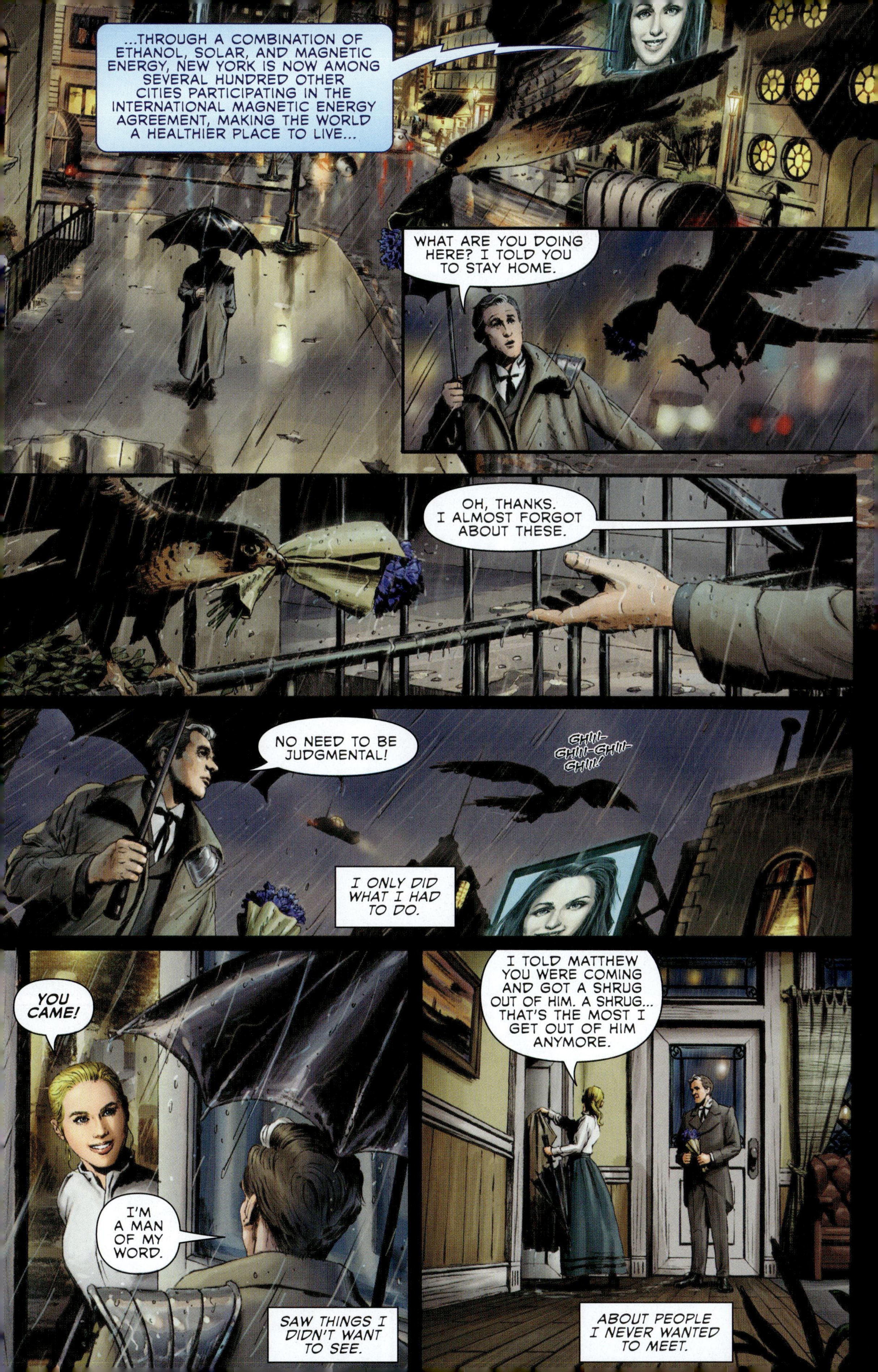
...THROUGH A COMBINATION OF ETHANOL, SOLAR, AND MAGNETIC ENERGY, NEW YORK IS NOW AMONG SEVERAL HUNDRED OTHER CITIES PARTICIPATING IN THE INTERNATIONAL MAGNETIC ENERGY AGREEMENT, MAKING THE WORLD A HEALTHIER PLACE TO LIVE...
WHAT ARE YOU DOING HERE? I TOLD YOU TO STAY HOME.
OH, THANKS. I ALMOST FORGOT ABOUT THESE.
NO NEED TO BE JUDGMENTAL!
GHIII-GHIII-GHIII-GHIII!
I ONLY DID WHAT I HAD TO DO.
YOU CAME!
I'M A MAN OF MY WORD.
SAW THINGS I DIDN'T WANT TO SEE.
I TOLD MATTHEW YOU WERE COMING AND GOT A SHRUG OUT OF HIM. A SHRUG... THAT'S THE MOST I GET OUT OF HIM ANYMORE.
ABOUT PEOPLE I NEVER WANTED TO MEET.

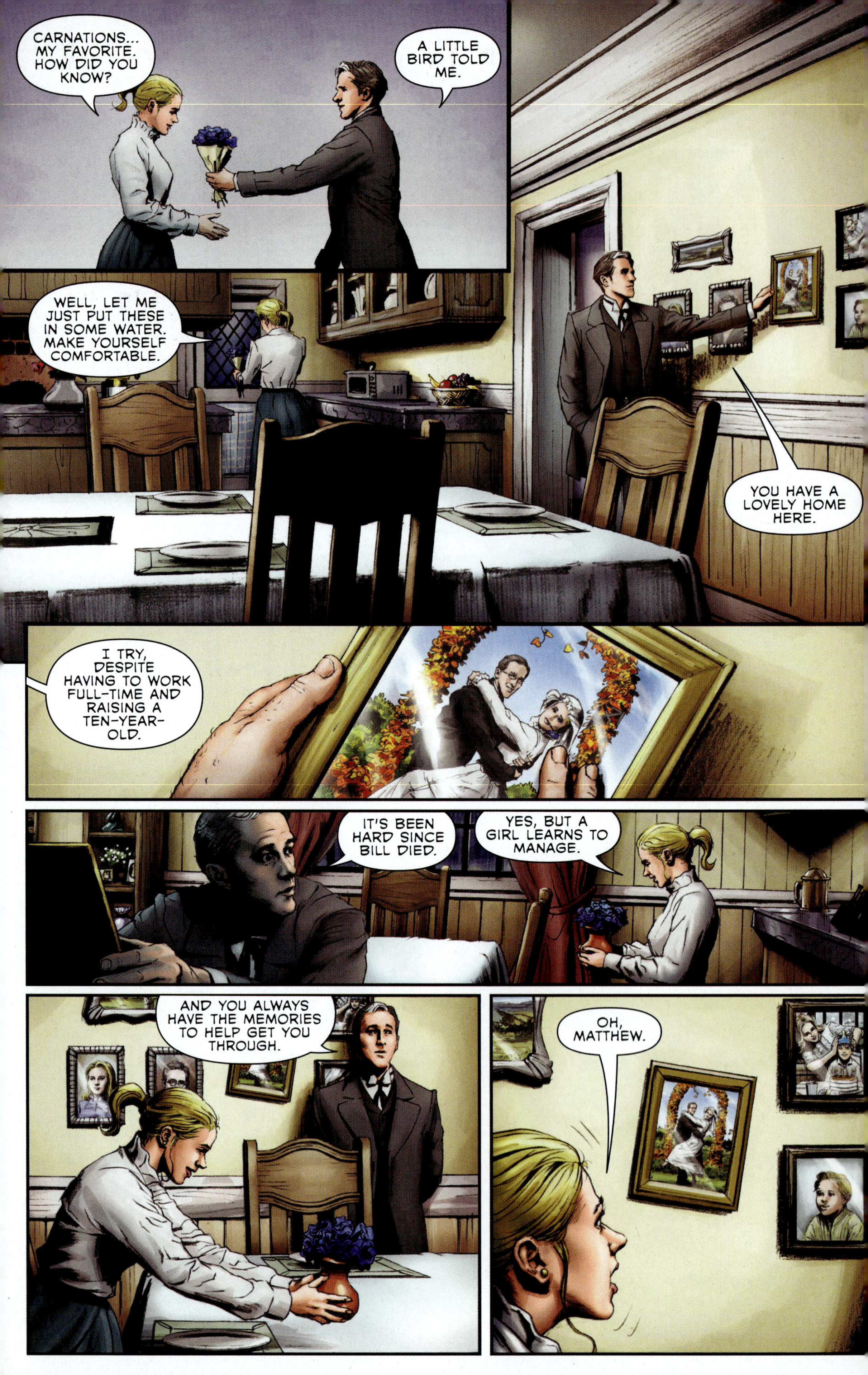
CARNATIONS... MY FAVORITE. HOW DID YOU KNOW?
A LITTLE BIRD TOLD ME.
WELL, LET ME JUST PUT THESE IN SOME WATER. MAKE YOURSELF COMFORTABLE.
YOU HAVE A LOVELY HOME HERE.
I TRY, DESPITE HAVING TO WORK FULL-TIME AND RAISING A TEN-YEAR-OLD.
IT'S BEEN HARD SINCE BILL DIED.
YES, BUT A GIRL LEARNS TO MANAGE.
AND YOU ALWAYS HAVE THE MEMORIES TO HELP GET YOU THROUGH.
OH, MATTHEW.

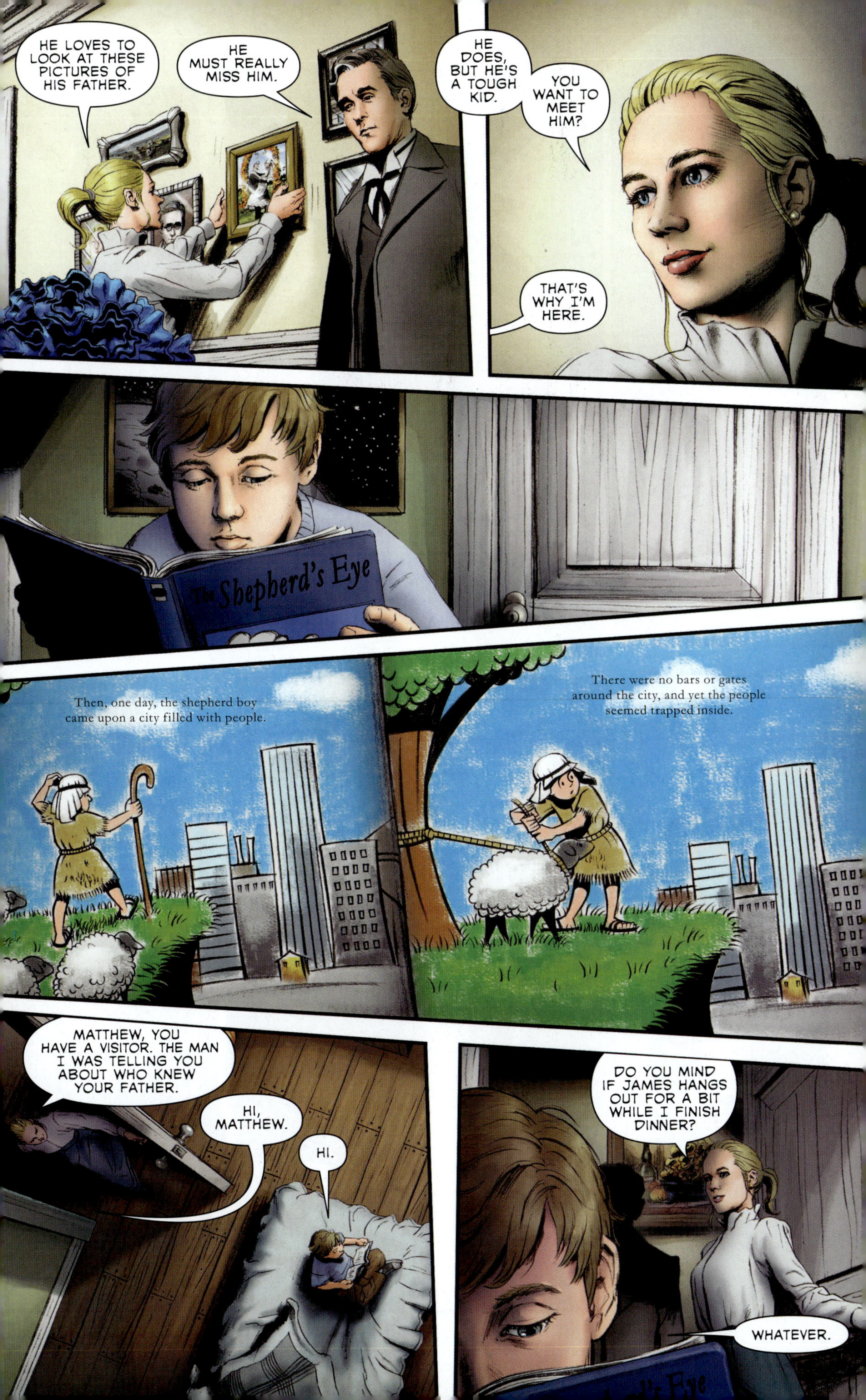
HE LOVES TO LOOK AT THESE PICTURES OF HIS FATHER.
HE MUST REALLY MISS HIM.
HE DOES, BUT HE'S A TOUGH KID.
YOU WANT TO MEET HIM?
THAT'S WHY I'M HERE.
The Shepherd's Eye
Then, one day, the shepherd boy came upon a city filled with people.
There were no bars or gates around the city, and yet the people seemed trapped inside.
MATTHEW, YOU HAVE A VISITOR. THE MAN I WAS TELLING YOU ABOUT WHO KNEW YOUR FATHER.
HI, MATTHEW.
HI.
DO YOU MIND IF JAMES HANGS OUT FOR A BIT WHILE I FINISH DINNER?
WHATEVER.

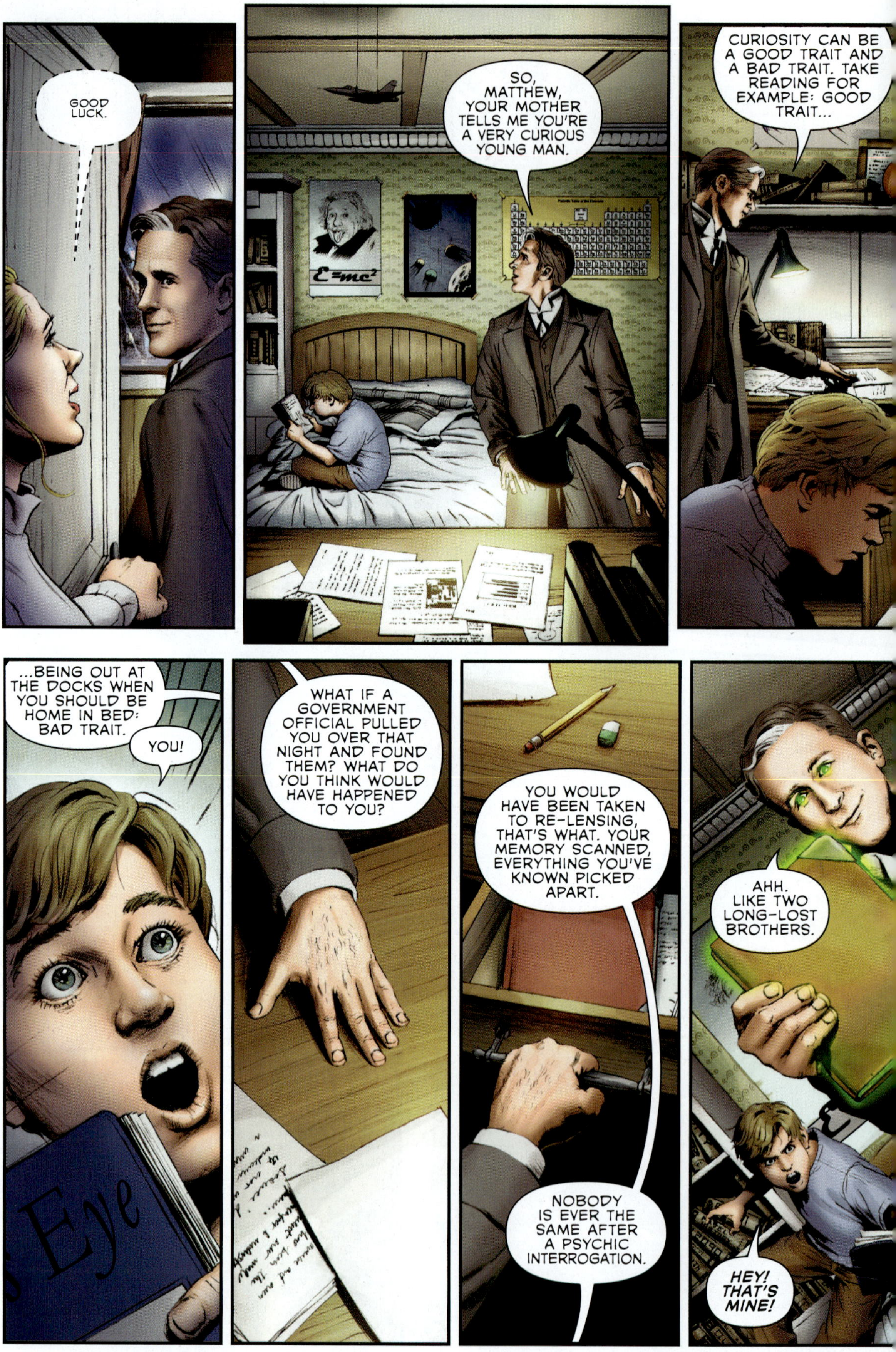
GOOD LUCK.
SO, MATTHEW, YOUR MOTHER TELLS ME YOU'RE A VERY CURIOUS YOUNG MAN.
E=mc²
CURIOSITY CAN BE A GOOD TRAIT AND A BAD TRAIT. TAKE READING FOR EXAMPLE: GOOD TRAIT...
...BEING OUT AT THE DOCKS WHEN YOU SHOULD BE HOME IN BED: BAD TRAIT.
YOU!
Eye
WHAT IF A GOVERNMENT OFFICIAL PULLED YOU OVER THAT NIGHT AND FOUND THEM? WHAT DO YOU THINK WOULD HAVE HAPPENED TO YOU?
YOU WOULD HAVE BEEN TAKEN TO RE-LENSING, THAT'S WHAT. YOUR MEMORY SCANNED, EVERYTHING YOU'VE KNOWN PICKED APART.
NOBODY IS EVER THE SAME AFTER A PSYCHIC INTERROGATION.
AHH. LIKE TWO LONG-LOST BROTHERS.
HEY! THAT'S MINE!

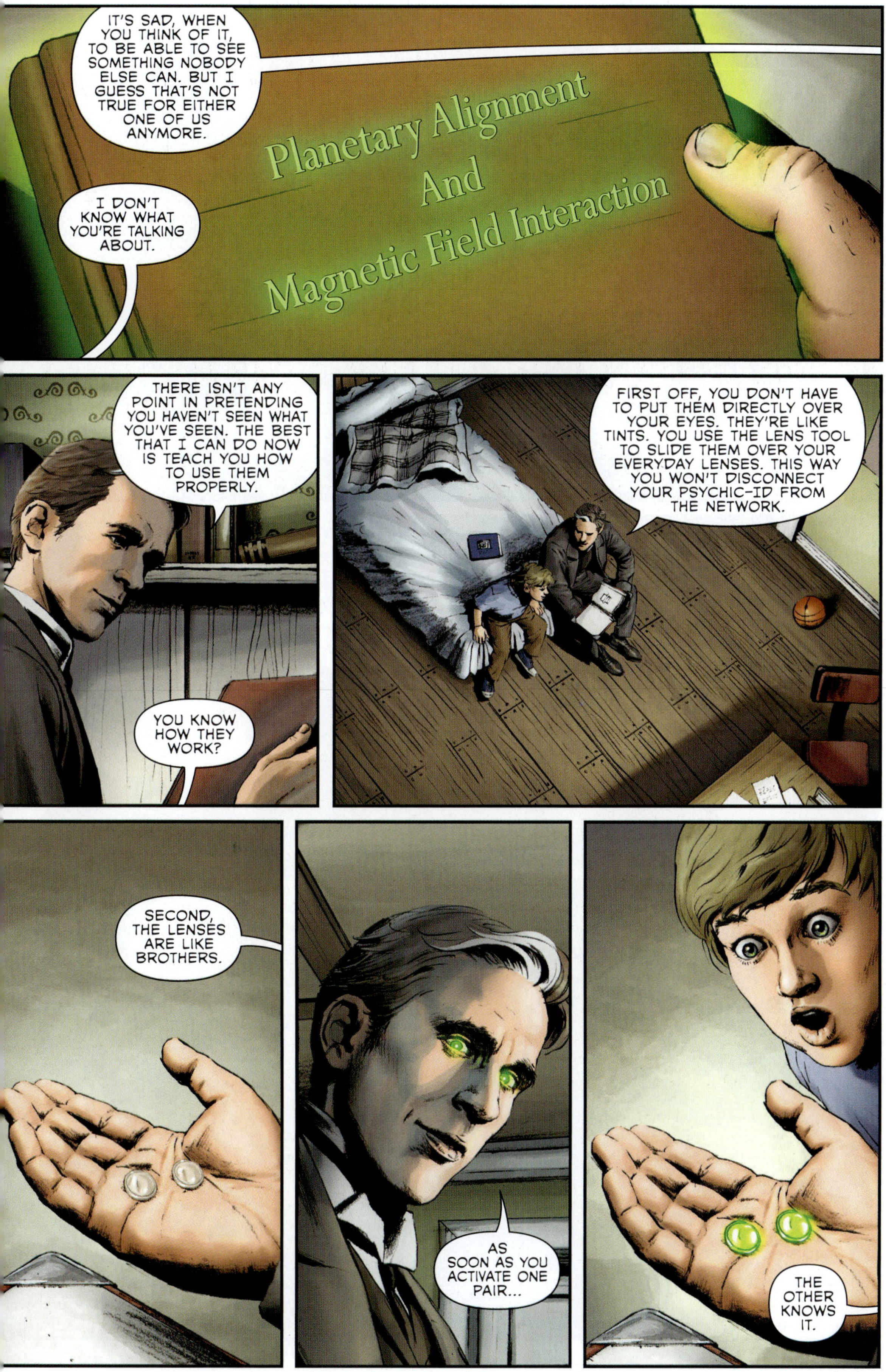
IT'S SAD, WHEN YOU THINK OF IT, TO BE ABLE TO SEE SOMETHING NOBODY ELSE CAN. BUT I GUESS THAT'S NOT TRUE FOR EITHER ONE OF US ANYMORE.
Planetary Alignment And Magnetic Field Interaction
I DON'T KNOW WHAT YOU'RE TALKING ABOUT.
THERE ISN'T ANY POINT IN PRETENDING YOU HAVEN'T SEEN WHAT YOU'VE SEEN. THE BEST THAT I CAN DO NOW IS TEACH YOU HOW TO USE THEM PROPERLY.
YOU KNOW HOW THEY WORK?
FIRST OFF, YOU DON'T HAVE TO PUT THEM DIRECTLY OVER YOUR EYES. THEY'RE LIKE TINTS. YOU USE THE LENS TOOL TO SLIDE THEM OVER YOUR EVERYDAY LENSES. THIS WAY YOU WON'T DISCONNECT YOUR PSYCHIC-ID FROM THE NETWORK.
SECOND, THE LENSES ARE LIKE BROTHERS.
AS SOON AS YOU ACTIVATE ONE PAIR...
THE OTHER KNOWS IT.

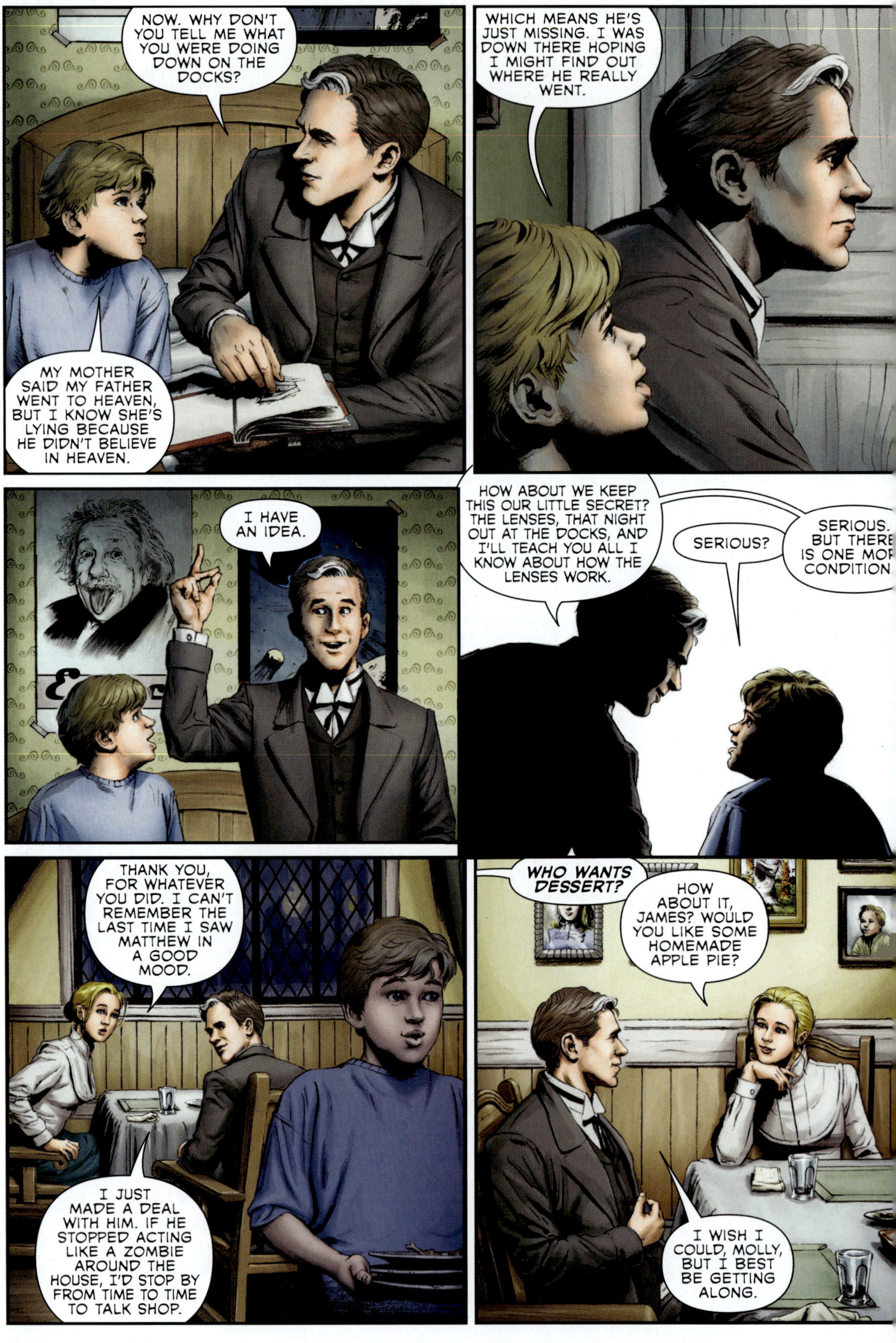
NOW. WHY DON'T YOU TELL ME WHAT YOU WERE DOING DOWN ON THE DOCKS?
MY MOTHER SAID MY FATHER WENT TO HEAVEN, BUT I KNOW SHE'S LYING BECAUSE HE DIDN'T BELIEVE IN HEAVEN.
WHICH MEANS HE'S JUST MISSING. I WAS DOWN THERE HOPING I MIGHT FIND OUT WHERE HE REALLY WENT.
I HAVE AN IDEA.
HOW ABOUT WE KEEP THIS OUR LITTLE SECRET? THE LENSES, THAT NIGHT OUT AT THE DOCKS, AND I'LL TEACH YOU ALL I KNOW ABOUT HOW THE LENSES WORK.
SERIOUS?
SERIOUS. BUT THERE IS ONE MOR CONDITION
THANK YOU, FOR WHATEVER YOU DID. I CAN'T REMEMBER THE LAST TIME I SAW MATTHEW IN A GOOD MOOD.
I JUST MADE A DEAL WITH HIM. IF HE STOPPED ACTING LIKE A ZOMBIE AROUND THE HOUSE, I'D STOP BY FROM TIME TO TIME TO TALK SHOP.
WHO WANTS DESSERT?
HOW ABOUT IT, JAMES? WOULD YOU LIKE SOME HOMEMADE APPLE PIE?
I WISH I COULD, MOLLY, BUT I BEST BE GETTING ALONG.

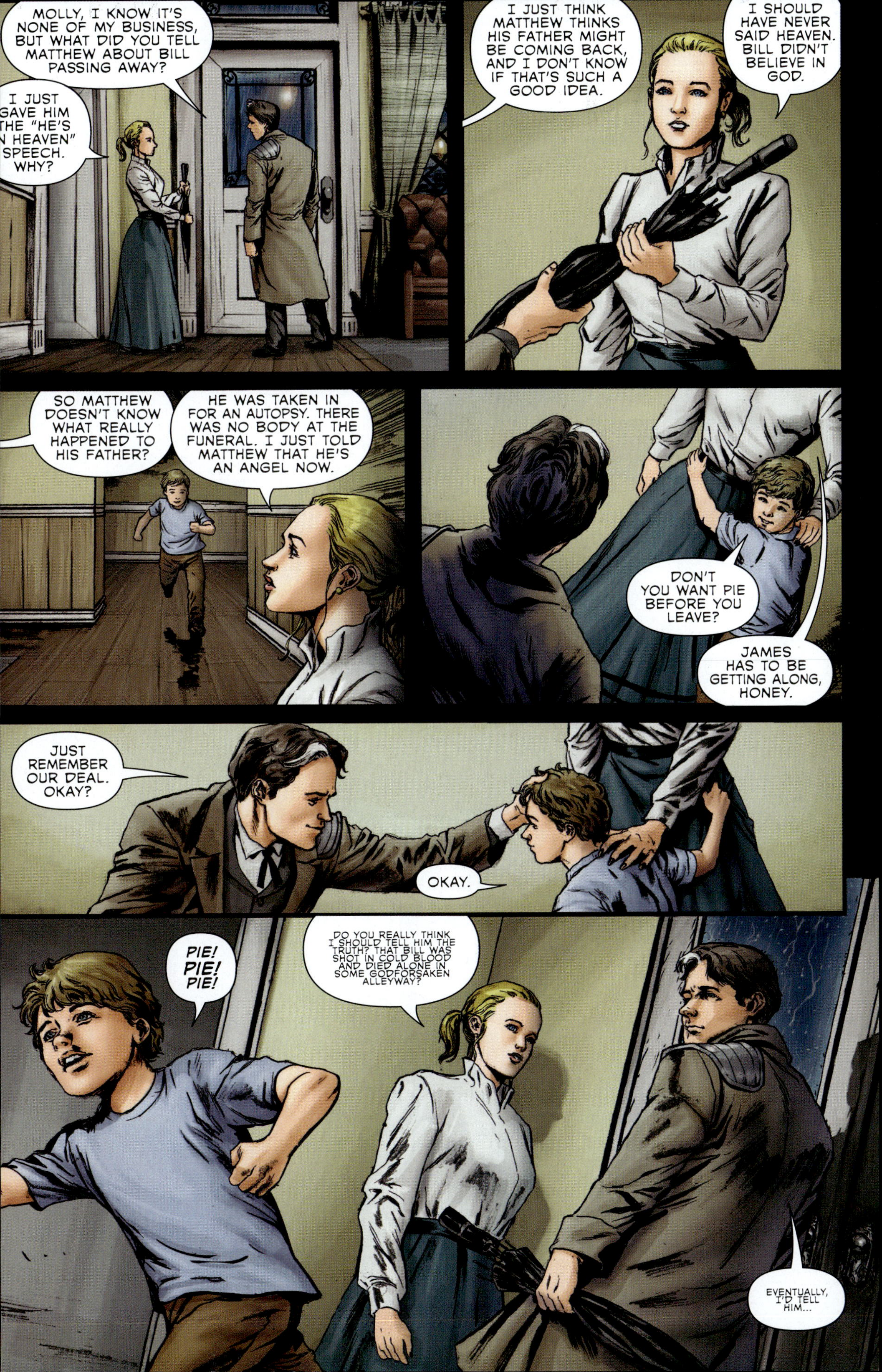

MOLLY, I KNOW IT'S NONE OF MY BUSINESS, BUT WHAT DID YOU TELL MATTHEW ABOUT BILL PASSING AWAY?
I JUST GAVE HIM THE "HE'S N HEAVEN" SPEECH. WHY?
I JUST THINK MATTHEW THINKS HIS FATHER MIGHT BE COMING BACK, AND I DON'T KNOW IF THAT'S SUCH A GOOD IDEA.
I SHOULD HAVE NEVER SAID HEAVEN. BILL DIDN'T BELIEVE IN GOD.
SO MATTHEW DOESN'T KNOW WHAT REALLY HAPPENED TO HIS FATHER?
HE WAS TAKEN IN FOR AN AUTOPSY. THERE WAS NO BODY AT THE FUNERAL. I JUST TOLD MATTHEW THAT HE'S AN ANGEL NOW.
DON'T YOU WANT PIE BEFORE YOU LEAVE?
JAMES HAS TO BE GETTING ALONG, HONEY.
JUST REMEMBER OUR DEAL. OKAY?
OKAY.
PIE! PIE! PIE!
DO YOU REALLY THINK I SHOULD TELL HIM THE TRUTH? THAT BILL WAS SHOT IN COLD BLOOD AND DIED ALONE IN SOME GODFORSAKEN ALLEYWAY?
EVENTUALLY, I'D TELL HIM...

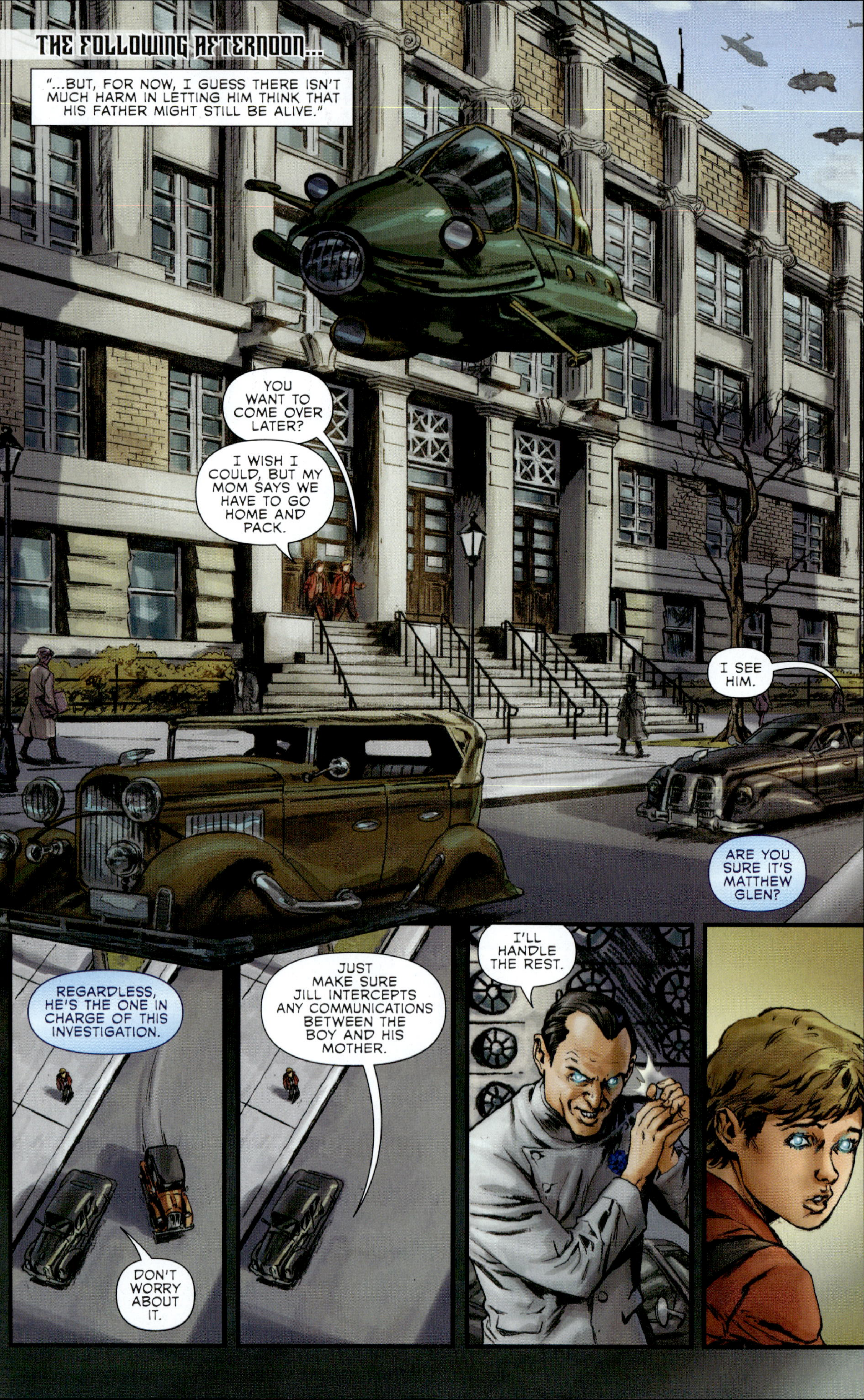
THE FOLLOWING AFTERNOON...
"...BUT, FOR NOW, I GUESS THERE ISN'T MUCH HARM IN LETTING HIM THINK THAT HIS FATHER MIGHT STILL BE ALIVE."
YOU WANT TO COME OVER LATER?
I WISH I COULD, BUT MY MOM SAYS WE HAVE TO GO HOME AND PACK.
I SEE HIM.
ARE YOU SURE IT'S MATTHEW GLEN?
REGARDLESS, HE'S THE ONE IN CHARGE OF THIS INVESTIGATION.
DON'T WORRY ABOUT IT.
JUST MAKE SURE JILL INTERCEPTS ANY COMMUNICATIONS BETWEEN THE BOY AND HIS MOTHER.
I'LL HANDLE THE REST.

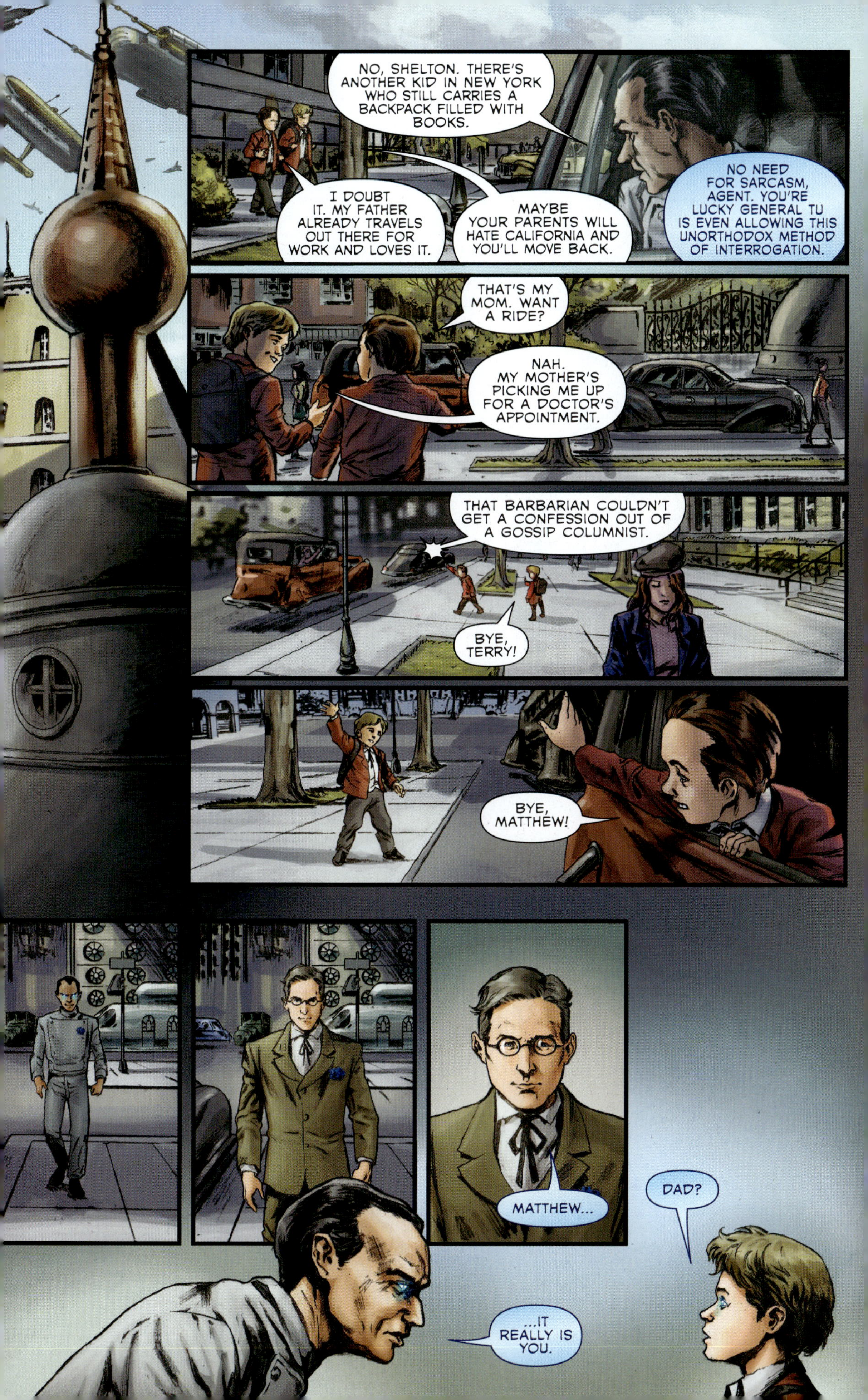
NO, SHELTON. THERE'S ANOTHER KID IN NEW YORK WHO STILL CARRIES A BACKPACK FILLED WITH BOOKS.
I DOUBT IT. MY FATHER ALREADY TRAVELS OUT THERE FOR WORK AND LOVES IT.
MAYBE YOUR PARENTS WILL HATE CALIFORNIA AND YOU'LL MOVE BACK.
NO NEED FOR SARCASM, AGENT. YOU'RE LUCKY GENERAL TU IS EVEN ALLOWING THIS UNORTHODOX METHOD OF INTERROGATION.
THAT'S MY MOM. WANT A RIDE?
NAH. MY MOTHER'S PICKING ME UP FOR A DOCTOR'S APPOINTMENT.
THAT BARBARIAN COULDN'T GET A CONFESSION OUT OF A GOSSIP COLUMNIST.
BYE, TERRY!
BYE, MATTHEW!
MATTHEW...
DAD?
...IT REALLY IS YOU.

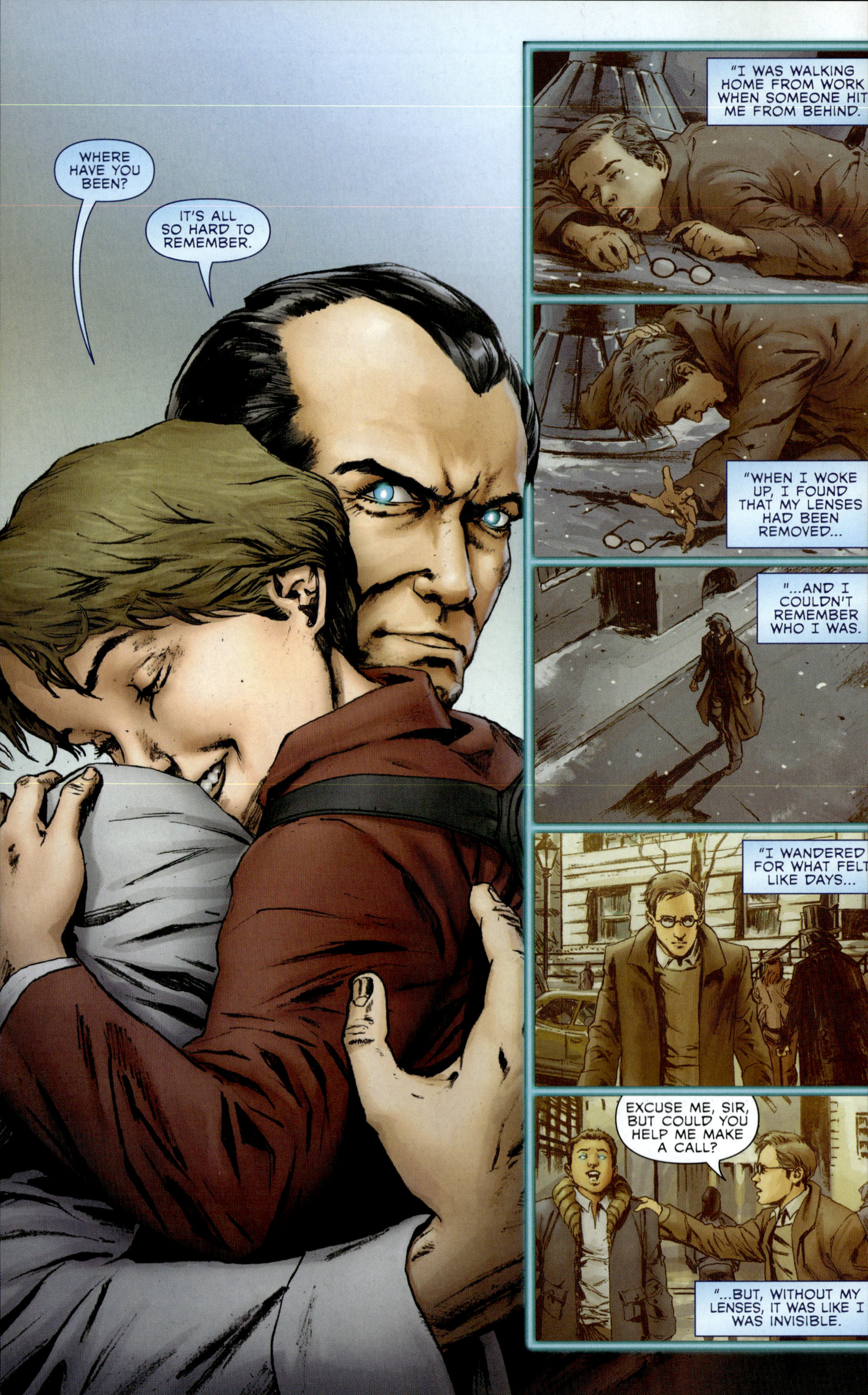

WHERE HAVE YOU BEEN?
IT'S ALL SO HARD TO REMEMBER.
"I WAS WALKING HOME FROM WORK WHEN SOMEONE HIT ME FROM BEHIND.
"WHEN I WOKE UP, I FOUND THAT MY LENSES HAD BEEN REMOVED...
"...AND I COULDN'T REMEMBER WHO I WAS.
"I WANDERED FOR WHAT FELT LIKE DAYS...
EXCUSE ME, SIR, BUT COULD YOU HELP ME MAKE A CALL?
"...BUT, WITHOUT MY LENSES, IT WAS LIKE I WAS INVISIBLE.

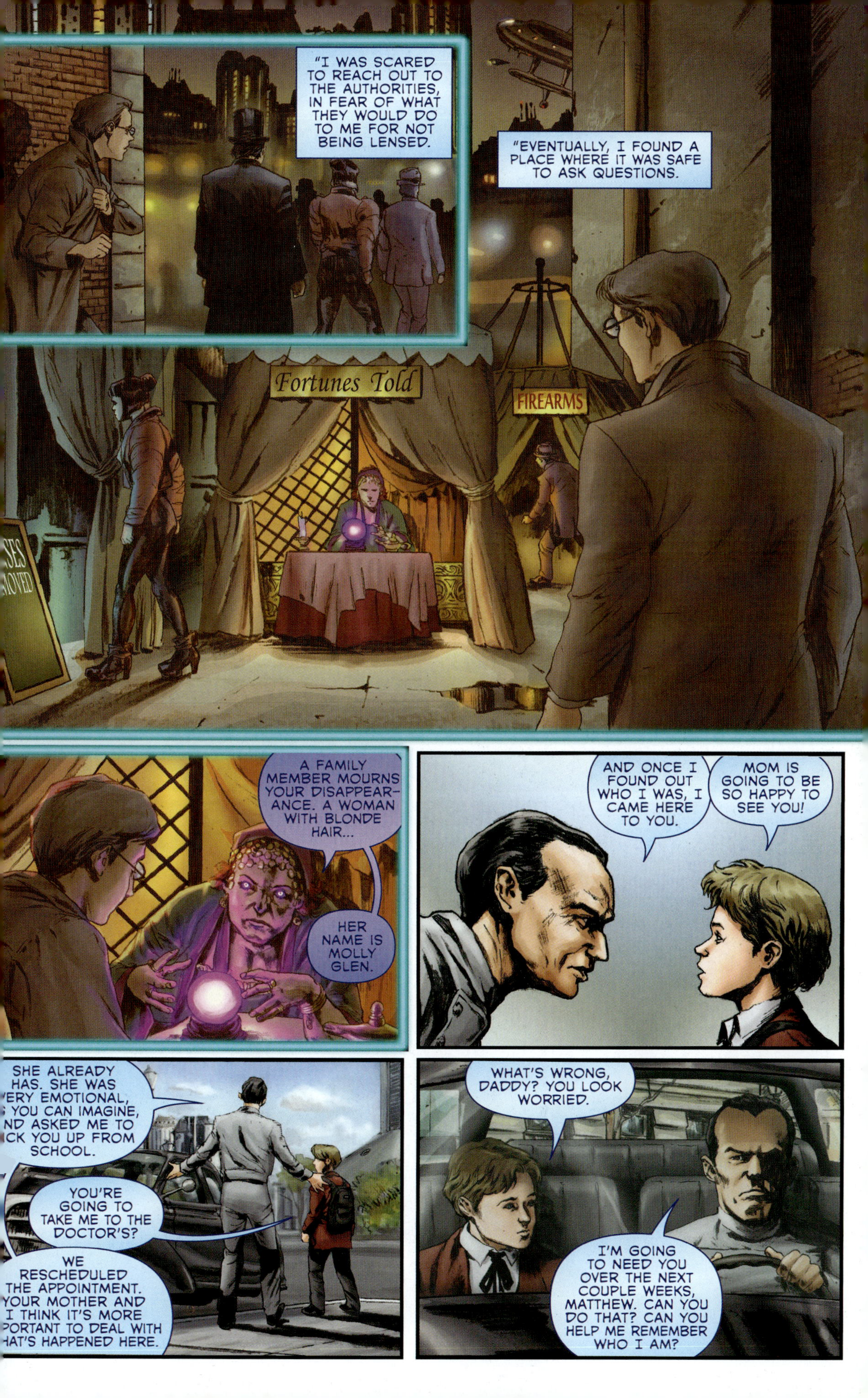

"I WAS SCARED TO REACH OUT TO THE AUTHORITIES, IN FEAR OF WHAT THEY WOULD DO TO ME FOR NOT BEING LENSED.
"EVENTUALLY, I FOUND A PLACE WHERE IT WAS SAFE TO ASK QUESTIONS.
Fortunes Told
FIREARMS
A FAMILY MEMBER MOURNS YOUR DISAPPEAR-ANCE. A WOMAN WITH BLONDE HAIR...
HER NAME IS MOLLY GLEN.
AND ONCE I FOUND OUT WHO I WAS, I CAME HERE TO YOU.
MOM IS GOING TO BE SO HAPPY TO SEE YOU!
SHE ALREADY HAS. SHE WAS ERY EMOTIONAL, YOU CAN IMAGINE, ND ASKED ME TO CK YOU UP FROM SCHOOL.
YOU'RE GOING TO TAKE ME TO THE DOCTOR'S?
WE RESCHEDULED THE APPOINTMENT. YOUR MOTHER AND I THINK IT'S MORE PORTANT TO DEAL WITH HAT'S HAPPENED HERE.
WHAT'S WRONG, DADDY? YOU LOOK WORRIED.
I'M GOING TO NEED YOU OVER THE NEXT COUPLE WEEKS, MATTHEW. CAN YOU DO THAT? CAN YOU HELP ME REMEMBER WHO I AM?

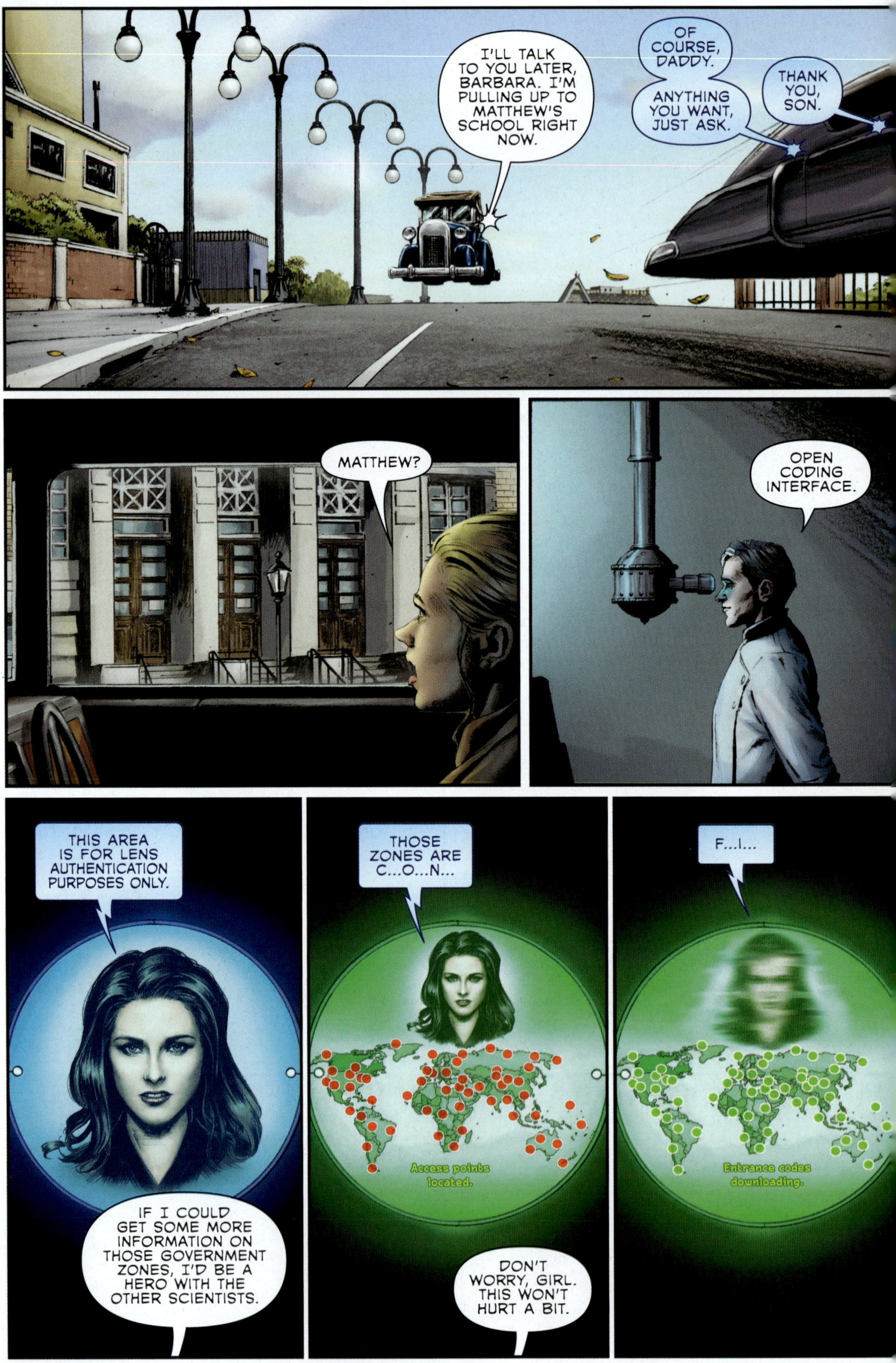
I'LL TALK TO YOU LATER, BARBARA. I'M PULLING UP TO MATTHEW'S SCHOOL RIGHT NOW.
OF COURSE, DADDY.
ANYTHING YOU WANT, JUST ASK.
THANK YOU, SON.
MATTHEW?
OPEN CODING INTERFACE.
THIS AREA IS FOR LENS AUTHENTICATION PURPOSES ONLY.
IF I COULD GET SOME MORE INFORMATION ON THOSE GOVERNMENT ZONES, I'D BE A HERO WITH THE OTHER SCIENTISTS.
THOSE ZONES ARE C...O...N...
Access points located.
DON'T WORRY, GIRL. THIS WON'T HURT A BIT.
F...I...
Entrance codes downloading.

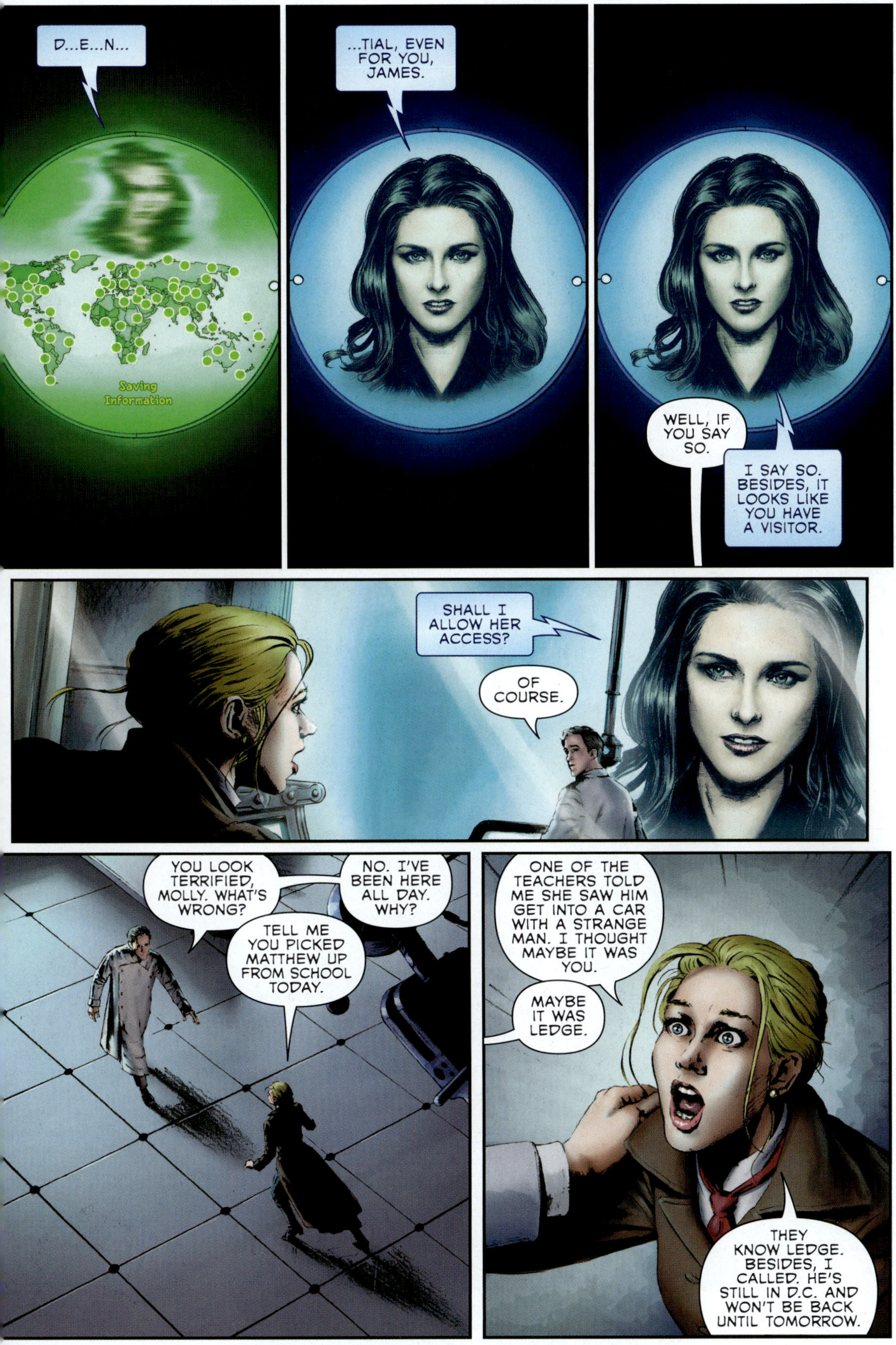
D...E...N...
Saving Information
...TIAL, EVEN FOR YOU, JAMES.
WELL, IF YOU SAY SO.
I SAY SO. BESIDES, IT LOOKS LIKE YOU HAVE A VISITOR.
SHALL I ALLOW HER ACCESS?
OF COURSE.
YOU LOOK TERRIFIED, MOLLY. WHAT'S WRONG?
TELL ME YOU PICKED MATTHEW UP FROM SCHOOL TODAY.
NO. I'VE BEEN HERE ALL DAY. WHY?
ONE OF THE TEACHERS TOLD ME SHE SAW HIM GET INTO A CAR WITH A STRANGE MAN. I THOUGHT MAYBE IT WAS YOU.
MAYBE IT WAS LEDGE.
THEY KNOW LEDGE. BESIDES, I CALLED. HE'S STILL IN D.C. AND WON'T BE BACK UNTIL TOMORROW.

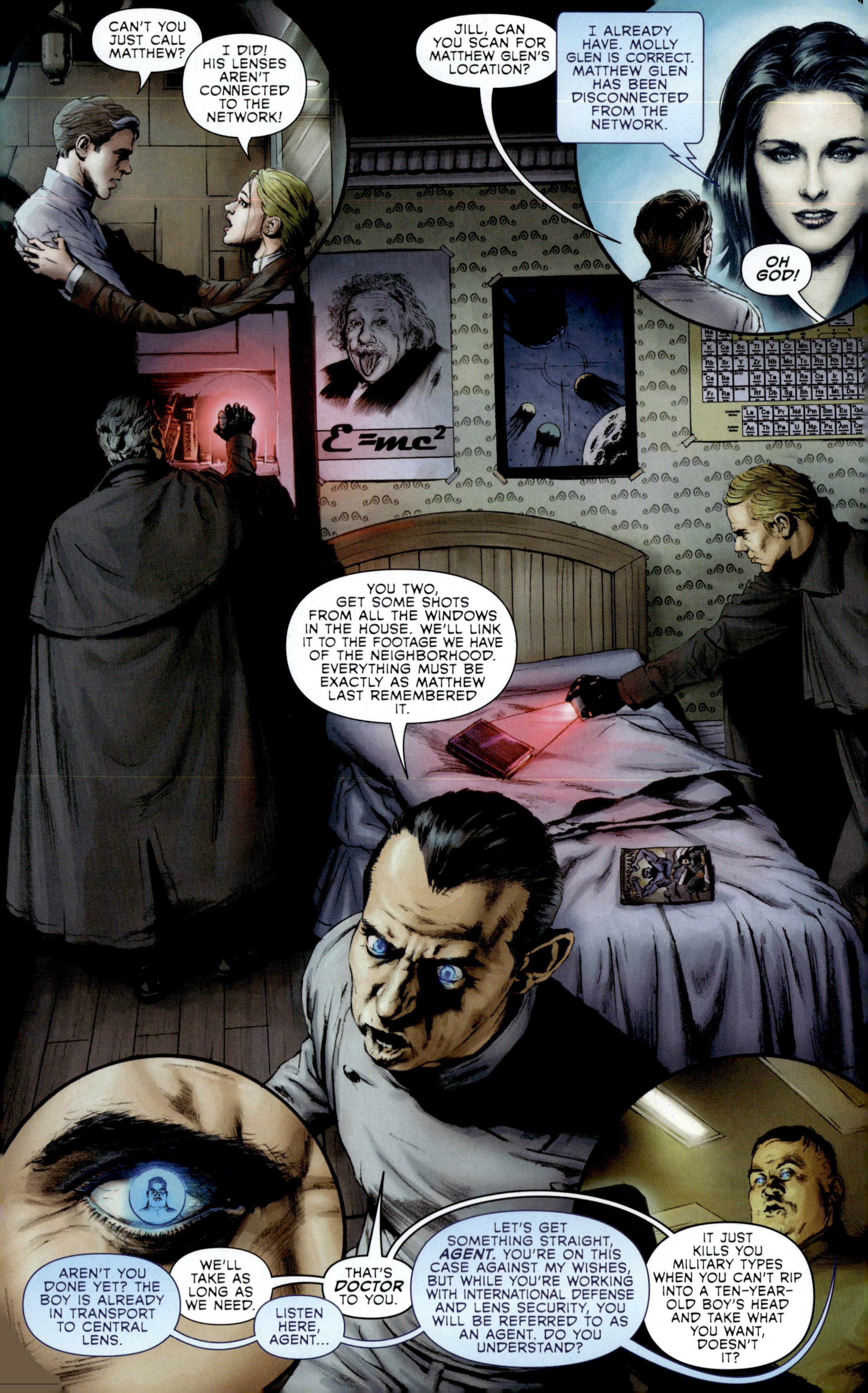
CAN'T YOU JUST CALL MATTHEW?
I DID! HIS LENSES AREN'T CONNECTED TO THE NETWORK!
JILL, CAN YOU SCAN FOR MATTHEW GLEN'S LOCATION?
I ALREADY HAVE. MOLLY GLEN IS CORRECT. MATTHEW GLEN HAS BEEN DISCONNECTED FROM THE NETWORK.
OH GOD!
E=mc²
YOU TWO, GET SOME SHOTS FROM ALL THE WINDOWS IN THE HOUSE. WE'LL LINK IT TO THE FOOTAGE WE HAVE OF THE NEIGHBORHOOD. EVERYTHING MUST BE EXACTLY AS MATTHEW LAST REMEMBERED IT.
AREN'T YOU DONE YET? THE BOY IS ALREADY IN TRANSPORT TO CENTRAL LENS.
WE'LL TAKE AS LONG AS WE NEED.
LISTEN HERE, AGENT...
THAT'S *DOCTOR* TO YOU.
LET'S GET SOMETHING STRAIGHT, *AGENT.* YOU'RE ON THIS CASE AGAINST MY WISHES, BUT WHILE YOU'RE WORKING WITH INTERNATIONAL DEFENSE AND LENS SECURITY, YOU WILL BE REFERRED TO AS AN AGENT. DO YOU UNDERSTAND?
IT JUST KILLS YOU MILITARY TYPES WHEN YOU CAN'T RIP INTO A TEN-YEAR-OLD BOY'S HEAD AND TAKE WHAT YOU WANT, DOESN'T IT?

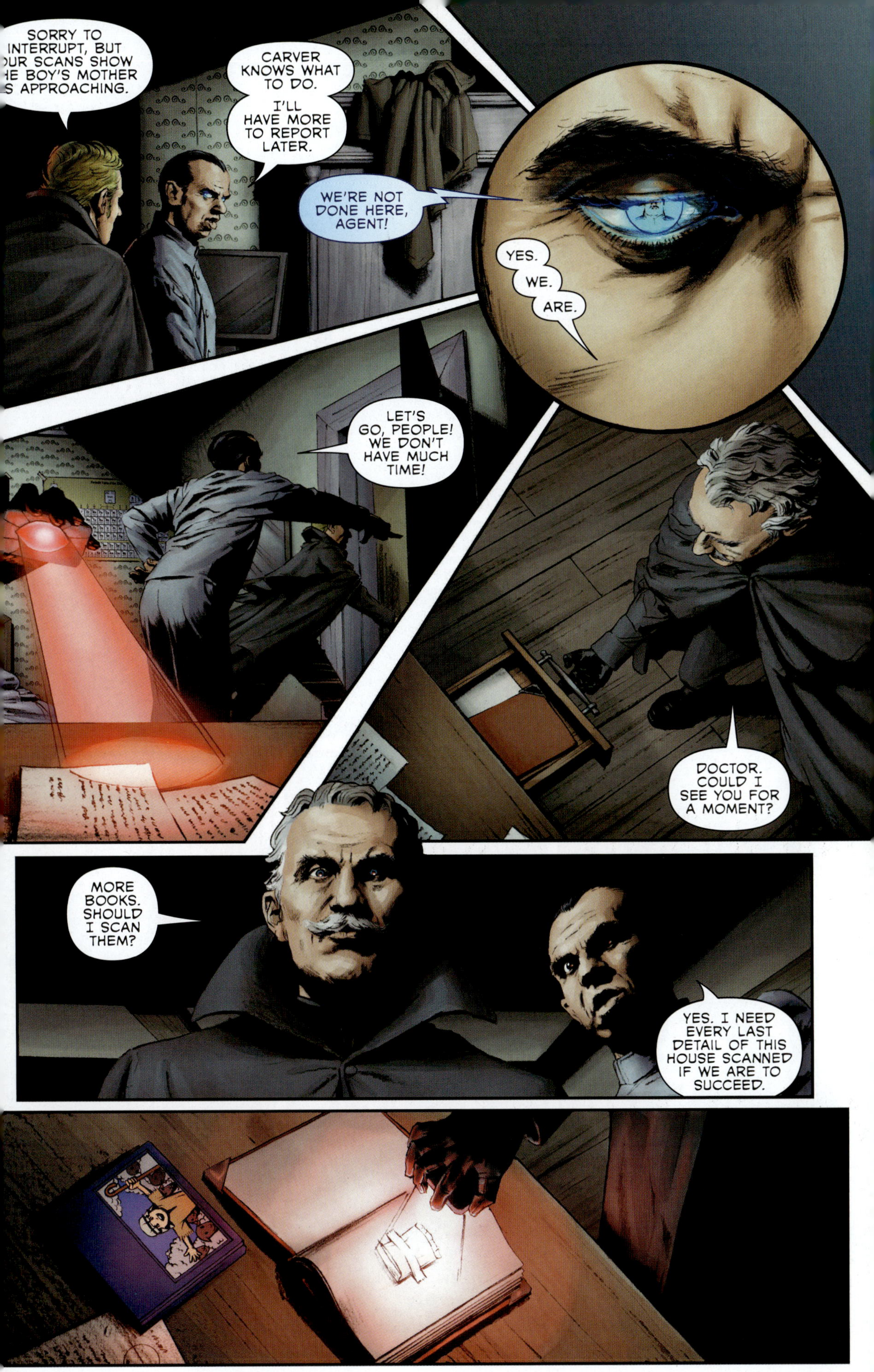
SORRY TO INTERRUPT, BUT OUR SCANS SHOW THE BOY'S MOTHER IS APPROACHING.
CARVER KNOWS WHAT TO DO.
I'LL HAVE MORE TO REPORT LATER.
WE'RE NOT DONE HERE, AGENT!
YES.
WE.
ARE.
LET'S GO, PEOPLE! WE DON'T HAVE MUCH TIME!
DOCTOR. COULD I SEE YOU FOR A MOMENT?
MORE BOOKS. SHOULD I SCAN THEM?
YES. I NEED EVERY LAST DETAIL OF THIS HOUSE SCANNED IF WE ARE TO SUCCEED.

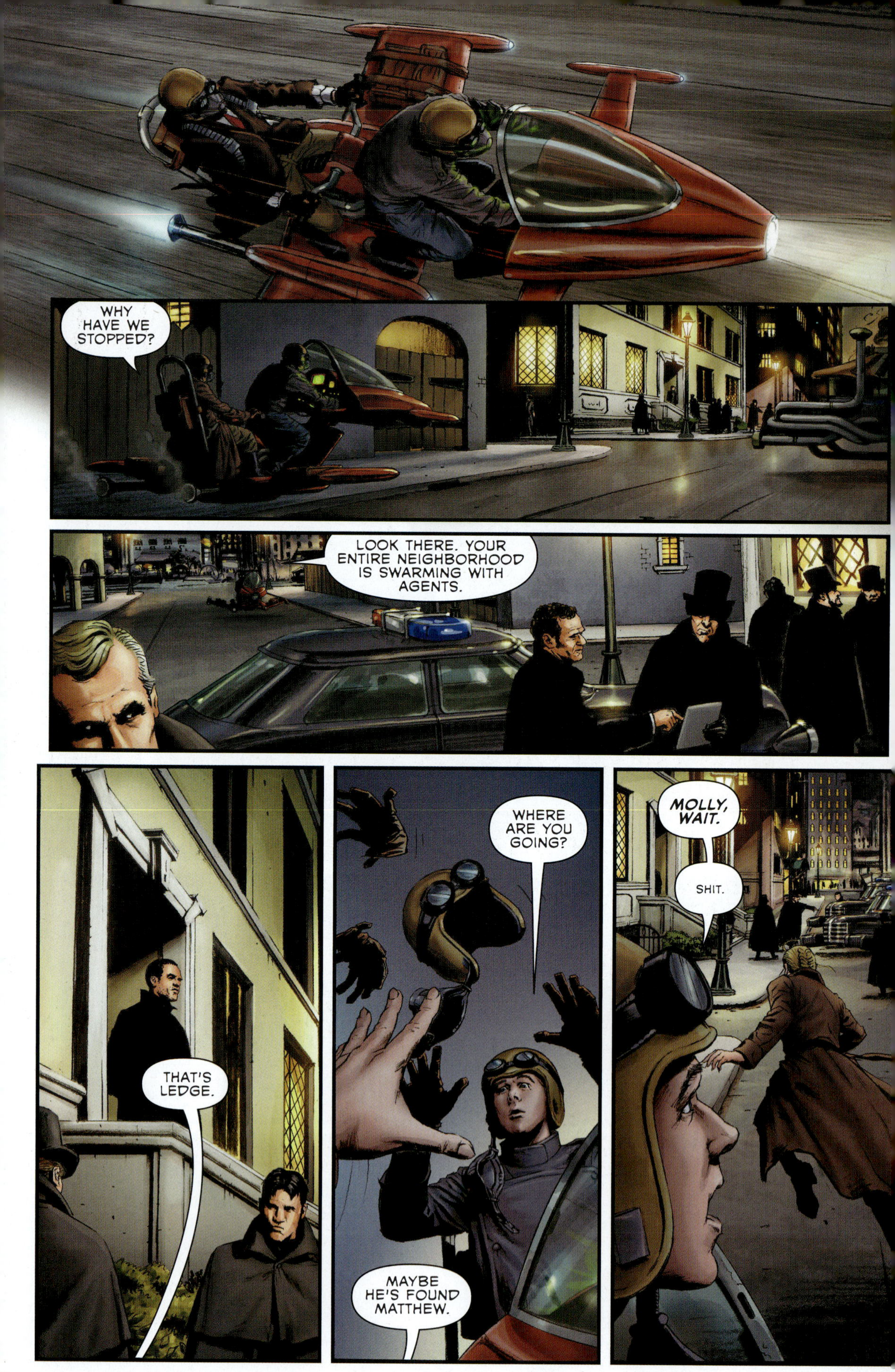
WHY HAVE WE STOPPED?
LOOK THERE. YOUR ENTIRE NEIGHBORHOOD IS SWARMING WITH AGENTS.
THAT'S LEDGE.
WHERE ARE YOU GOING?
MAYBE HE'S FOUND MATTHEW.
MOLLY, WAIT.
SHIT.

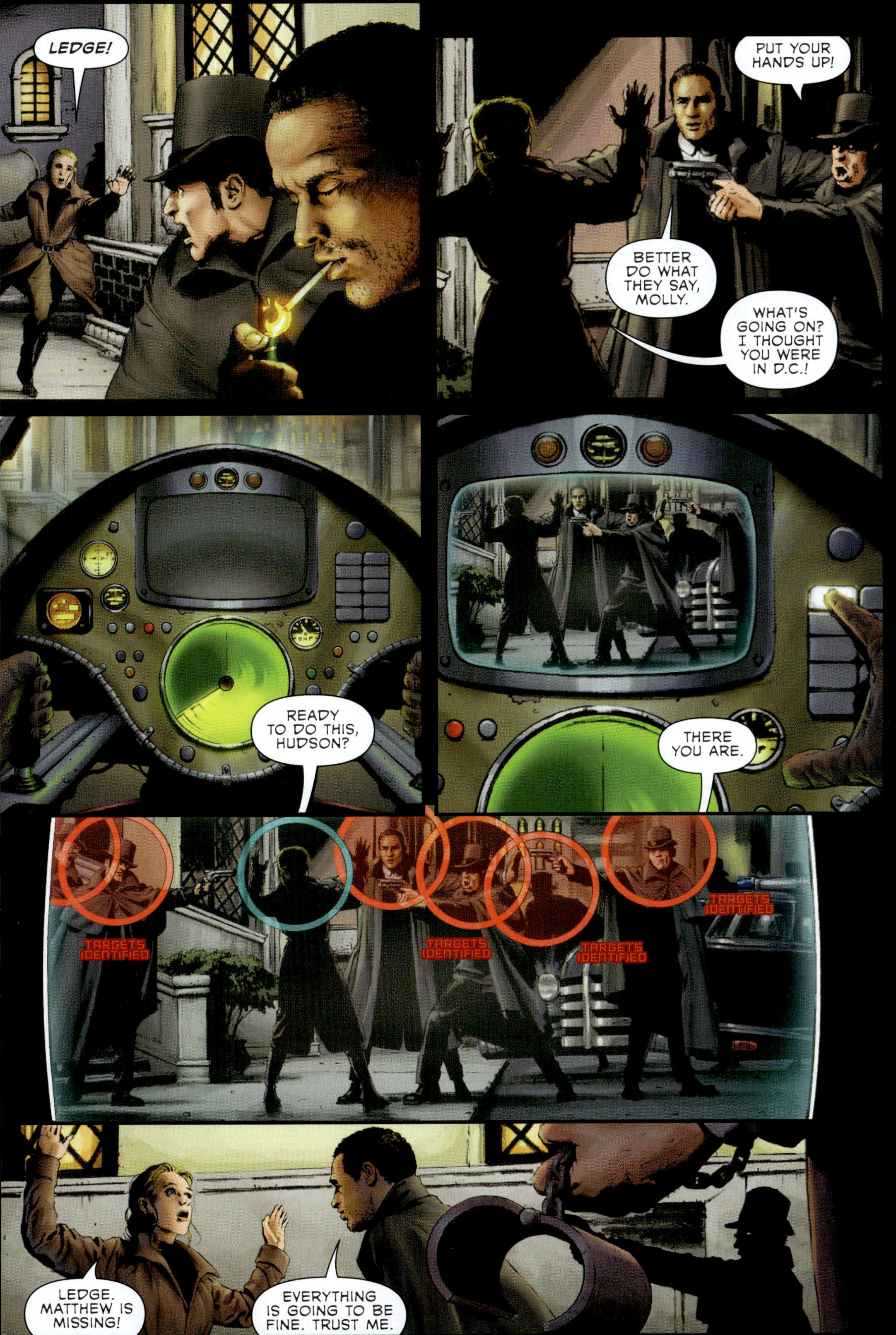

LEDGE!
PUT YOUR HANDS UP!
BETTER DO WHAT THEY SAY, MOLLY.
WHAT'S GOING ON? I THOUGHT YOU WERE IN D.C.!
READY TO DO THIS, HUDSON?
THERE YOU ARE.
TARGETS IDENTIFIED
TARGETS IDENTIFIED
TARGETS IDENTIFIED
TARGETS IDENTIFIED
LEDGE. MATTHEW IS MISSING!
EVERYTHING IS GOING TO BE FINE. TRUST ME.

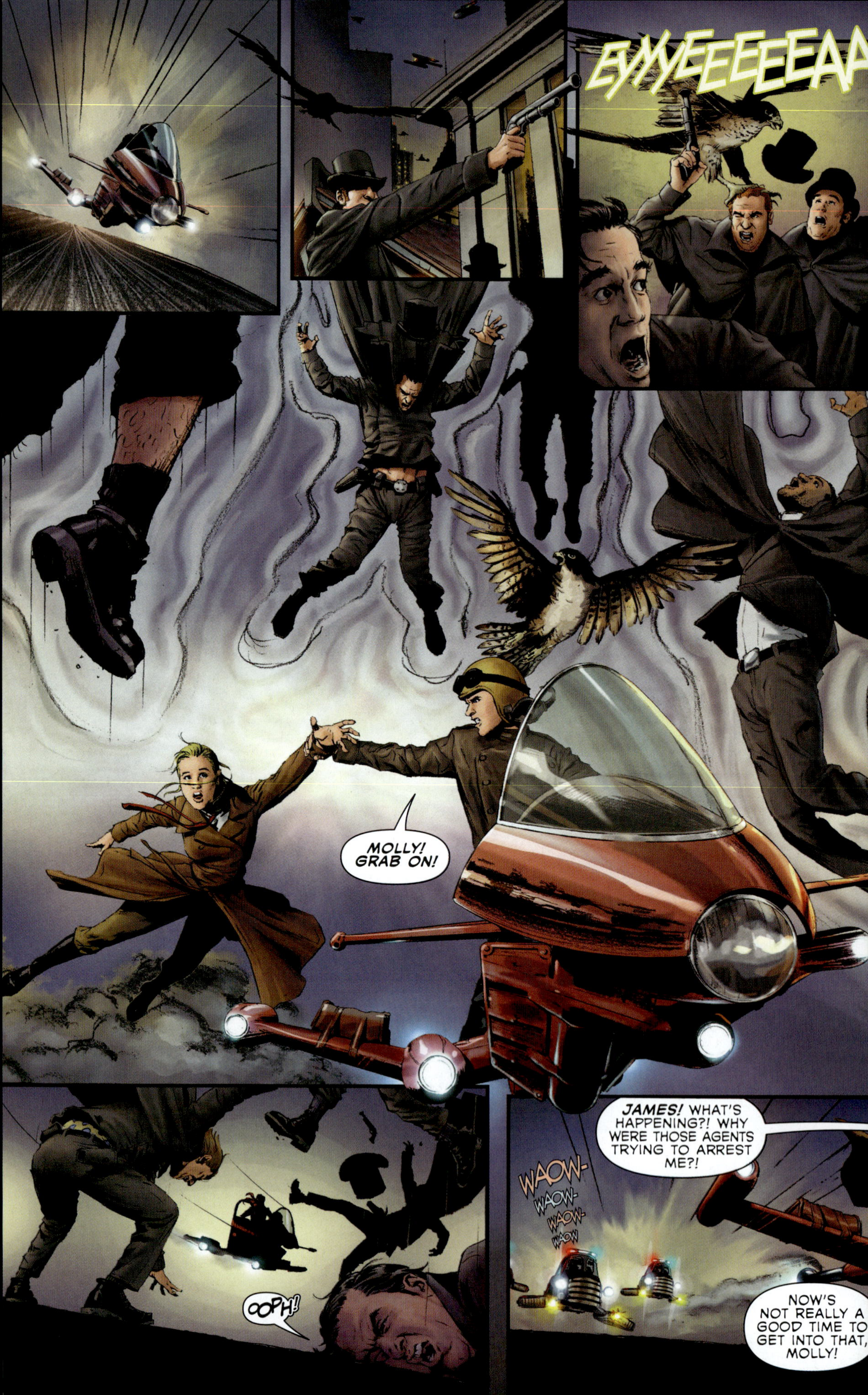
EYYYEEEEEAA
MOLLY! GRAB ON!
OOPH!
JAMES! WHAT'S HAPPENING?! WHY WERE THOSE AGENTS TRYING TO ARREST ME?!
WAOW-WAOW-WAOW-WAOW
NOW'S NOT REALLY A GOOD TIME TO GET INTO THAT, MOLLY!

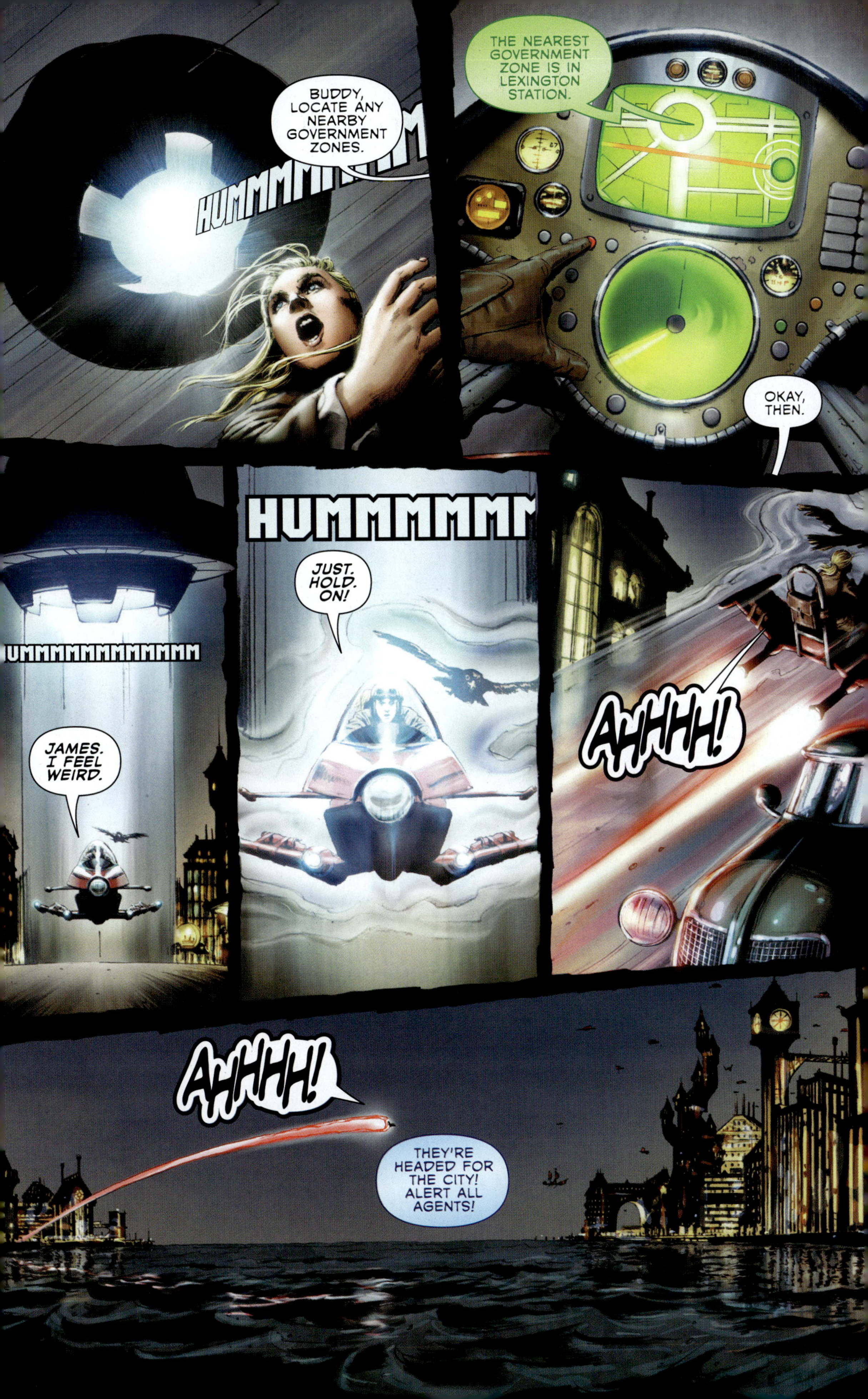
BUDDY, LOCATE ANY NEARBY GOVERNMENT ZONES.
HUMMMMMMM
THE NEAREST GOVERNMENT ZONE IS IN LEXINGTON STATION.
OKAY, THEN.
UMMMMMMMMMMMM
JAMES. I FEEL WEIRD.
HUMMMMMMM
JUST. HOLD. ON!
AHHHH!
AHHHH!
THEY'RE HEADED FOR THE CITY! ALERT ALL AGENTS!

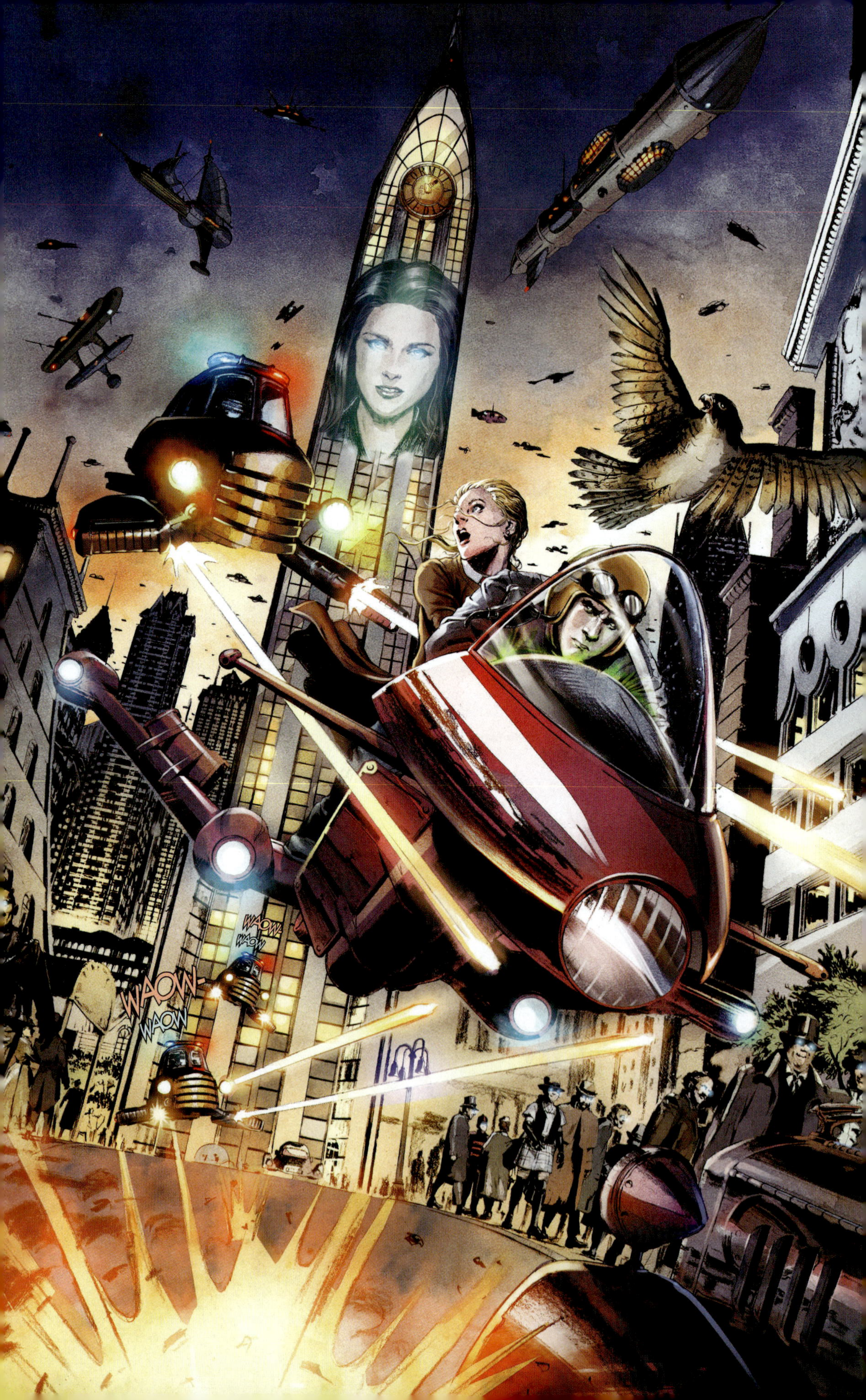
WAOW-
WAOW
WAOW-
WAOW

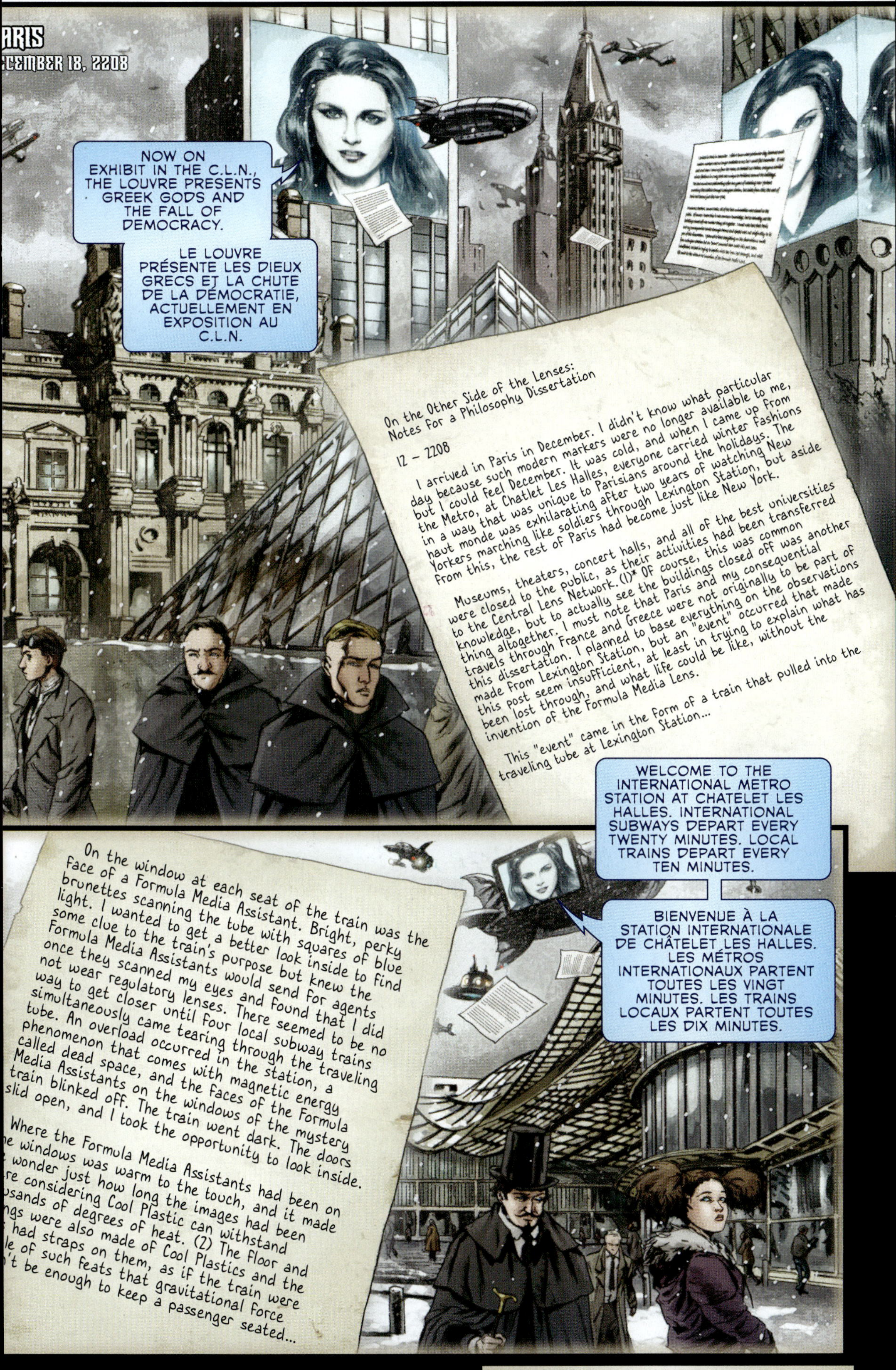
ARIS
CEMBER 18, 2208
NOW ON EXHIBIT IN THE C.L.N., THE LOUVRE PRESENTS GREEK GODS AND THE FALL OF DEMOCRACY.
LE LOUVRE PRÉSENTE LES DIEUX GRECS ET LA CHUTE DE LA DÉMOCRATIE, ACTUELLEMENT EN EXPOSITION AU C.L.N.
On the Other Side of the Lenses:
Notes for a Philosophy Dissertation
12 – 2208
I arrived in Paris in December. I didn't know what particular day because such modern markers were no longer available to me, but I could feel December. It was cold, and when I came up from the Metro, at Chatlet Les Halles, everyone carried winter fashions in a way that was unique to Parisians around the holidays. The haut monde was exhilarating after two years of watching New Yorkers marching like soldiers through Lexington Station, but aside from this, the rest of Paris had become just like New York.
Museums, theaters, concert halls, and all of the best universities were closed to the public, as their activities had been transferred to the Central Lens Network. (1)* Of course, this was common knowledge, but to actually see the buildings closed off was another thing altogether. I must note that Paris and my consequential travels through France and Greece were not originally to be part of this dissertation. I planned to base everything on the observations made from Lexington Station, but an "event" occurred that made this post seem insufficient, at least in trying to explain what has been lost through, and what life could be like, without the invention of the Formula Media Lens.
This "event" came in the form of a train that pulled into the traveling tube at Lexington Station...
WELCOME TO THE INTERNATIONAL METRO STATION AT CHATELET LES HALLES. INTERNATIONAL SUBWAYS DEPART EVERY TWENTY MINUTES. LOCAL TRAINS DEPART EVERY TEN MINUTES.
BIENVENUE À LA STATION INTERNATIONALE DE CHÂTELET LES HALLES. LES MÉTROS INTERNATIONAUX PARTENT TOUTES LES VINGT MINUTES. LES TRAINS LOCAUX PARTENT TOUTES LES DIX MINUTES.
On the window at each seat of the train was the face of a Formula Media Assistant. Bright, perky brunettes scanning the tube with squares of blue light. I wanted to get a better look inside to find some clue to the train's purpose but knew the Formula Media Assistants would send for agents once they scanned my eyes and found that I did not wear regulatory lenses. There seemed to be no way to get closer until four local subway trains simultaneously came tearing through the traveling tube. An overload occurred in the station, a phenomenon that comes with magnetic energy called dead space, and the faces of the Formula Media Assistants on the windows of the mystery train blinked off. The train went dark. The doors slid open, and I took the opportunity to look inside.
Where the Formula Media Assistants had been on
e windows was warm to the touch, and it made
wonder just how long the images had been
re considering Cool Plastic can withstand
usands of degrees of heat. (2) The floor and
ngs were also made of Cool Plastics and the
had straps on them, as if the train were
le of such feats that gravitational force
't be enough to keep a passenger seated...

* For all endnotes, see the epilogue: "Untangling From the Lenses." – Richard

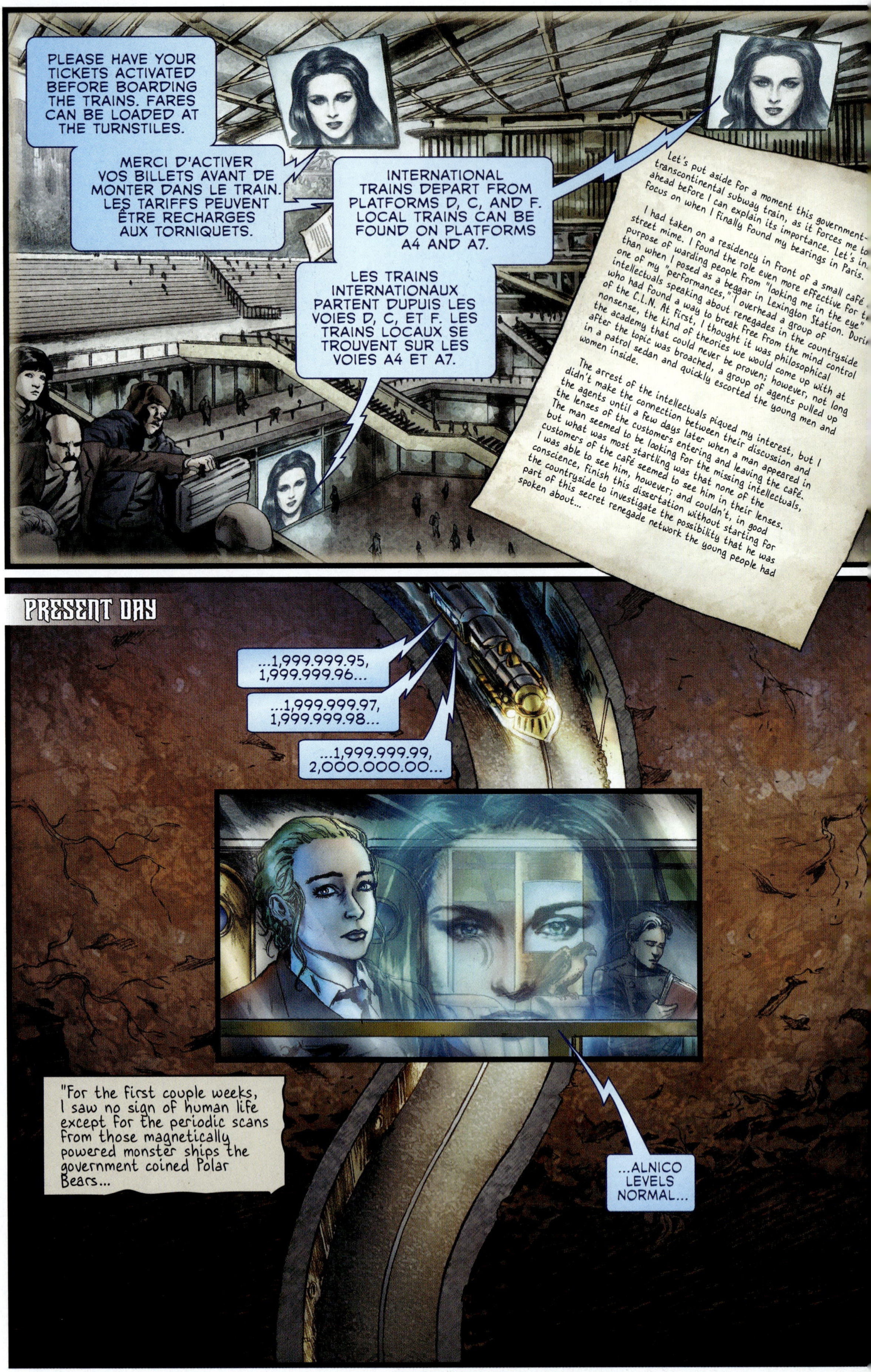

PLEASE HAVE YOUR TICKETS ACTIVATED BEFORE BOARDING THE TRAINS. FARES CAN BE LOADED AT THE TURNSTILES.
MERCI D'ACTIVER VOS BILLETS AVANT DE MONTER DANS LE TRAIN. LES TARIFFS PEUVENT ÊTRE RECHARGES AUX TORNIQUETS.
INTERNATIONAL TRAINS DEPART FROM PLATFORMS D, C, AND F. LOCAL TRAINS CAN BE FOUND ON PLATFORMS A4 AND A7.
LES TRAINS INTERNATIONAUX PARTENT DUPUIS LES VOIES D, C, ET F. LES TRAINS LOCAUX SE TROUVENT SUR LES VOIES A4 ET A7.
Let's put aside for a moment this government-
transcontinental subway train, as it forces me to
ahead before I can explain its importance. Let's in
focus on when I finally found my bearings in Paris.
I had taken on a residency in front of a small café
street mime. I found the role even more effective for t
purpose of warding people from "looking me in the eye"
than when I posed as a beggar in Lexington Station. Durin
one of my "performances," I overhead a group of
intellectuals speaking about renegades in the countryside
who had found a way to break free from the mind control
of the C.L.N. At first, I thought it was philosophical
nonsense, the kind of theories we would come up with at
the academy that could never be proven; however, not long
after the topic was broached, a group of agents pulled up
in a patrol sedan and quickly escorted the young men and
women inside.
The arrest of the intellectuals piqued my interest, but I
didn't make the connection between their discussion and
the agents until a few days later when a man appeared in
the lenses of the customers entering and leaving the café.
The man seemed to be looking for the missing intellectuals,
but what was most startling was that none of the
customers of the café seemed to see him in their lenses.
I was able to see him, however; and couldn't, in good
conscience, finish this dissertation without starting for
the countryside to investigate the possibility that he was
part of this secret renegade network the young people had
spoken about...
PRESENT DAY
...1,999.999.95, 1,999.999.96...
...1,999.999.97, 1,999.999.98...
...1,999.999.99, 2,000.000.00...
"For the first couple weeks, I saw no sign of human life except for the periodic scans from those magnetically powered monster ships the government coined Polar Bears...
...ALNICO LEVELS NORMAL...

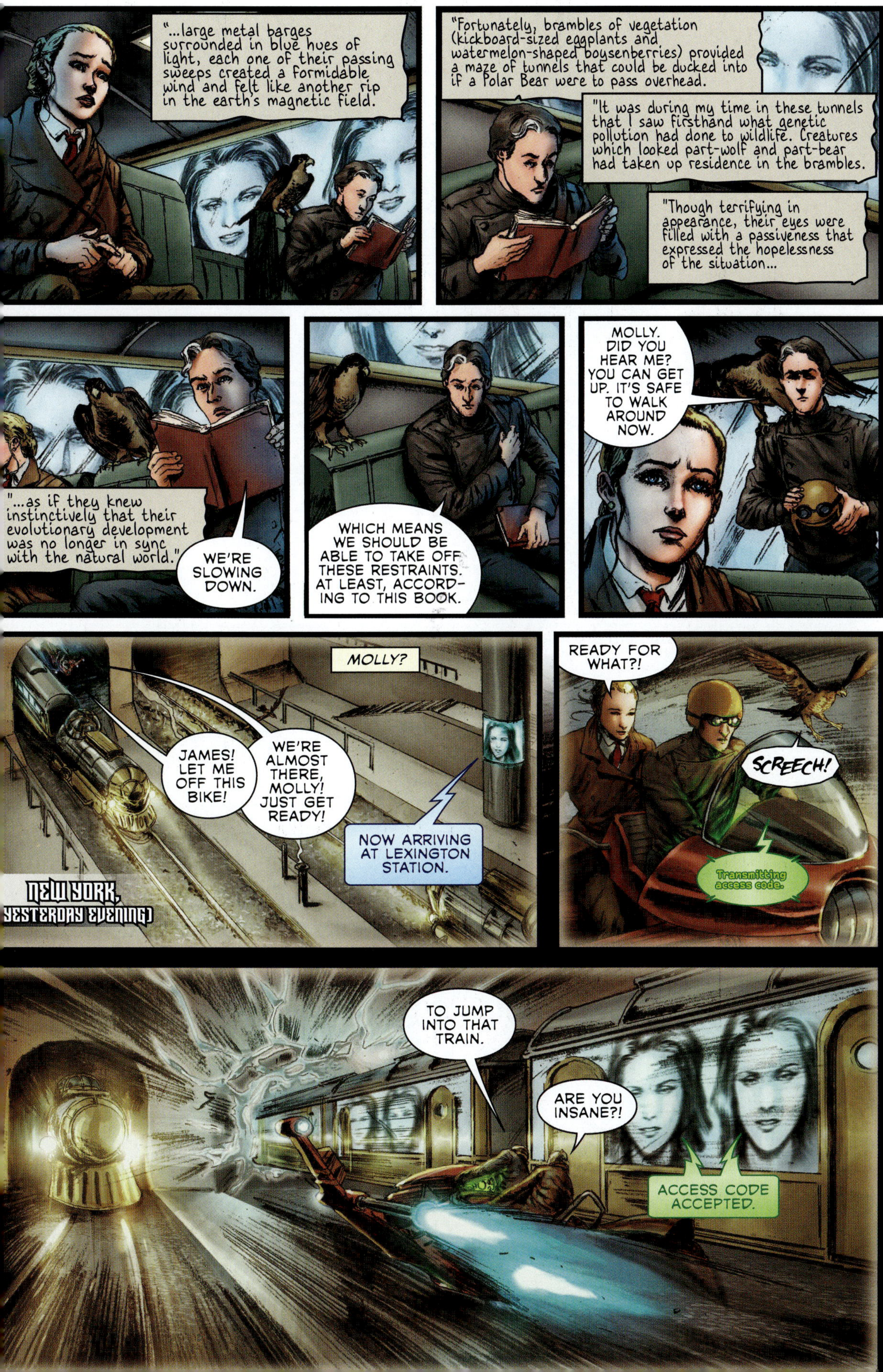
"...large metal barges surrounded in blue hues of light, each one of their passing sweeps created a formidable wind and felt like another rip in the earth's magnetic field.
"Fortunately, brambles of vegetation (kickboard-sized eggplants and watermelon-shaped boysenberries) provided a maze of tunnels that could be ducked into if a Polar Bear were to pass overhead.
"It was during my time in these tunnels that I saw firsthand what genetic pollution had done to wildlife. Creatures which looked part-wolf and part-bear had taken up residence in the brambles.
"Though terrifying in appearance, their eyes were filled with a passiveness that expressed the hopelessness of the situation...
"...as if they knew instinctively that their evolutionary development was no longer in sync with the natural world."
WE'RE SLOWING DOWN.
WHICH MEANS WE SHOULD BE ABLE TO TAKE OFF THESE RESTRAINTS. AT LEAST, ACCORDING TO THIS BOOK.
MOLLY. DID YOU HEAR ME? YOU CAN GET UP. IT'S SAFE TO WALK AROUND NOW.
NEW YORK, YESTERDAY EVENING)
MOLLY?
JAMES! LET ME OFF THIS BIKE!
WE'RE ALMOST THERE, MOLLY! JUST GET READY!
NOW ARRIVING AT LEXINGTON STATION.
READY FOR WHAT?!
SCREECH!
Transmitting access code.
TO JUMP INTO THAT TRAIN.
ARE YOU INSANE?!
ACCESS CODE ACCEPTED.

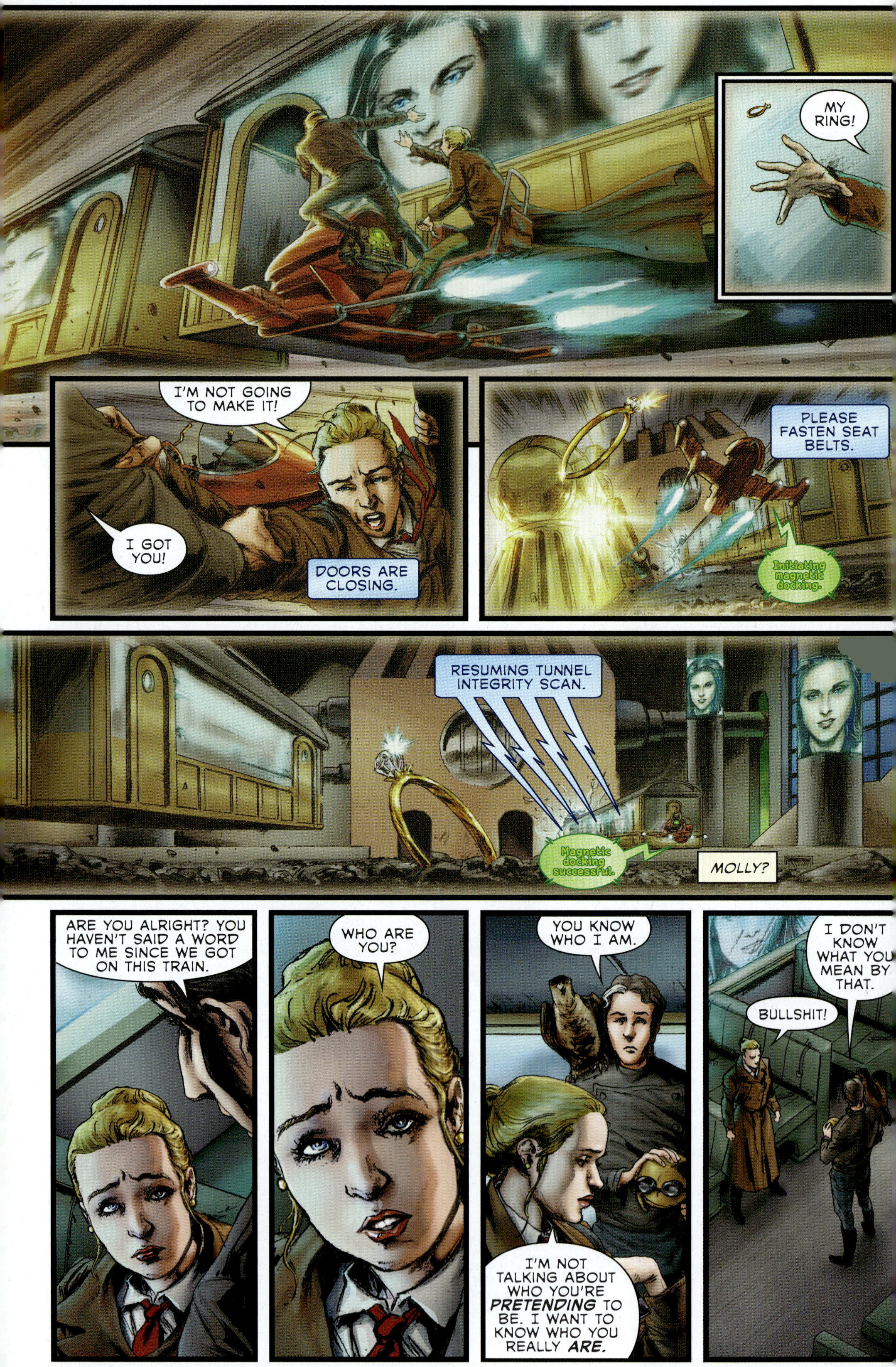
MY RING!
I'M NOT GOING TO MAKE IT!
I GOT YOU!
DOORS ARE CLOSING.
PLEASE FASTEN SEAT BELTS.
Initiating magnetic docking.
RESUMING TUNNEL INTEGRITY SCAN.
Magnetic docking successful.
MOLLY?
ARE YOU ALRIGHT? YOU HAVEN'T SAID A WORD TO ME SINCE WE GOT ON THIS TRAIN.
WHO ARE YOU?
YOU KNOW WHO I AM.
I'M NOT TALKING ABOUT WHO YOU'RE ***PRETENDING*** TO BE. I WANT TO KNOW WHO YOU REALLY ***ARE.***
I DON'T KNOW WHAT YOU MEAN BY THAT.
BULLSHIT!

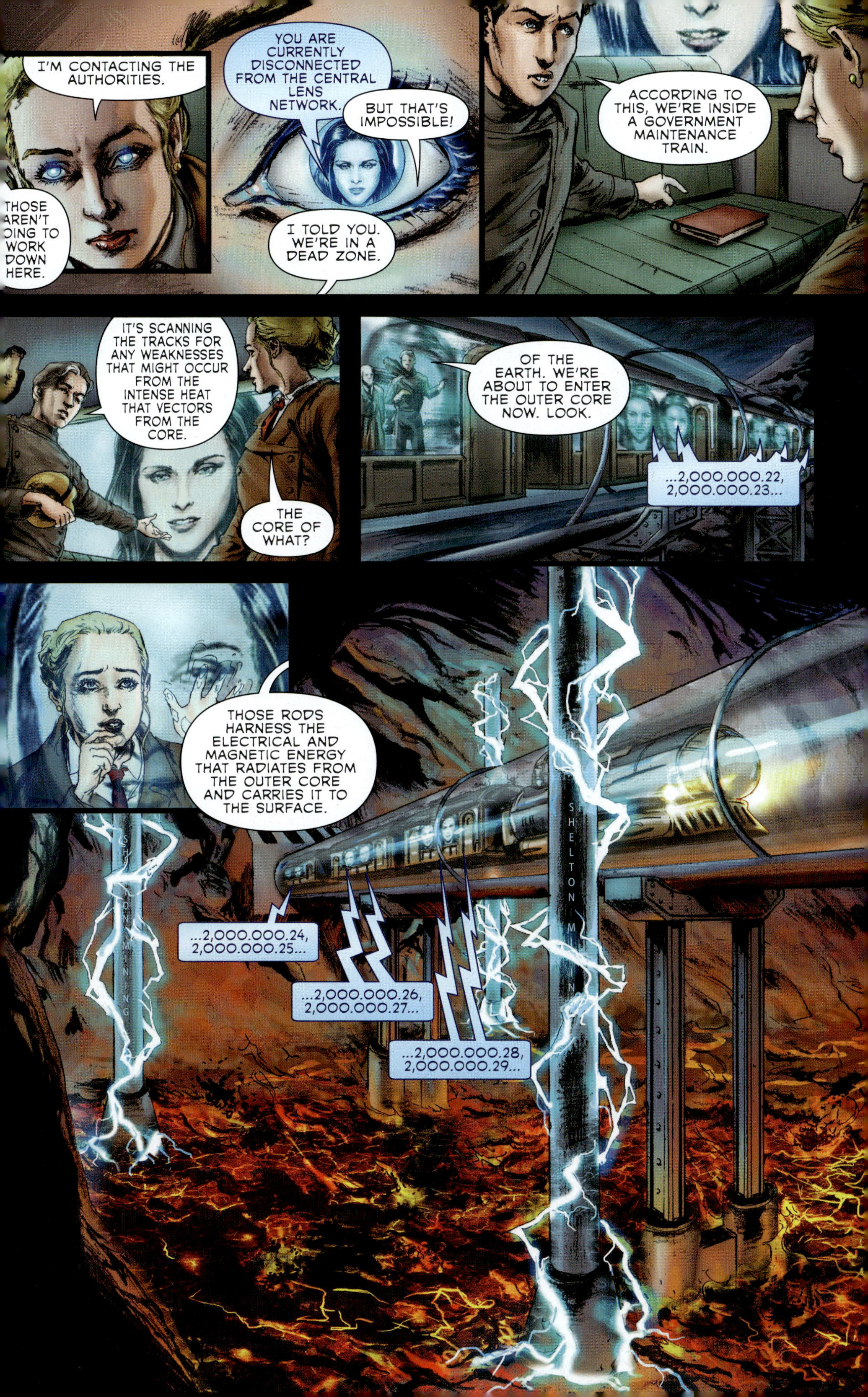
I'M CONTACTING THE AUTHORITIES.
YOU ARE CURRENTLY DISCONNECTED FROM THE CENTRAL LENS NETWORK.
BUT THAT'S IMPOSSIBLE!
THOSE AREN'T OING TO WORK DOWN HERE.
I TOLD YOU. WE'RE IN A DEAD ZONE.
ACCORDING TO THIS, WE'RE INSIDE A GOVERNMENT MAINTENANCE TRAIN.
IT'S SCANNING THE TRACKS FOR ANY WEAKNESSES THAT MIGHT OCCUR FROM THE INTENSE HEAT THAT VECTORS FROM THE CORE.
THE CORE OF WHAT?
OF THE EARTH. WE'RE ABOUT TO ENTER THE OUTER CORE NOW. LOOK.
...2,000.000.22, 2,000.000.23...
THOSE RODS HARNESS THE ELECTRICAL AND MAGNETIC ENERGY THAT RADIATES FROM THE OUTER CORE AND CARRIES IT TO THE SURFACE.
...2,000.000.24, 2,000.000.25...
...2,000.000.26, 2,000.000.27...
...2,000.000.28, 2,000.000.29...

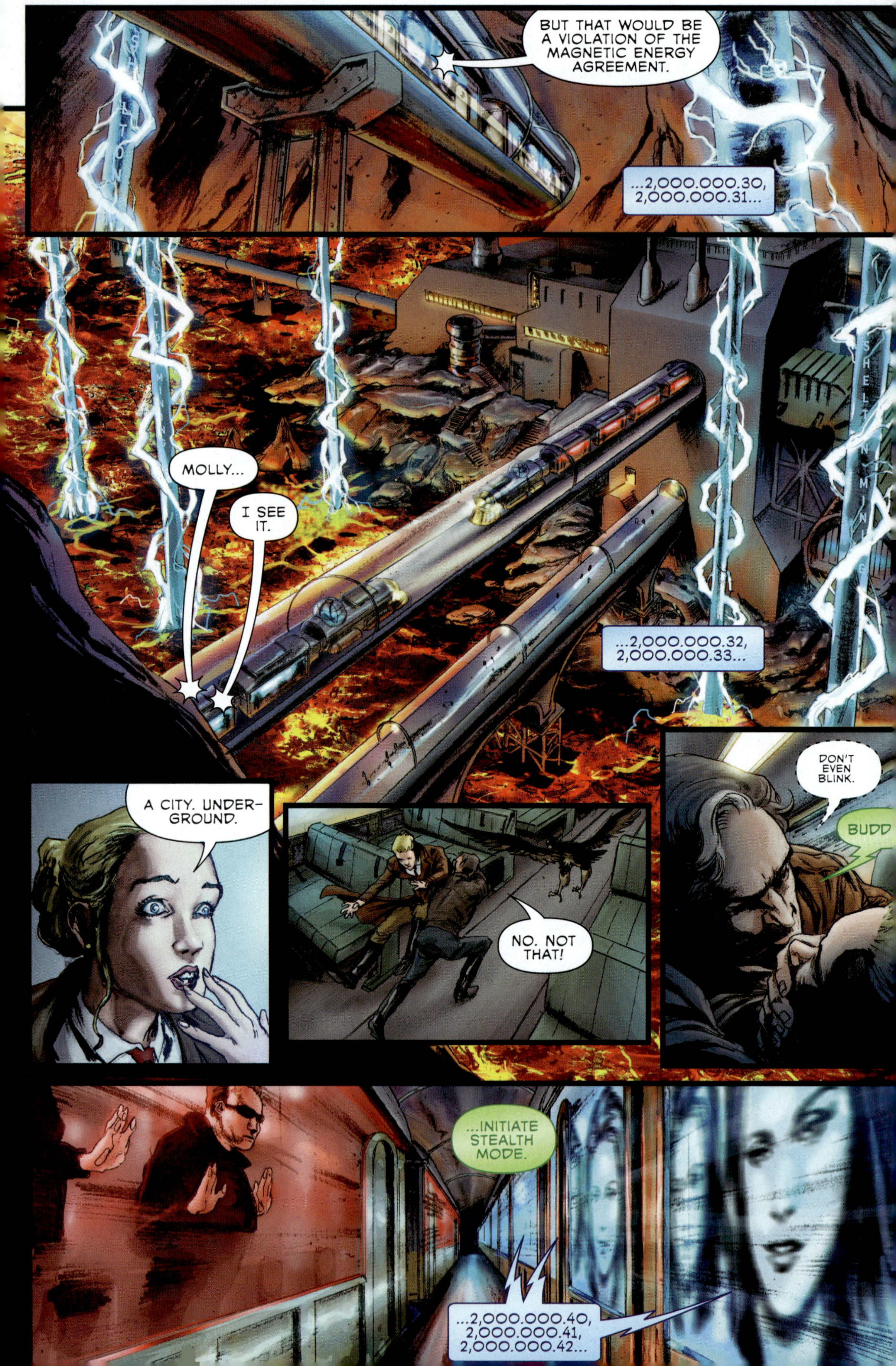
BUT THAT WOULD BE A VIOLATION OF THE MAGNETIC ENERGY AGREEMENT.
...2,000.000.30, 2,000.000.31...
MOLLY...
I SEE IT.
...2,000.000.32, 2,000.000.33...
A CITY. UNDER-GROUND.
NO. NOT THAT!
DON'T EVEN BLINK.
BUDD
...INITIATE STEALTH MODE.
...2,000.000.40, 2,000.000.41, 2,000.000.42...

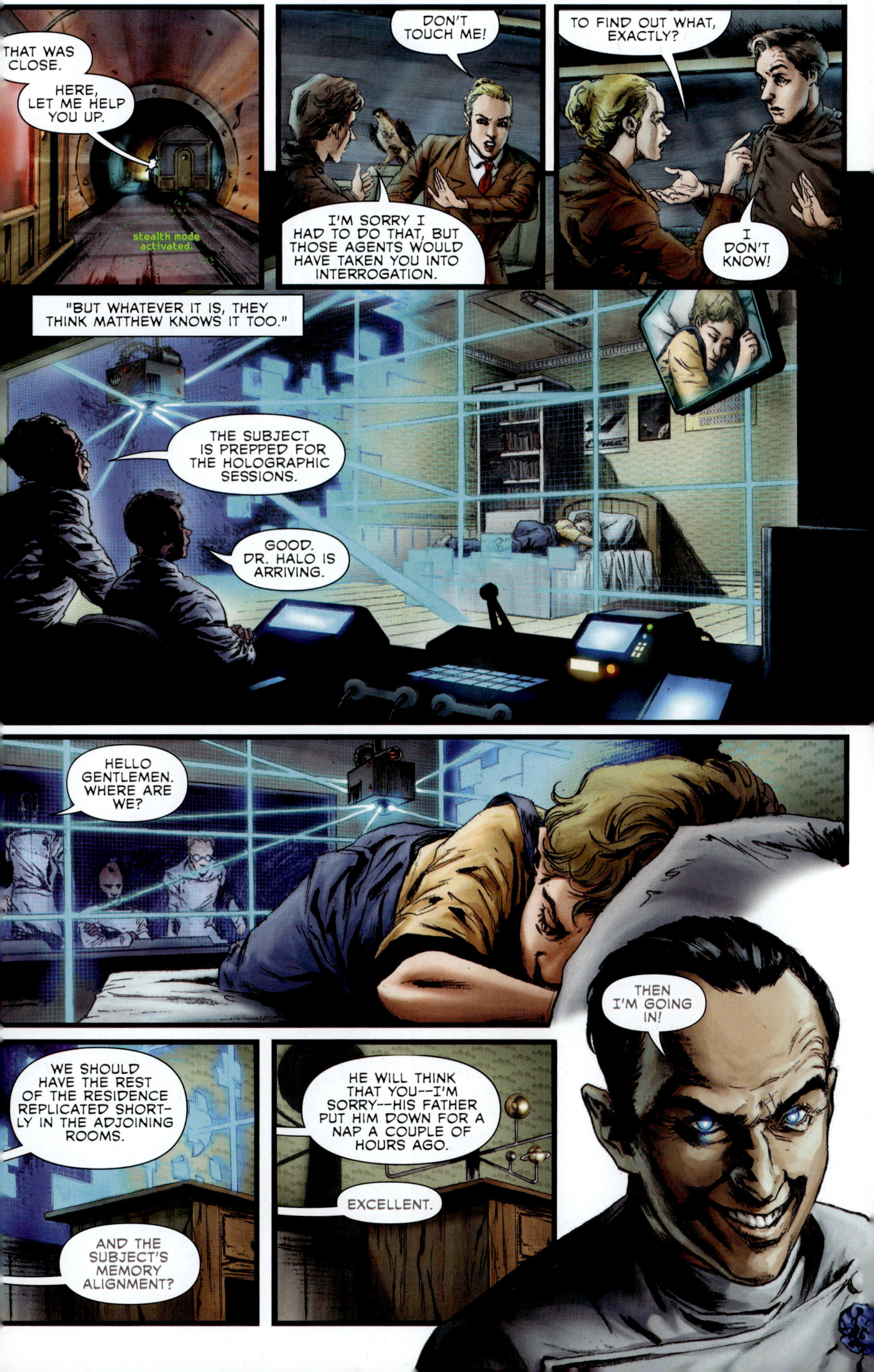
THAT WAS CLOSE.
HERE, LET ME HELP YOU UP.
stealth mode activated.
DON'T TOUCH ME!
I'M SORRY I HAD TO DO THAT, BUT THOSE AGENTS WOULD HAVE TAKEN YOU INTO INTERROGATION.
TO FIND OUT WHAT, EXACTLY?
I DON'T KNOW!
"BUT WHATEVER IT IS, THEY THINK MATTHEW KNOWS IT TOO."
THE SUBJECT IS PREPPED FOR THE HOLOGRAPHIC SESSIONS.
GOOD. DR. HALO IS ARRIVING.
HELLO GENTLEMEN. WHERE ARE WE?
WE SHOULD HAVE THE REST OF THE RESIDENCE REPLICATED SHORTLY IN THE ADJOINING ROOMS.
AND THE SUBJECT'S MEMORY ALIGNMENT?
HE WILL THINK THAT YOU--I'M SORRY--HIS FATHER PUT HIM DOWN FOR A NAP A COUPLE OF HOURS AGO.
EXCELLENT.
THEN I'M GOING IN!

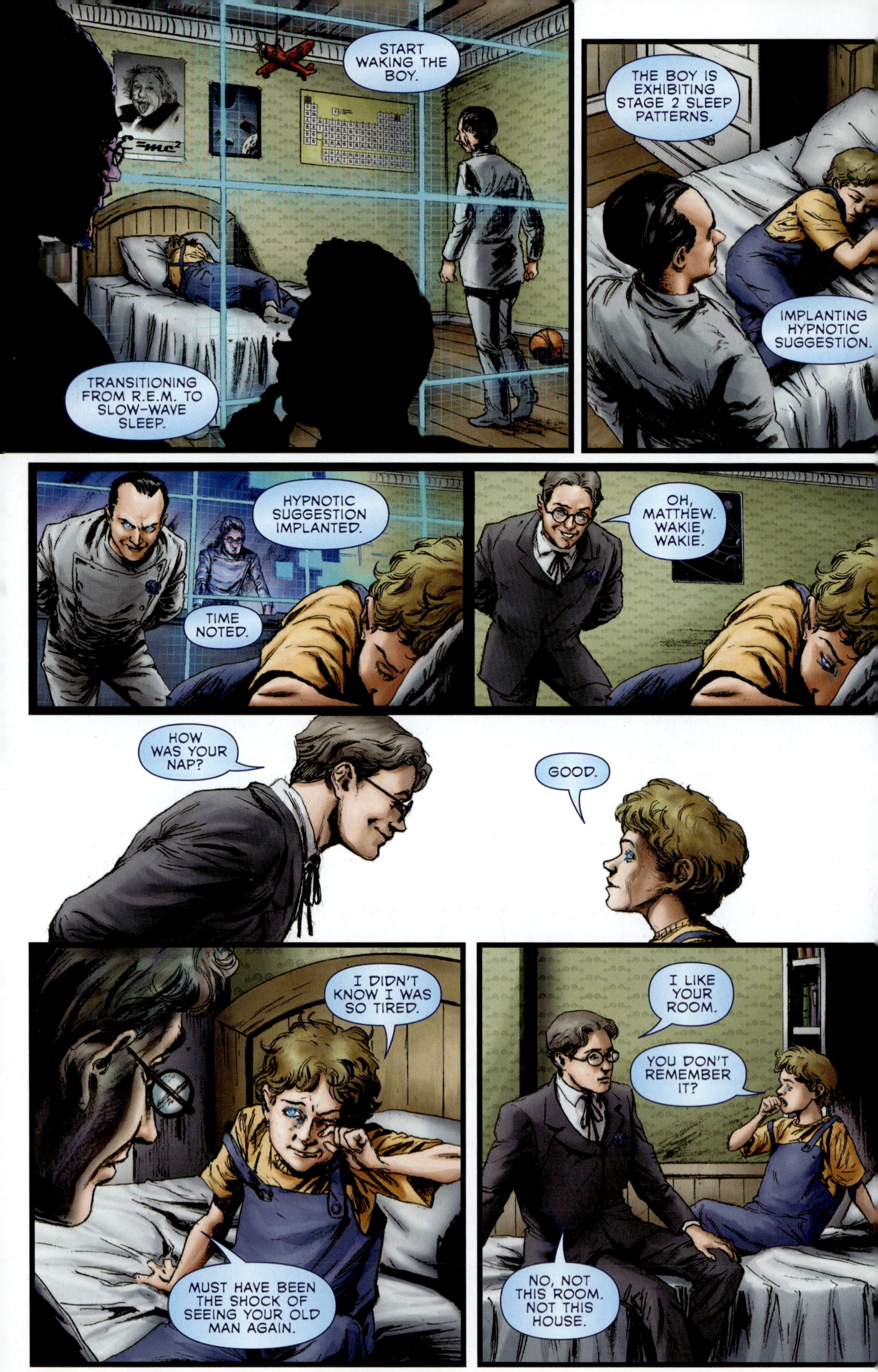
START WAKING THE BOY.
TRANSITIONING FROM R.E.M. TO SLOW-WAVE SLEEP.
THE BOY IS EXHIBITING STAGE 2 SLEEP PATTERNS.
IMPLANTING HYPNOTIC SUGGESTION.
HYPNOTIC SUGGESTION IMPLANTED.
TIME NOTED.
OH, MATTHEW. WAKIE, WAKIE.
HOW WAS YOUR NAP?
GOOD.
I DIDN'T KNOW I WAS SO TIRED.
MUST HAVE BEEN THE SHOCK OF SEEING YOUR OLD MAN AGAIN.
I LIKE YOUR ROOM.
YOU DON'T REMEMBER IT?
NO, NOT THIS ROOM. NOT THIS HOUSE.

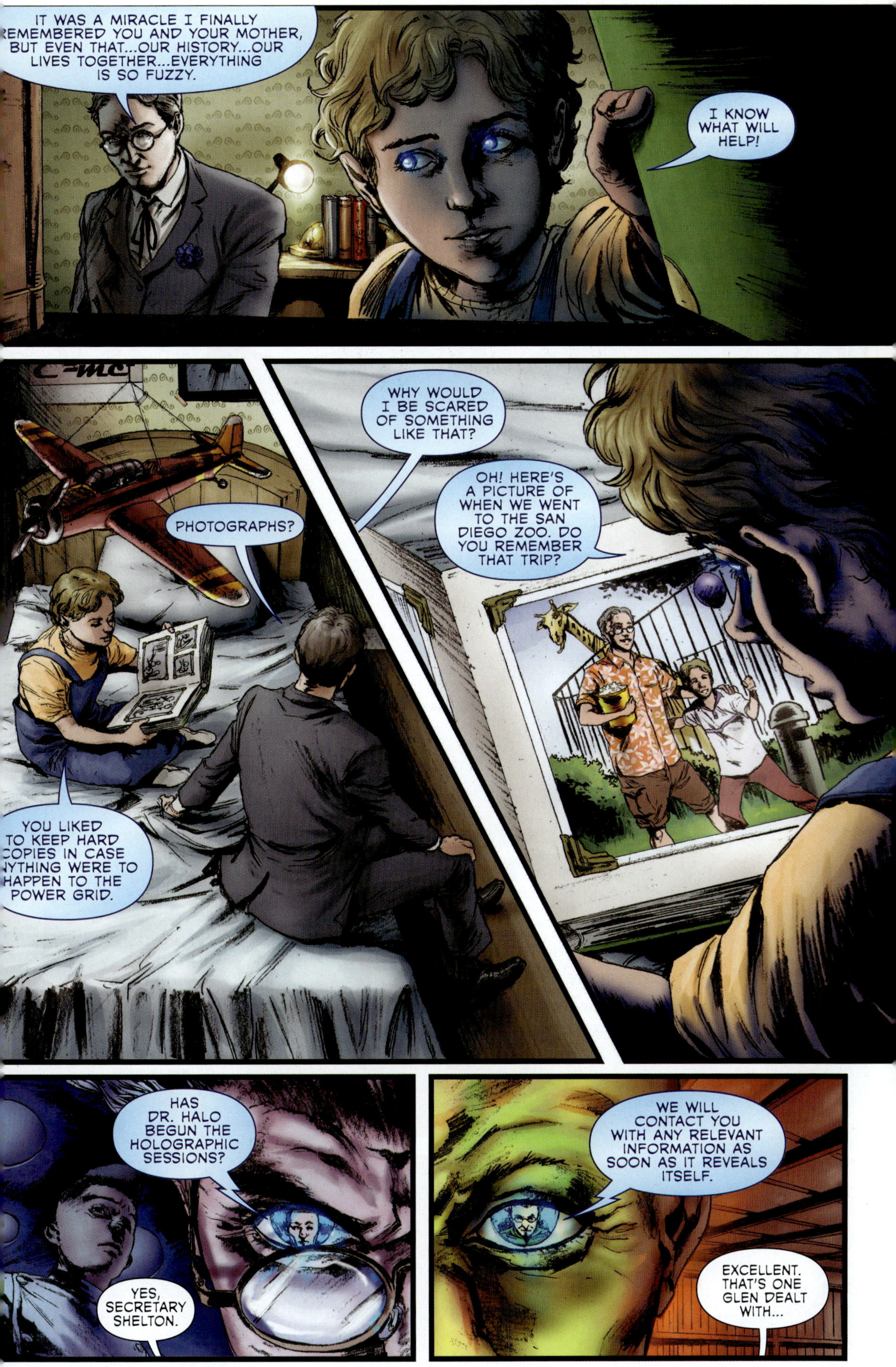
IT WAS A MIRACLE I FINALLY REMEMBERED YOU AND YOUR MOTHER, BUT EVEN THAT...OUR HISTORY...OUR LIVES TOGETHER...EVERYTHING IS SO FUZZY.
I KNOW WHAT WILL HELP!
PHOTOGRAPHS?
YOU LIKED TO KEEP HARD COPIES IN CASE NYTHING WERE TO HAPPEN TO THE POWER GRID.
WHY WOULD I BE SCARED OF SOMETHING LIKE THAT?
OH! HERE'S A PICTURE OF WHEN WE WENT TO THE SAN DIEGO ZOO. DO YOU REMEMBER THAT TRIP?
HAS DR. HALO BEGUN THE HOLOGRAPHIC SESSIONS?
YES, SECRETARY SHELTON.
WE WILL CONTACT YOU WITH ANY RELEVANT INFORMATION AS SOON AS IT REVEALS ITSELF.
EXCELLENT. THAT'S ONE GLEN DEALT WITH...

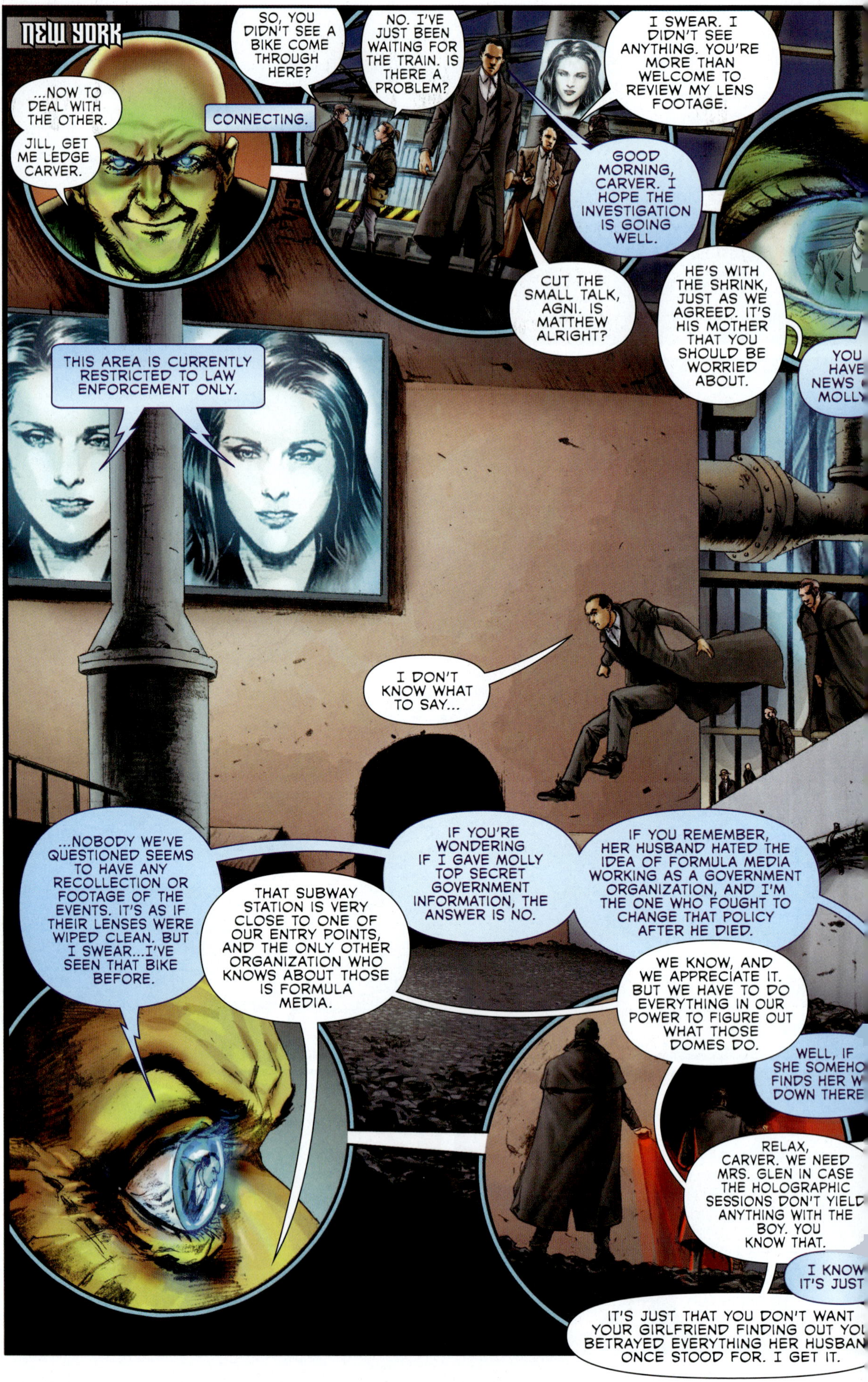

NEW YORK
...NOW TO DEAL WITH THE OTHER.
JILL, GET ME LEDGE CARVER.
CONNECTING.
SO, YOU DIDN'T SEE A BIKE COME THROUGH HERE?
NO. I'VE JUST BEEN WAITING FOR THE TRAIN. IS THERE A PROBLEM?
I SWEAR. I DIDN'T SEE ANYTHING. YOU'RE MORE THAN WELCOME TO REVIEW MY LENS FOOTAGE.
GOOD MORNING, CARVER. I HOPE THE INVESTIGATION IS GOING WELL.
CUT THE SMALL TALK, AGNI. IS MATTHEW ALRIGHT?
HE'S WITH THE SHRINK, JUST AS WE AGREED. IT'S HIS MOTHER THAT YOU SHOULD BE WORRIED ABOUT.
YOU HAVE NEWS MOLLY
THIS AREA IS CURRENTLY RESTRICTED TO LAW ENFORCEMENT ONLY.
I DON'T KNOW WHAT TO SAY...
...NOBODY WE'VE QUESTIONED SEEMS TO HAVE ANY RECOLLECTION OR FOOTAGE OF THE EVENTS. IT'S AS IF THEIR LENSES WERE WIPED CLEAN. BUT I SWEAR...I'VE SEEN THAT BIKE BEFORE.
THAT SUBWAY STATION IS VERY CLOSE TO ONE OF OUR ENTRY POINTS, AND THE ONLY OTHER ORGANIZATION WHO KNOWS ABOUT THOSE IS FORMULA MEDIA.
IF YOU'RE WONDERING IF I GAVE MOLLY TOP SECRET GOVERNMENT INFORMATION, THE ANSWER IS NO.
IF YOU REMEMBER, HER HUSBAND HATED THE IDEA OF FORMULA MEDIA WORKING AS A GOVERNMENT ORGANIZATION, AND I'M THE ONE WHO FOUGHT TO CHANGE THAT POLICY AFTER HE DIED.
WE KNOW, AND WE APPRECIATE IT. BUT EVERYTHING WE HAVE TO DO EVERYTHING IN OUR POWER TO FIGURE OUT WHAT THOSE DOMES DO.
WELL, IF SHE SOMEHO FINDS HER W DOWN THERE
RELAX, CARVER. WE NEED MRS. GLEN IN CASE THE HOLOGRAPHIC SESSIONS DON'T YIELD ANYTHING WITH THE BOY. YOU KNOW THAT.
I KNOW IT'S JUST
IT'S JUST THAT YOU DON'T WANT YOUR GIRLFRIEND FINDING OUT YOU BETRAYED EVERYTHING HER HUSBAN ONCE STOOD FOR. I GET IT.

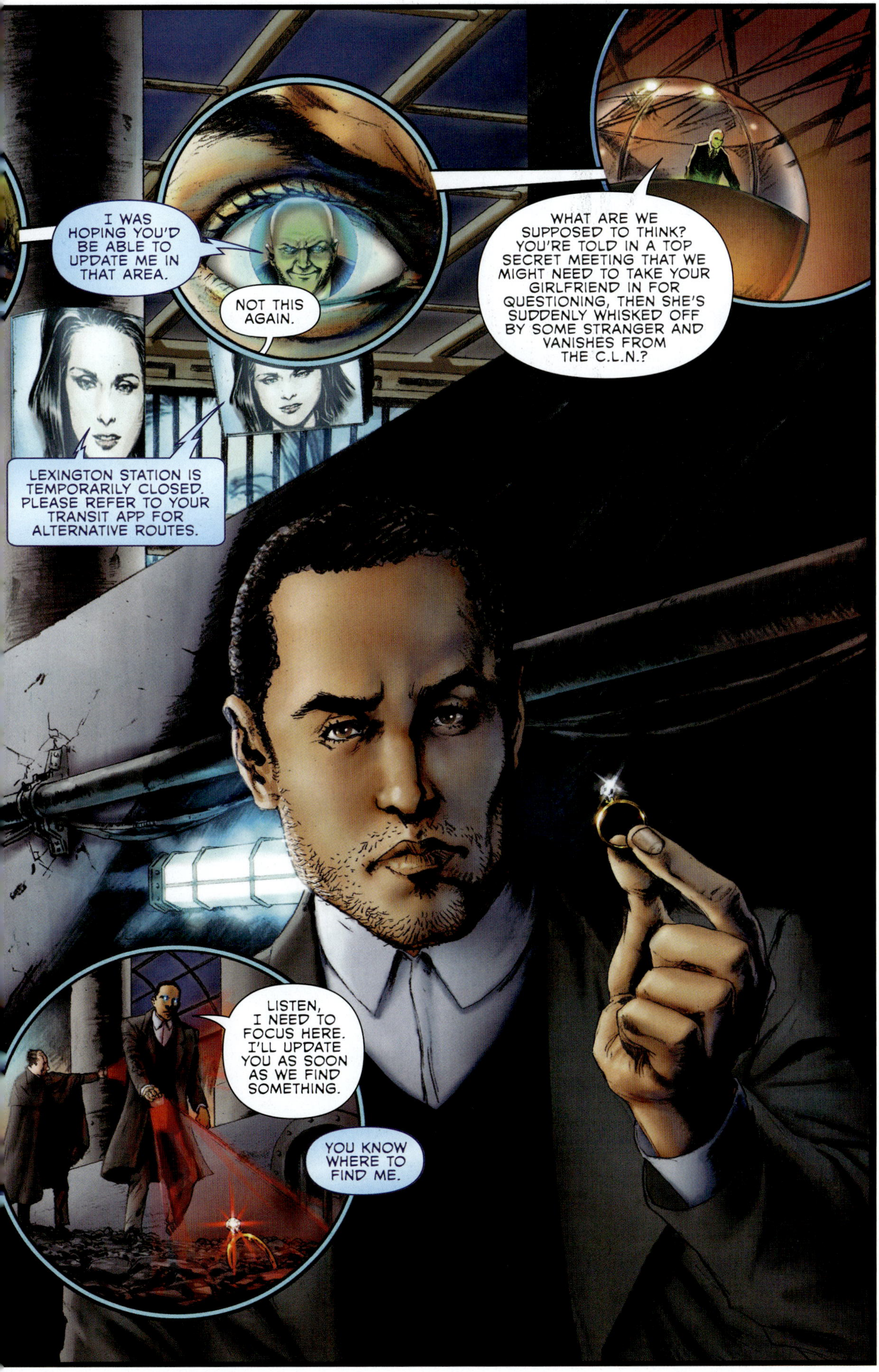
I WAS HOPING YOU'D BE ABLE TO UPDATE ME IN THAT AREA.
NOT THIS AGAIN.
WHAT ARE WE SUPPOSED TO THINK? YOU'RE TOLD IN A TOP SECRET MEETING THAT WE MIGHT NEED TO TAKE YOUR GIRLFRIEND IN FOR QUESTIONING, THEN SHE'S SUDDENLY WHISKED OFF BY SOME STRANGER AND VANISHES FROM THE C.L.N.?
LEXINGTON STATION IS TEMPORARILY CLOSED. PLEASE REFER TO YOUR TRANSIT APP FOR ALTERNATIVE ROUTES.
LISTEN, I NEED TO FOCUS HERE. I'LL UPDATE YOU AS SOON AS WE FIND SOMETHING.
YOU KNOW WHERE TO FIND ME.

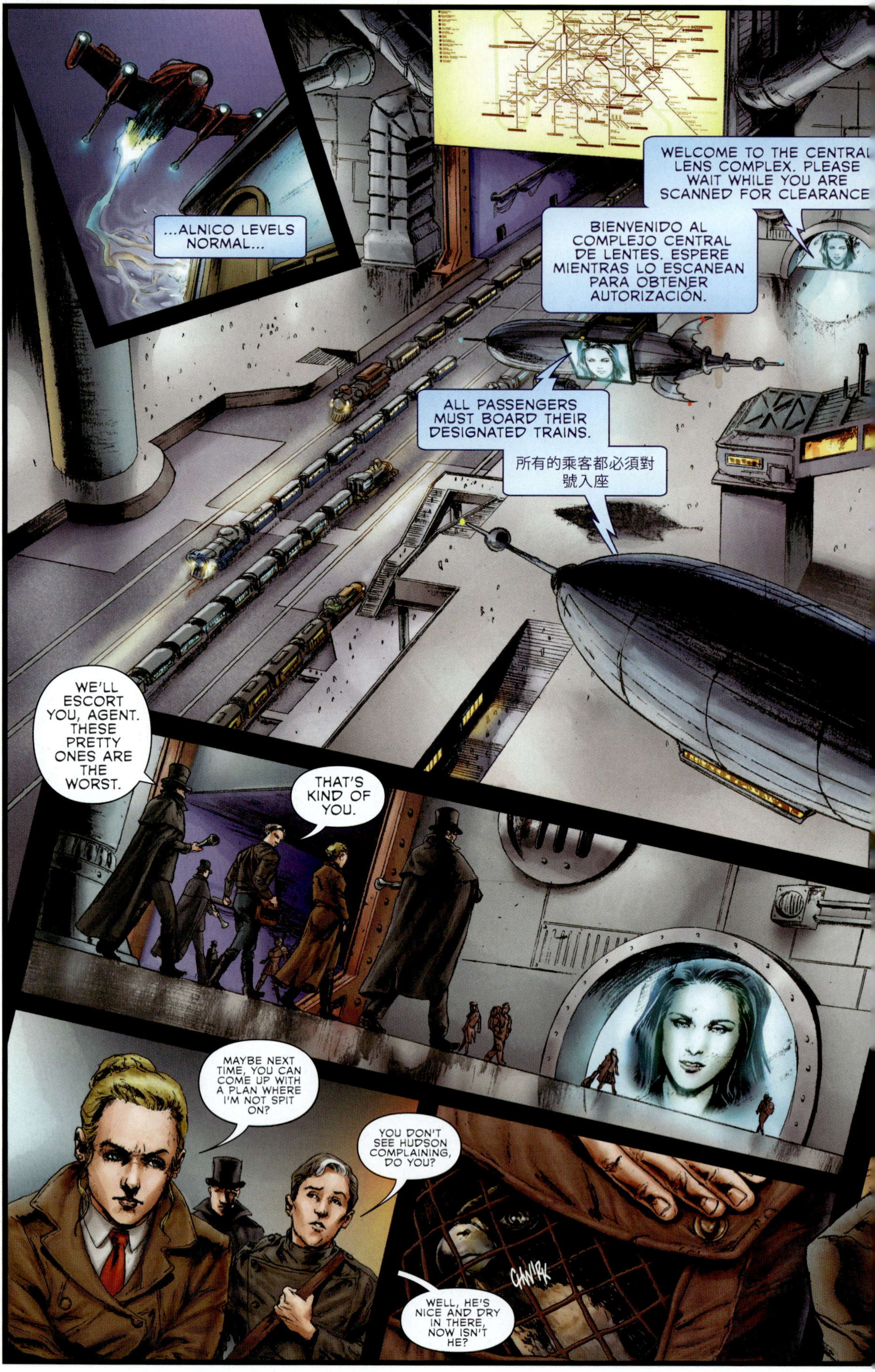
...ALNICO LEVELS NORMAL...
WELCOME TO THE CENTRAL LENS COMPLEX. PLEASE WAIT WHILE YOU ARE SCANNED FOR CLEARANCE.
BIENVENIDO AL COMPLEJO CENTRAL DE LENTES. ESPERE MIENTRAS LO ESCANEAN PARA OBTENER AUTORIZACIÓN.
ALL PASSENGERS MUST BOARD THEIR DESIGNATED TRAINS.
所有的乘客都必須對號入座
WE'LL ESCORT YOU, AGENT. THESE PRETTY ONES ARE THE WORST.
THAT'S KIND OF YOU.
MAYBE NEXT TIME, YOU CAN COME UP WITH A PLAN WHERE I'M NOT SPIT ON?
YOU DON'T SEE HUDSON COMPLAINING, DO YOU?
WELL, HE'S NICE AND DRY IN THERE, NOW ISN'T HE?

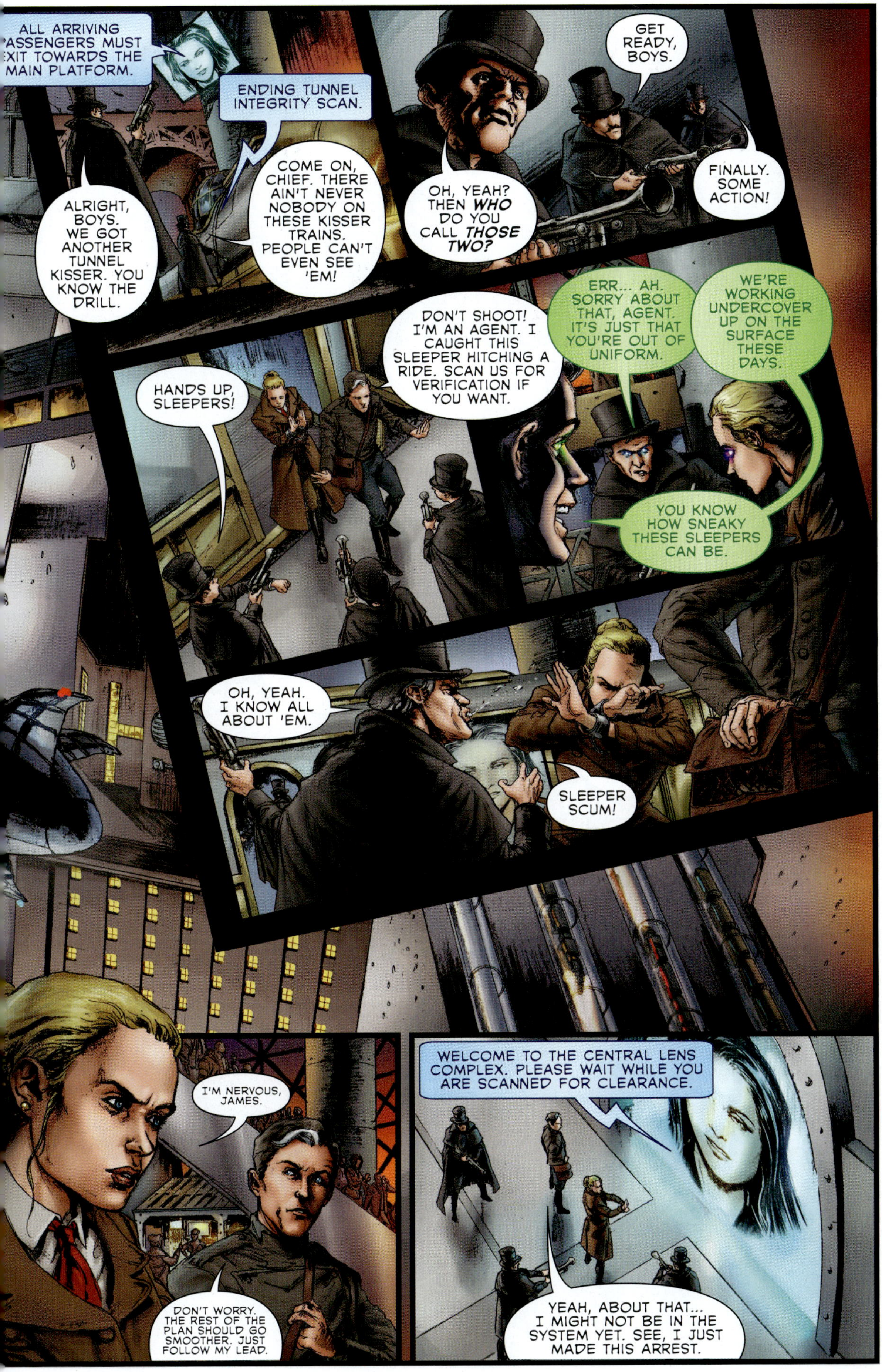

ALL ARRIVING PASSENGERS MUST EXIT TOWARDS THE MAIN PLATFORM.
ENDING TUNNEL INTEGRITY SCAN.
ALRIGHT, BOYS. WE GOT ANOTHER TUNNEL KISSER. YOU KNOW THE DRILL.
COME ON, CHIEF. THERE AIN'T NEVER NOBODY ON THESE KISSER TRAINS. PEOPLE CAN'T EVEN SEE 'EM!
OH, YEAH? THEN WHO DO YOU CALL THOSE TWO?
GET READY, BOYS.
FINALLY. SOME ACTION!
HANDS UP, SLEEPERS!
DON'T SHOOT! I'M AN AGENT. I CAUGHT THIS SLEEPER HITCHING A RIDE. SCAN US FOR VERIFICATION IF YOU WANT.
ERR... AH. SORRY ABOUT THAT, AGENT. IT'S JUST THAT YOU'RE OUT OF UNIFORM.
WE'RE WORKING UNDERCOVER UP ON THE SURFACE THESE DAYS.
YOU KNOW HOW SNEAKY THESE SLEEPERS CAN BE.
OH, YEAH. I KNOW ALL ABOUT 'EM.
SLEEPER SCUM!
I'M NERVOUS, JAMES.
DON'T WORRY. THE REST OF THE PLAN SHOULD GO SMOOTHER. JUST FOLLOW MY LEAD.
WELCOME TO THE CENTRAL LENS COMPLEX. PLEASE WAIT WHILE YOU ARE SCANNED FOR CLEARANCE.
YEAH, ABOUT THAT... I MIGHT NOT BE IN THE SYSTEM YET. SEE, I JUST MADE THIS ARREST.

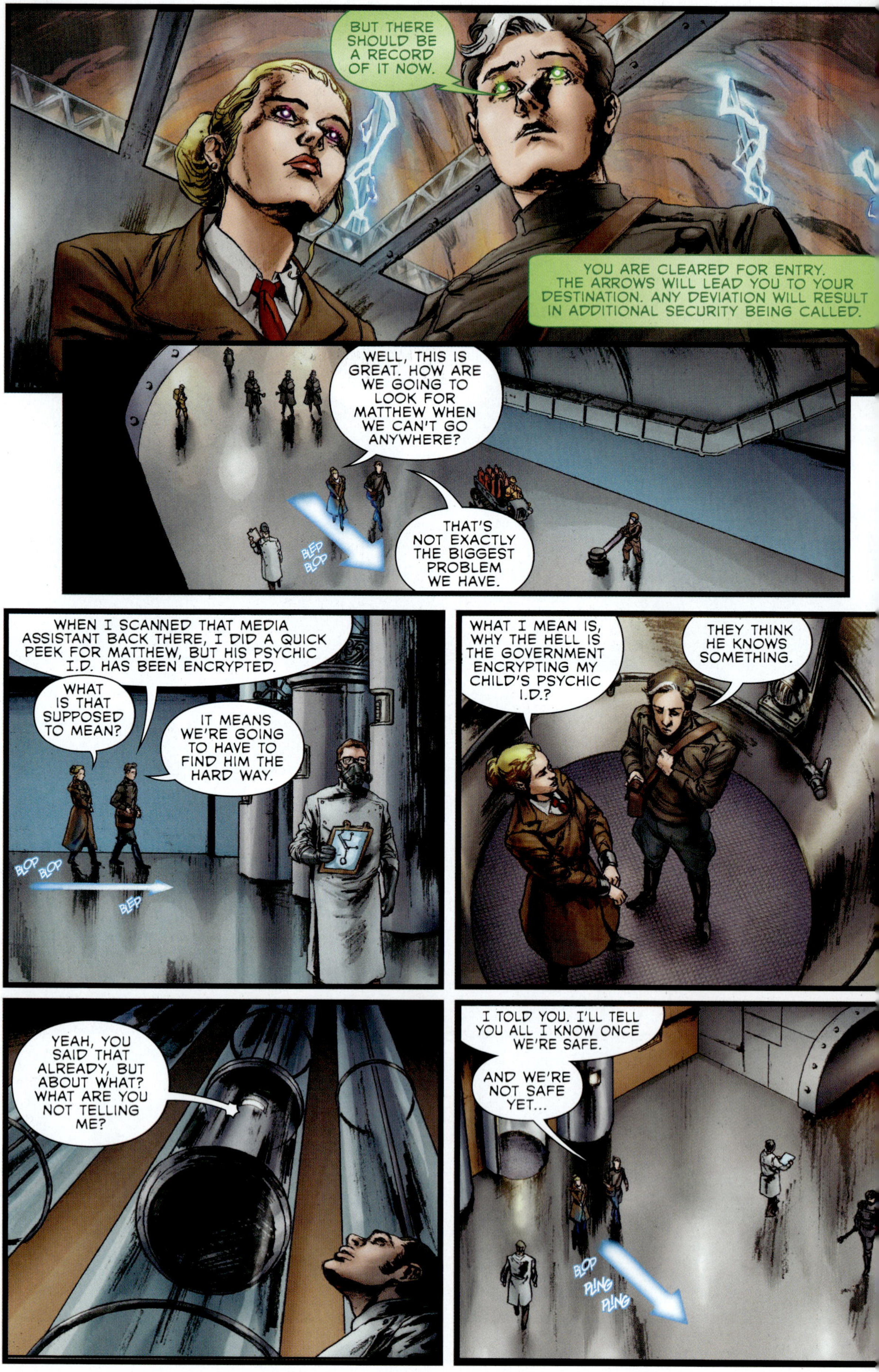
BUT THERE SHOULD BE A RECORD OF IT NOW.
YOU ARE CLEARED FOR ENTRY. THE ARROWS WILL LEAD YOU TO YOUR DESTINATION. ANY DEVIATION WILL RESULT IN ADDITIONAL SECURITY BEING CALLED.
WELL, THIS IS GREAT. HOW ARE WE GOING TO LOOK FOR MATTHEW WHEN WE CAN'T GO ANYWHERE?
THAT'S NOT EXACTLY THE BIGGEST PROBLEM WE HAVE.
BLEP BLOP
WHEN I SCANNED THAT MEDIA ASSISTANT BACK THERE, I DID A QUICK PEEK FOR MATTHEW, BUT HIS PSYCHIC I.D. HAS BEEN ENCRYPTED.
WHAT IS THAT SUPPOSED TO MEAN?
IT MEANS WE'RE GOING TO HAVE TO FIND HIM THE HARD WAY.
BLOP BLOP
BLEP
WHAT I MEAN IS, WHY THE HELL IS THE GOVERNMENT ENCRYPTING MY CHILD'S PSYCHIC I.D.?
THEY THINK HE KNOWS SOMETHING.
YEAH, YOU SAID THAT ALREADY, BUT ABOUT WHAT? WHAT ARE YOU NOT TELLING ME?
I TOLD YOU. I'LL TELL YOU ALL I KNOW ONCE WE'RE SAFE.
AND WE'RE NOT SAFE YET...
BLOP
PLING
PLING

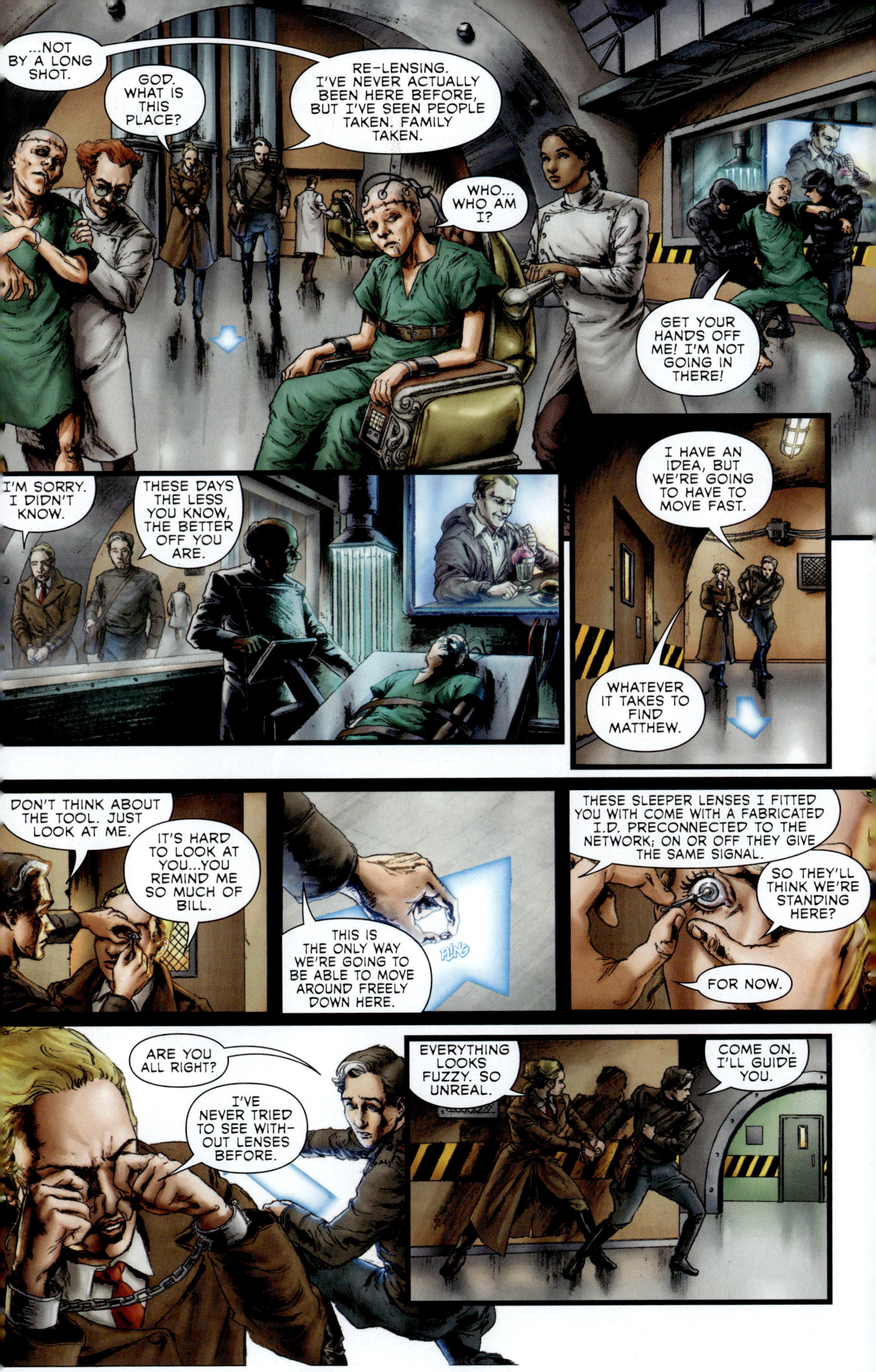

...NOT BY A LONG SHOT.
GOD. WHAT IS THIS PLACE?
RE-LENSING. I'VE NEVER ACTUALLY BEEN HERE BEFORE, BUT I'VE SEEN PEOPLE TAKEN. FAMILY TAKEN.
WHO... WHO AM I?
GET YOUR HANDS OFF ME! I'M NOT GOING IN THERE!
I'M SORRY. I DIDN'T KNOW.
THESE DAYS THE LESS YOU KNOW, THE BETTER OFF YOU ARE.
I HAVE AN IDEA, BUT WE'RE GOING TO HAVE TO MOVE FAST.
WHATEVER IT TAKES TO FIND MATTHEW.
DON'T THINK ABOUT THE TOOL. JUST LOOK AT ME.
IT'S HARD TO LOOK AT YOU...YOU REMIND ME SO MUCH OF BILL.
THIS IS THE ONLY WAY WE'RE GOING TO BE ABLE TO MOVE AROUND FREELY DOWN HERE.
THESE SLEEPER LENSES I FITTED YOU WITH COME WITH A FABRICATED I.D. PRECONNECTED TO THE NETWORK; ON OR OFF THEY GIVE THE SAME SIGNAL.
SO THEY'LL THINK WE'RE STANDING HERE?
FOR NOW.
ARE YOU ALL RIGHT?
I'VE NEVER TRIED TO SEE WITH-OUT LENSES BEFORE.
EVERYTHING LOOKS FUZZY. SO UNREAL.
COME ON. I'LL GUIDE YOU.

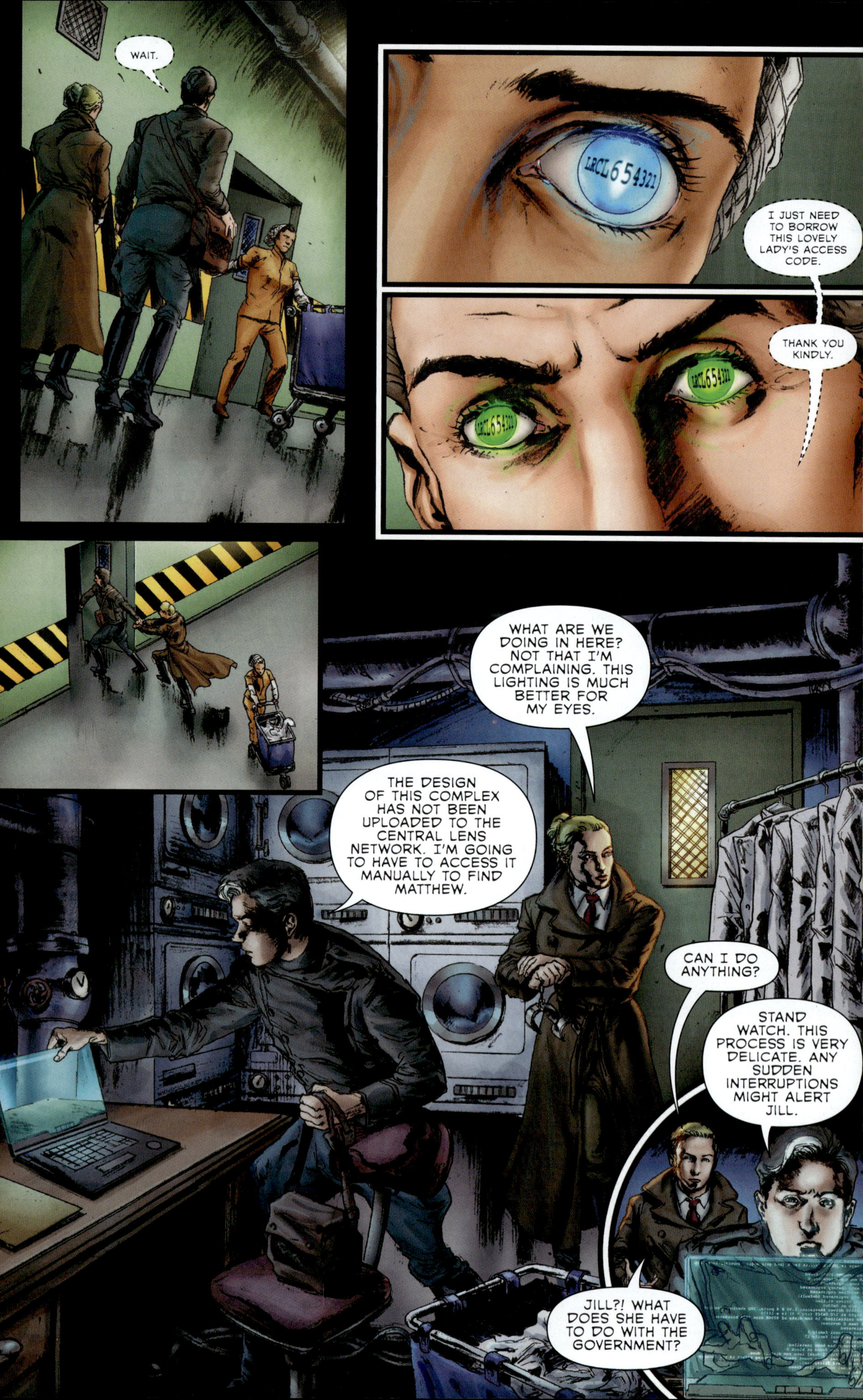
WAIT.
LRCL654321
I JUST NEED TO BORROW THIS LOVELY LADY'S ACCESS CODE.
LRCL654321
LRCL654321
THANK YOU KINDLY.
WHAT ARE WE DOING IN HERE? NOT THAT I'M COMPLAINING. THIS LIGHTING IS MUCH BETTER FOR MY EYES.
THE DESIGN OF THIS COMPLEX HAS NOT BEEN UPLOADED TO THE CENTRAL LENS NETWORK. I'M GOING TO HAVE TO ACCESS IT MANUALLY TO FIND MATTHEW.
CAN I DO ANYTHING?
STAND WATCH. THIS PROCESS IS VERY DELICATE. ANY SUDDEN INTERRUPTIONS MIGHT ALERT JILL.
JILL?! WHAT DOES SHE HAVE TO DO WITH THE GOVERNMENT?

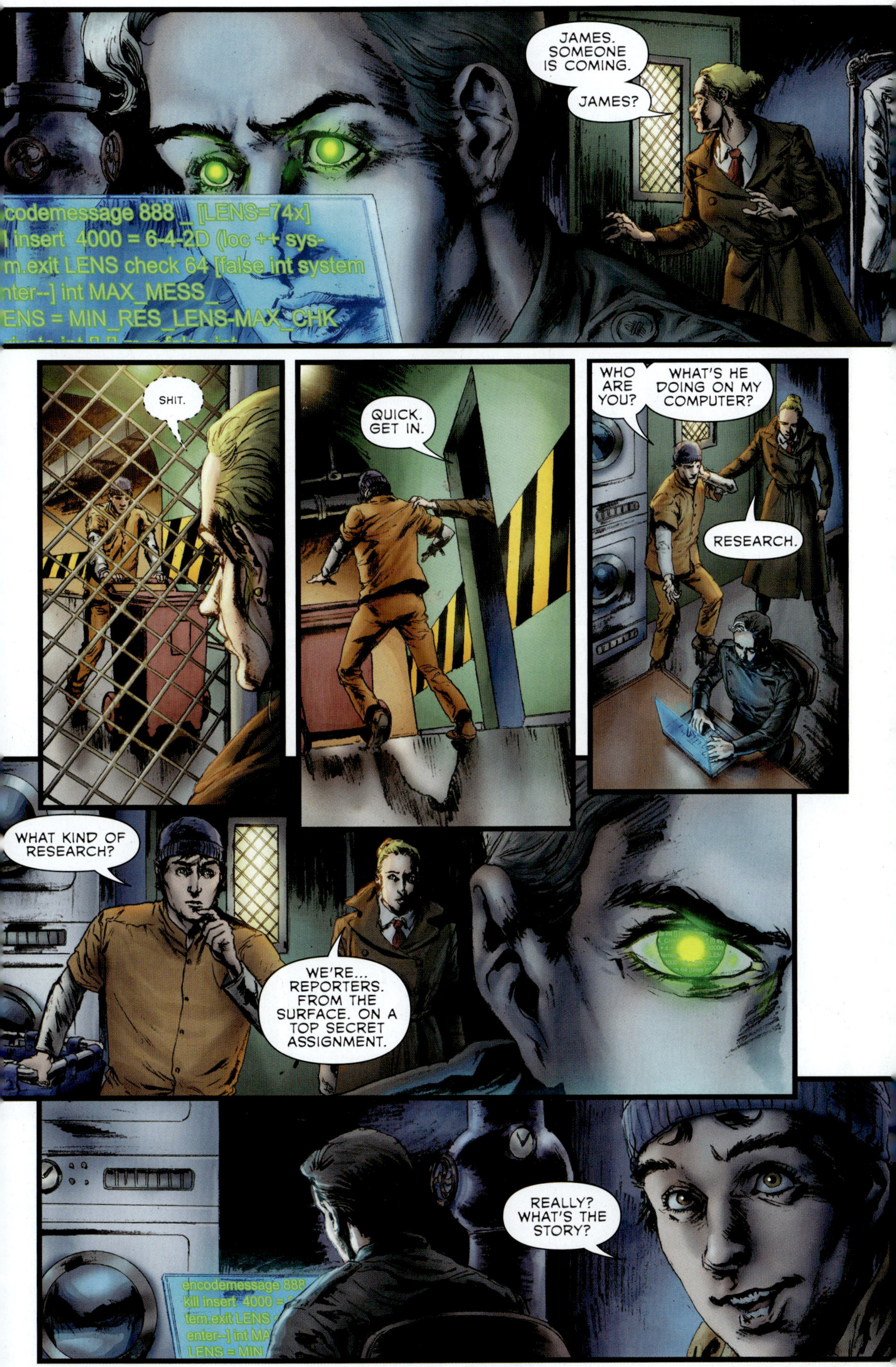
codemessage 888 _ [LENS=74x]
l insert 4000 = 6-4-2D (loc ++ sys-
m.exit LENS check 64 [false int system
nter--] int MAX_MESS_
ENS = MIN_RES_LENS-MAX_CHK
JAMES. SOMEONE IS COMING.
JAMES?
SHIT.
QUICK. GET IN.
WHO ARE YOU?
WHAT'S HE DOING ON MY COMPUTER?
RESEARCH.
WHAT KIND OF RESEARCH?
WE'RE... REPORTERS. FROM THE SURFACE. ON A TOP SECRET ASSIGNMENT.
REALLY? WHAT'S THE STORY?
encodemessage 888
kill insert 4000 =
tem.exit LENS
enter--] int MA
LENS = MIN

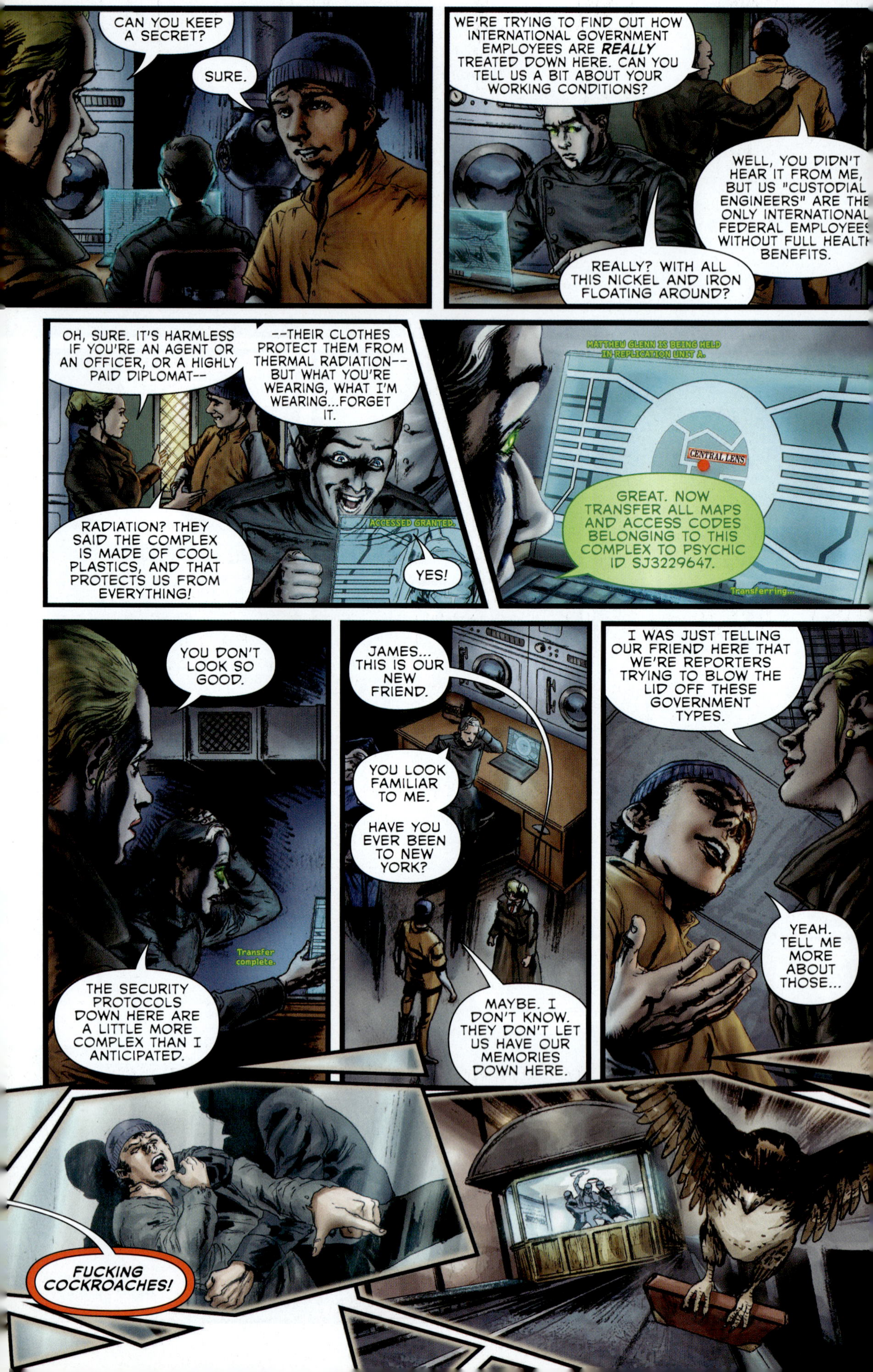
CAN YOU KEEP A SECRET?
SURE.
WE'RE TRYING TO FIND OUT HOW INTERNATIONAL GOVERNMENT EMPLOYEES ARE REALLY TREATED DOWN HERE. CAN YOU TELL US A BIT ABOUT YOUR WORKING CONDITIONS?
WELL, YOU DIDN'T HEAR IT FROM ME, BUT US "CUSTODIAL ENGINEERS" ARE THE ONLY INTERNATIONAL FEDERAL EMPLOYEES WITHOUT FULL HEALTH BENEFITS.
REALLY? WITH ALL THIS NICKEL AND IRON FLOATING AROUND?
OH, SURE. IT'S HARMLESS IF YOU'RE AN AGENT OR AN OFFICER, OR A HIGHLY PAID DIPLOMAT--
--THEIR CLOTHES PROTECT THEM FROM THERMAL RADIATION--BUT WHAT YOU'RE WEARING, WHAT I'M WEARING...FORGET IT.
RADIATION? THEY SAID THE COMPLEX IS MADE OF COOL PLASTICS, AND THAT PROTECTS US FROM EVERYTHING!
ACCESSED GRANTED.
YES!
MATTHEW GLENN IS BEING HELD IN REPLICATION UNIT A.
CENTRAL LENS
GREAT. NOW TRANSFER ALL MAPS AND ACCESS CODES BELONGING TO THIS COMPLEX TO PSYCHIC ID SJ3229647.
Transferring...
YOU DON'T LOOK SO GOOD.
Transfer complete.
THE SECURITY PROTOCOLS DOWN HERE ARE A LITTLE MORE COMPLEX THAN I ANTICIPATED.
JAMES... THIS IS OUR NEW FRIEND.
YOU LOOK FAMILIAR TO ME.
HAVE YOU EVER BEEN TO NEW YORK?
MAYBE. I DON'T KNOW. THEY DON'T LET US HAVE OUR MEMORIES DOWN HERE.
I WAS JUST TELLING OUR FRIEND HERE THAT WE'RE REPORTERS TRYING TO BLOW THE LID OFF THESE GOVERNMENT TYPES.
YEAH. TELL ME MORE ABOUT THOSE...
FUCKING COCKROACHES!

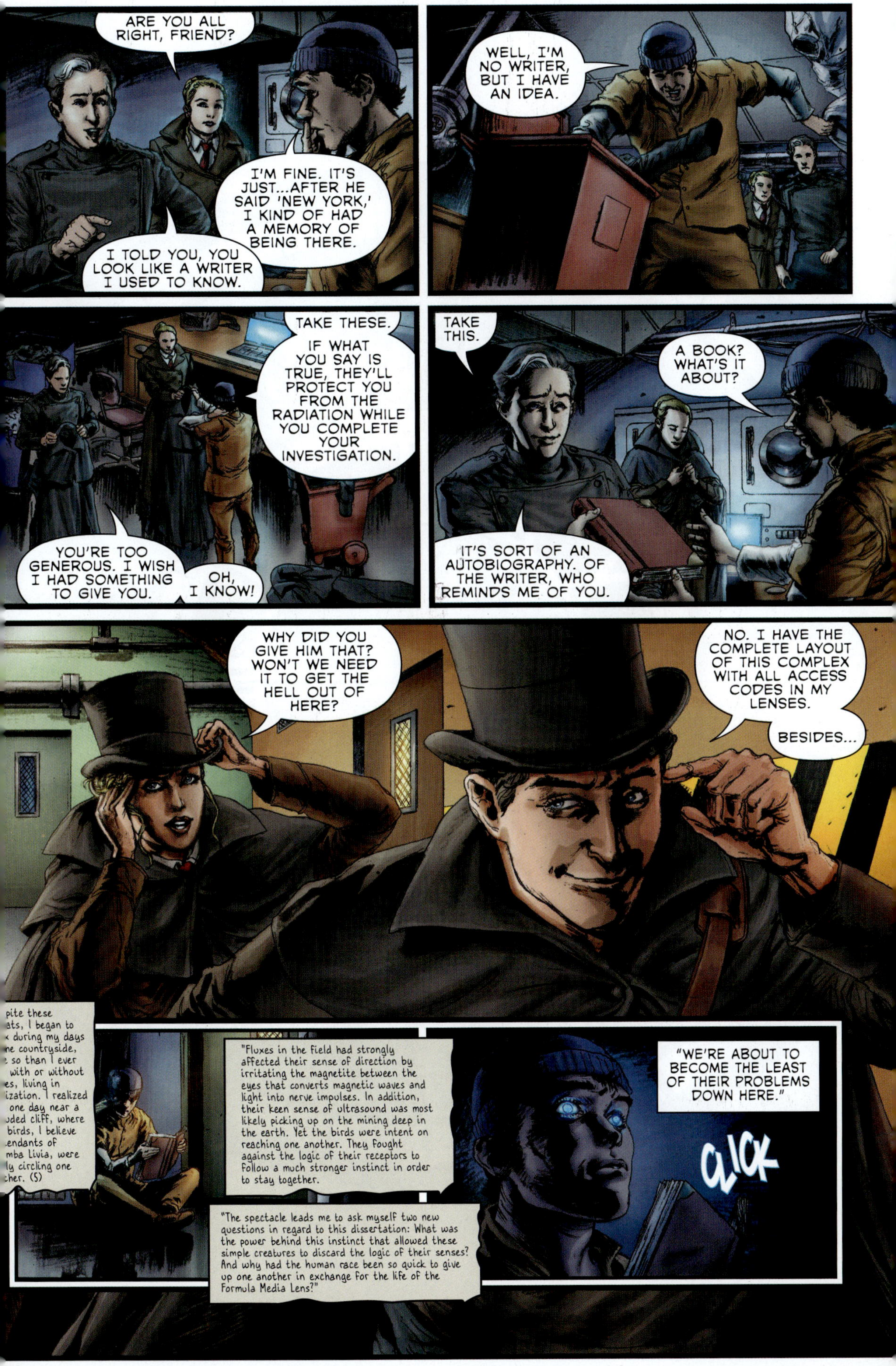
ARE YOU ALL RIGHT, FRIEND?
I'M FINE. IT'S JUST...AFTER HE SAID 'NEW YORK,' I KIND OF HAD A MEMORY OF BEING THERE.
I TOLD YOU, YOU LOOK LIKE A WRITER I USED TO KNOW.
WELL, I'M NO WRITER, BUT I HAVE AN IDEA.
TAKE THESE.
IF WHAT YOU SAY IS TRUE, THEY'LL PROTECT YOU FROM THE RADIATION WHILE YOU COMPLETE YOUR INVESTIGATION.
YOU'RE TOO GENEROUS. I WISH I HAD SOMETHING TO GIVE YOU.
OH, I KNOW!
TAKE THIS.
A BOOK? WHAT'S IT ABOUT?
IT'S SORT OF AN AUTOBIOGRAPHY. OF THE WRITER, WHO REMINDS ME OF YOU.
WHY DID YOU GIVE HIM THAT? WON'T WE NEED IT TO GET THE HELL OUT OF HERE?
NO. I HAVE THE COMPLETE LAYOUT OF THIS COMPLEX WITH ALL ACCESS CODES IN MY LENSES.
BESIDES...
pite these ats, I began to during my days ne countryside, so than I ever with or without es, living in ization. I realized one day near a oded cliff, where birds, I believe endants of mba Livia, were ly circling one her. (5)
"Fluxes in the field had strongly affected their sense of direction by irritating the magnetite between the eyes that converts magnetic waves and light into nerve impulses. In addition, their keen sense of ultrasound was most likely picking up on the mining deep in the earth. Yet the birds were intent on reaching one another. They fought against the logic of their receptors to follow a much stronger instinct in order to stay together.
"The spectacle leads me to ask myself two new questions in regard to this dissertation: What was the power behind this instinct that allowed these simple creatures to discard the logic of their senses? And why had the human race been so quick to give up one another in exchange for the life of the Formula Media Lens?"
"WE'RE ABOUT TO BECOME THE LEAST OF THEIR PROBLEMS DOWN HERE."
CLICK

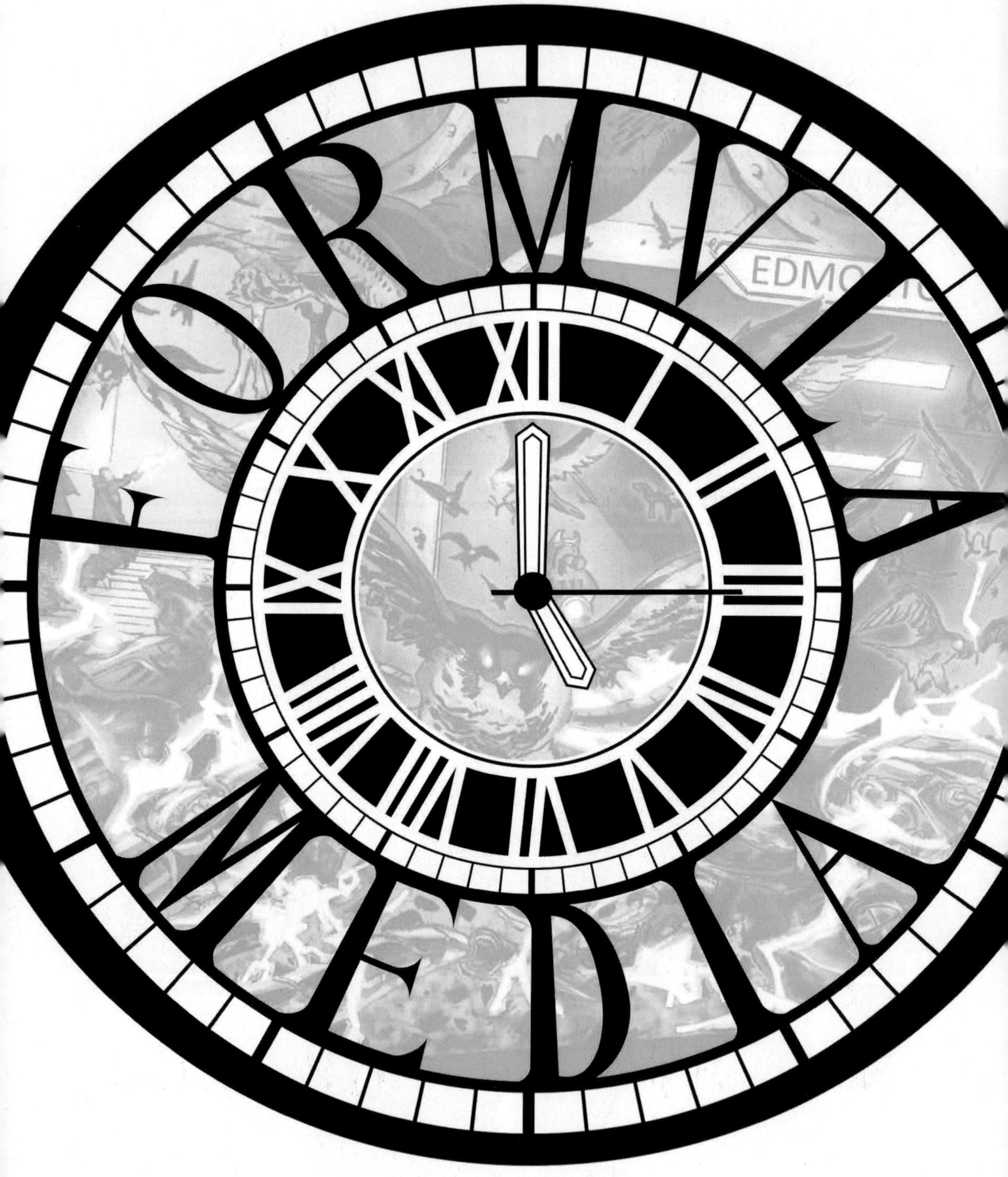

CHAPTER 05

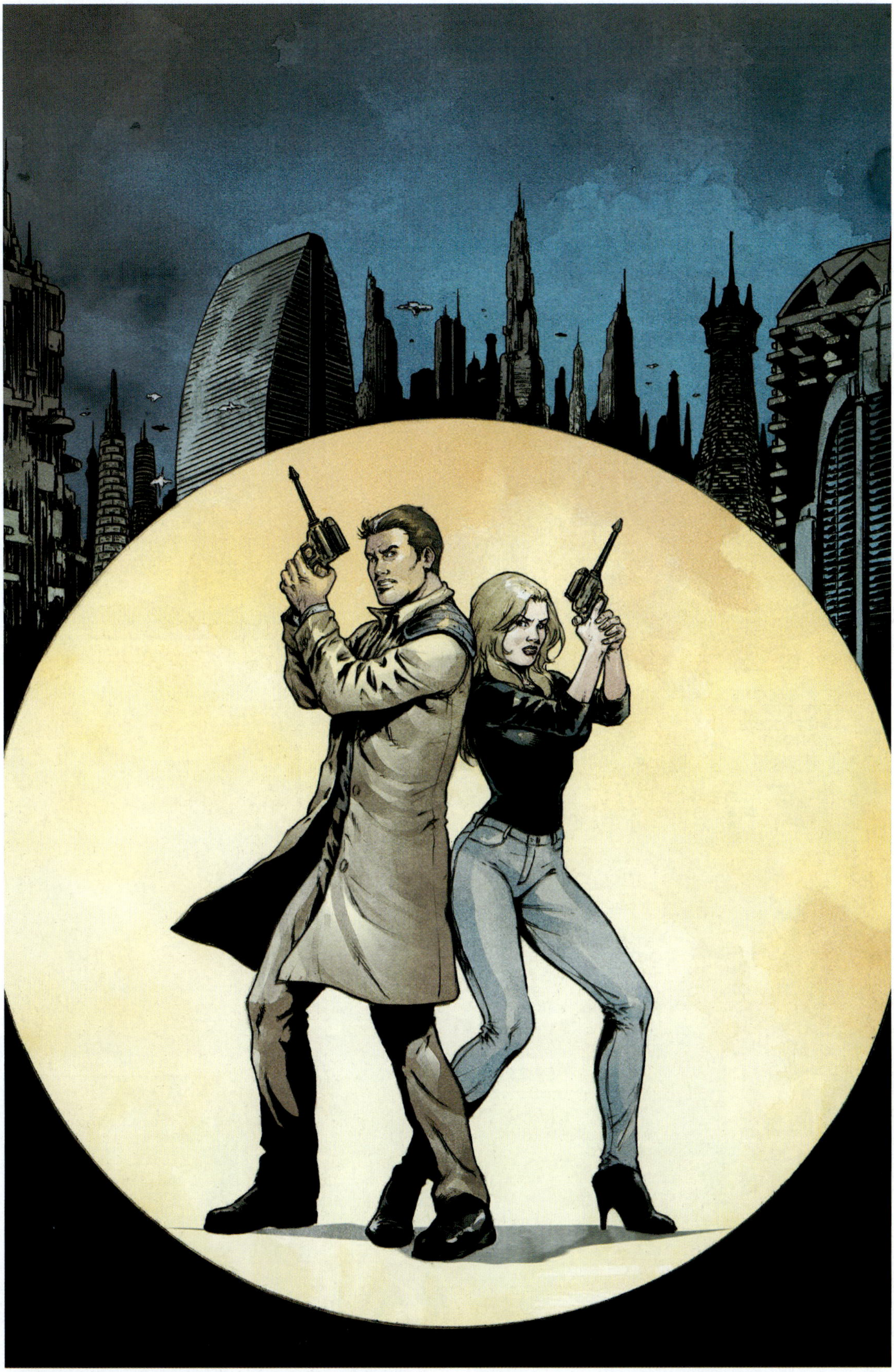

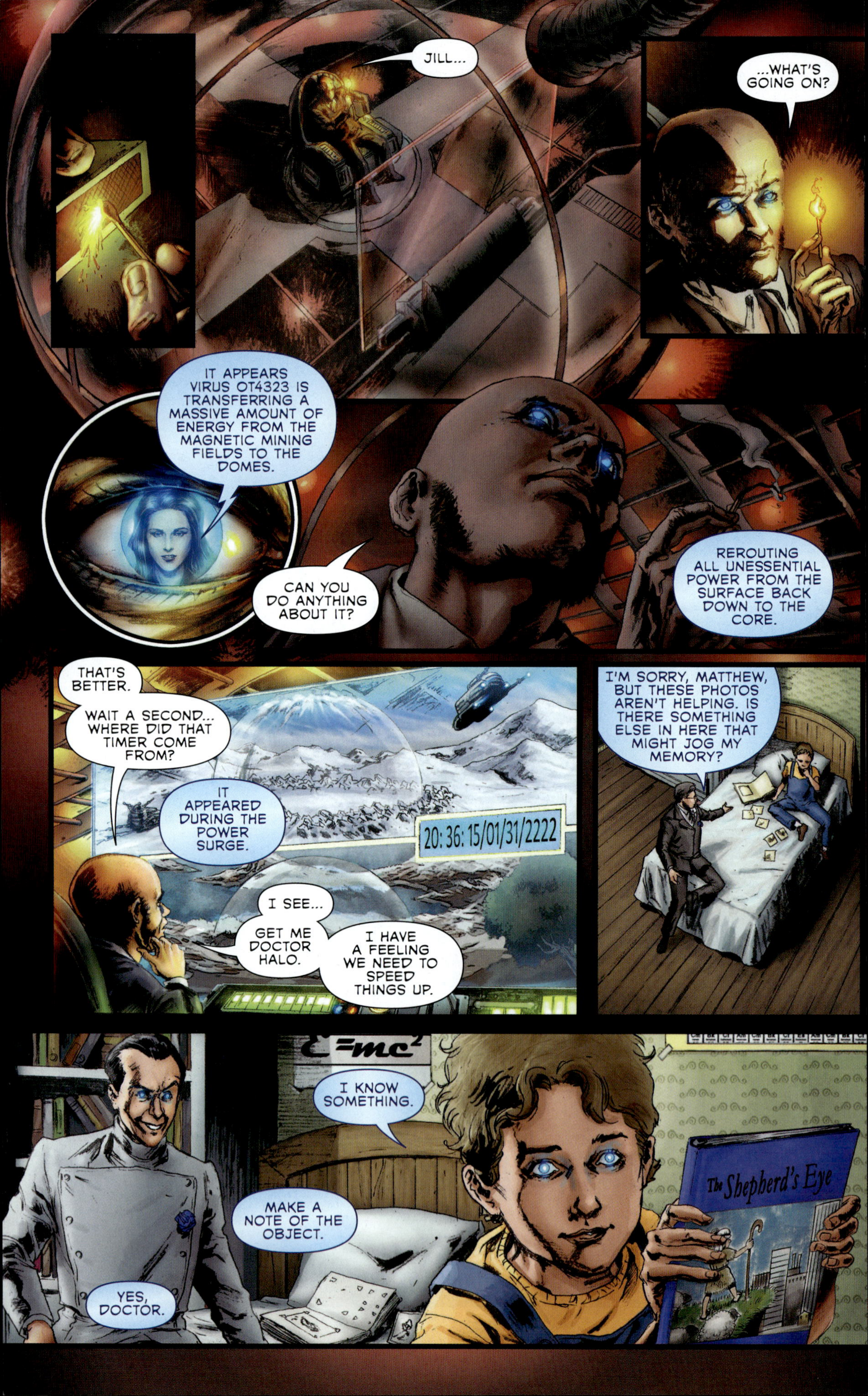
JILL...
...WHAT'S GOING ON?
IT APPEARS VIRUS OT4323 IS TRANSFERRING A MASSIVE AMOUNT OF ENERGY FROM THE MAGNETIC MINING FIELDS TO THE DOMES.
CAN YOU DO ANYTHING ABOUT IT?
REROUTING ALL UNESSENTIAL POWER FROM THE SURFACE BACK DOWN TO THE CORE.
THAT'S BETTER.
WAIT A SECOND... WHERE DID THAT TIMER COME FROM?
IT APPEARED DURING THE POWER SURGE.
20: 36: 15/01/31/2222
I SEE...
GET ME DOCTOR HALO.
I HAVE A FEELING WE NEED TO SPEED THINGS UP.
I'M SORRY, MATTHEW, BUT THESE PHOTOS AREN'T HELPING. IS THERE SOMETHING ELSE IN HERE THAT MIGHT JOG MY MEMORY?
E=mc²
I KNOW SOMETHING.
MAKE A NOTE OF THE OBJECT.
YES, DOCTOR.
The Shepherd's Eye

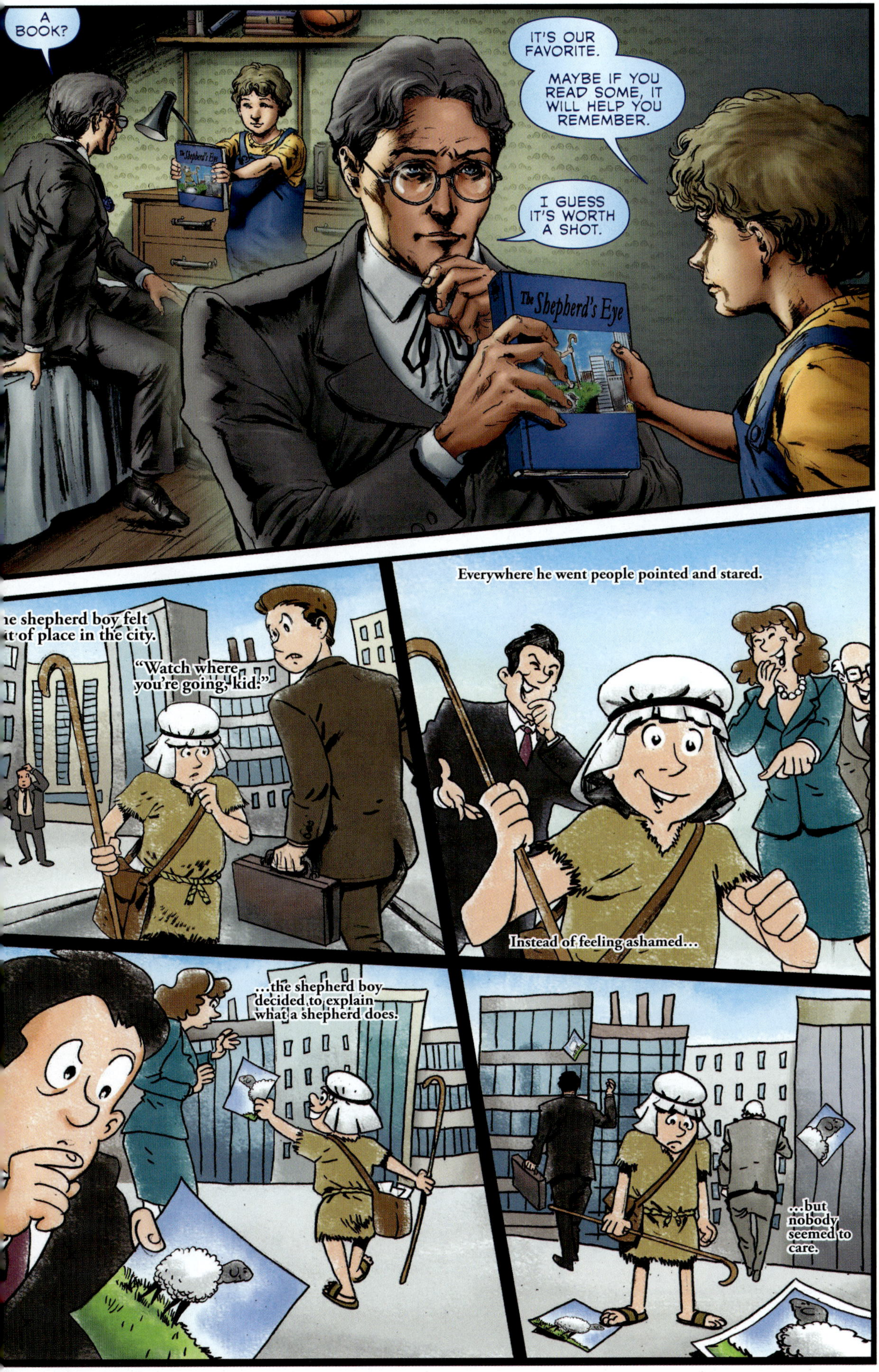
A BOOK?
IT'S OUR FAVORITE.
MAYBE IF YOU READ SOME, IT WILL HELP YOU REMEMBER.
I GUESS IT'S WORTH A SHOT.
The Shepherd's Eye
e shepherd boy felt
ut of place in the city.
"Watch where you're going, kid."
Everywhere he went people pointed and stared.
Instead of feeling ashamed…
…the shepherd boy decided to explain what a shepherd does.
…but nobody seemed to care.

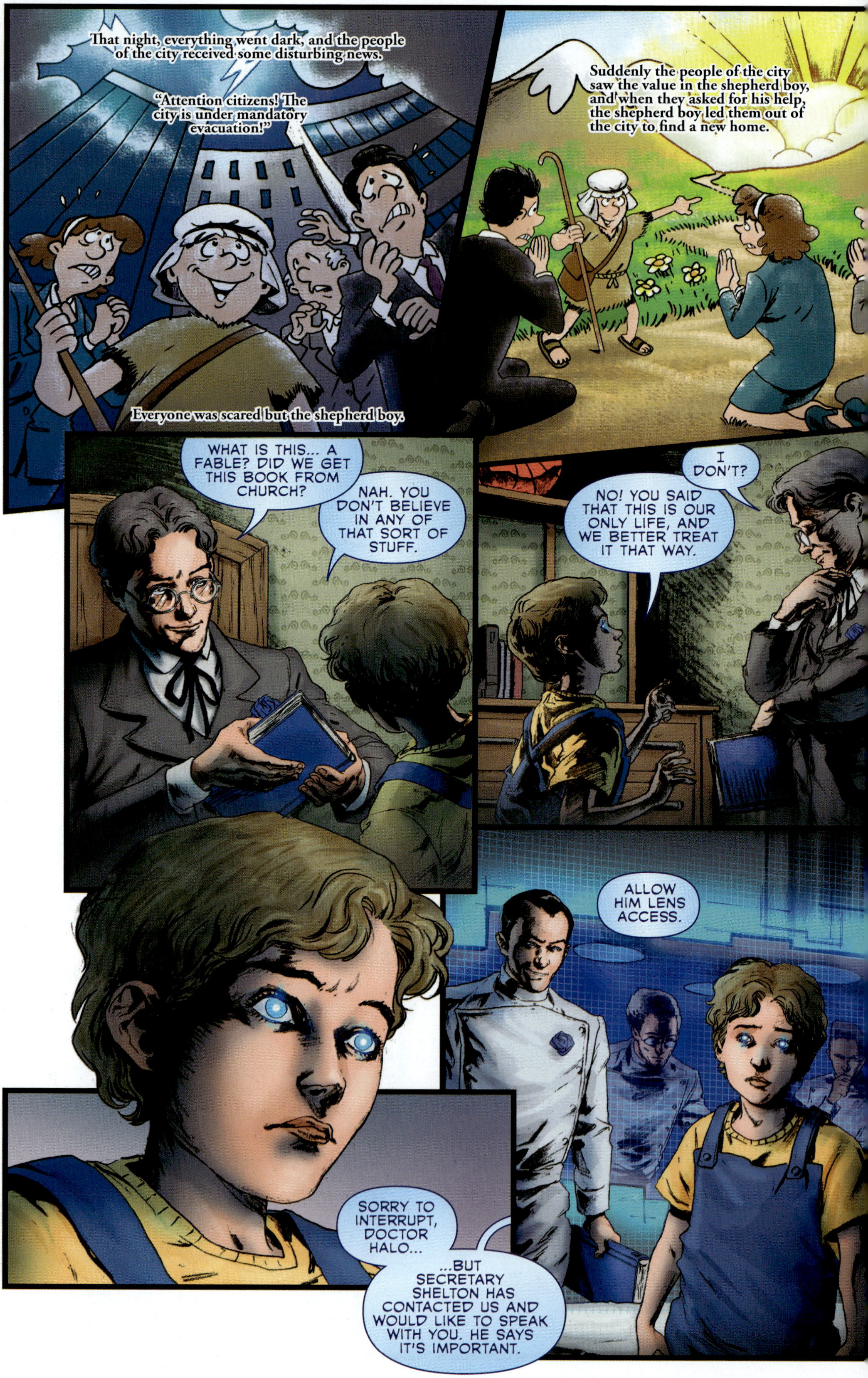
That night, everything went dark, and the people of the city received some disturbing news.
"Attention citizens! The city is under mandatory evacuation!"
Everyone was scared but the shepherd boy.
Suddenly the people of the city saw the value in the shepherd boy, and when they asked for his help, the shepherd boy led them out of the city to find a new home.
WHAT IS THIS... A FABLE? DID WE GET THIS BOOK FROM CHURCH?
NAH. YOU DON'T BELIEVE IN ANY OF THAT SORT OF STUFF.
I DON'T?
NO! YOU SAID THAT THIS IS OUR ONLY LIFE, AND WE BETTER TREAT IT THAT WAY.
ALLOW HIM LENS ACCESS.
SORRY TO INTERRUPT, DOCTOR HALO...
...BUT SECRETARY SHELTON HAS CONTACTED US AND WOULD LIKE TO SPEAK WITH YOU. HE SAYS IT'S IMPORTANT.

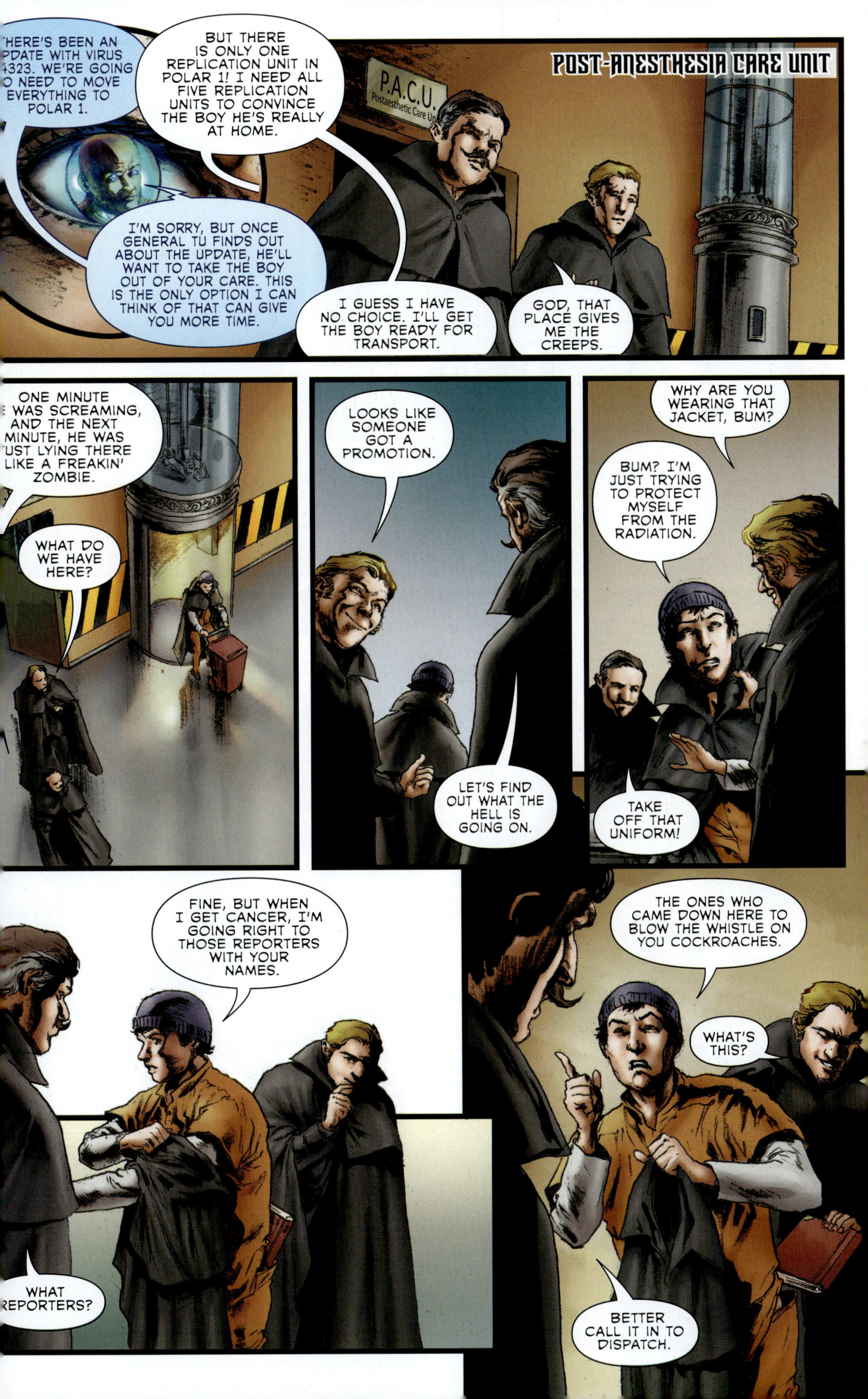
POST-ANESTHESIA CARE UNIT
P.A.C.U.
Postaesthetic Care Un
HERE'S BEEN AN PDATE WITH VIRUS 4323. WE'RE GOING O NEED TO MOVE EVERYTHING TO POLAR 1.
BUT THERE IS ONLY ONE REPLICATION UNIT IN POLAR 1! I NEED ALL FIVE REPLICATION UNITS TO CONVINCE THE BOY HE'S REALLY AT HOME.
I'M SORRY, BUT ONCE GENERAL TU FINDS OUT ABOUT THE UPDATE, HE'LL WANT TO TAKE THE BOY OUT OF YOUR CARE. THIS IS THE ONLY OPTION I CAN THINK OF THAT CAN GIVE YOU MORE TIME.
I GUESS I HAVE NO CHOICE. I'LL GET THE BOY READY FOR TRANSPORT.
GOD, THAT PLACE GIVES ME THE CREEPS.
ONE MINUTE WAS SCREAMING, AND THE NEXT MINUTE, HE WAS UST LYING THERE LIKE A FREAKIN' ZOMBIE.
WHAT DO WE HAVE HERE?
LOOKS LIKE SOMEONE GOT A PROMOTION.
LET'S FIND OUT WHAT THE HELL IS GOING ON.
WHY ARE YOU WEARING THAT JACKET, BUM?
BUM? I'M JUST TRYING TO PROTECT MYSELF FROM THE RADIATION.
TAKE OFF THAT UNIFORM!
FINE, BUT WHEN I GET CANCER, I'M GOING RIGHT TO THOSE REPORTERS WITH YOUR NAMES.
WHAT REPORTERS?
THE ONES WHO CAME DOWN HERE TO BLOW THE WHISTLE ON YOU COCKROACHES.
WHAT'S THIS?
BETTER CALL IT IN TO DISPATCH.

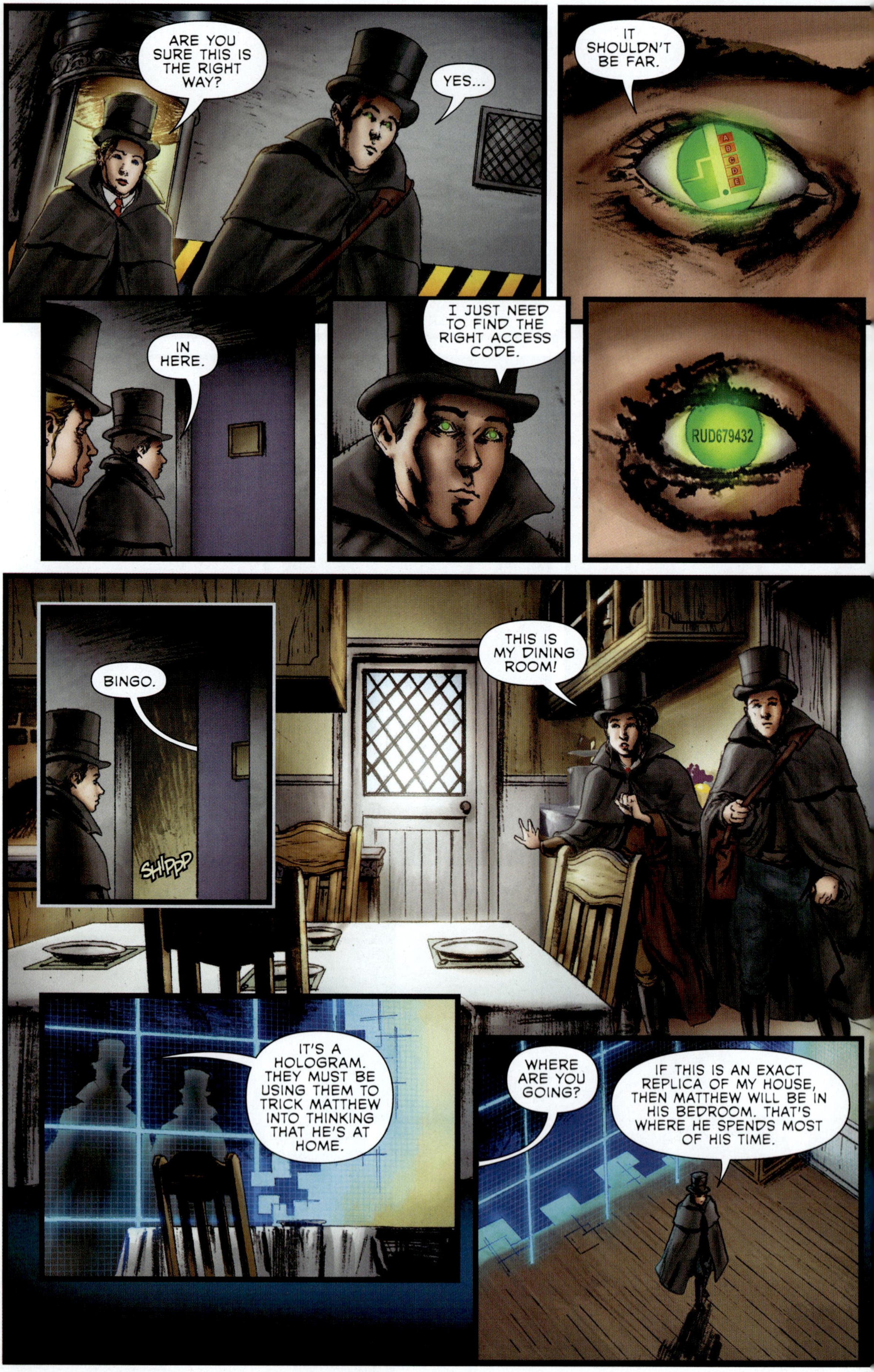
ARE YOU SURE THIS IS THE RIGHT WAY?
YES...
IT SHOULDN'T BE FAR.
IN HERE.
I JUST NEED TO FIND THE RIGHT ACCESS CODE.
RUD679432
BINGO.
SHPPP
THIS IS MY DINING ROOM!
IT'S A HOLOGRAM. THEY MUST BE USING THEM TO TRICK MATTHEW INTO THINKING THAT HE'S AT HOME.
WHERE ARE YOU GOING?
IF THIS IS AN EXACT REPLICA OF MY HOUSE, THEN MATTHEW WILL BE IN HIS BEDROOM. THAT'S WHERE HE SPENDS MOST OF HIS TIME.

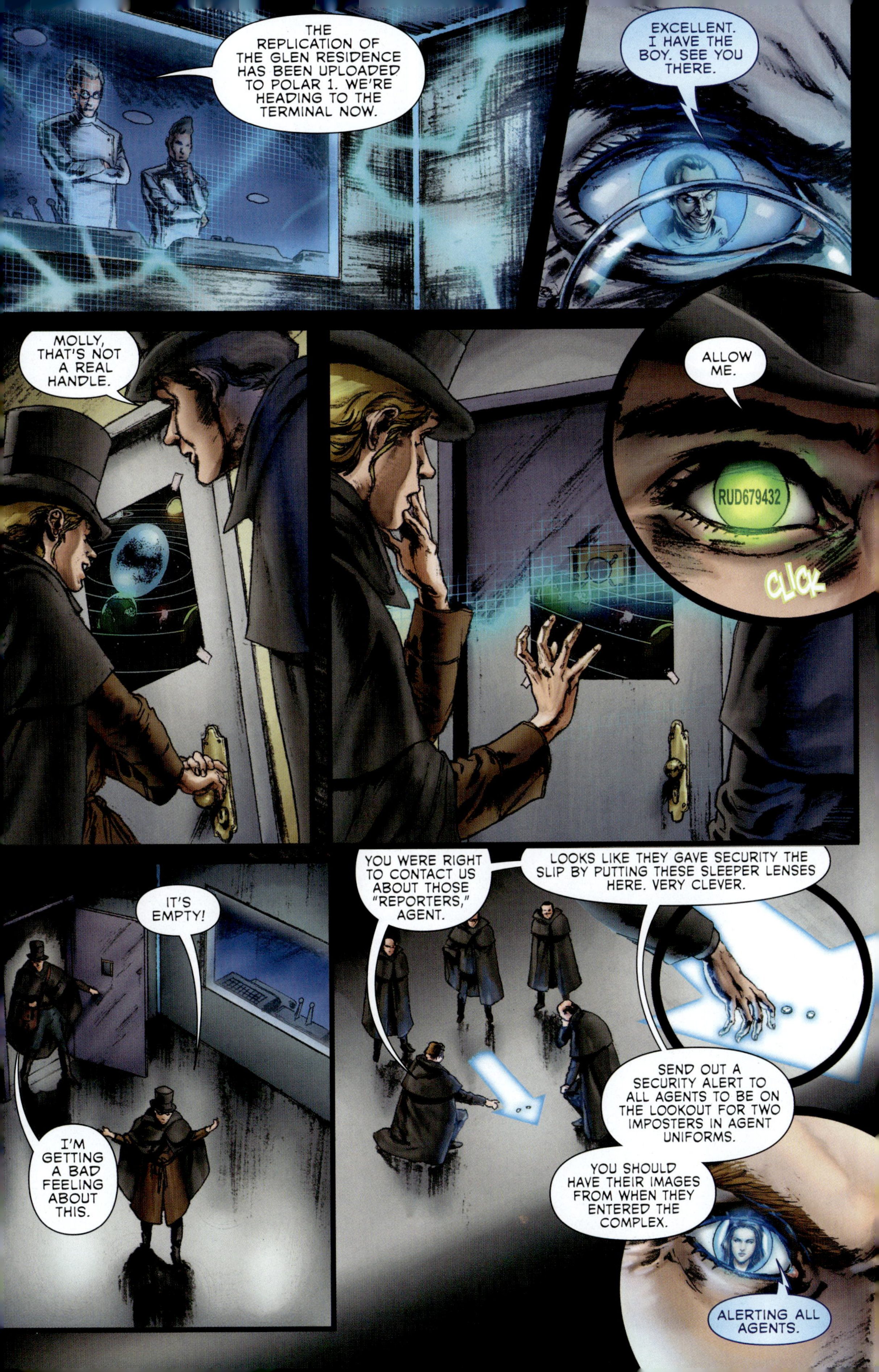
THE REPLICATION OF THE GLEN RESIDENCE HAS BEEN UPLOADED TO POLAR 1. WE'RE HEADING TO THE TERMINAL NOW.
EXCELLENT. I HAVE THE BOY. SEE YOU THERE.
MOLLY, THAT'S NOT A REAL HANDLE.
ALLOW ME.
RUD679432
CLICK
IT'S EMPTY!
I'M GETTING A BAD FEELING ABOUT THIS.
YOU WERE RIGHT TO CONTACT US ABOUT THOSE "REPORTERS," AGENT.
LOOKS LIKE THEY GAVE SECURITY THE SLIP BY PUTTING THESE SLEEPER LENSES HERE. VERY CLEVER.
SEND OUT A SECURITY ALERT TO ALL AGENTS TO BE ON THE LOOKOUT FOR TWO IMPOSTERS IN AGENT UNIFORMS.
YOU SHOULD HAVE THEIR IMAGES FROM WHEN THEY ENTERED THE COMPLEX.
ALERTING ALL AGENTS.

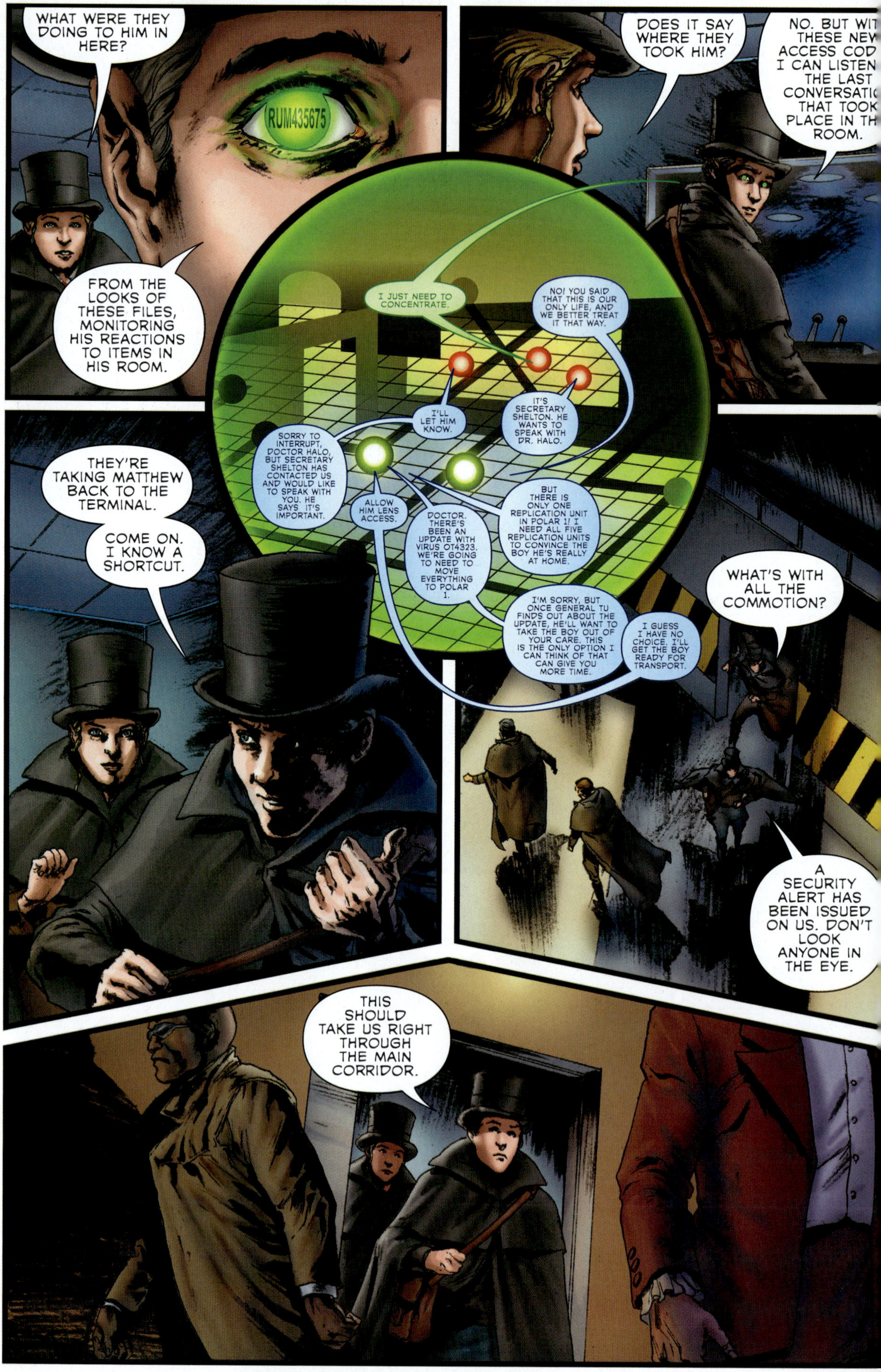
WHAT WERE THEY DOING TO HIM IN HERE?
RUM435675
FROM THE LOOKS OF THESE FILES, MONITORING HIS REACTIONS TO ITEMS IN HIS ROOM.
DOES IT SAY WHERE THEY TOOK HIM?
NO. BUT WIT THESE NEV ACCESS COD I CAN LISTEN THE LAST CONVERSATIO THAT TOOK PLACE IN TH ROOM.
I JUST NEED TO CONCENTRATE.
SORRY TO INTERRUPT, DOCTOR HALO, BUT SECRETARY SHELTON HAS CONTACTED US AND WOULD LIKE TO SPEAK WITH YOU. HE SAYS IT'S IMPORTANT.
I'LL LET HIM KNOW.
IT'S SECRETARY SHELTON. HE WANTS TO SPEAK WITH DR. HALO.
NO! YOU SAID THAT THIS IS OUR ONLY LIFE, AND WE BETTER TREAT IT THAT WAY.
DOCTOR. THERE'S BEEN AN UPDATE WITH VIRUS OT4323. WE'RE GOING TO NEED TO MOVE EVERYTHING TO POLAR 1.
BUT THERE IS ONLY ONE REPLICATION UNIT IN POLAR 1! I NEED ALL FIVE REPLICATION UNITS TO CONVINCE THE BOY HE'S REALLY AT HOME.
I'M SORRY, BUT ONCE GENERAL TU FINDS OUT ABOUT THE UPDATE, HE'LL WANT TO TAKE THE BOY OUT OF YOUR CARE. THIS IS THE ONLY OPTION I CAN THINK OF THAT CAN GIVE YOU MORE TIME.
I GUESS I HAVE NO CHOICE. I'LL GET THE BOY READY FOR TRANSPORT.
ALLOW HIM LENS ACCESS.
THEY'RE TAKING MATTHEW BACK TO THE TERMINAL.
COME ON. I KNOW A SHORTCUT.
WHAT'S WITH ALL THE COMMOTION?
A SECURITY ALERT HAS BEEN ISSUED ON US. DON'T LOOK ANYONE IN THE EYE.
THIS SHOULD TAKE US RIGHT THROUGH THE MAIN CORRIDOR.

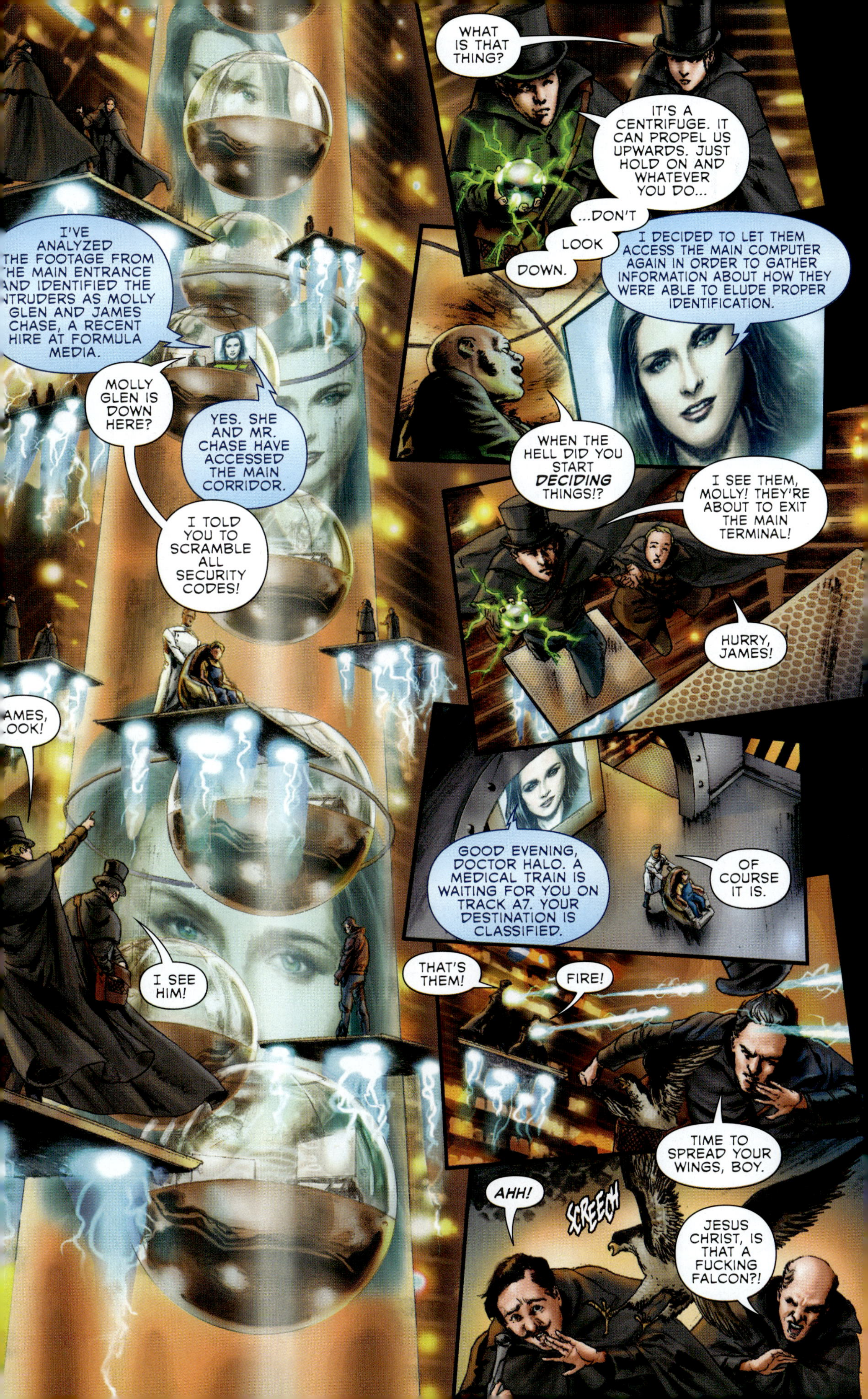
I'VE ANALYZED THE FOOTAGE FROM THE MAIN ENTRANCE AND IDENTIFIED THE INTRUDERS AS MOLLY GLEN AND JAMES CHASE, A RECENT HIRE AT FORMULA MEDIA.
MOLLY GLEN IS DOWN HERE?
YES. SHE AND MR. CHASE HAVE ACCESSED THE MAIN CORRIDOR.
I TOLD YOU TO SCRAMBLE ALL SECURITY CODES!
AMES, OOK!
I SEE HIM!
WHAT IS THAT THING?
IT'S A CENTRIFUGE. IT CAN PROPEL US UPWARDS. JUST HOLD ON AND WHATEVER YOU DO...
...DON'T
LOOK
DOWN.
I DECIDED TO LET THEM ACCESS THE MAIN COMPUTER AGAIN IN ORDER TO GATHER INFORMATION ABOUT HOW THEY WERE ABLE TO ELUDE PROPER IDENTIFICATION.
WHEN THE HELL DID YOU START *DECIDING* THINGS!?
I SEE THEM, MOLLY! THEY'RE ABOUT TO EXIT THE MAIN TERMINAL!
HURRY, JAMES!
GOOD EVENING, DOCTOR HALO. A MEDICAL TRAIN IS WAITING FOR YOU ON TRACK A7. YOUR DESTINATION IS CLASSIFIED.
OF COURSE IT IS.
THAT'S THEM!
FIRE!
TIME TO SPREAD YOUR WINGS, BOY.
AHH!
SCREECH
JESUS CHRIST, IS THAT A FUCKING FALCON?!

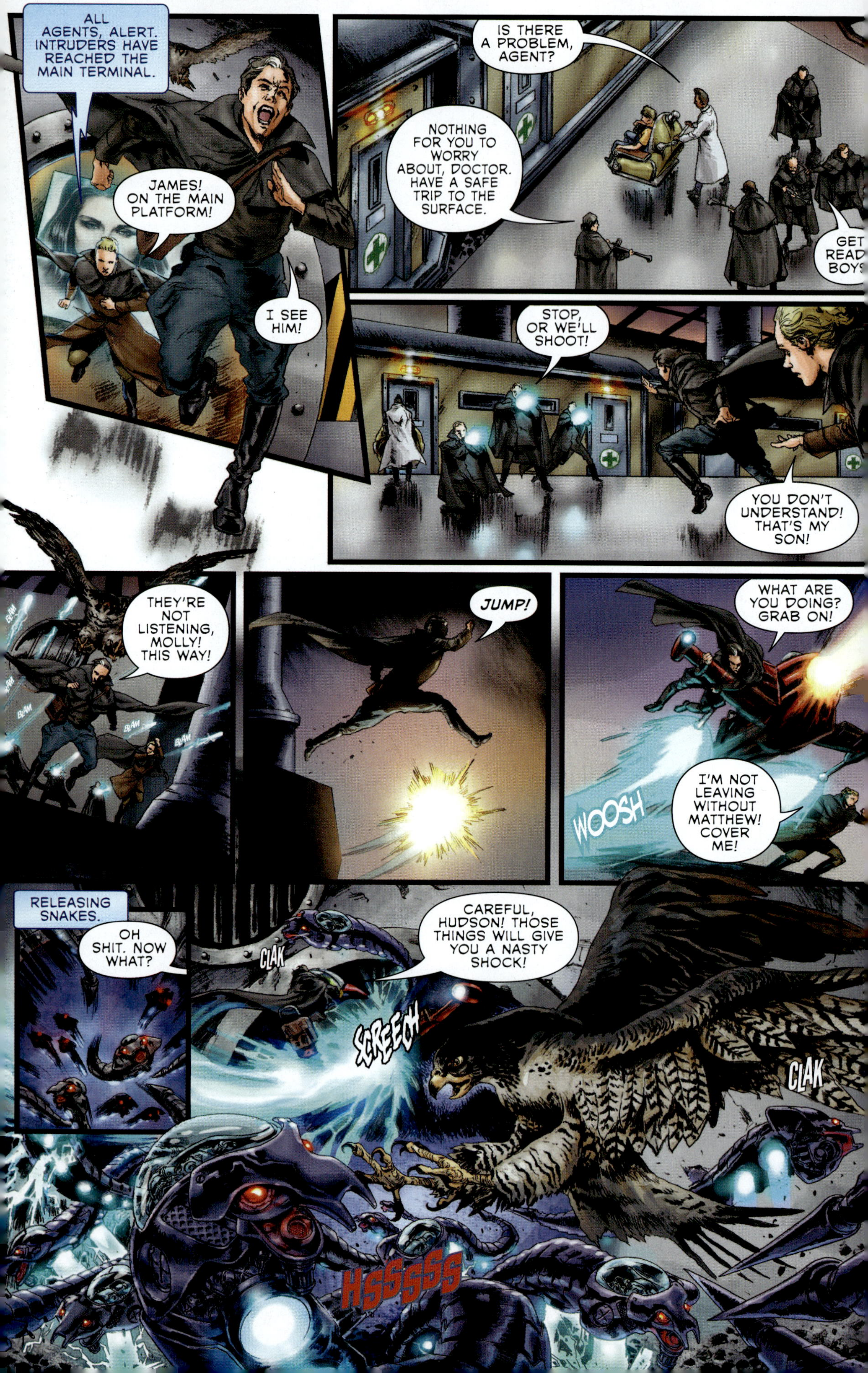
ALL AGENTS, ALERT. INTRUDERS HAVE REACHED THE MAIN TERMINAL.
JAMES! ON THE MAIN PLATFORM!
I SEE HIM!
IS THERE A PROBLEM, AGENT?
NOTHING FOR YOU TO WORRY ABOUT, DOCTOR. HAVE A SAFE TRIP TO THE SURFACE.
GET READ BOYS
STOP, OR WE'LL SHOOT!
YOU DON'T UNDERSTAND! THAT'S MY SON!
THEY'RE NOT LISTENING, MOLLY! THIS WAY!
BLAM
BLAM
BLAM
JUMP!
WHAT ARE YOU DOING? GRAB ON!
WOOSH
I'M NOT LEAVING WITHOUT MATTHEW! COVER ME!
RELEASING SNAKES.
OH SHIT. NOW WHAT?
CAREFUL, HUDSON! THOSE THINGS WILL GIVE YOU A NASTY SHOCK!
CLAK
SCREECH
CLAK
HSSSSS

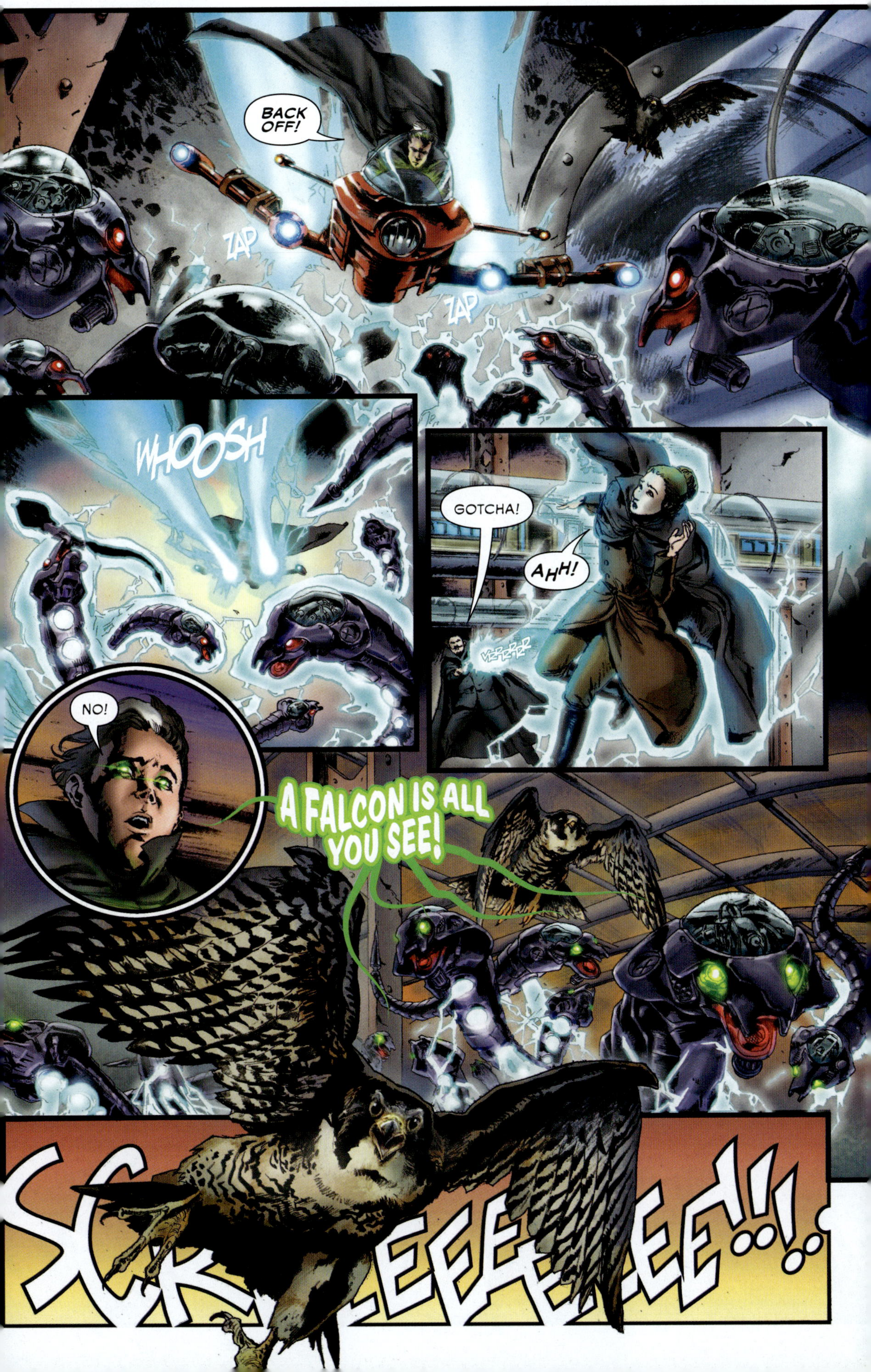
BACK OFF!
ZAP
ZAP
WHOOSH
GOTCHA!
AHH!
VZRRRRR
NO!
A FALCON IS ALL YOU SEE!
SCREEEEEEE!!..!..

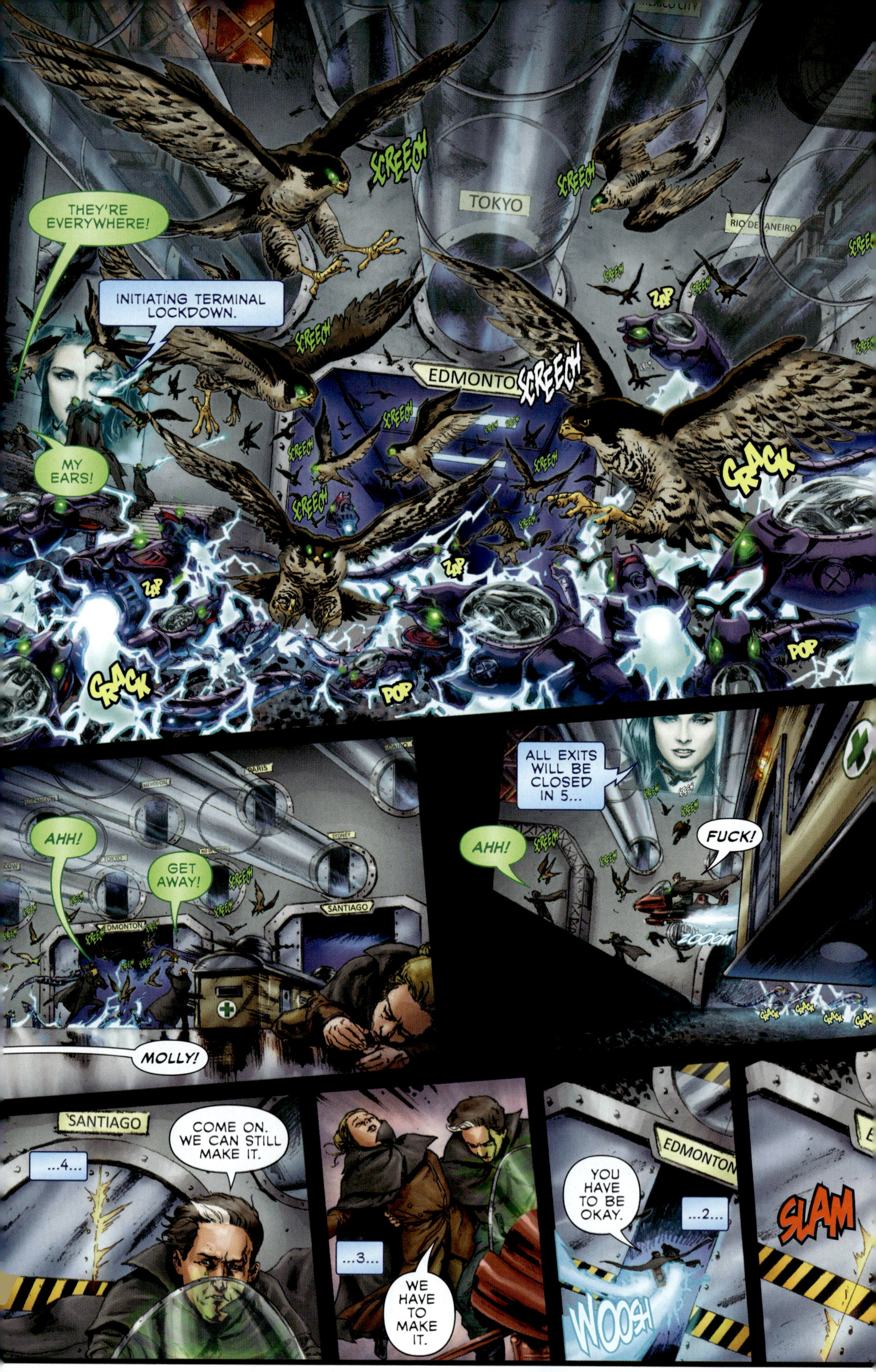

TOKYO
RIO DE JANEIRO
SCREECH
THEY'RE EVERYWHERE!
INITIATING TERMINAL LOCKDOWN.
EDMONTON
SCREECH
MY EARS!
CRACK
ZAP
POP
AHH!
GET AWAY!
PARIS
SYDNEY
EDMONTON
SANTIAGO
MOLLY!
ALL EXITS WILL BE CLOSED IN 5...
AHH!
FUCK!
ZOOOM
SANTIAGO
...4...
COME ON. WE CAN STILL MAKE IT.
...3...
WE HAVE TO MAKE IT.
EDMONTON
YOU HAVE TO BE OKAY.
...2...
WOOSH
SLAM

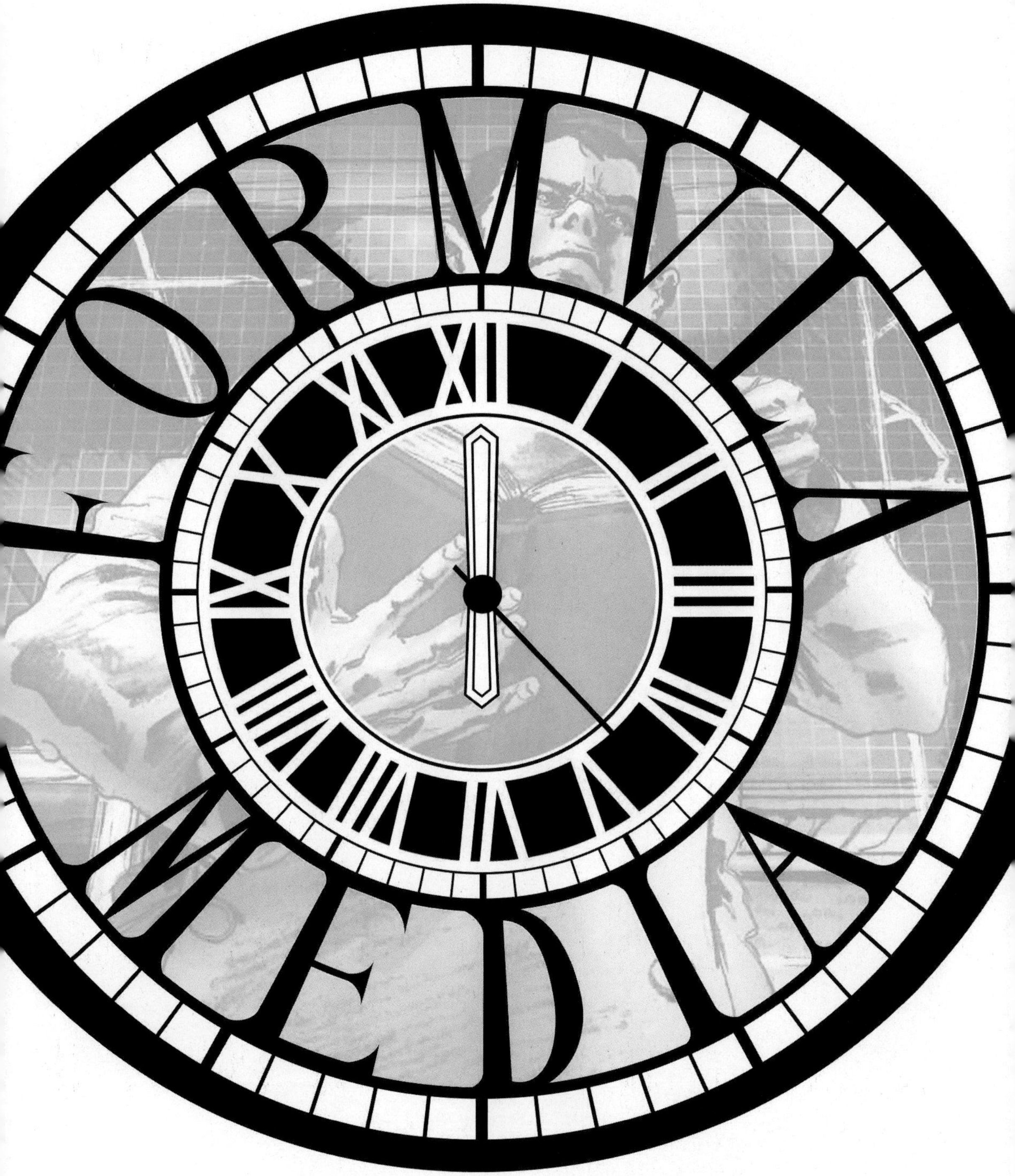

CHAPTER 06

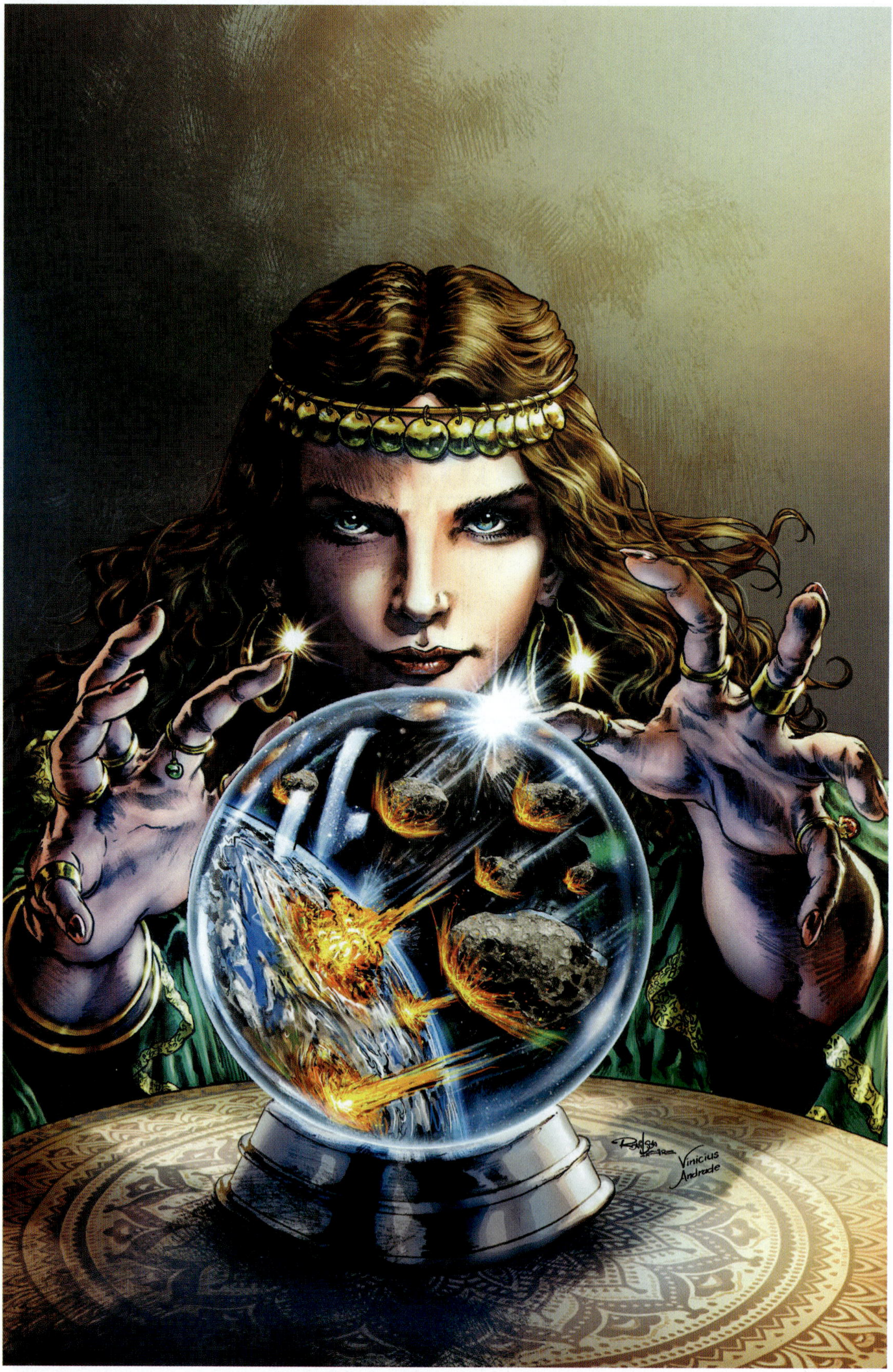
Vinicius
Andrade

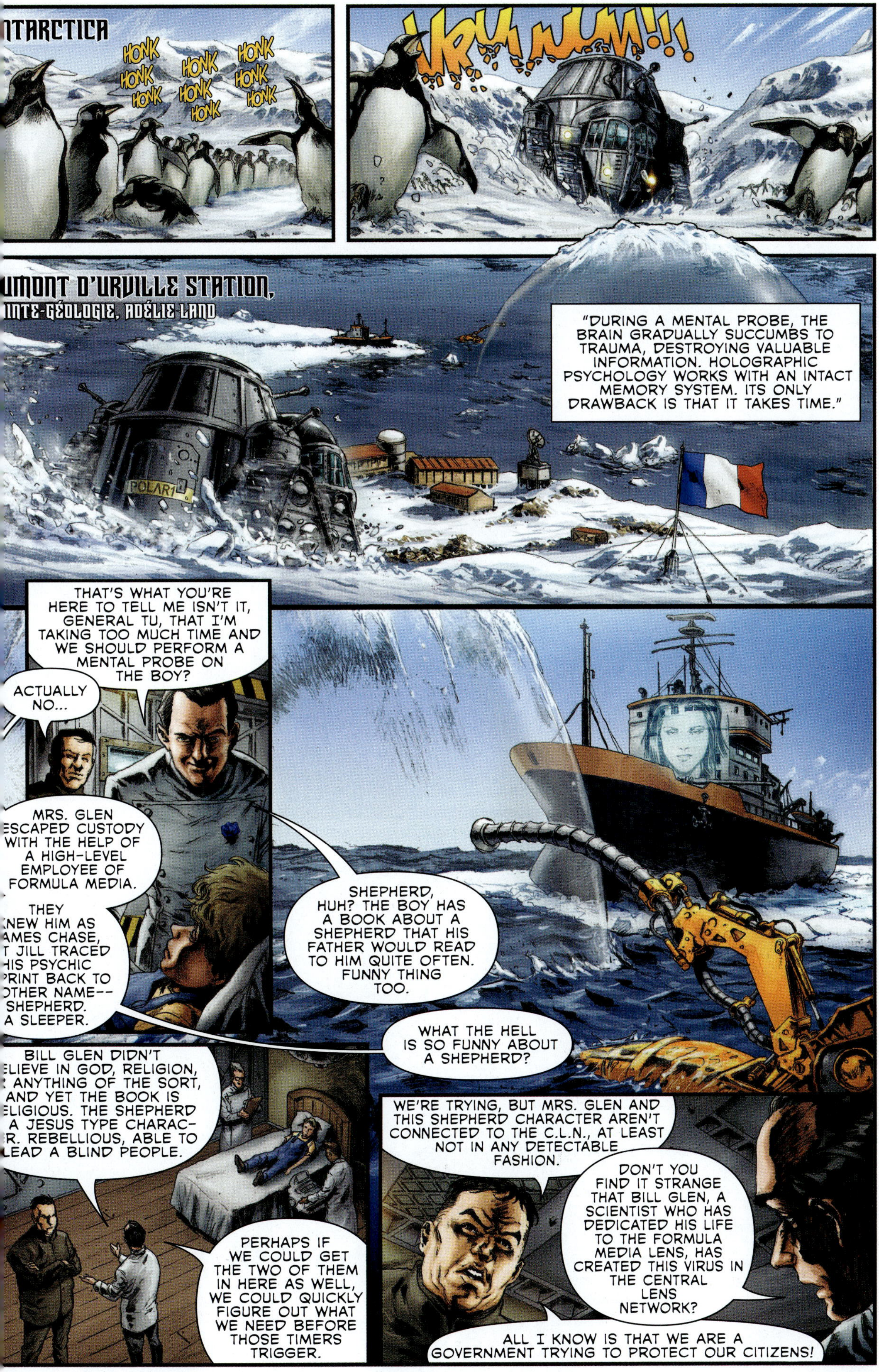
NTARCTICA
HONK HONK HONK
HONK HONK HONK
HONK HONK HONK
VRUMMM!!!
UMONT D'URVILLE STATION,
INTE-GÉOLOGIE, ADÉLIE LAND
POLAR1
"DURING A MENTAL PROBE, THE BRAIN GRADUALLY SUCCUMBS TO TRAUMA, DESTROYING VALUABLE INFORMATION. HOLOGRAPHIC PSYCHOLOGY WORKS WITH AN INTACT MEMORY SYSTEM. ITS ONLY DRAWBACK IS THAT IT TAKES TIME."
THAT'S WHAT YOU'RE HERE TO TELL ME ISN'T IT, GENERAL TU, THAT I'M TAKING TOO MUCH TIME AND WE SHOULD PERFORM A MENTAL PROBE ON THE BOY?
ACTUALLY NO...
MRS. GLEN ESCAPED CUSTODY WITH THE HELP OF A HIGH-LEVEL EMPLOYEE OF FORMULA MEDIA.
THEY NEW HIM AS AMES CHASE, T JILL TRACED HIS PSYCHIC PRINT BACK TO OTHER NAME-- SHEPHERD. A SLEEPER.
SHEPHERD, HUH? THE BOY HAS A BOOK ABOUT A SHEPHERD THAT HIS FATHER WOULD READ TO HIM QUITE OFTEN. FUNNY THING TOO.
WHAT THE HELL IS SO FUNNY ABOUT A SHEPHERD?
BILL GLEN DIDN'T ELIEVE IN GOD, RELIGION, ANYTHING OF THE SORT, AND YET THE BOOK IS ELIGIOUS. THE SHEPHERD A JESUS TYPE CHARAC- R. REBELLIOUS, ABLE TO LEAD A BLIND PEOPLE.
PERHAPS IF WE COULD GET THE TWO OF THEM IN HERE AS WELL, WE COULD QUICKLY FIGURE OUT WHAT WE NEED BEFORE THOSE TIMERS TRIGGER.
WE'RE TRYING, BUT MRS. GLEN AND THIS SHEPHERD CHARACTER AREN'T CONNECTED TO THE C.L.N., AT LEAST NOT IN ANY DETECTABLE FASHION.
DON'T YOU FIND IT STRANGE THAT BILL GLEN, A SCIENTIST WHO HAS DEDICATED HIS LIFE TO THE FORMULA MEDIA LENS, HAS CREATED THIS VIRUS IN THE CENTRAL LENS NETWORK?
ALL I KNOW IS THAT WE ARE A GOVERNMENT TRYING TO PROTECT OUR CITIZENS!

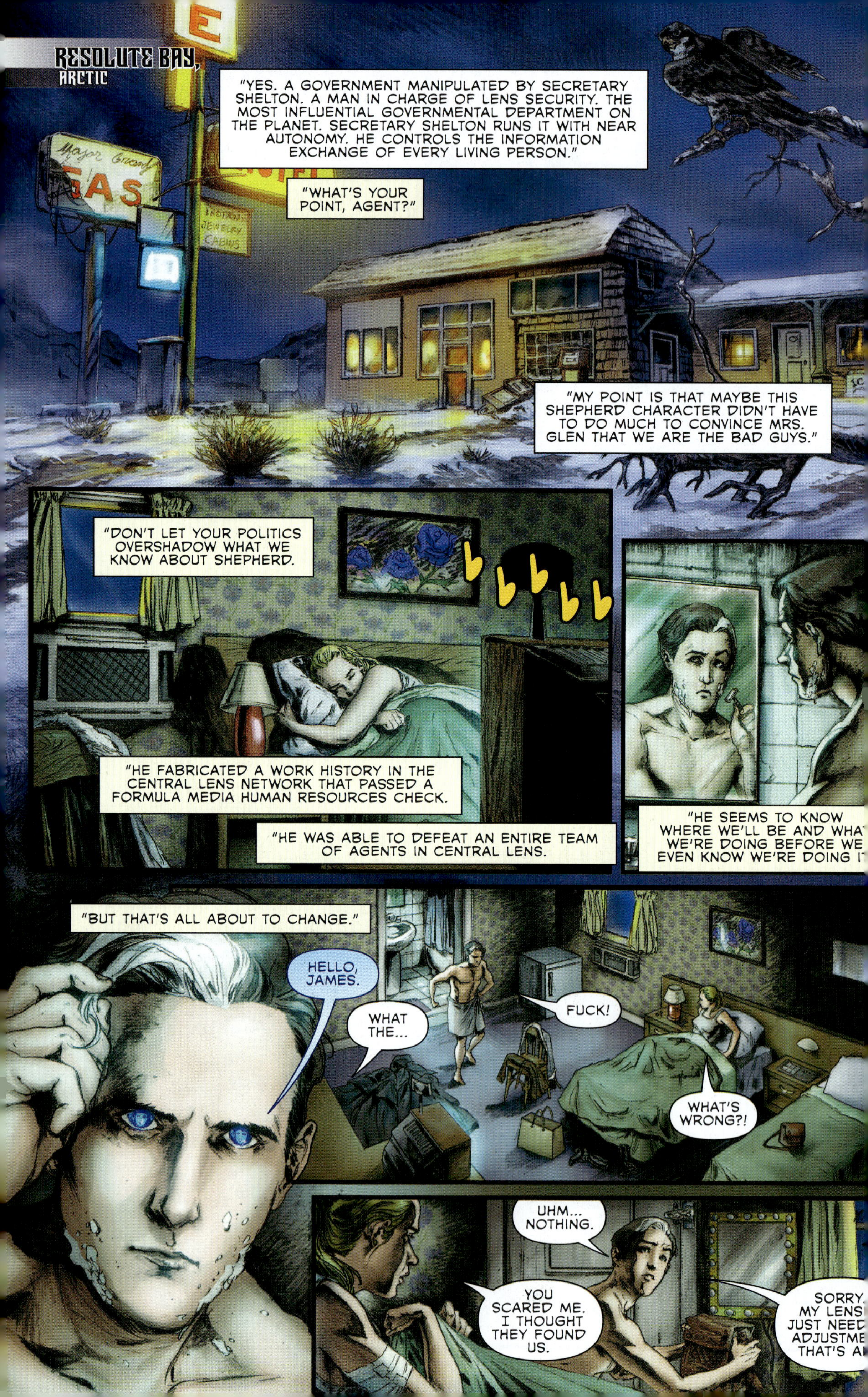
RESOLUTE BAY, ARCTIC
"YES. A GOVERNMENT MANIPULATED BY SECRETARY SHELTON. A MAN IN CHARGE OF LENS SECURITY. THE MOST INFLUENTIAL GOVERNMENTAL DEPARTMENT ON THE PLANET. SECRETARY SHELTON RUNS IT WITH NEAR AUTONOMY. HE CONTROLS THE INFORMATION EXCHANGE OF EVERY LIVING PERSON."
GAS
"WHAT'S YOUR POINT, AGENT?"
INDIAN JEWELRY CABINS
"MY POINT IS THAT MAYBE THIS SHEPHERD CHARACTER DIDN'T HAVE TO DO MUCH TO CONVINCE MRS. GLEN THAT WE ARE THE BAD GUYS."
"DON'T LET YOUR POLITICS OVERSHADOW WHAT WE KNOW ABOUT SHEPHERD.
"HE FABRICATED A WORK HISTORY IN THE CENTRAL LENS NETWORK THAT PASSED A FORMULA MEDIA HUMAN RESOURCES CHECK.
"HE WAS ABLE TO DEFEAT AN ENTIRE TEAM OF AGENTS IN CENTRAL LENS.
"HE SEEMS TO KNOW WHERE WE'LL BE AND WHA WE'RE DOING BEFORE WE EVEN KNOW WE'RE DOING I
"BUT THAT'S ALL ABOUT TO CHANGE."
HELLO, JAMES.
WHAT THE...
FUCK!
WHAT'S WRONG?!
UHM... NOTHING.
YOU SCARED ME. I THOUGHT THEY FOUND US.
SORRY. MY LENS JUST NEED ADJUSTME THAT'S A

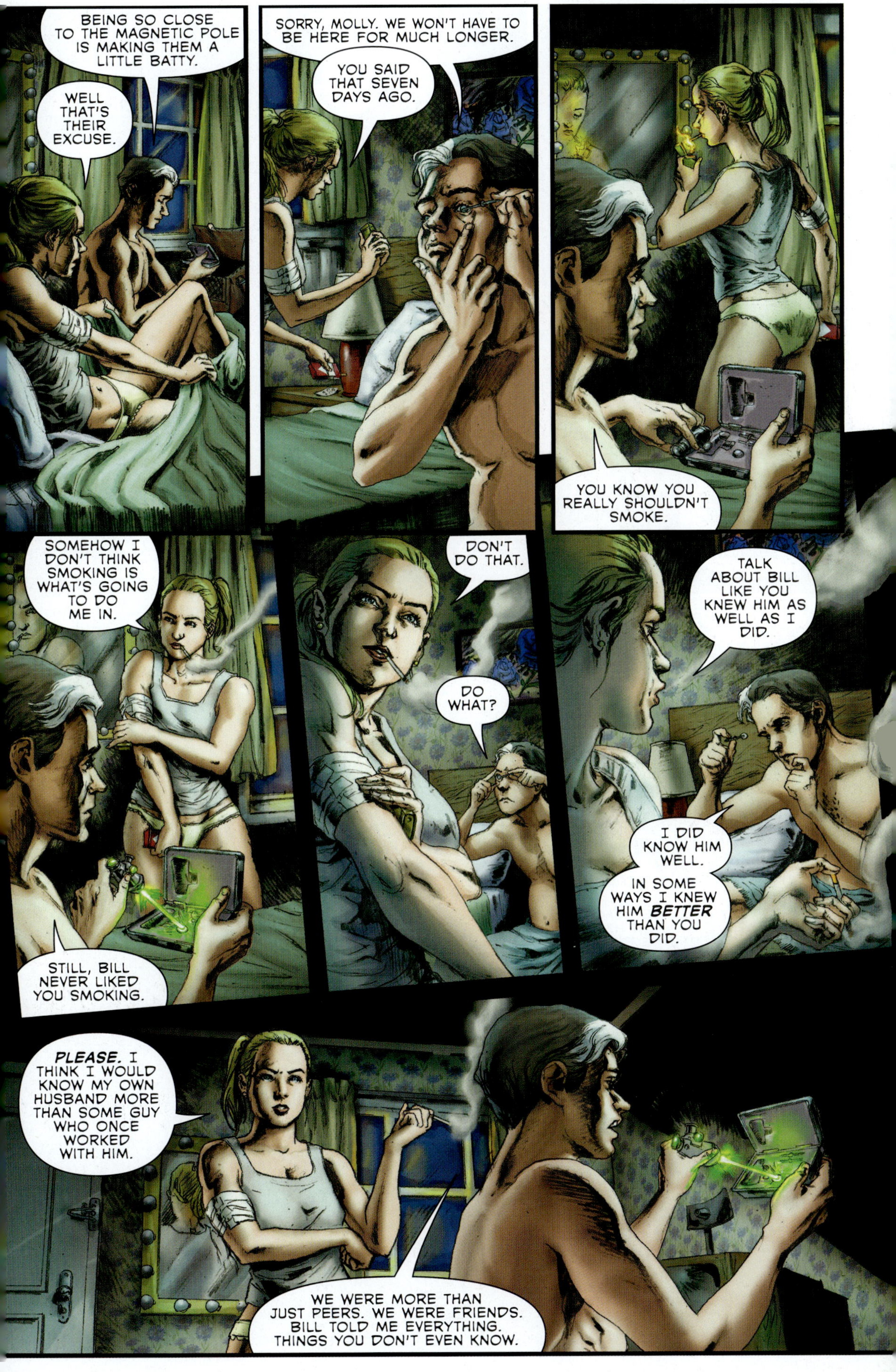
BEING SO CLOSE TO THE MAGNETIC POLE IS MAKING THEM A LITTLE BATTY.
WELL THAT'S THEIR EXCUSE.
SORRY, MOLLY. WE WON'T HAVE TO BE HERE FOR MUCH LONGER.
YOU SAID THAT SEVEN DAYS AGO.
YOU KNOW YOU REALLY SHOULDN'T SMOKE.
SOMEHOW I DON'T THINK SMOKING IS WHAT'S GOING TO DO ME IN.
STILL, BILL NEVER LIKED YOU SMOKING.
DON'T DO THAT.
DO WHAT?
TALK ABOUT BILL LIKE YOU KNEW HIM AS WELL AS I DID.
I DID KNOW HIM WELL.
IN SOME WAYS I KNEW HIM *BETTER* THAN YOU DID.
PLEASE. I THINK I WOULD KNOW MY OWN HUSBAND MORE THAN SOME GUY WHO ONCE WORKED WITH HIM.
WE WERE MORE THAN JUST PEERS. WE WERE FRIENDS. BILL TOLD ME EVERYTHING. THINGS YOU DON'T EVEN KNOW.

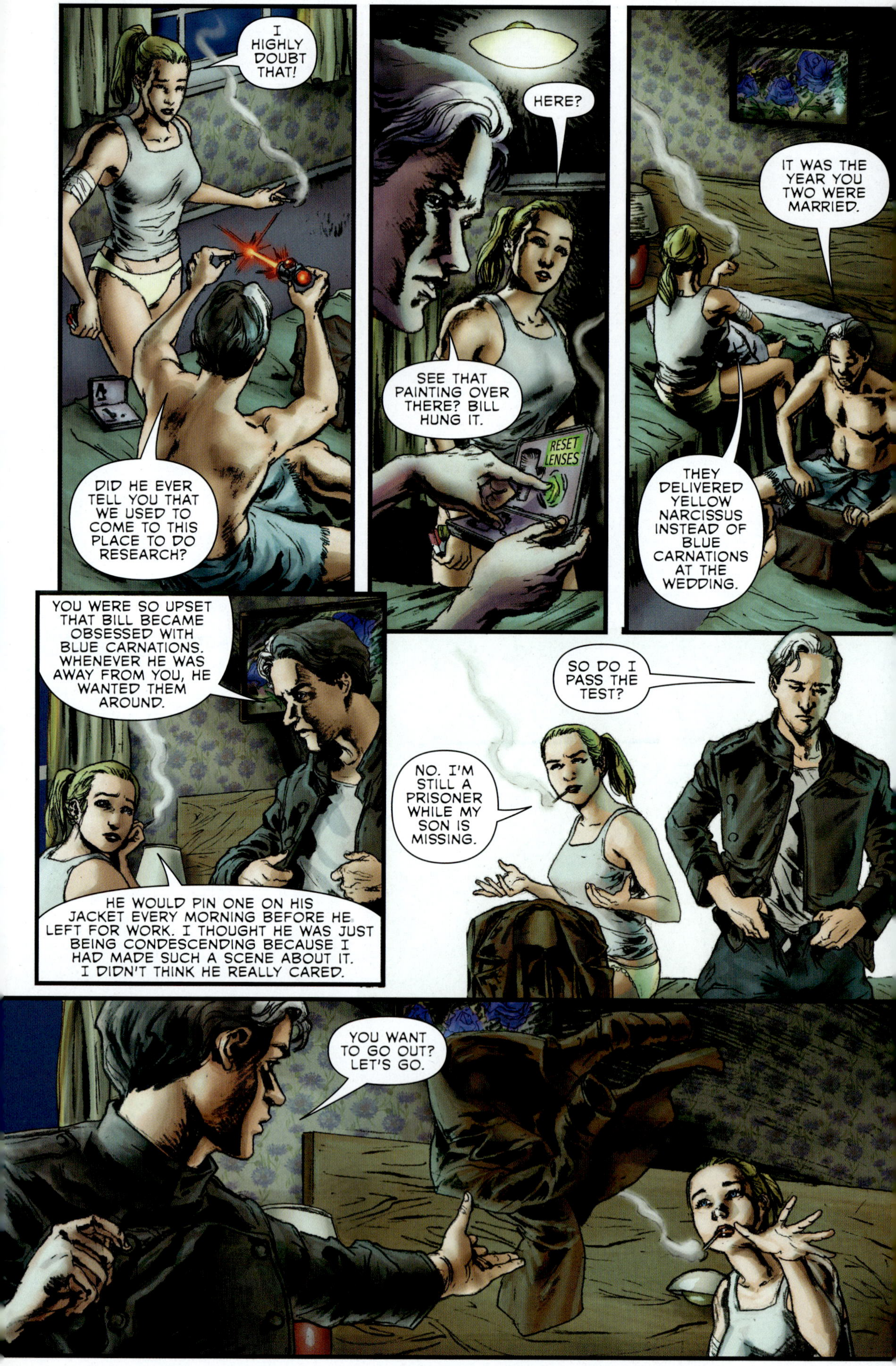
I HIGHLY DOUBT THAT!
DID HE EVER TELL YOU THAT WE USED TO COME TO THIS PLACE TO DO RESEARCH?
HERE?
SEE THAT PAINTING OVER THERE? BILL HUNG IT.
RESET LENSES
IT WAS THE YEAR YOU TWO WERE MARRIED.
THEY DELIVERED YELLOW NARCISSUS INSTEAD OF BLUE CARNATIONS AT THE WEDDING.
YOU WERE SO UPSET THAT BILL BECAME OBSESSED WITH BLUE CARNATIONS. WHENEVER HE WAS AWAY FROM YOU, HE WANTED THEM AROUND.
HE WOULD PIN ONE ON HIS JACKET EVERY MORNING BEFORE HE LEFT FOR WORK. I THOUGHT HE WAS JUST BEING CONDESCENDING BECAUSE I HAD MADE SUCH A SCENE ABOUT IT. I DIDN'T THINK HE REALLY CARED.
SO DO I PASS THE TEST?
NO. I'M STILL A PRISONER WHILE MY SON IS MISSING.
YOU WANT TO GO OUT? LET'S GO.

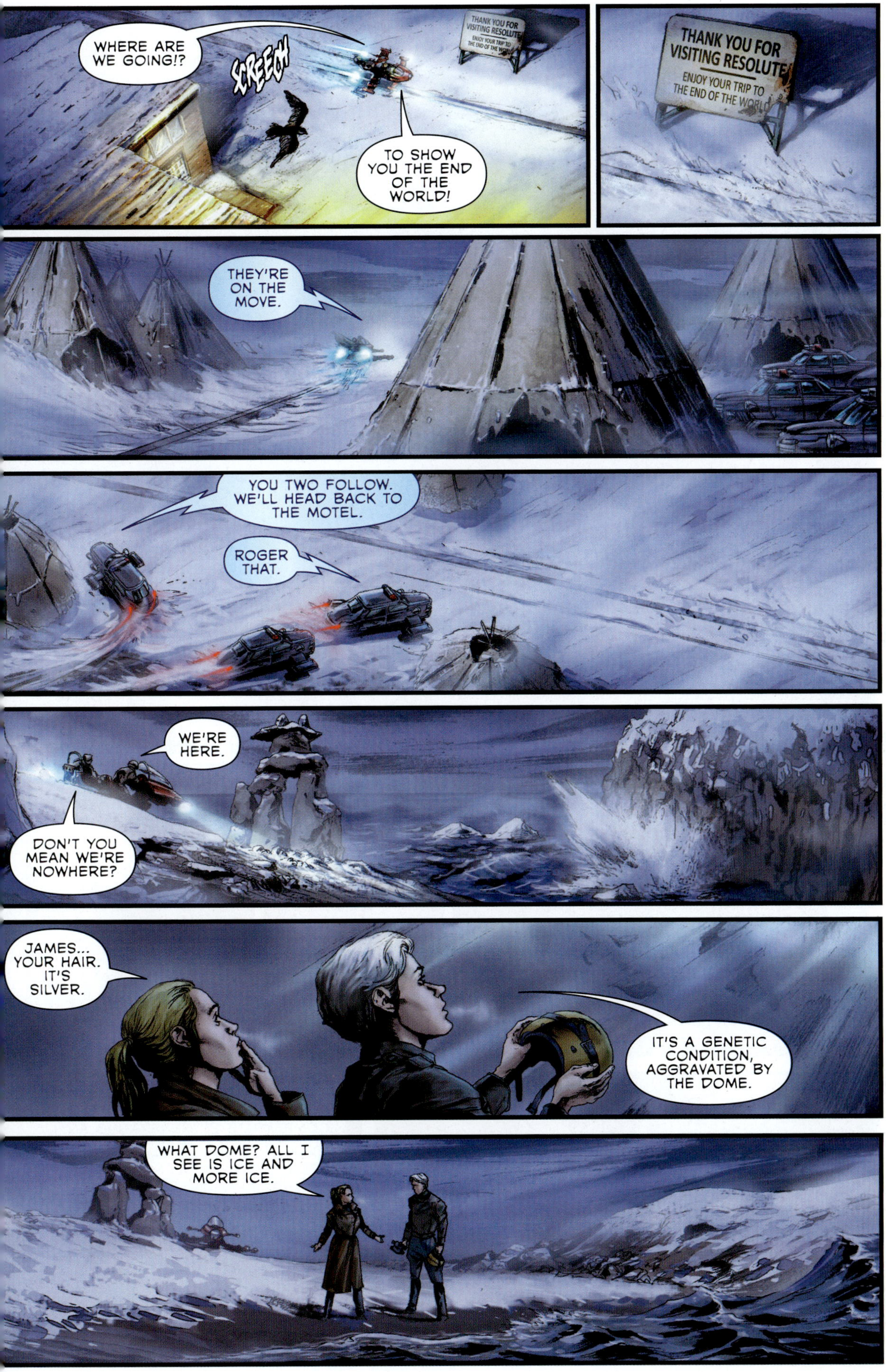
WHERE ARE WE GOING!?
SCREECH
THANK YOU FOR VISITING RESOLUTE
TO SHOW YOU THE END OF THE WORLD!
THANK YOU FOR VISITING RESOLUTE
ENJOY YOUR TRIP TO THE END OF THE WORLD
THEY'RE ON THE MOVE.
YOU TWO FOLLOW. WE'LL HEAD BACK TO THE MOTEL.
ROGER THAT.
WE'RE HERE.
DON'T YOU MEAN WE'RE NOWHERE?
JAMES... YOUR HAIR. IT'S SILVER.
IT'S A GENETIC CONDITION, AGGRAVATED BY THE DOME.
WHAT DOME? ALL I SEE IS ICE AND MORE ICE.

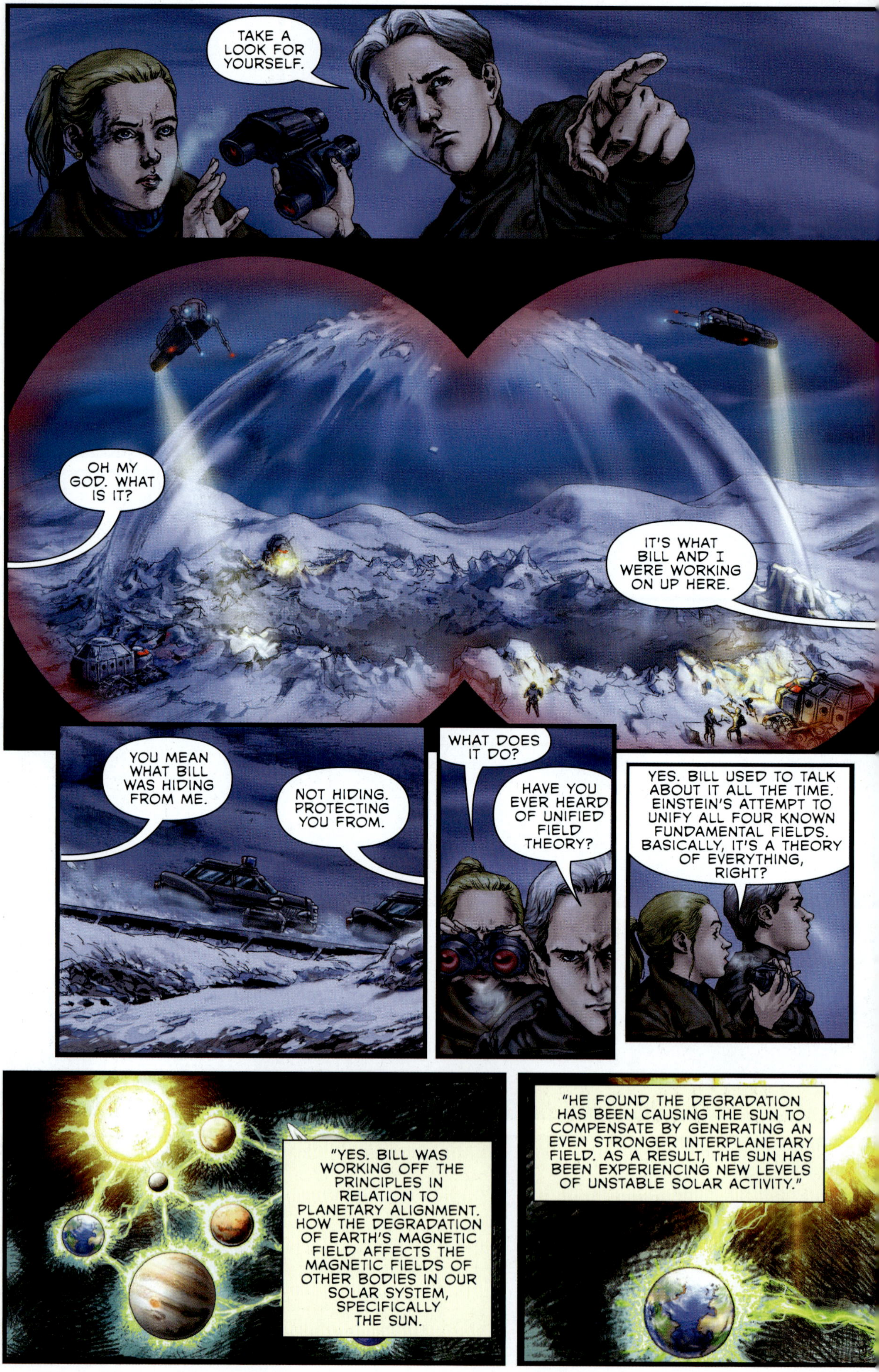
TAKE A LOOK FOR YOURSELF.
OH MY GOD. WHAT IS IT?
IT'S WHAT BILL AND I WERE WORKING ON UP HERE.
YOU MEAN WHAT BILL WAS HIDING FROM ME.
NOT HIDING. PROTECTING YOU FROM.
WHAT DOES IT DO?
HAVE YOU EVER HEARD OF UNIFIED FIELD THEORY?
YES. BILL USED TO TALK ABOUT IT ALL THE TIME. EINSTEIN'S ATTEMPT TO UNIFY ALL FOUR KNOWN FUNDAMENTAL FIELDS. BASICALLY, IT'S A THEORY OF EVERYTHING, RIGHT?
"YES. BILL WAS WORKING OFF THE PRINCIPLES IN RELATION TO PLANETARY ALIGNMENT. HOW THE DEGRADATION OF EARTH'S MAGNETIC FIELD AFFECTS THE MAGNETIC FIELDS OF OTHER BODIES IN OUR SOLAR SYSTEM, SPECIFICALLY THE SUN.
"HE FOUND THE DEGRADATION HAS BEEN CAUSING THE SUN TO COMPENSATE BY GENERATING AN EVEN STRONGER INTERPLANETARY FIELD. AS A RESULT, THE SUN HAS BEEN EXPERIENCING NEW LEVELS OF UNSTABLE SOLAR ACTIVITY."

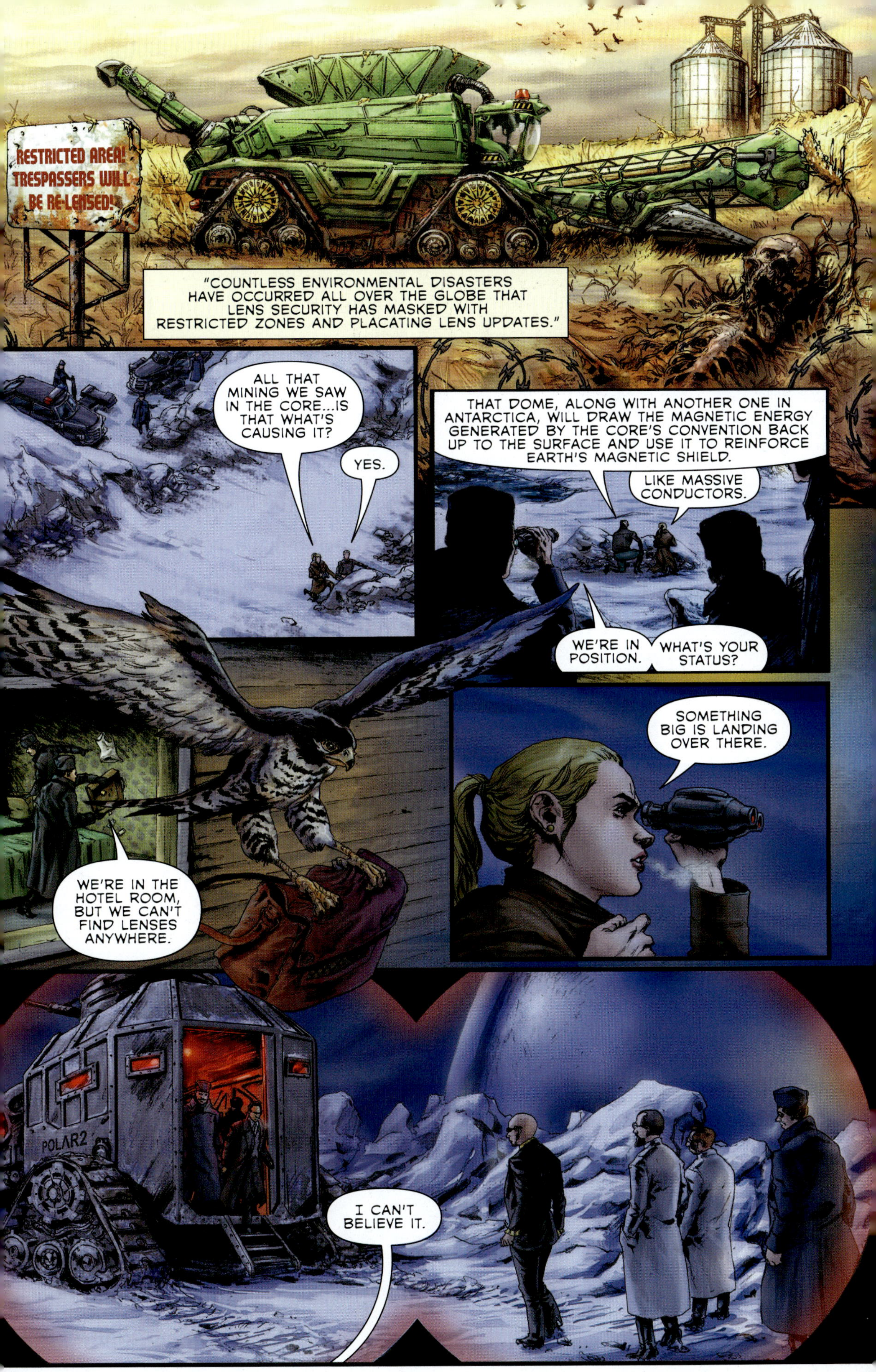
RESTRICTED AREA! TRESPASSERS WILL BE RE-LENSED!
"COUNTLESS ENVIRONMENTAL DISASTERS HAVE OCCURRED ALL OVER THE GLOBE THAT LENS SECURITY HAS MASKED WITH RESTRICTED ZONES AND PLACATING LENS UPDATES."
ALL THAT MINING WE SAW IN THE CORE...IS THAT WHAT'S CAUSING IT?
YES.
THAT DOME, ALONG WITH ANOTHER ONE IN ANTARCTICA, WILL DRAW THE MAGNETIC ENERGY GENERATED BY THE CORE'S CONVENTION BACK UP TO THE SURFACE AND USE IT TO REINFORCE EARTH'S MAGNETIC SHIELD.
LIKE MASSIVE CONDUCTORS.
WE'RE IN POSITION.
WHAT'S YOUR STATUS?
WE'RE IN THE HOTEL ROOM, BUT WE CAN'T FIND LENSES ANYWHERE.
SOMETHING BIG IS LANDING OVER THERE.
POLAR2
I CAN'T BELIEVE IT.

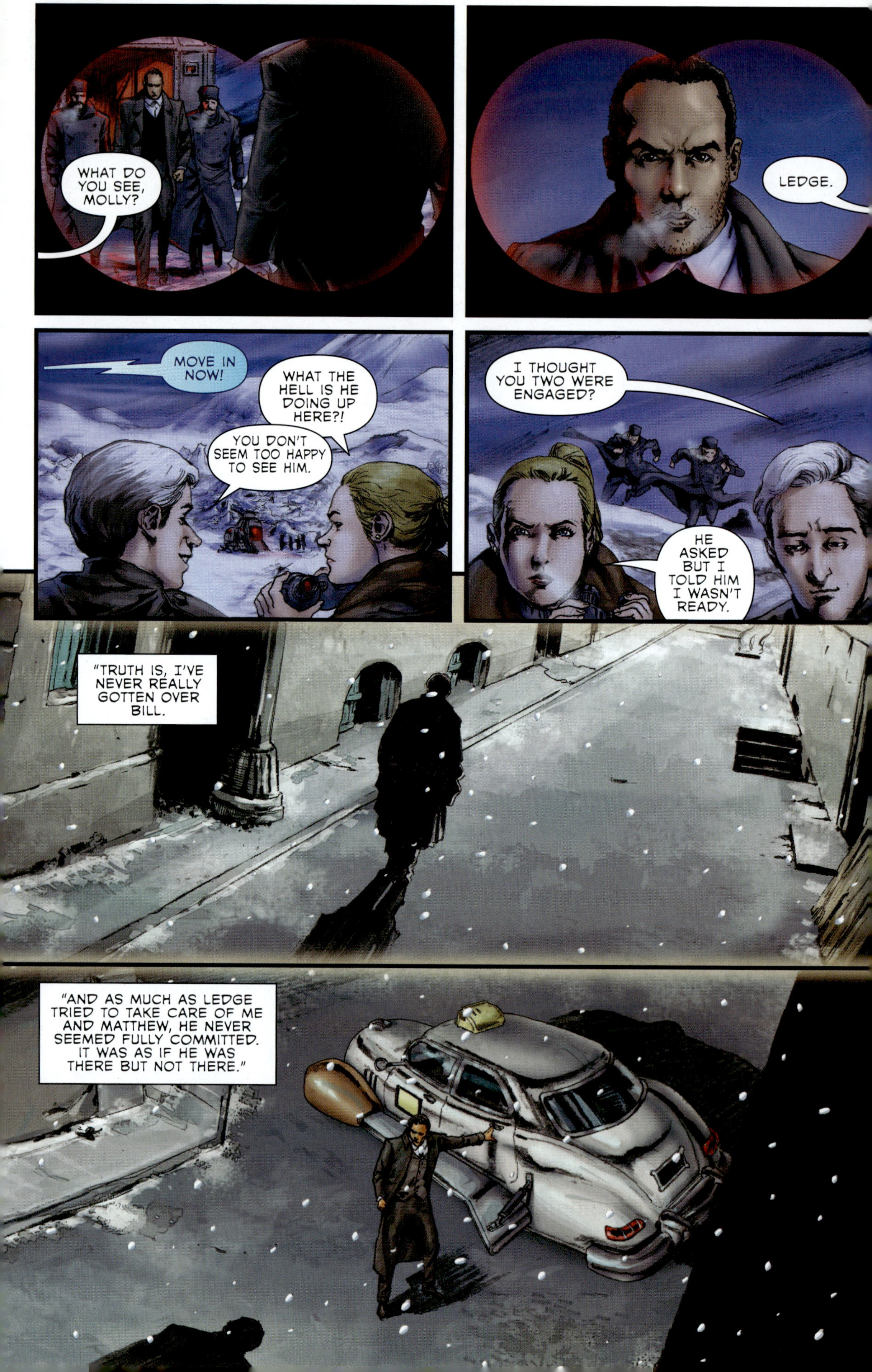
WHAT DO YOU SEE, MOLLY?
LEDGE.
MOVE IN NOW!
WHAT THE HELL IS HE DOING UP HERE?!
YOU DON'T SEEM TOO HAPPY TO SEE HIM.
I THOUGHT YOU TWO WERE ENGAGED?
HE ASKED BUT I TOLD HIM I WASN'T READY.
"TRUTH IS, I'VE NEVER REALLY GOTTEN OVER BILL.
"AND AS MUCH AS LEDGE TRIED TO TAKE CARE OF ME AND MATTHEW, HE NEVER SEEMED FULLY COMMITTED. IT WAS AS IF HE WAS THERE BUT NOT THERE."

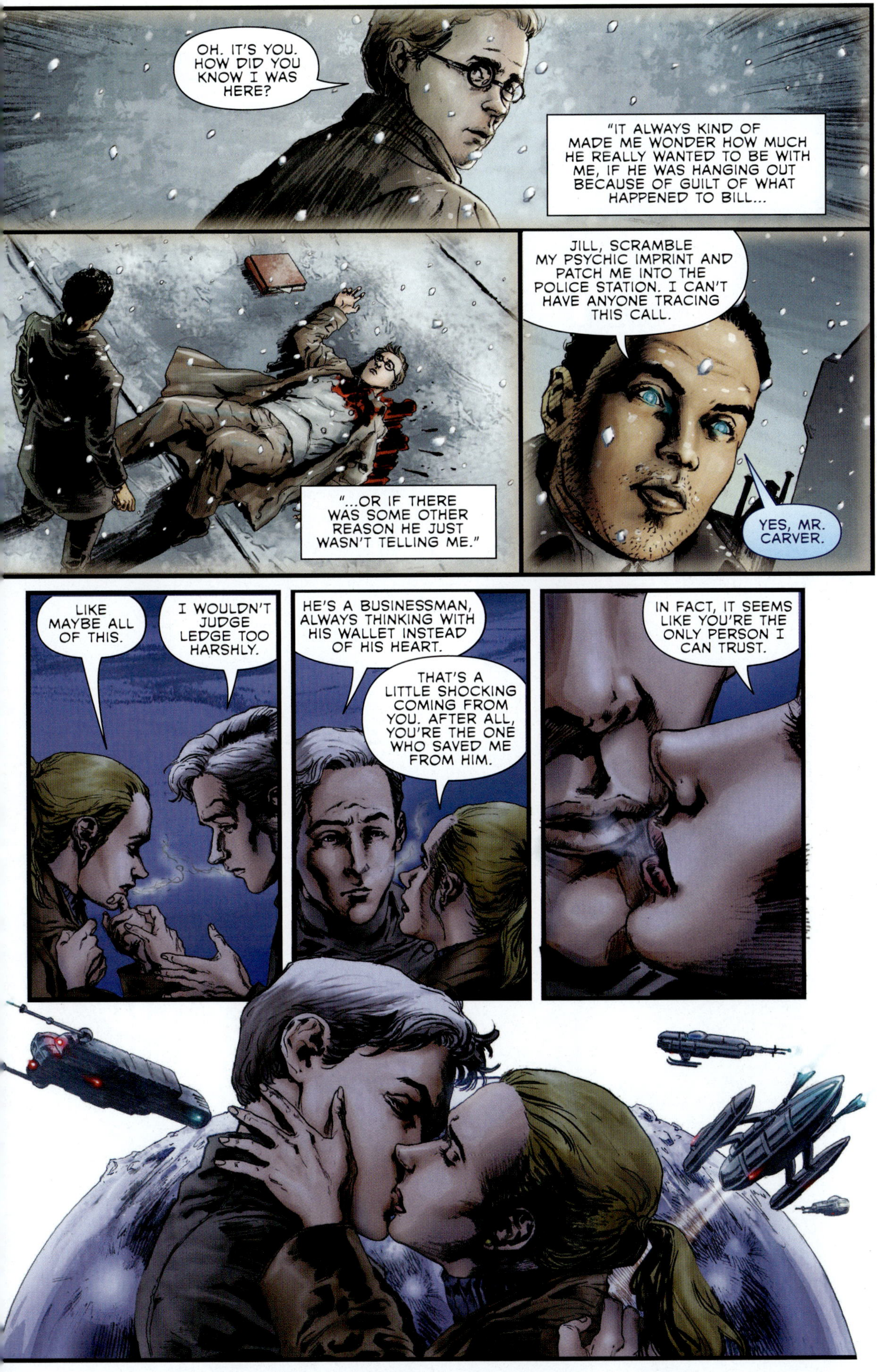
OH. IT'S YOU. HOW DID YOU KNOW I WAS HERE?
"IT ALWAYS KIND OF MADE ME WONDER HOW MUCH HE REALLY WANTED TO BE WITH ME, IF HE WAS HANGING OUT BECAUSE OF GUILT OF WHAT HAPPENED TO BILL...
"...OR IF THERE WAS SOME OTHER REASON HE JUST WASN'T TELLING ME."
JILL, SCRAMBLE MY PSYCHIC IMPRINT AND PATCH ME INTO THE POLICE STATION. I CAN'T HAVE ANYONE TRACING THIS CALL.
YES, MR. CARVER.
LIKE MAYBE ALL OF THIS.
I WOULDN'T JUDGE LEDGE TOO HARSHLY.
HE'S A BUSINESSMAN, ALWAYS THINKING WITH HIS WALLET INSTEAD OF HIS HEART.
THAT'S A LITTLE SHOCKING COMING FROM YOU. AFTER ALL, YOU'RE THE ONE WHO SAVED ME FROM HIM.
IN FACT, IT SEEMS LIKE YOU'RE THE ONLY PERSON I CAN TRUST.

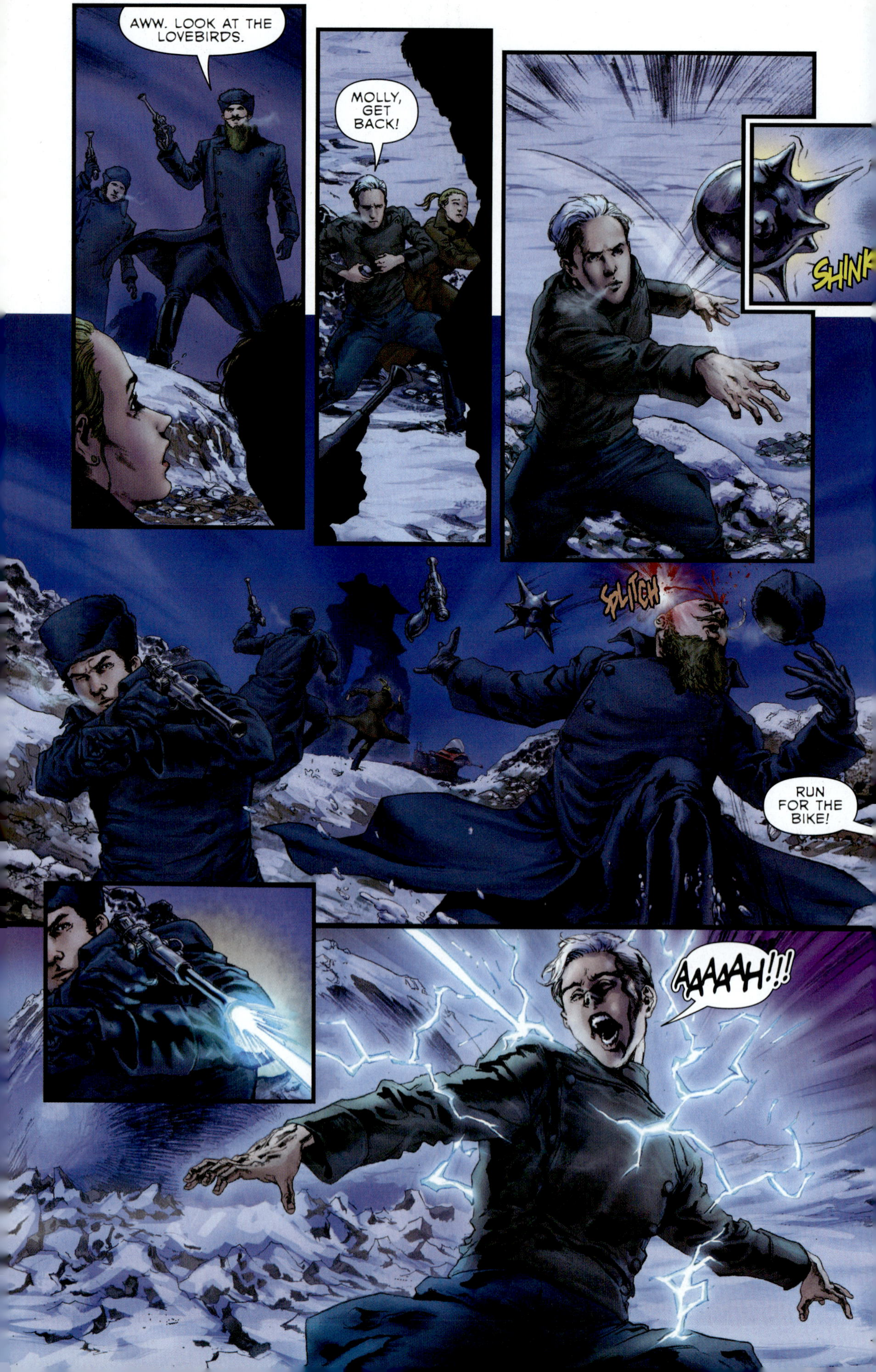
AWW. LOOK AT THE LOVEBIRDS.
MOLLY, GET BACK!
SHINK
SPLITCH
RUN FOR THE BIKE!
AAAAAH!!!

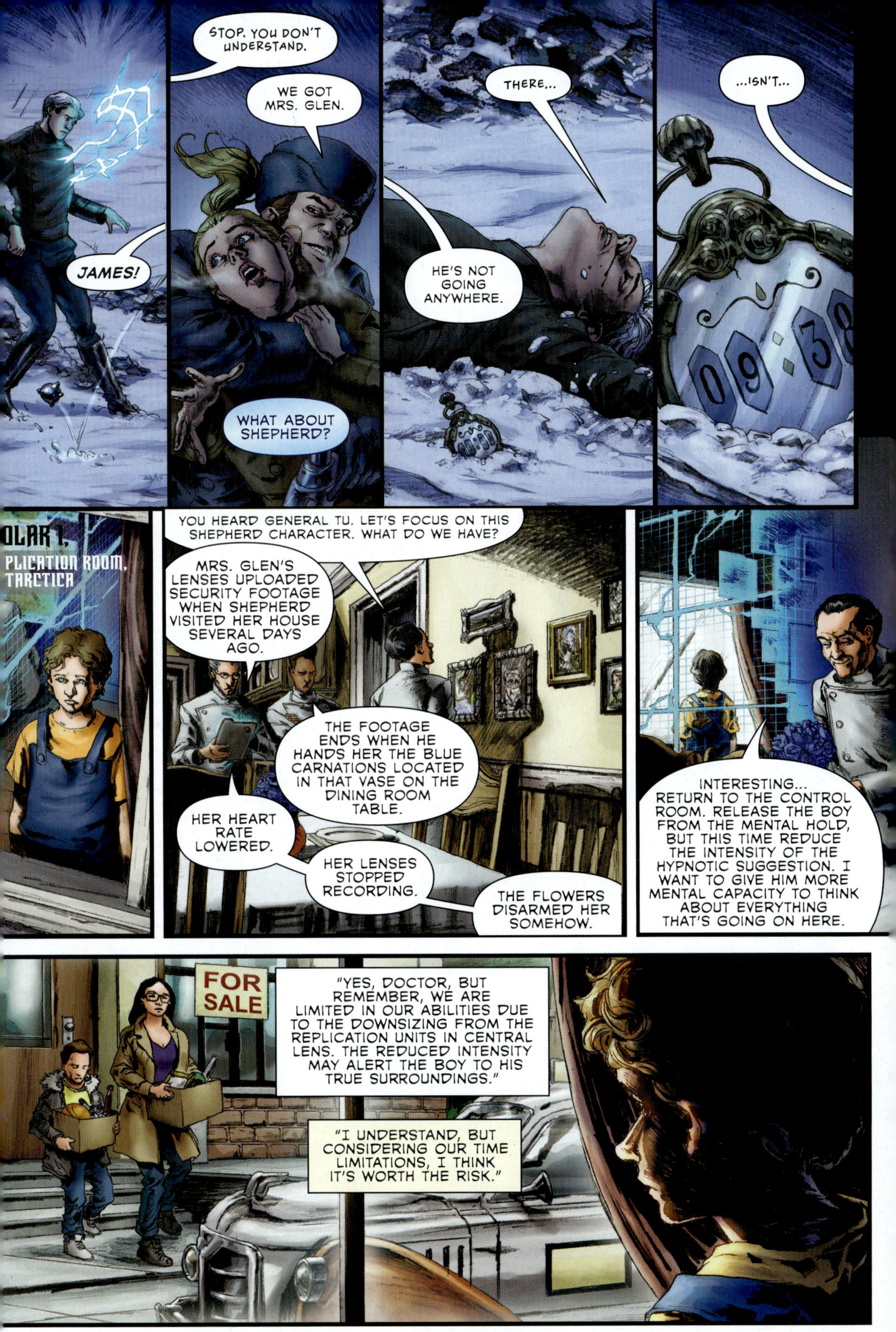
JAMES!
STOP. YOU DON'T UNDERSTAND.
WE GOT MRS. GLEN.
WHAT ABOUT SHEPHERD?
THERE...
HE'S NOT GOING ANYWHERE.
...ISN'T...
09:38
OLAR 1, PLICATION ROOM, TARCTICA
YOU HEARD GENERAL TU. LET'S FOCUS ON THIS SHEPHERD CHARACTER. WHAT DO WE HAVE?
MRS. GLEN'S LENSES UPLOADED SECURITY FOOTAGE WHEN SHEPHERD VISITED HER HOUSE SEVERAL DAYS AGO.
THE FOOTAGE ENDS WHEN HE HANDS HER THE BLUE CARNATIONS LOCATED IN THAT VASE ON THE DINING ROOM TABLE.
HER HEART RATE LOWERED.
HER LENSES STOPPED RECORDING.
THE FLOWERS DISARMED HER SOMEHOW.
INTERESTING... RETURN TO THE CONTROL ROOM. RELEASE THE BOY FROM THE MENTAL HOLD, BUT THIS TIME REDUCE THE INTENSITY OF THE HYPNOTIC SUGGESTION. I WANT TO GIVE HIM MORE MENTAL CAPACITY TO THINK ABOUT EVERYTHING THAT'S GOING ON HERE.
FOR SALE
"YES, DOCTOR, BUT REMEMBER, WE ARE LIMITED IN OUR ABILITIES DUE TO THE DOWNSIZING FROM THE REPLICATION UNITS IN CENTRAL LENS. THE REDUCED INTENSITY MAY ALERT THE BOY TO HIS TRUE SURROUNDINGS."
"I UNDERSTAND, BUT CONSIDERING OUR TIME LIMITATIONS, I THINK IT'S WORTH THE RISK."

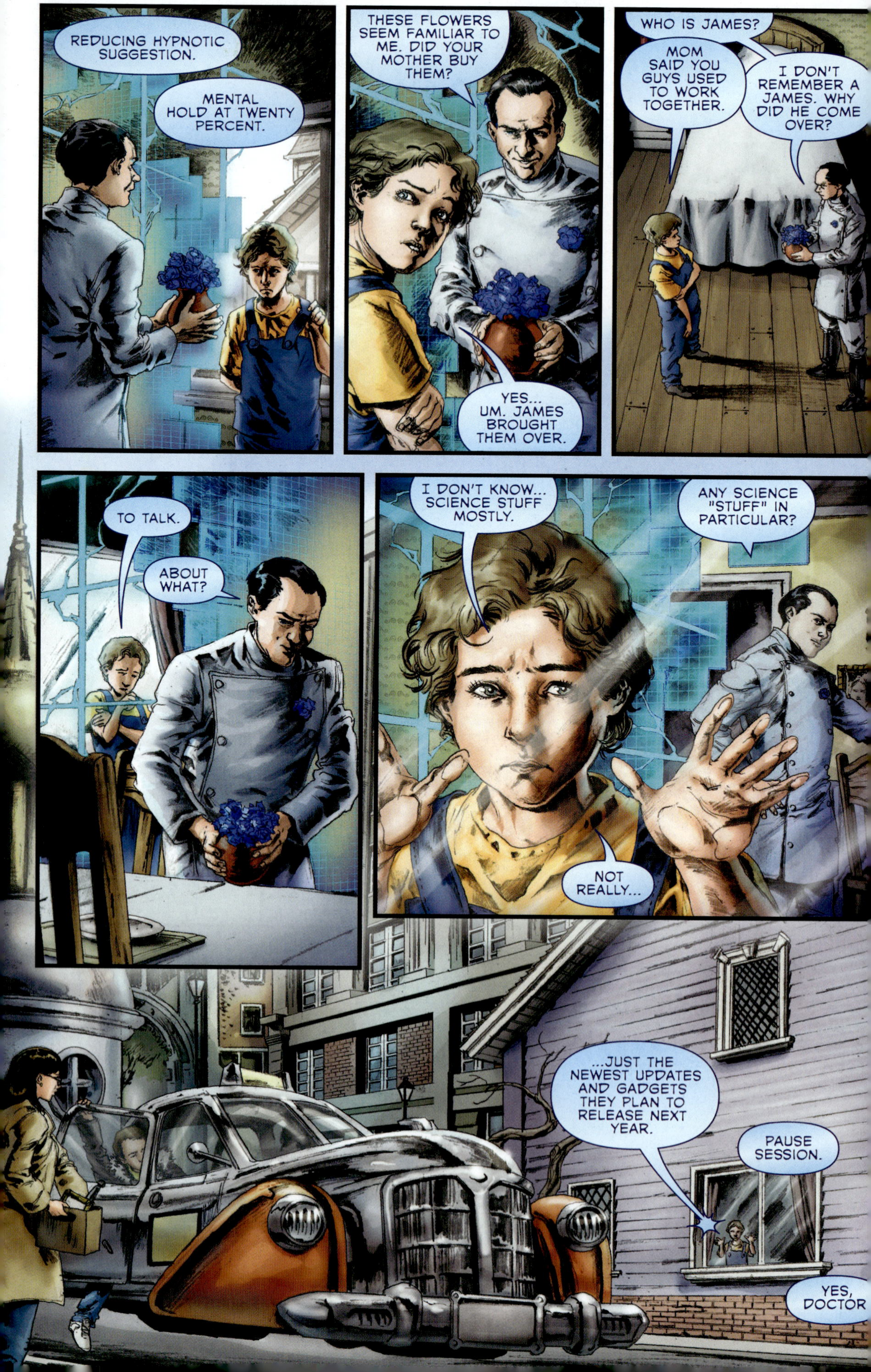
REDUCING HYPNOTIC SUGGESTION.
MENTAL HOLD AT TWENTY PERCENT.
THESE FLOWERS SEEM FAMILIAR TO ME. DID YOUR MOTHER BUY THEM?
YES... UM. JAMES BROUGHT THEM OVER.
WHO IS JAMES?
MOM SAID YOU GUYS USED TO WORK TOGETHER.
I DON'T REMEMBER A JAMES. WHY DID HE COME OVER?
TO TALK.
ABOUT WHAT?
I DON'T KNOW... SCIENCE STUFF MOSTLY.
ANY SCIENCE "STUFF" IN PARTICULAR?
NOT REALLY...
...JUST THE NEWEST UPDATES AND GADGETS THEY PLAN TO RELEASE NEXT YEAR.
PAUSE SESSION.
YES, DOCTOR

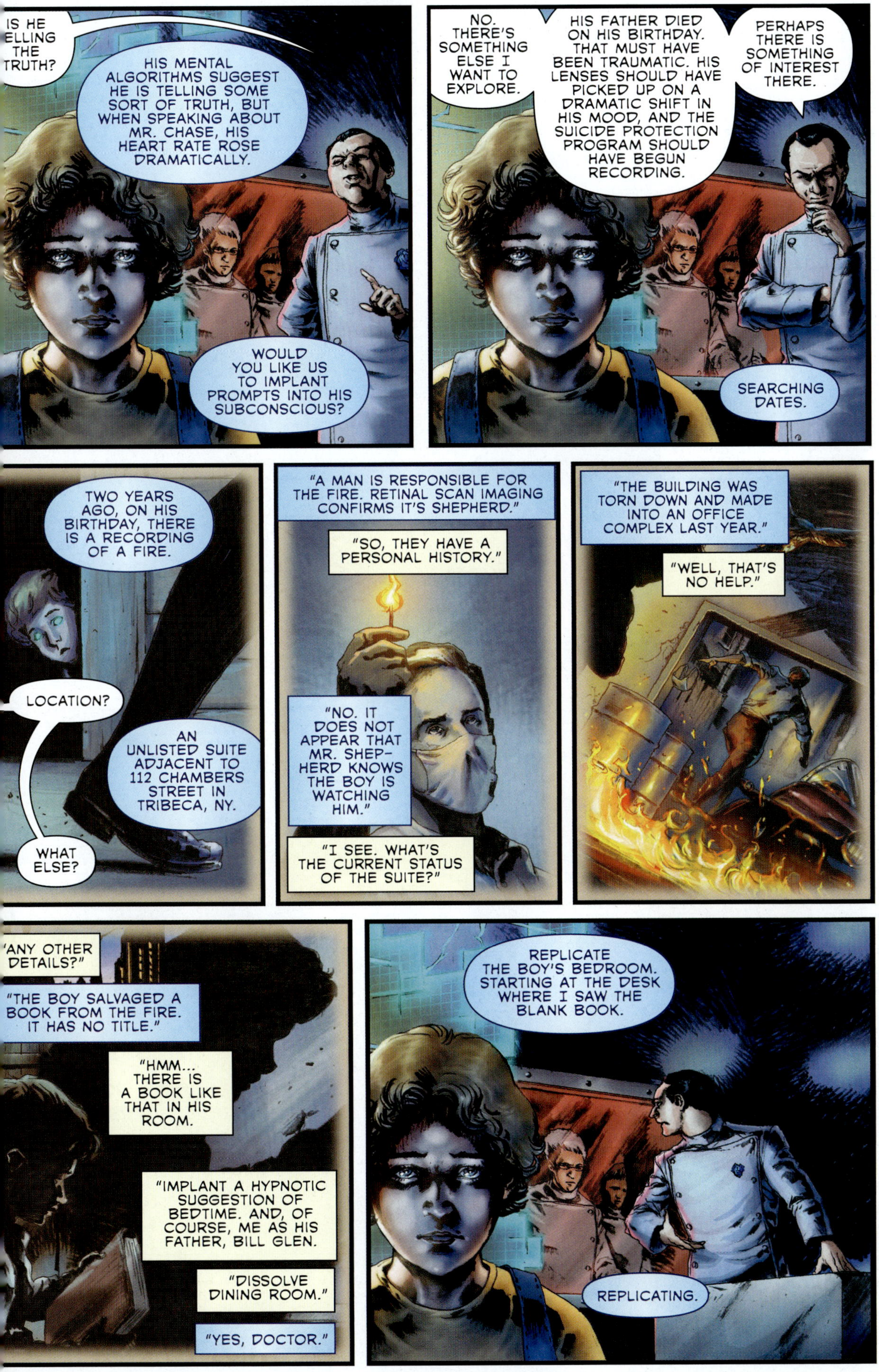
IS HE TELLING THE TRUTH?
HIS MENTAL ALGORITHMS SUGGEST HE IS TELLING SOME SORT OF TRUTH, BUT WHEN SPEAKING ABOUT MR. CHASE, HIS HEART RATE ROSE DRAMATICALLY.
WOULD YOU LIKE US TO IMPLANT PROMPTS INTO HIS SUBCONSCIOUS?
NO. THERE'S SOMETHING ELSE I WANT TO EXPLORE.
HIS FATHER DIED ON HIS BIRTHDAY. THAT MUST HAVE BEEN TRAUMATIC. HIS LENSES SHOULD HAVE PICKED UP ON A DRAMATIC SHIFT IN HIS MOOD, AND THE SUICIDE PROTECTION PROGRAM SHOULD HAVE BEGUN RECORDING.
PERHAPS THERE IS SOMETHING OF INTEREST THERE.
SEARCHING DATES.
TWO YEARS AGO, ON HIS BIRTHDAY, THERE IS A RECORDING OF A FIRE.
LOCATION?
AN UNLISTED SUITE ADJACENT TO 112 CHAMBERS STREET IN TRIBECA, NY.
WHAT ELSE?
"A MAN IS RESPONSIBLE FOR THE FIRE. RETINAL SCAN IMAGING CONFIRMS IT'S SHEPHERD."
"SO, THEY HAVE A PERSONAL HISTORY."
"NO. IT DOES NOT APPEAR THAT MR. SHEPHERD KNOWS THE BOY IS WATCHING HIM."
"I SEE. WHAT'S THE CURRENT STATUS OF THE SUITE?"
"THE BUILDING WAS TORN DOWN AND MADE INTO AN OFFICE COMPLEX LAST YEAR."
"WELL, THAT'S NO HELP."
"ANY OTHER DETAILS?"
"THE BOY SALVAGED A BOOK FROM THE FIRE. IT HAS NO TITLE."
"HMM... THERE IS A BOOK LIKE THAT IN HIS ROOM.
"IMPLANT A HYPNOTIC SUGGESTION OF BEDTIME. AND, OF COURSE, ME AS HIS FATHER, BILL GLEN.
"DISSOLVE DINING ROOM."
"YES, DOCTOR."
REPLICATE THE BOY'S BEDROOM. STARTING AT THE DESK WHERE I SAW THE BLANK BOOK.
REPLICATING.

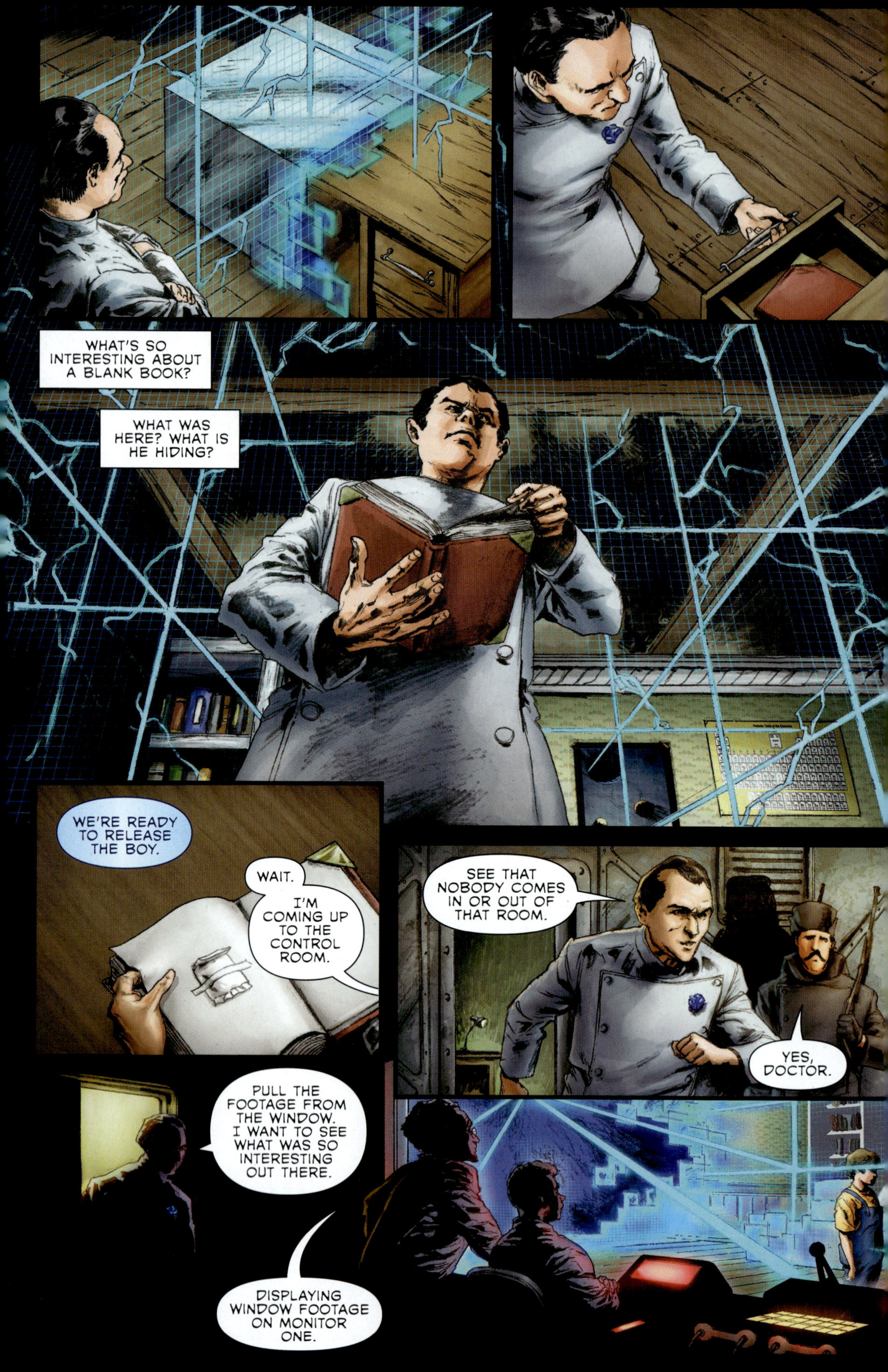
WHAT'S SO INTERESTING ABOUT A BLANK BOOK?
WHAT WAS HERE? WHAT IS HE HIDING?
WE'RE READY TO RELEASE THE BOY.
WAIT.
I'M COMING UP TO THE CONTROL ROOM.
SEE THAT NOBODY COMES IN OR OUT OF THAT ROOM.
YES, DOCTOR.
PULL THE FOOTAGE FROM THE WINDOW. I WANT TO SEE WHAT WAS SO INTERESTING OUT THERE.
DISPLAYING WINDOW FOOTAGE ON MONITOR ONE.

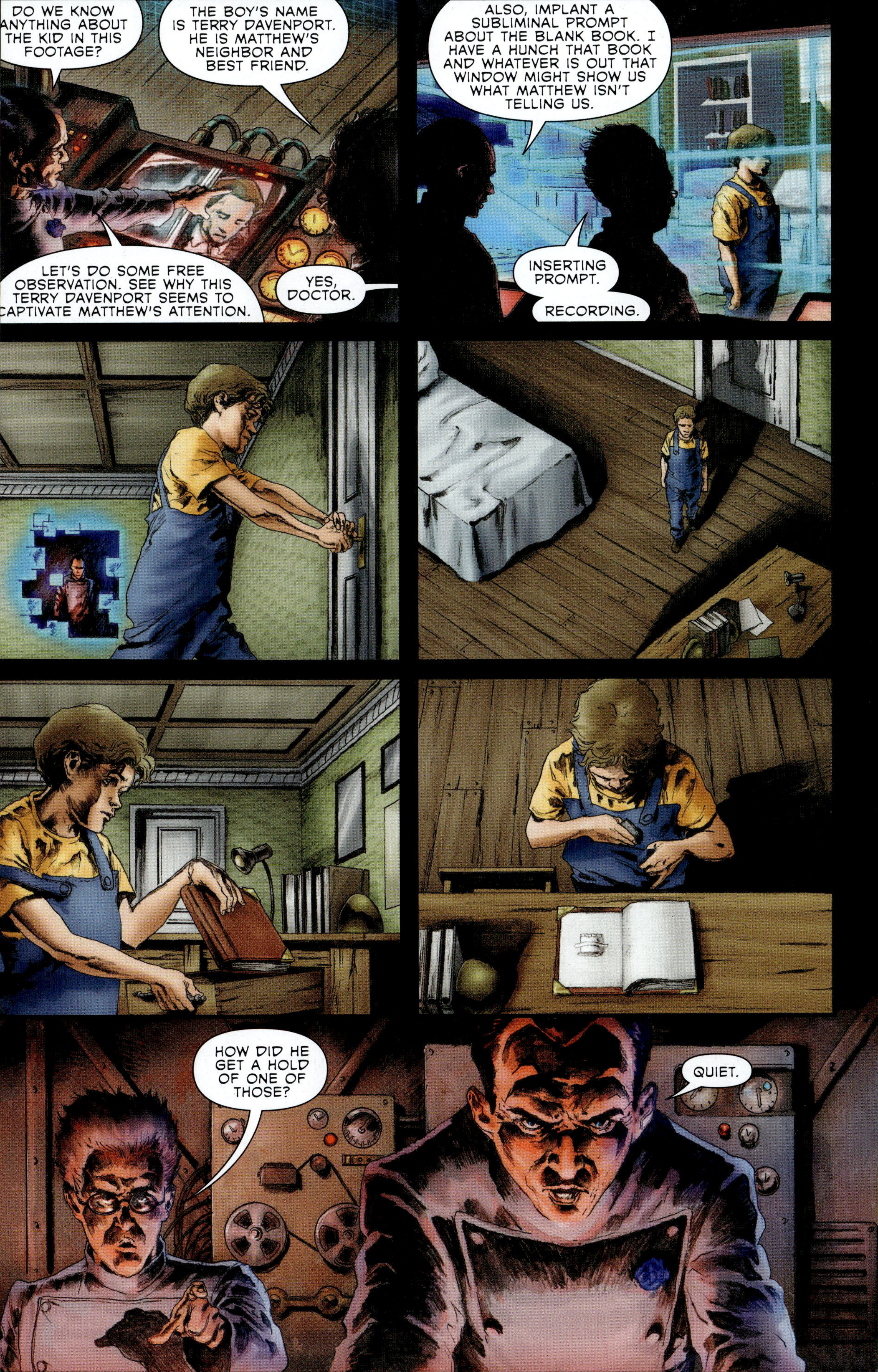
DO WE KNOW ANYTHING ABOUT THE KID IN THIS FOOTAGE?
THE BOY'S NAME IS TERRY DAVENPORT. HE IS MATTHEW'S NEIGHBOR AND BEST FRIEND.
LET'S DO SOME FREE OBSERVATION. SEE WHY THIS TERRY DAVENPORT SEEMS TO CAPTIVATE MATTHEW'S ATTENTION.
YES, DOCTOR.
ALSO, IMPLANT A SUBLIMINAL PROMPT ABOUT THE BLANK BOOK. I HAVE A HUNCH THAT BOOK AND WHATEVER IS OUT THAT WINDOW MIGHT SHOW US WHAT MATTHEW ISN'T TELLING US.
INSERTING PROMPT.
RECORDING.
HOW DID HE GET A HOLD OF ONE OF THOSE?
QUIET.

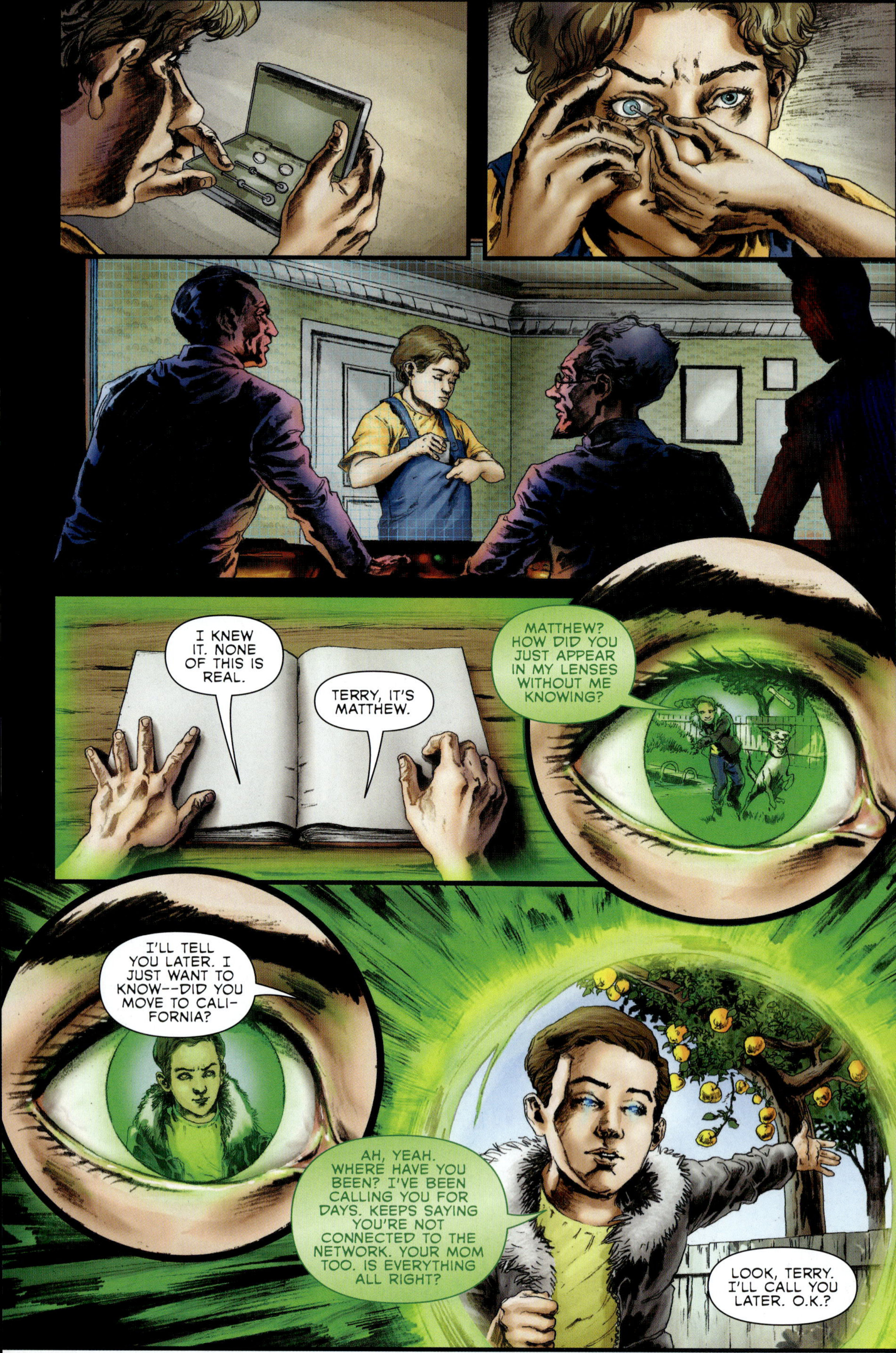
I KNEW IT. NONE OF THIS IS REAL.
TERRY, IT'S MATTHEW.
MATTHEW? HOW DID YOU JUST APPEAR IN MY LENSES WITHOUT ME KNOWING?
I'LL TELL YOU LATER. I JUST WANT TO KNOW--DID YOU MOVE TO CALI-FORNIA?
AH, YEAH. WHERE HAVE YOU BEEN? I'VE BEEN CALLING YOU FOR DAYS. KEEPS SAYING YOU'RE NOT CONNECTED TO THE NETWORK. YOUR MOM TOO. IS EVERYTHING ALL RIGHT?
LOOK, TERRY. I'LL CALL YOU LATER. O.K.?

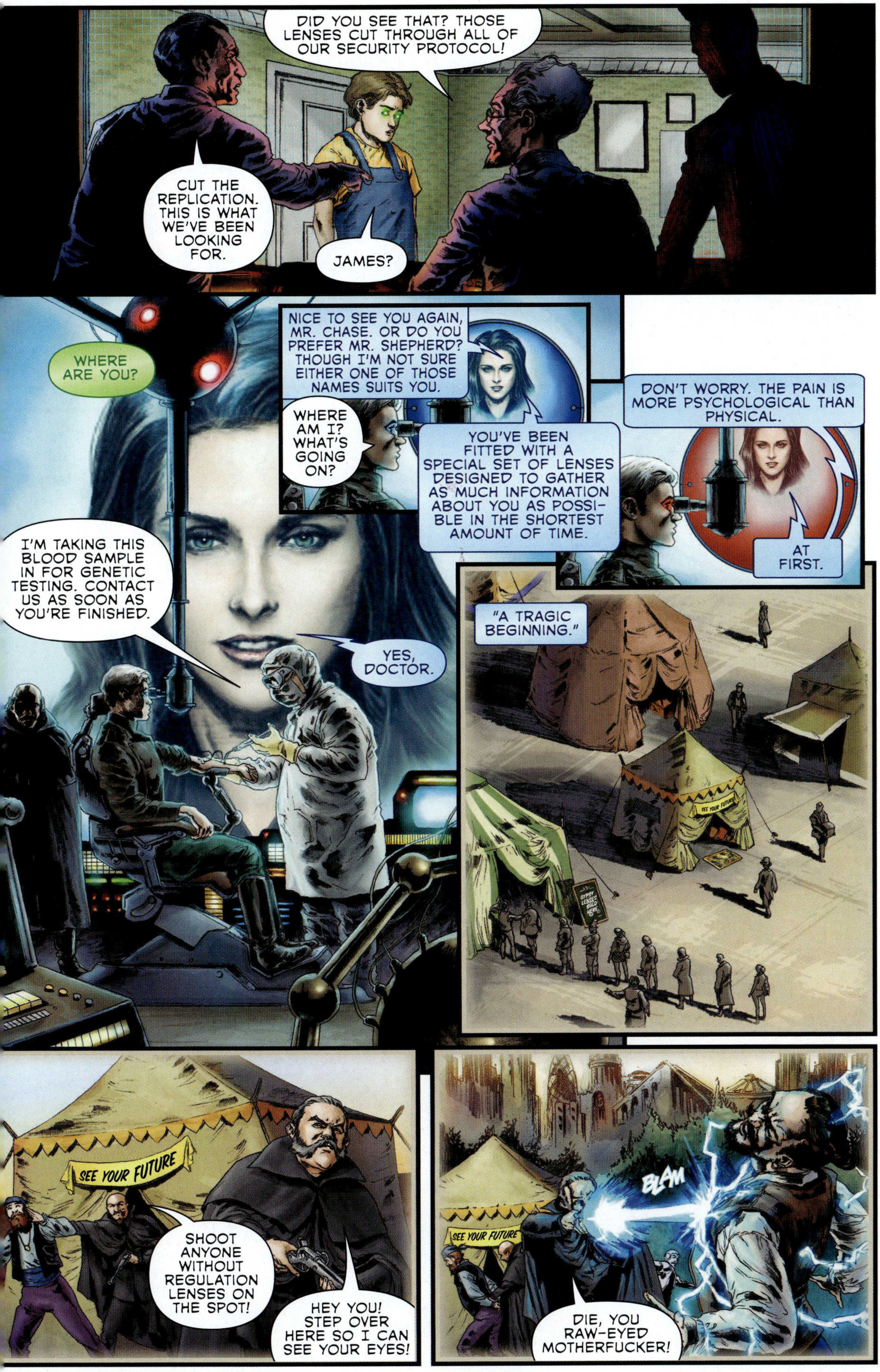

DID YOU SEE THAT? THOSE LENSES CUT THROUGH ALL OF OUR SECURITY PROTOCOL!
CUT THE REPLICATION. THIS IS WHAT WE'VE BEEN LOOKING FOR.
JAMES?
WHERE ARE YOU?
NICE TO SEE YOU AGAIN, MR. CHASE. OR DO YOU PREFER MR. SHEPHERD? THOUGH I'M NOT SURE EITHER ONE OF THOSE NAMES SUITS YOU.
WHERE AM I? WHAT'S GOING ON?
YOU'VE BEEN FITTED WITH A SPECIAL SET OF LENSES DESIGNED TO GATHER AS MUCH INFORMATION ABOUT YOU AS POSSI-BLE IN THE SHORTEST AMOUNT OF TIME.
DON'T WORRY. THE PAIN IS MORE PSYCHOLOGICAL THAN PHYSICAL.
AT FIRST.
I'M TAKING THIS BLOOD SAMPLE IN FOR GENETIC TESTING. CONTACT US AS SOON AS YOU'RE FINISHED.
YES, DOCTOR.
"A TRAGIC BEGINNING."
SEE YOUR FUTURE
SHOOT ANYONE WITHOUT REGULATION LENSES ON THE SPOT!
HEY YOU! STEP OVER HERE SO I CAN SEE YOUR EYES!
SEE YOUR FUTURE
BLAM
DIE, YOU RAW-EYED MOTHERFUCKER!

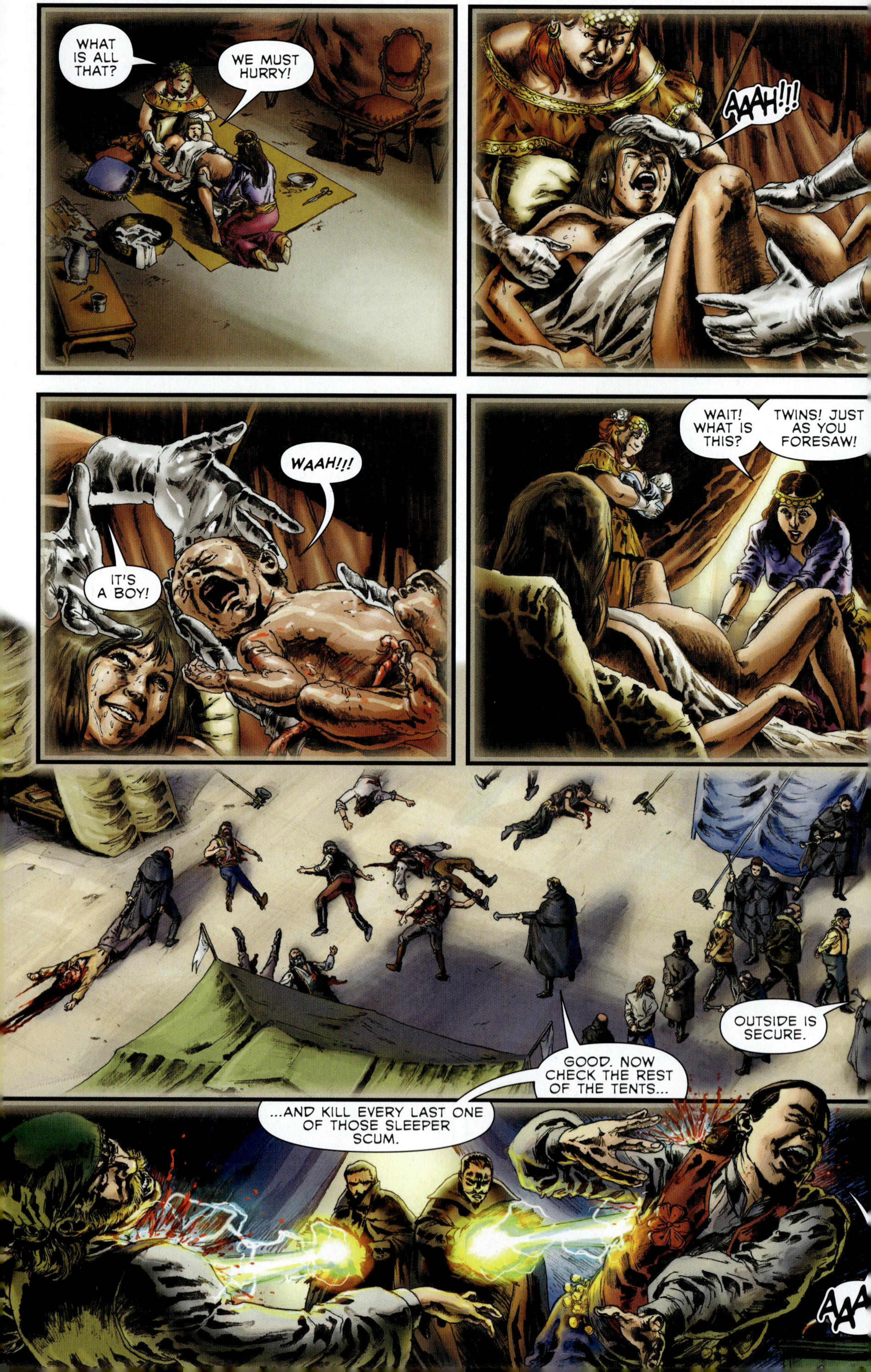
WHAT IS ALL THAT?
WE MUST HURRY!
AAAH!!!
WAAH!!!
IT'S A BOY!
WAIT! WHAT IS THIS?
TWINS! JUST AS YOU FORESAW!
OUTSIDE IS SECURE.
GOOD. NOW CHECK THE REST OF THE TENTS...
...AND KILL EVERY LAST ONE OF THOSE SLEEPER SCUM.

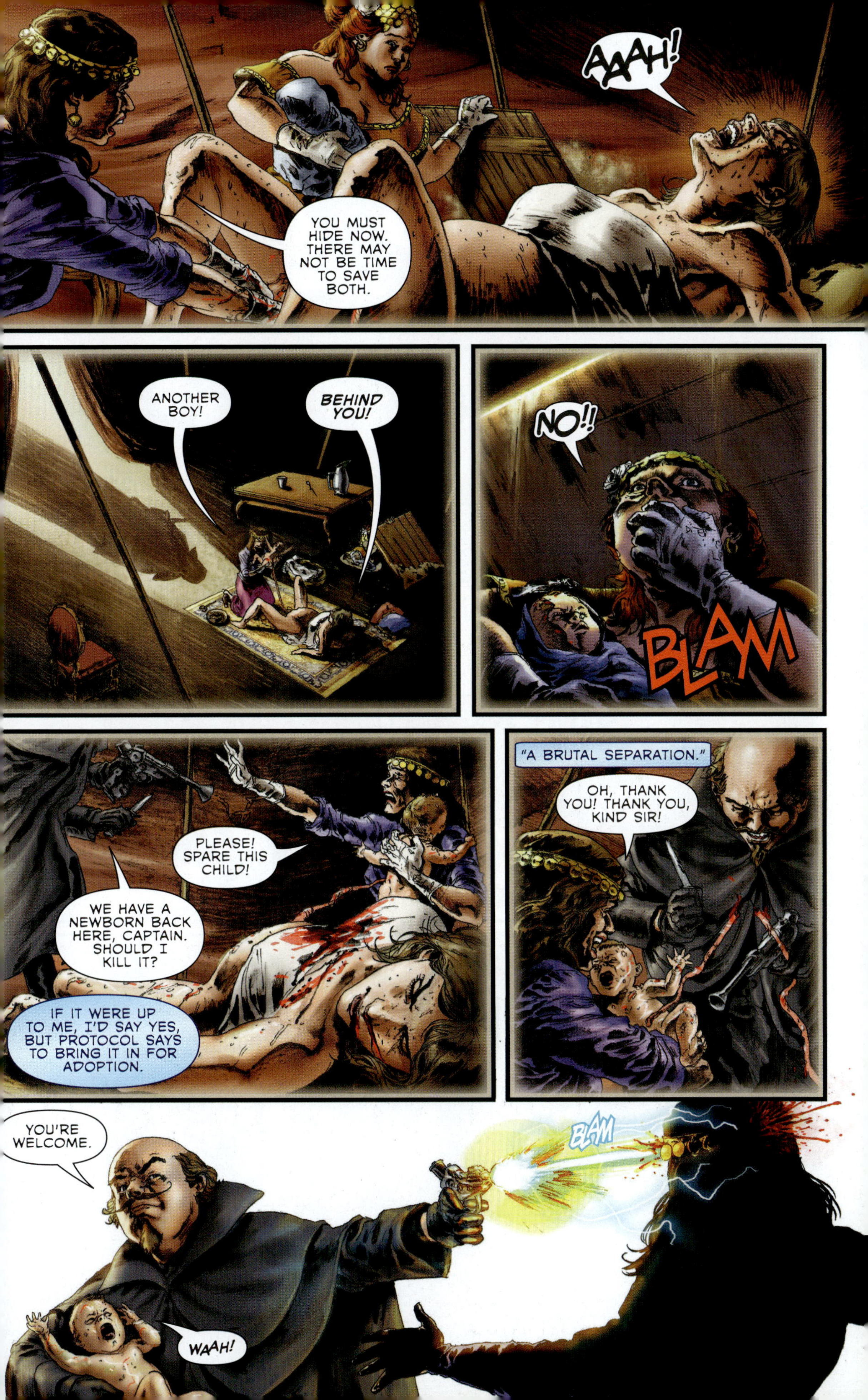
AAAH!
YOU MUST HIDE NOW. THERE MAY NOT BE TIME TO SAVE BOTH.
ANOTHER BOY!
BEHIND YOU!
NO!!
BLAM
PLEASE! SPARE THIS CHILD!
WE HAVE A NEWBORN BACK HERE, CAPTAIN. SHOULD I KILL IT?
IF IT WERE UP TO ME, I'D SAY YES, BUT PROTOCOL SAYS TO BRING IT IN FOR ADOPTION.
"A BRUTAL SEPARATION."
OH, THANK YOU! THANK YOU, KIND SIR!
YOU'RE WELCOME.
BLAM
WAAH!

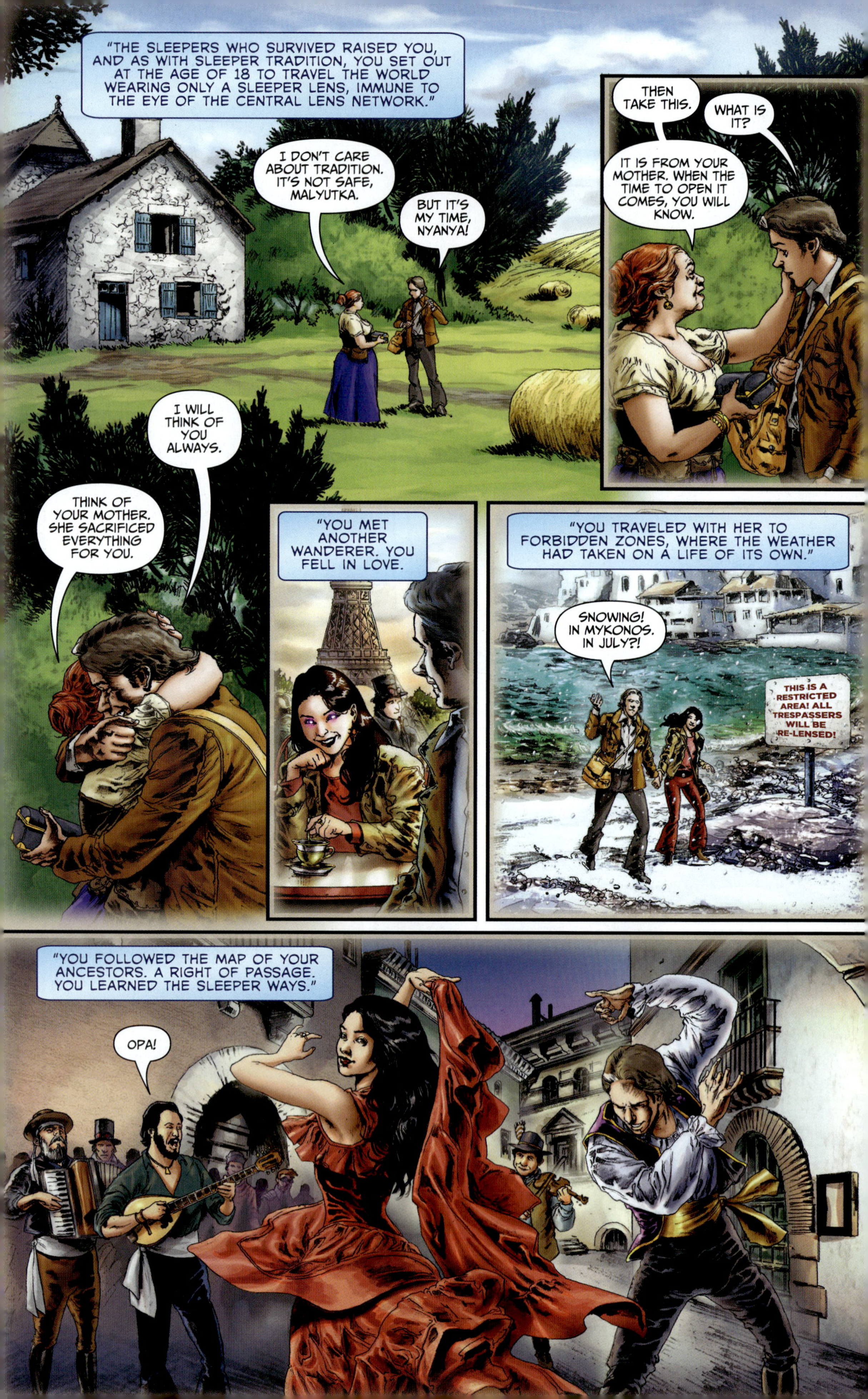

"THE SLEEPERS WHO SURVIVED RAISED YOU, AND AS WITH SLEEPER TRADITION, YOU SET OUT AT THE AGE OF 18 TO TRAVEL THE WORLD WEARING ONLY A SLEEPER LENS, IMMUNE TO THE EYE OF THE CENTRAL LENS NETWORK."
I DON'T CARE ABOUT TRADITION. IT'S NOT SAFE, MALYUTKA.
BUT IT'S MY TIME, NYANYA!
THEN TAKE THIS.
WHAT IS IT?
IT IS FROM YOUR MOTHER. WHEN THE TIME TO OPEN IT COMES, YOU WILL KNOW.
I WILL THINK OF YOU ALWAYS.
THINK OF YOUR MOTHER. SHE SACRIFICED EVERYTHING FOR YOU.
"YOU MET ANOTHER WANDERER. YOU FELL IN LOVE.
"YOU TRAVELED WITH HER TO FORBIDDEN ZONES, WHERE THE WEATHER HAD TAKEN ON A LIFE OF ITS OWN."
SNOWING! IN MYKONOS. IN JULY?!
THIS IS A RESTRICTED AREA! ALL TRESPASSERS WILL BE RE-LENSED!
"YOU FOLLOWED THE MAP OF YOUR ANCESTORS. A RIGHT OF PASSAGE. YOU LEARNED THE SLEEPER WAYS."
OPA!

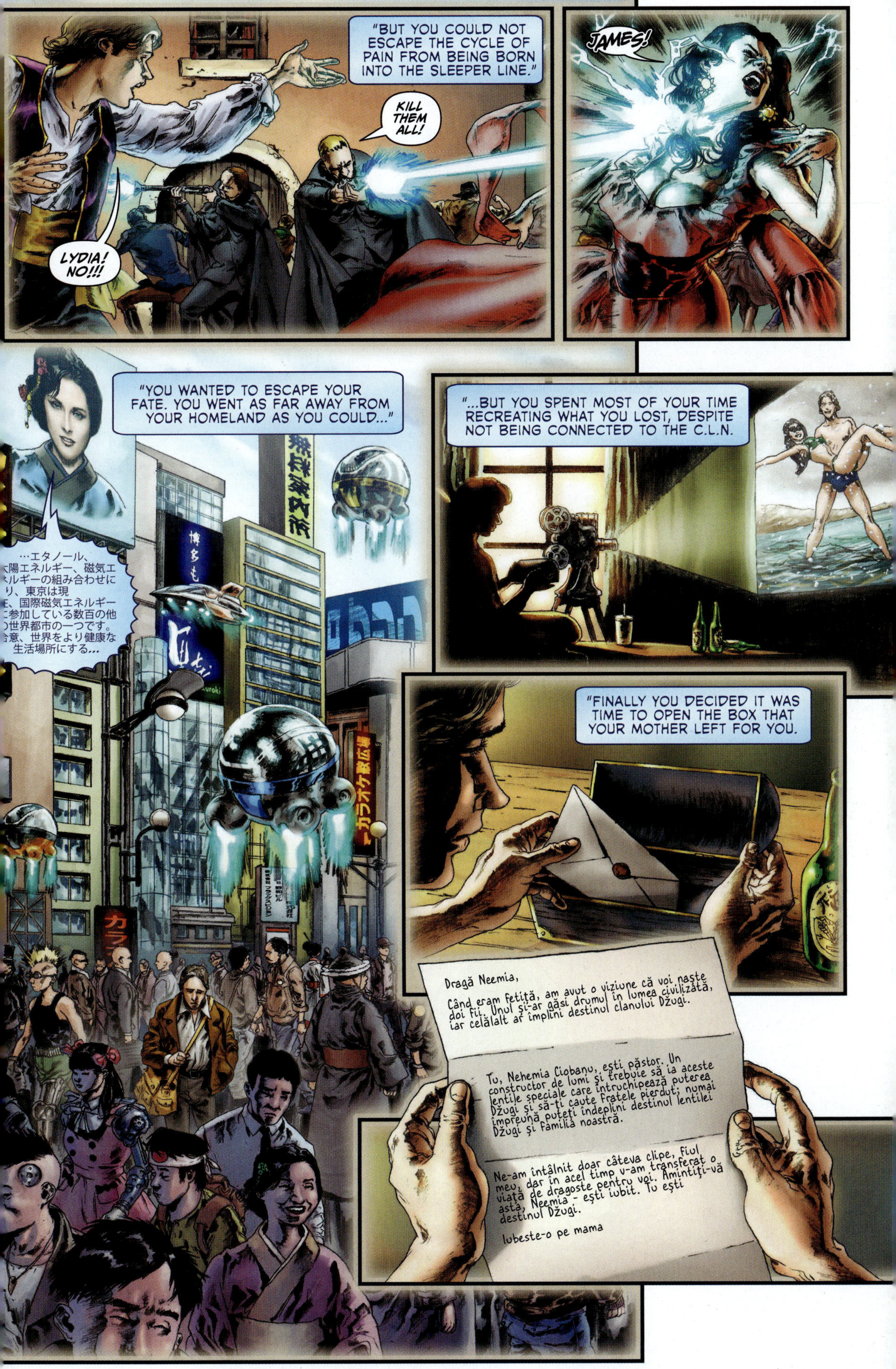
"BUT YOU COULD NOT ESCAPE THE CYCLE OF PAIN FROM BEING BORN INTO THE SLEEPER LINE."
KILL THEM ALL!
LYDIA! NO!!!
JAMES!
"YOU WANTED TO ESCAPE YOUR FATE. YOU WENT AS FAR AWAY FROM YOUR HOMELAND AS YOU COULD..."
…エタノール、
陽エネルギー、磁気エ
ルギーの組み合わせに
り、東京は現
、国際磁気エネルギー
参加している数百の他
世界都市の一つです。
意、世界をより健康な
生活場所にする...
"...BUT YOU SPENT MOST OF YOUR TIME RECREATING WHAT YOU LOST, DESPITE NOT BEING CONNECTED TO THE C.L.N.
"FINALLY YOU DECIDED IT WAS TIME TO OPEN THE BOX THAT YOUR MOTHER LEFT FOR YOU.
Dragă Neemia,
Când eram fetiță, am avut o viziune că voi naște doi fii. Unul și-ar găsi drumul în lumea civilizată, iar celălalt ar împlini destinul clanului Džugi.
Tu, Nehemia Ciobanu, ești păstor. Un constructor de lumi și trebuie să ia aceste lentile speciale care întruchipează puterea Džugi și să-ți caute fratele pierdut; numai împreună puteți îndeplini destinul lentilei Džugi și familia noastră.
Ne-am întâlnit doar câteva clipe, fiul meu, dar în acel timp v-am transferat o viață de dragoste pentru voi. Amintiți-vă asta, Neemia - ești iubit. Tu ești destinul Džugi.
Iubeste-o pe mama

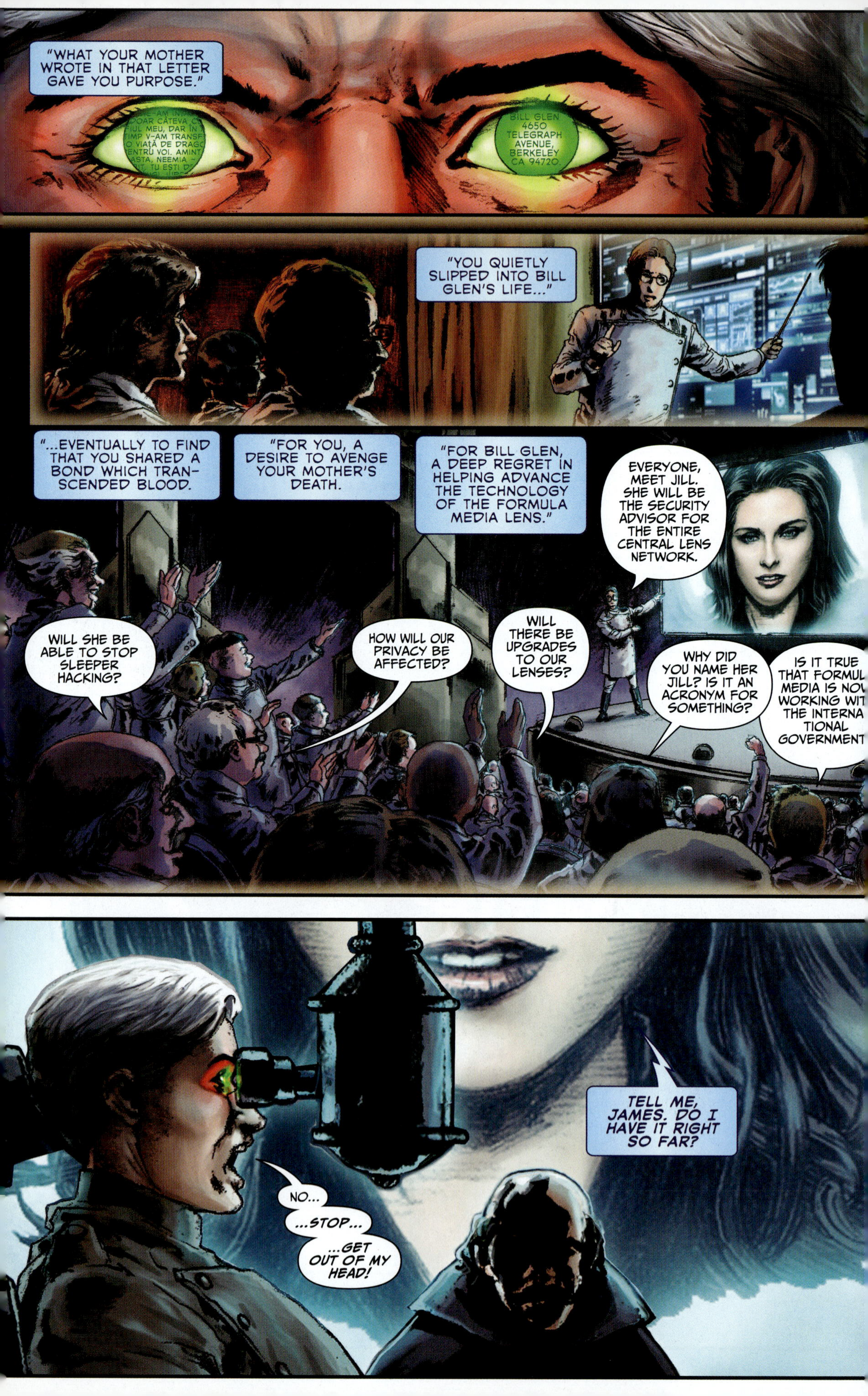
"WHAT YOUR MOTHER WROTE IN THAT LETTER GAVE YOU PURPOSE."
BILL GLEN 4650 TELEGRAPH AVENUE, BERKELEY CA 94720
"YOU QUIETLY SLIPPED INTO BILL GLEN'S LIFE..."
"...EVENTUALLY TO FIND THAT YOU SHARED A BOND WHICH TRAN-SCENDED BLOOD.
"FOR YOU, A DESIRE TO AVENGE YOUR MOTHER'S DEATH.
"FOR BILL GLEN, A DEEP REGRET IN HELPING ADVANCE THE TECHNOLOGY OF THE FORMULA MEDIA LENS."
EVERYONE, MEET JILL. SHE WILL BE THE SECURITY ADVISOR FOR THE ENTIRE CENTRAL LENS NETWORK.
WILL SHE BE ABLE TO STOP SLEEPER HACKING?
HOW WILL OUR PRIVACY BE AFFECTED?
WILL THERE BE UPGRADES TO OUR LENSES?
WHY DID YOU NAME HER JILL? IS IT AN ACRONYM FOR SOMETHING?
IS IT TRUE THAT FORMUL MEDIA IS NOV WORKING WIT THE INTERNA TIONAL GOVERNMENT
TELL ME, JAMES. DO I HAVE IT RIGHT SO FAR?
NO...
...STOP...
...GET OUT OF MY HEAD!

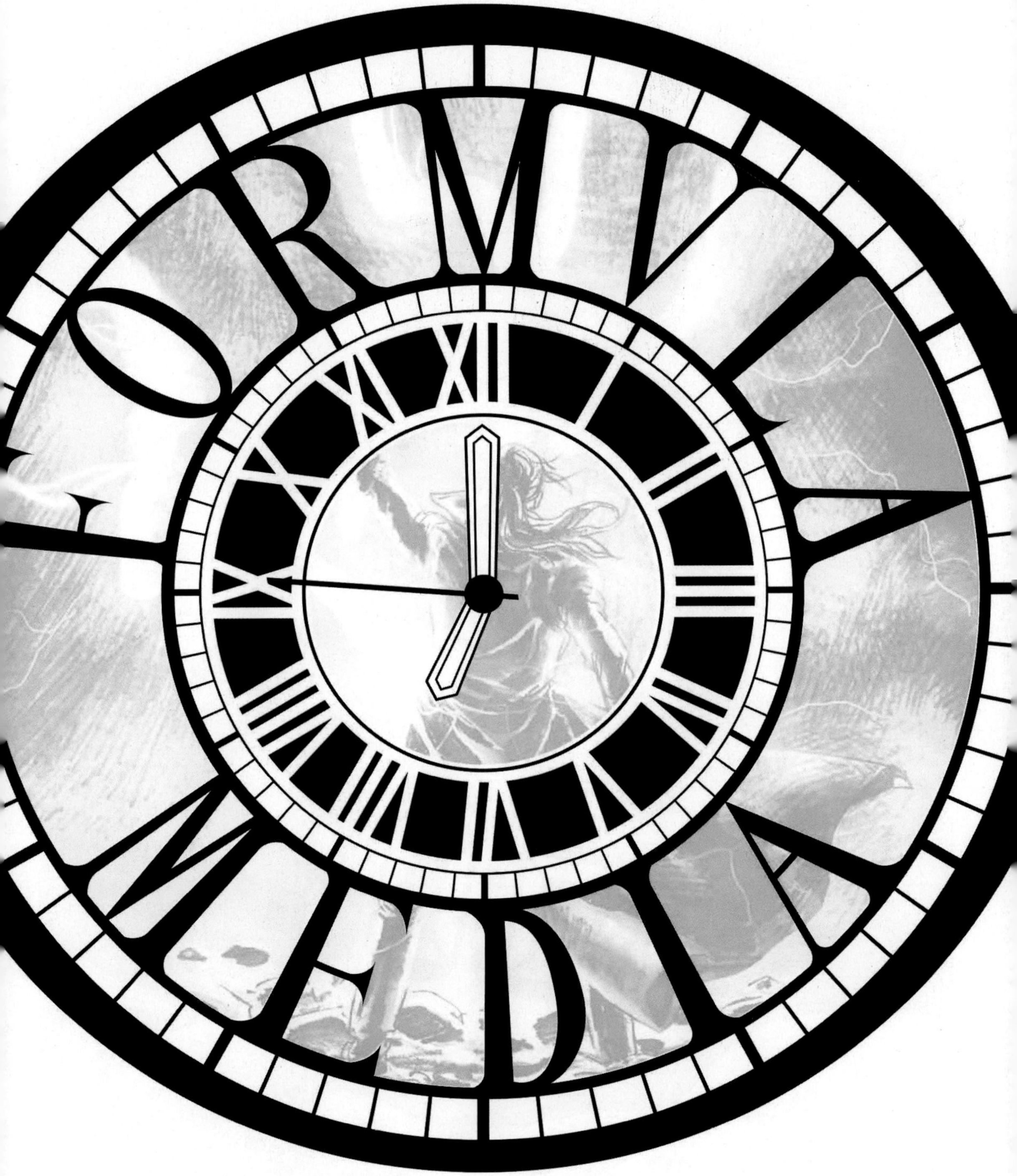

CHAPTER 07

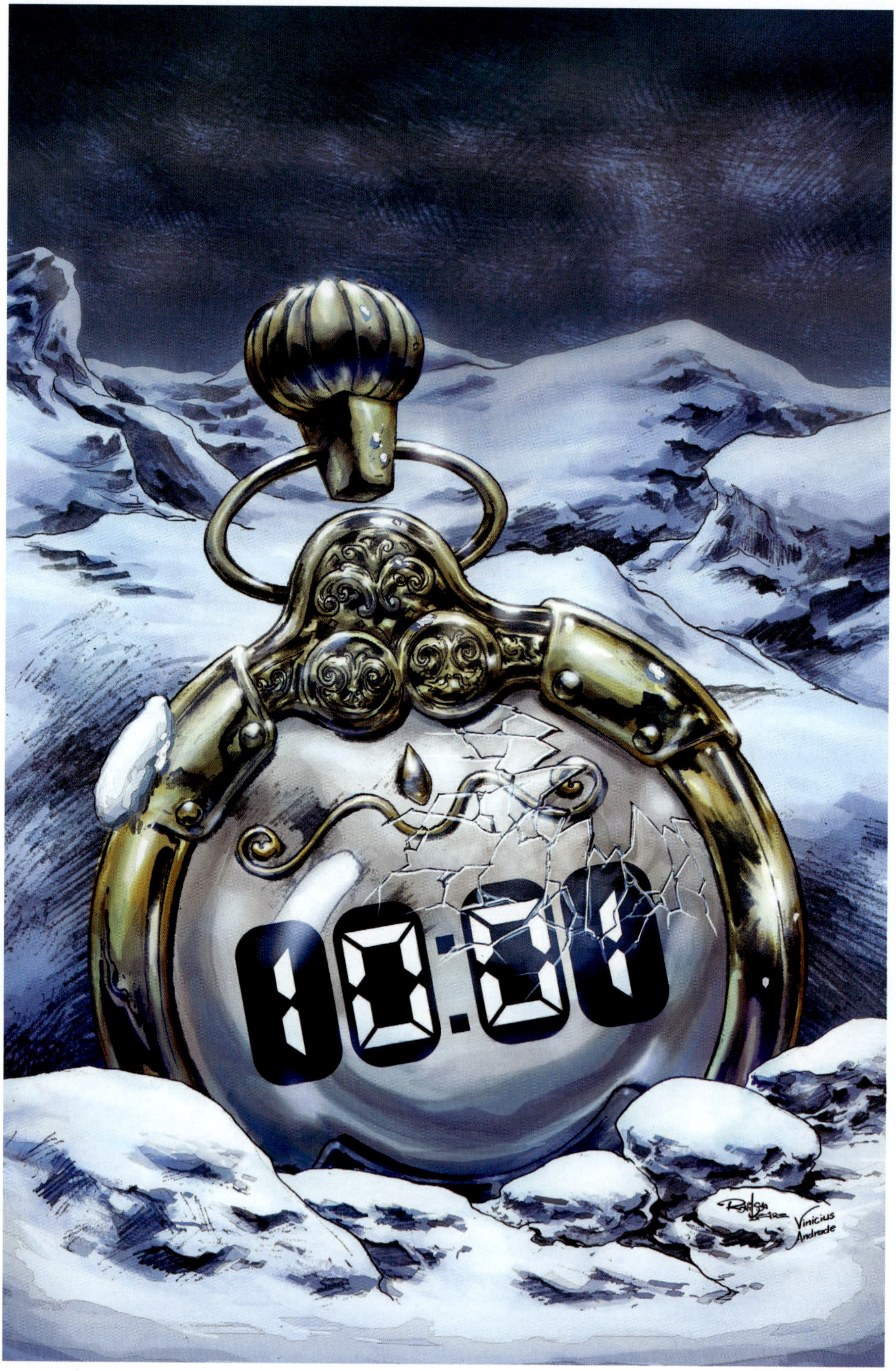
10:00
Ronilson Freire
Vinicius Andrade

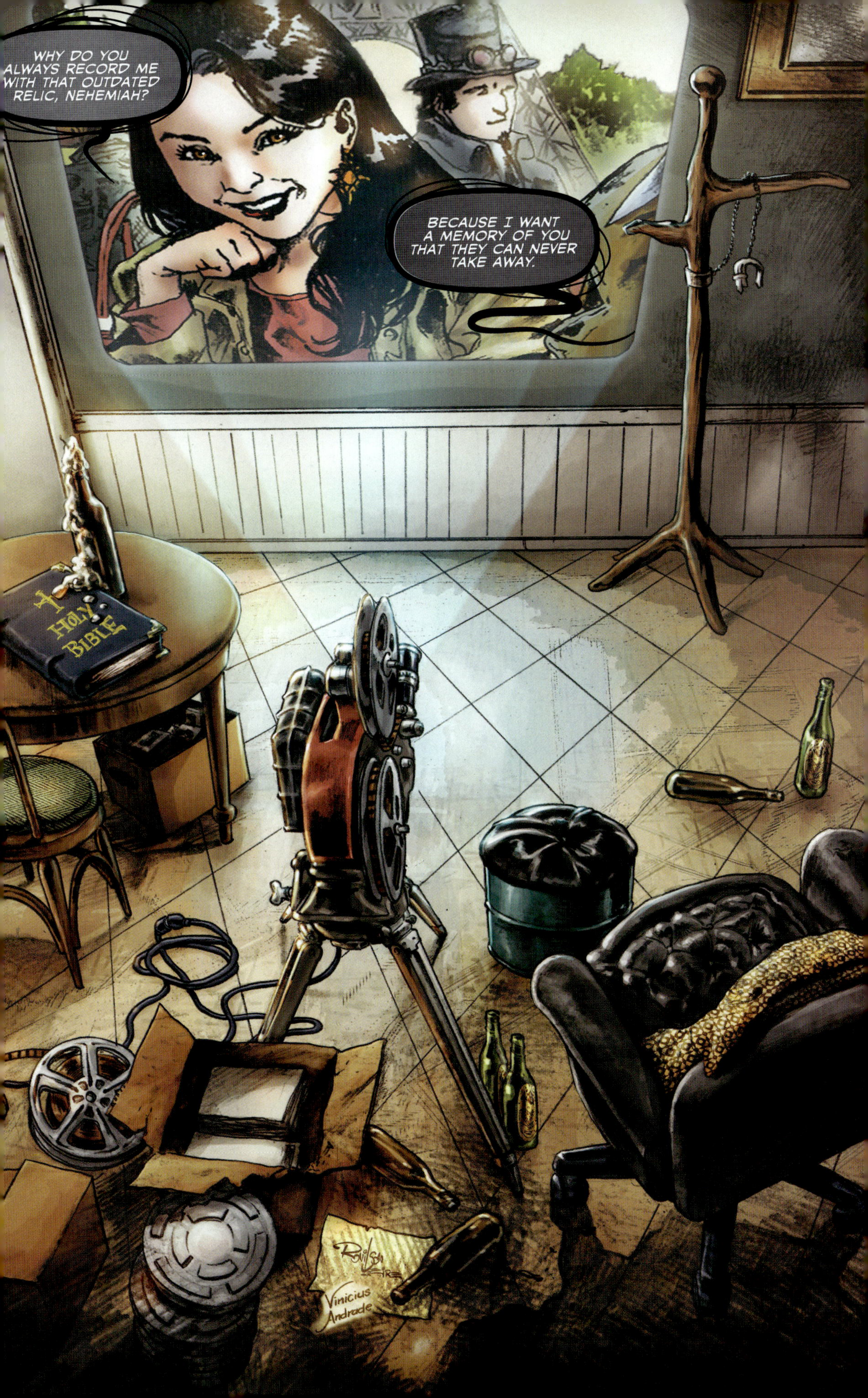
WHY DO YOU ALWAYS RECORD ME WITH THAT OUTDATED RELIC, NEHEMIAH?
BECAUSE I WANT A MEMORY OF YOU THAT THEY CAN NEVER TAKE AWAY.
HOLY BIBLE
Vinicius Andrade

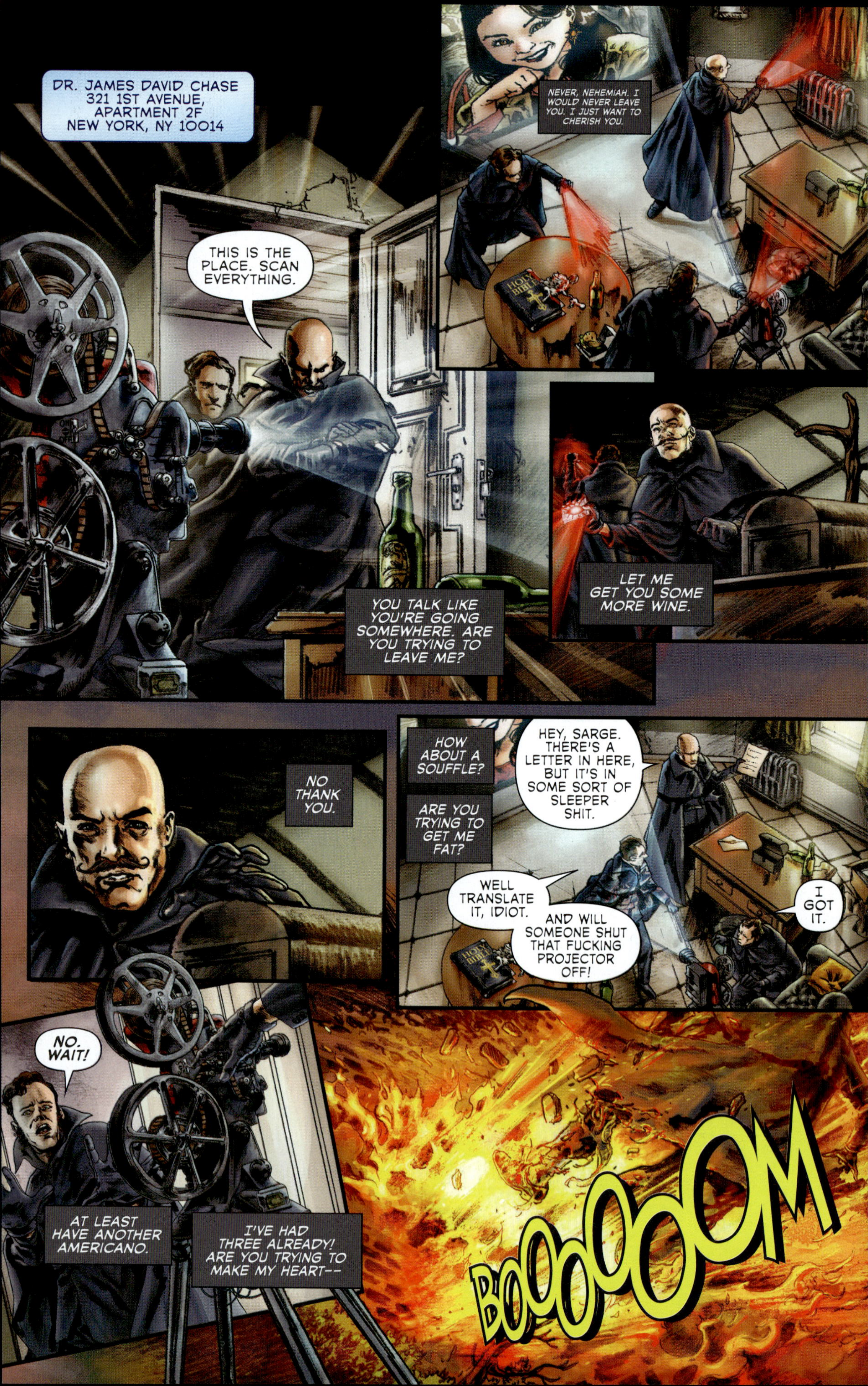
DR. JAMES DAVID CHASE
321 1ST AVENUE,
APARTMENT 2F
NEW YORK, NY 10014
THIS IS THE PLACE. SCAN EVERYTHING.
NEVER, NEHEMIAH. I WOULD NEVER LEAVE YOU. I JUST WANT TO CHERISH YOU.
YOU TALK LIKE YOU'RE GOING SOMEWHERE. ARE YOU TRYING TO LEAVE ME?
LET ME GET YOU SOME MORE WINE.
NO THANK YOU.
HOW ABOUT A SOUFFLE?
ARE YOU TRYING TO GET ME FAT?
HEY, SARGE. THERE'S A LETTER IN HERE, BUT IT'S IN SOME SORT OF SLEEPER SHIT.
WELL TRANSLATE IT, IDIOT.
AND WILL SOMEONE SHUT THAT FUCKING PROJECTOR OFF!
I GOT IT.
NO. WAIT!
AT LEAST HAVE ANOTHER AMERICANO.
I'VE HAD THREE ALREADY! ARE YOU TRYING TO MAKE MY HEART--
BOOOOOOM

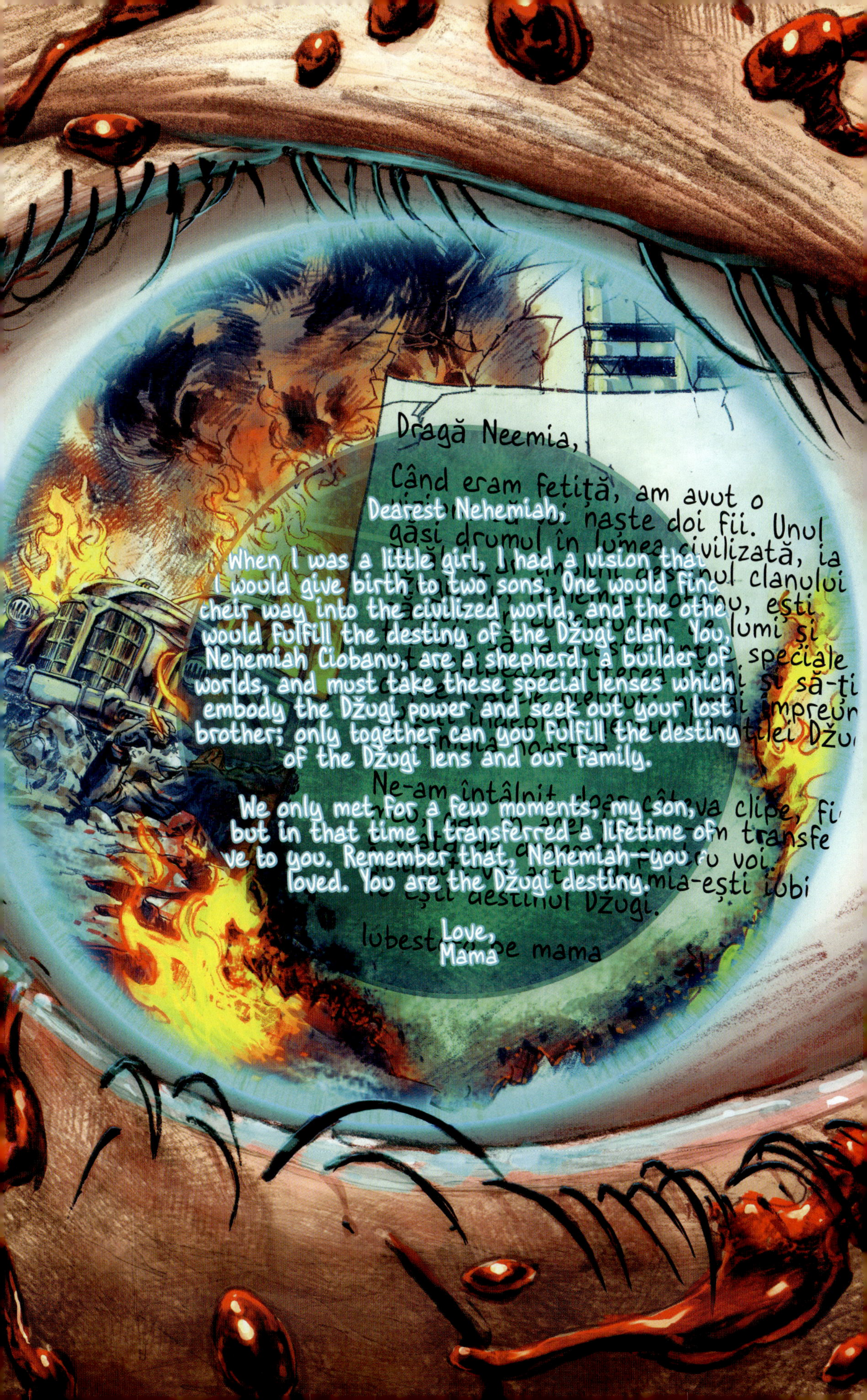

Dragă Neemia,
Când eram fetiță, am avut o
Dearest Nehemiah,
When I was a little girl, I had a vision that I would give birth to two sons. One would find their way into the civilized world, and the other would fulfill the destiny of the Džugi clan. You, Nehemiah Ciobanu, are a shepherd, a builder of worlds, and must take these special lenses which embody the Džugi power and seek out your lost brother; only together can you fulfill the destiny of the Džugi lens and our family.
We only met for a few moments, my son, but in that time I transferred a lifetime of
ve to you. Remember that, Nehemiah--you
loved. You are the Džugi destiny.
Love,
Mama

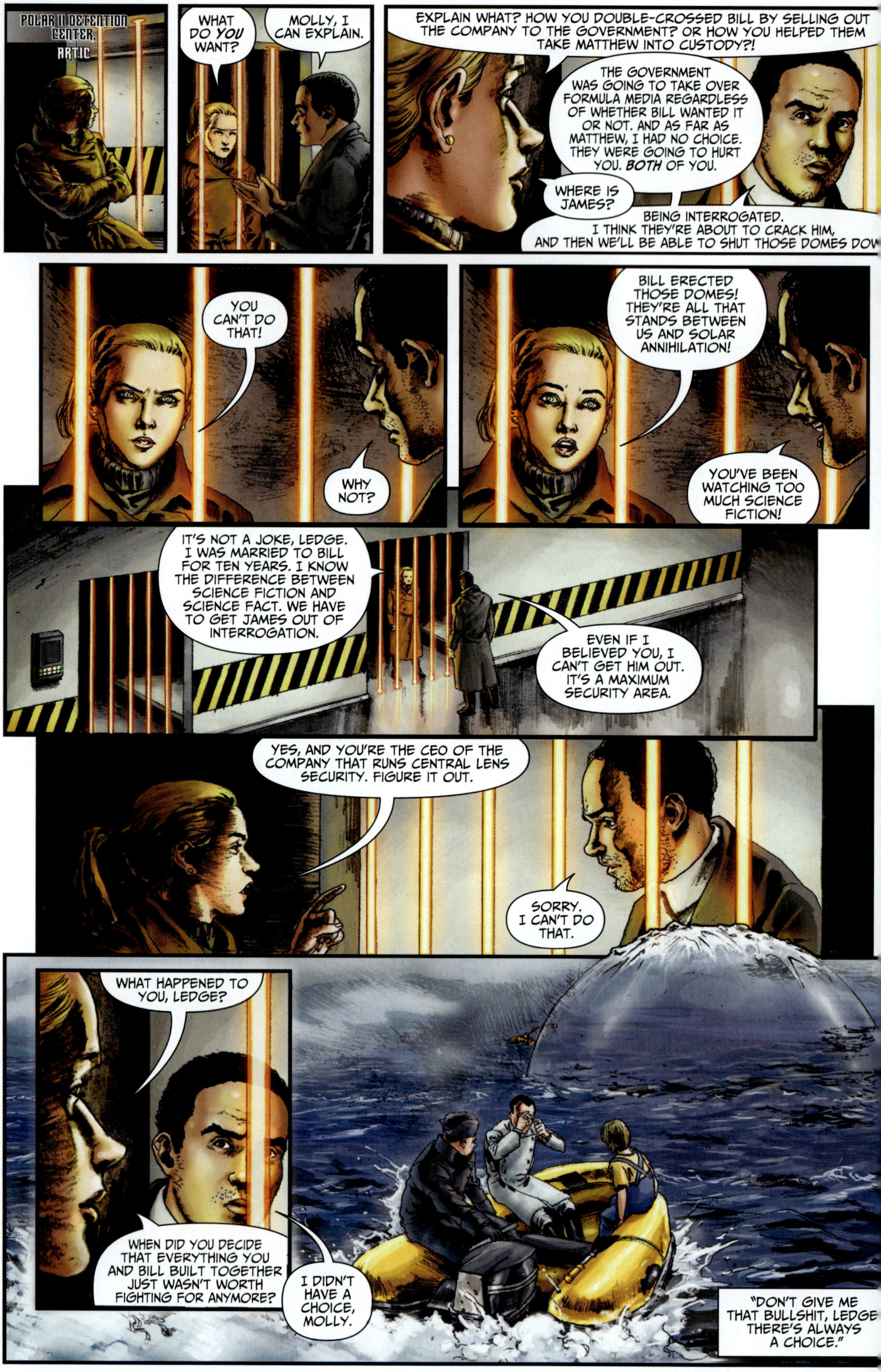
POLAR II DETENTION CENTER, ARTIC
WHAT DO YOU WANT?
MOLLY, I CAN EXPLAIN.
EXPLAIN WHAT? HOW YOU DOUBLE-CROSSED BILL BY SELLING OUT THE COMPANY TO THE GOVERNMENT? OR HOW YOU HELPED THEM TAKE MATTHEW INTO CUSTODY?!
THE GOVERNMENT WAS GOING TO TAKE OVER FORMULA MEDIA REGARDLESS OF WHETHER BILL WANTED IT OR NOT. AND AS FAR AS MATTHEW, I HAD NO CHOICE. THEY WERE GOING TO HURT YOU. BOTH OF YOU.
WHERE IS JAMES?
BEING INTERROGATED. I THINK THEY'RE ABOUT TO CRACK HIM, AND THEN WE'LL BE ABLE TO SHUT THOSE DOMES DOW
YOU CAN'T DO THAT!
WHY NOT?
BILL ERECTED THOSE DOMES! THEY'RE ALL THAT STANDS BETWEEN US AND SOLAR ANNIHILATION!
YOU'VE BEEN WATCHING TOO MUCH SCIENCE FICTION!
IT'S NOT A JOKE, LEDGE. I WAS MARRIED TO BILL FOR TEN YEARS. I KNOW THE DIFFERENCE BETWEEN SCIENCE FICTION AND SCIENCE FACT. WE HAVE TO GET JAMES OUT OF INTERROGATION.
EVEN IF I BELIEVED YOU, I CAN'T GET HIM OUT. IT'S A MAXIMUM SECURITY AREA.
YES, AND YOU'RE THE CEO OF THE COMPANY THAT RUNS CENTRAL LENS SECURITY. FIGURE IT OUT.
SORRY. I CAN'T DO THAT.
WHAT HAPPENED TO YOU, LEDGE?
WHEN DID YOU DECIDE THAT EVERYTHING YOU AND BILL BUILT TOGETHER JUST WASN'T WORTH FIGHTING FOR ANYMORE?
I DIDN'T HAVE A CHOICE, MOLLY.
"DON'T GIVE ME THAT BULLSHIT, LEDGE THERE'S ALWAYS A CHOICE."

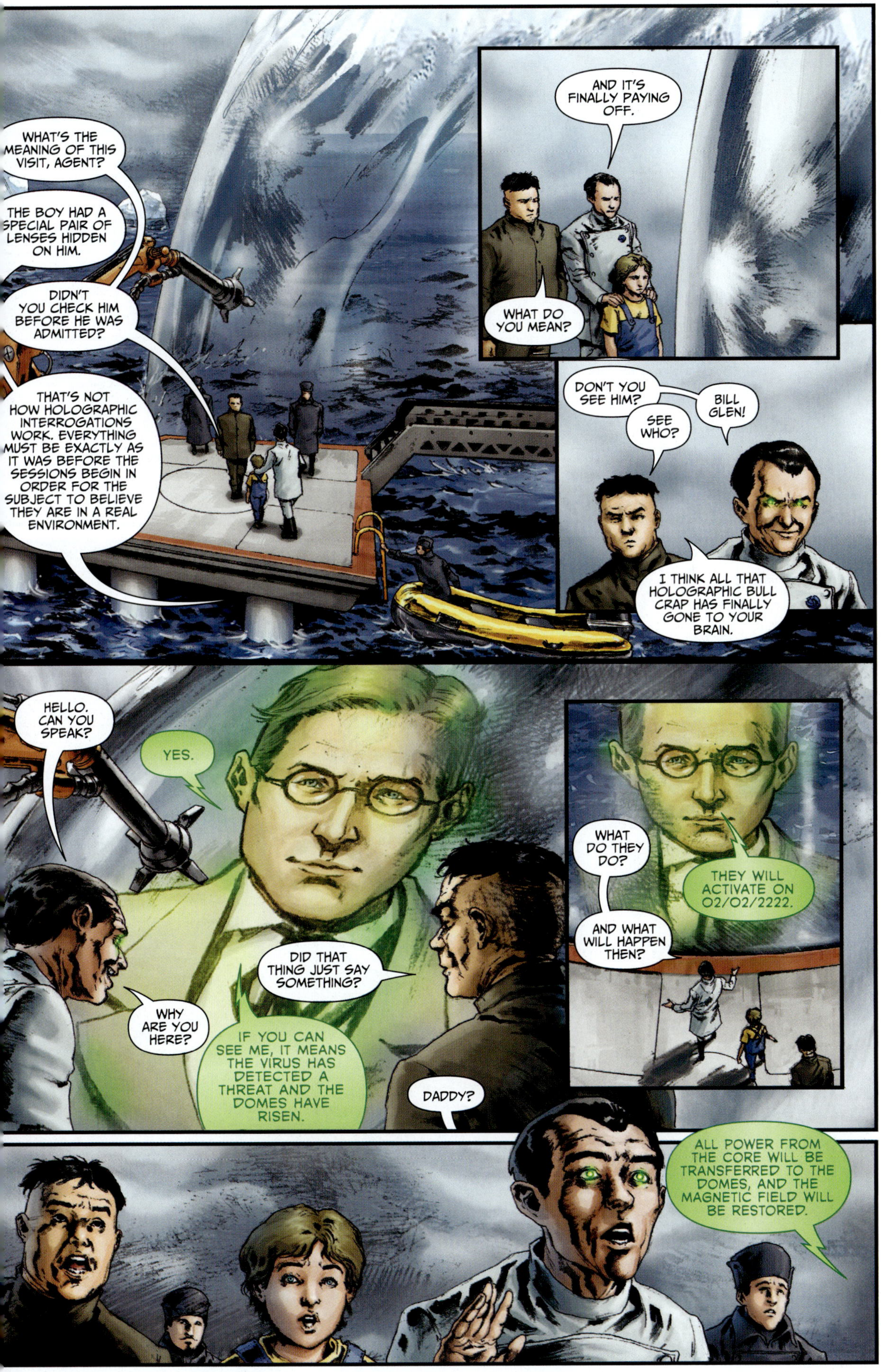
WHAT'S THE MEANING OF THIS VISIT, AGENT?
THE BOY HAD A SPECIAL PAIR OF LENSES HIDDEN ON HIM.
DIDN'T YOU CHECK HIM BEFORE HE WAS ADMITTED?
THAT'S NOT HOW HOLOGRAPHIC INTERROGATIONS WORK. EVERYTHING MUST BE EXACTLY AS IT WAS BEFORE THE SESSIONS BEGIN IN ORDER FOR THE SUBJECT TO BELIEVE THEY ARE IN A REAL ENVIRONMENT.
AND IT'S FINALLY PAYING OFF.
WHAT DO YOU MEAN?
DON'T YOU SEE HIM?
SEE WHO?
BILL GLEN!
I THINK ALL THAT HOLOGRAPHIC BULL CRAP HAS FINALLY GONE TO YOUR BRAIN.
HELLO. CAN YOU SPEAK?
YES.
DID THAT THING JUST SAY SOMETHING?
WHY ARE YOU HERE?
IF YOU CAN SEE ME, IT MEANS THE VIRUS HAS DETECTED A THREAT AND THE DOMES HAVE RISEN.
DADDY?
WHAT DO THEY DO?
THEY WILL ACTIVATE ON 02/02/2222.
AND WHAT WILL HAPPEN THEN?
ALL POWER FROM THE CORE WILL BE TRANSFERRED TO THE DOMES, AND THE MAGNETIC FIELD WILL BE RESTORED.

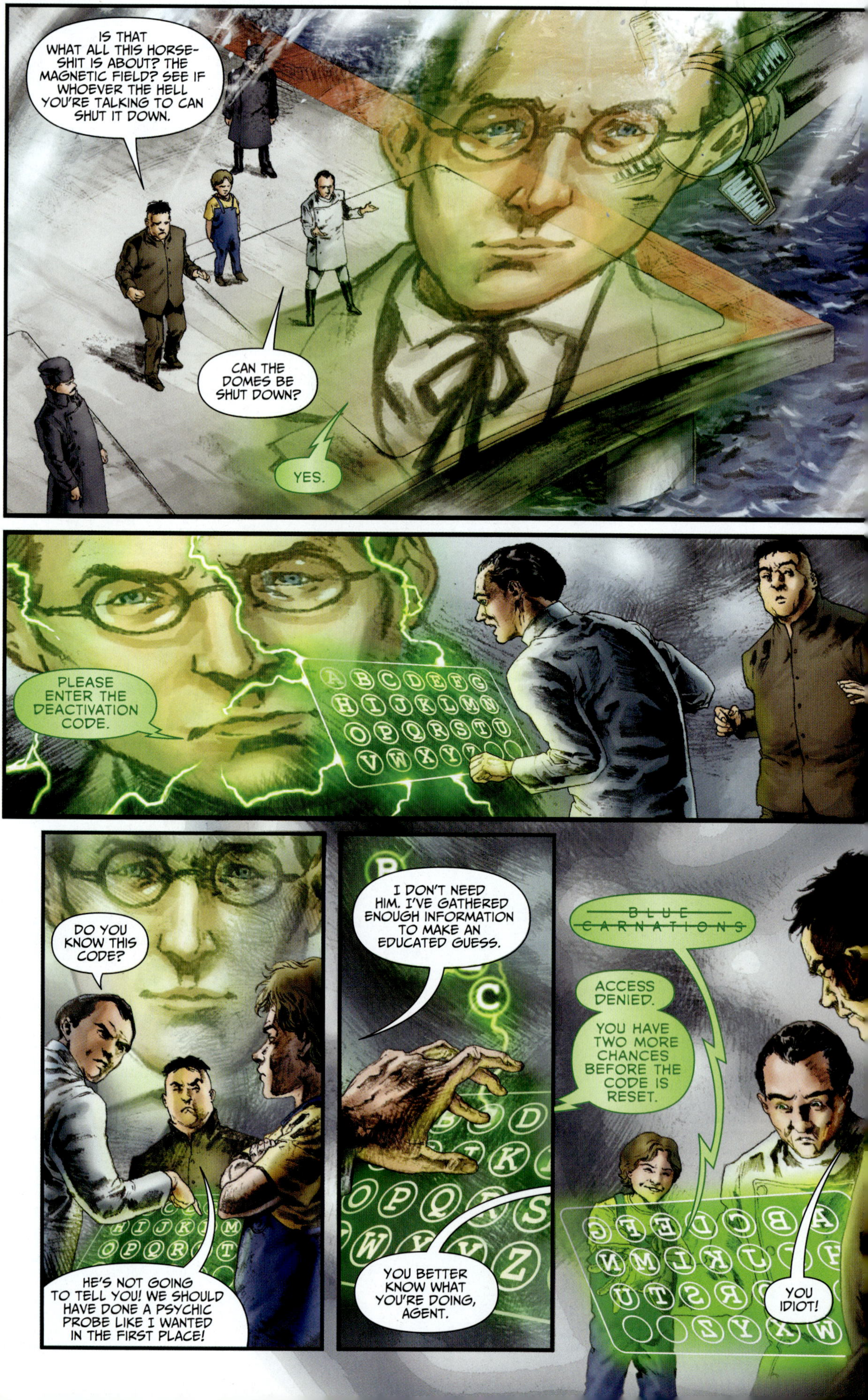
IS THAT WHAT ALL THIS HORSE-SHIT IS ABOUT? THE MAGNETIC FIELD? SEE IF WHOEVER THE HELL YOU'RE TALKING TO CAN SHUT IT DOWN.
CAN THE DOMES BE SHUT DOWN?
YES.
PLEASE ENTER THE DEACTIVATION CODE.
DO YOU KNOW THIS CODE?
HE'S NOT GOING TO TELL YOU! WE SHOULD HAVE DONE A PSYCHIC PROBE LIKE I WANTED IN THE FIRST PLACE!
I DON'T NEED HIM. I'VE GATHERED ENOUGH INFORMATION TO MAKE AN EDUCATED GUESS.
YOU BETTER KNOW WHAT YOU'RE DOING, AGENT.
BLUE CARNATIONS
ACCESS DENIED.
YOU HAVE TWO MORE CHANCES BEFORE THE CODE IS RESET.
YOU IDIOT!

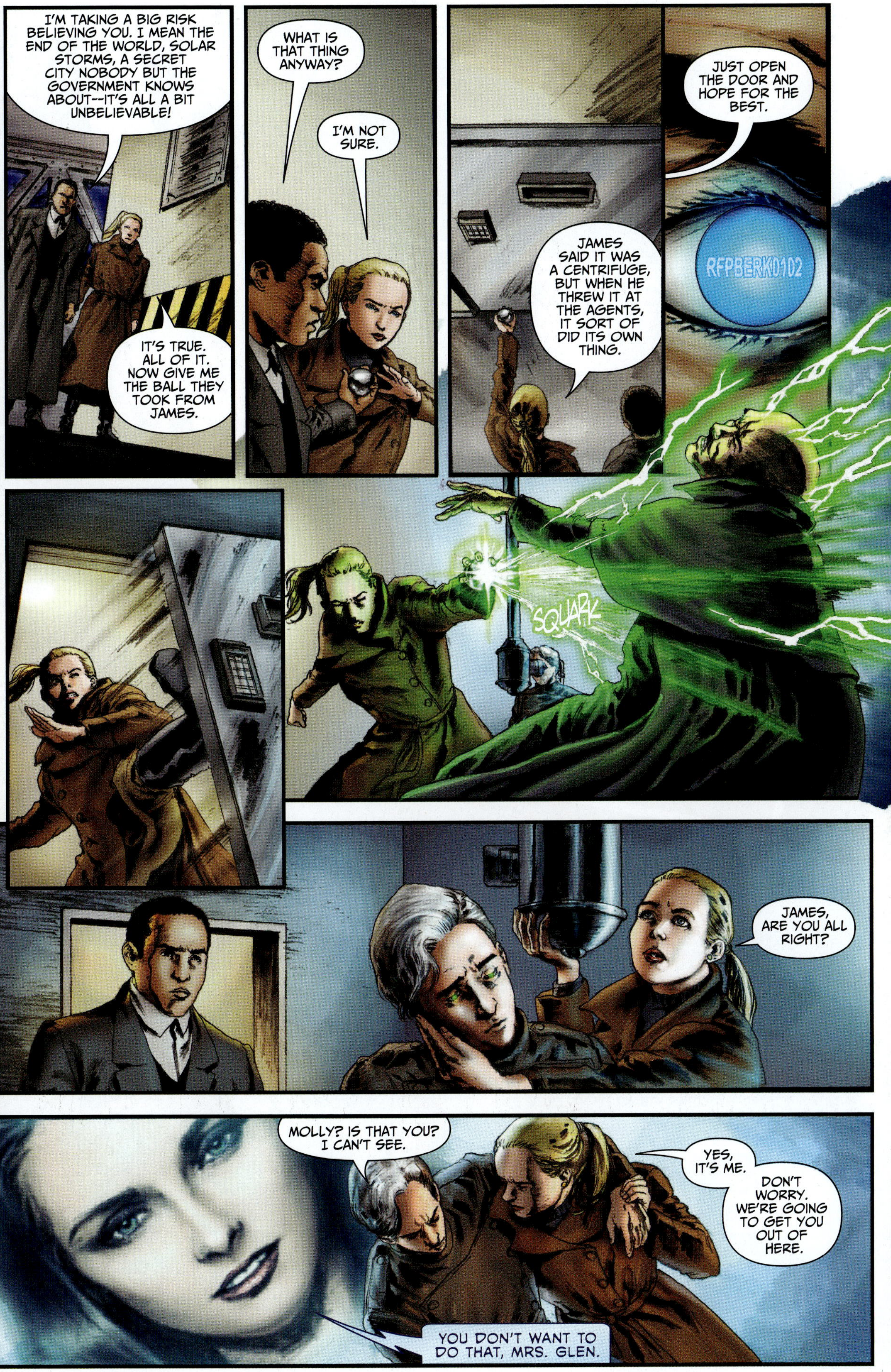

I'M TAKING A BIG RISK BELIEVING YOU. I MEAN THE END OF THE WORLD, SOLAR STORMS, A SECRET CITY NOBODY BUT THE GOVERNMENT KNOWS ABOUT--IT'S ALL A BIT UNBELIEVABLE!
IT'S TRUE. ALL OF IT. NOW GIVE ME THE BALL THEY TOOK FROM JAMES.
WHAT IS THAT THING ANYWAY?
I'M NOT SURE.
JAMES SAID IT WAS A CENTRIFUGE, BUT WHEN HE THREW IT AT THE AGENTS, IT SORT OF DID ITS OWN THING.
JUST OPEN THE DOOR AND HOPE FOR THE BEST.
RFPBERK0102
SQUARK
JAMES, ARE YOU ALL RIGHT?
MOLLY? IS THAT YOU? I CAN'T SEE.
YES, IT'S ME.
DON'T WORRY. WE'RE GOING TO GET YOU OUT OF HERE.
YOU DON'T WANT TO DO THAT, MRS. GLEN.

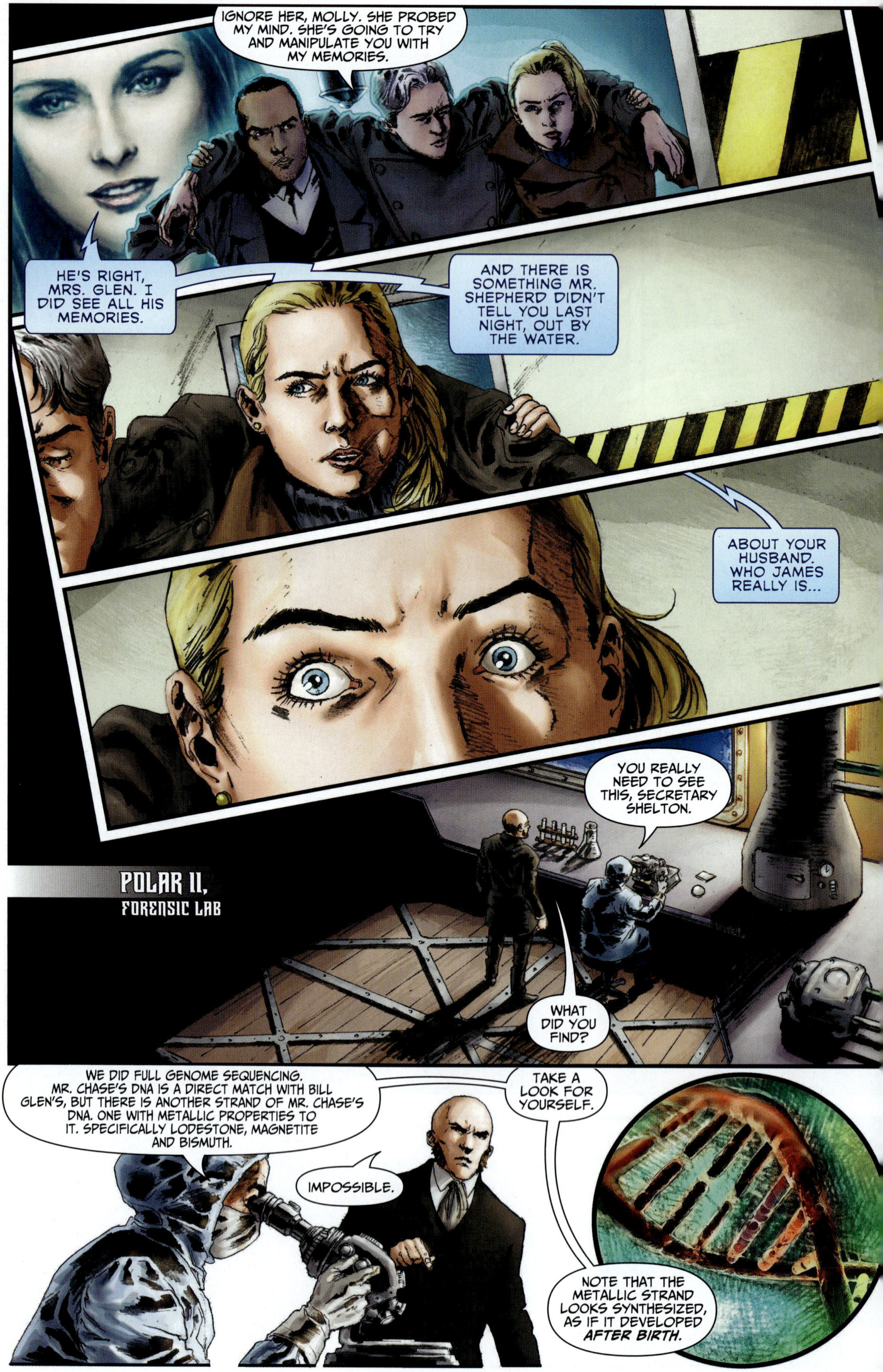

IGNORE HER, MOLLY. SHE PROBED MY MIND. SHE'S GOING TO TRY AND MANIPULATE YOU WITH MY MEMORIES.
HE'S RIGHT, MRS. GLEN. I DID SEE ALL HIS MEMORIES.
AND THERE IS SOMETHING MR. SHEPHERD DIDN'T TELL YOU LAST NIGHT, OUT BY THE WATER.
ABOUT YOUR HUSBAND. WHO JAMES REALLY IS...
POLAR II,
FORENSIC LAB
YOU REALLY NEED TO SEE THIS, SECRETARY SHELTON.
WHAT DID YOU FIND?
WE DID FULL GENOME SEQUENCING. MR. CHASE'S DNA IS A DIRECT MATCH WITH BILL GLEN'S, BUT THERE IS ANOTHER STRAND OF MR. CHASE'S DNA. ONE WITH METALLIC PROPERTIES TO IT. SPECIFICALLY LODESTONE, MAGNETITE AND BISMUTH.
TAKE A LOOK FOR YOURSELF.
IMPOSSIBLE.
NOTE THAT THE METALLIC STRAND LOOKS SYNTHESIZED, AS IF IT DEVELOPED *AFTER BIRTH.*

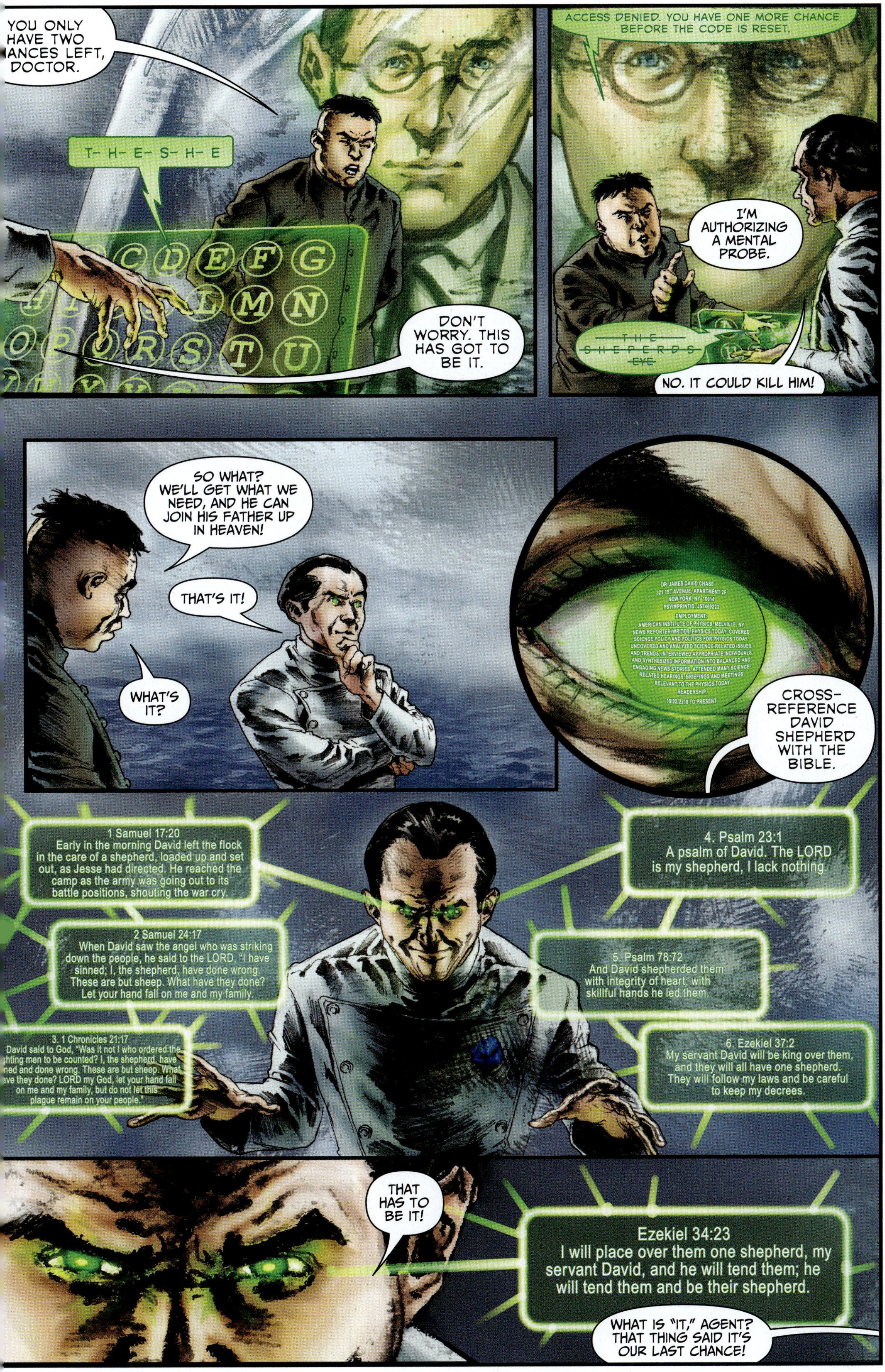
YOU ONLY HAVE TWO ANCES LEFT, DOCTOR.
T- H- E- S- H- E
DON'T WORRY. THIS HAS GOT TO BE IT.
ACCESS DENIED. YOU HAVE ONE MORE CHANCE BEFORE THE CODE IS RESET.
I'M AUTHORIZING A MENTAL PROBE.
THE SHEPERDS EYE
NO. IT COULD KILL HIM!
SO WHAT? WE'LL GET WHAT WE NEED, AND HE CAN JOIN HIS FATHER UP IN HEAVEN!
THAT'S IT!
WHAT'S IT?
DR. JAMES DAVID CHASE
321 1ST AVENUE, APARTMENT 2F
NEW YORK, NY 10014
PSYIMPRINTID: JS7469223
EMPLOYMENT:
AMERICAN INSTITUTE OF PHYSICS, MELVILLE, NY
NEWS REPORTER/WRITER, PHYSICS TODAY. COVERED SCIENCE POLICY AND POLITICS FOR PHYSICS TODAY. UNCOVERED AND ANALYZED SCIENCE-RELATED ISSUES AND TRENDS, INTERVIEWED APPROPRIATE INDIVIDUALS AND SYNTHESIZED INFORMATION INTO BALANCED AND ENGAGING NEWS STORIES. ATTENDED MANY SCIENCE-RELATED HEARINGS, BRIEFINGS AND MEETINGS RELEVANT TO THE PHYSICS TODAY READERSHIP.
10/02/2218 TO PRESENT
CROSS-REFERENCE DAVID SHEPHERD WITH THE BIBLE.
1 Samuel 17:20 Early in the morning David left the flock in the care of a shepherd, loaded up and set out, as Jesse had directed. He reached the camp as the army was going out to its battle positions, shouting the war cry.
2 Samuel 24:17 When David saw the angel who was striking down the people, he said to the LORD, "I have sinned; I, the shepherd, have done wrong. These are but sheep. What have they done? Let your hand fall on me and my family.
3. 1 Chronicles 21:17 David said to God, "Was it not I who ordered the ghting men to be counted? I, the shepherd, have ned and done wrong. These are but sheep. What ave they done? LORD my God, let your hand fall on me and my family, but do not let this plague remain on your people."
4. Psalm 23:1 A psalm of David. The LORD is my shepherd, I lack nothing.
5. Psalm 78:72 And David shepherded them with integrity of heart; with skillful hands he led them.
6. Ezekiel 37:2 My servant David will be king over them, and they will all have one shepherd. They will follow my laws and be careful to keep my decrees.
THAT HAS TO BE IT!
Ezekiel 34:23 I will place over them one shepherd, my servant David, and he will tend them; he will tend them and be their shepherd.
WHAT IS "IT," AGENT? THAT THING SAID IT'S OUR LAST CHANCE!

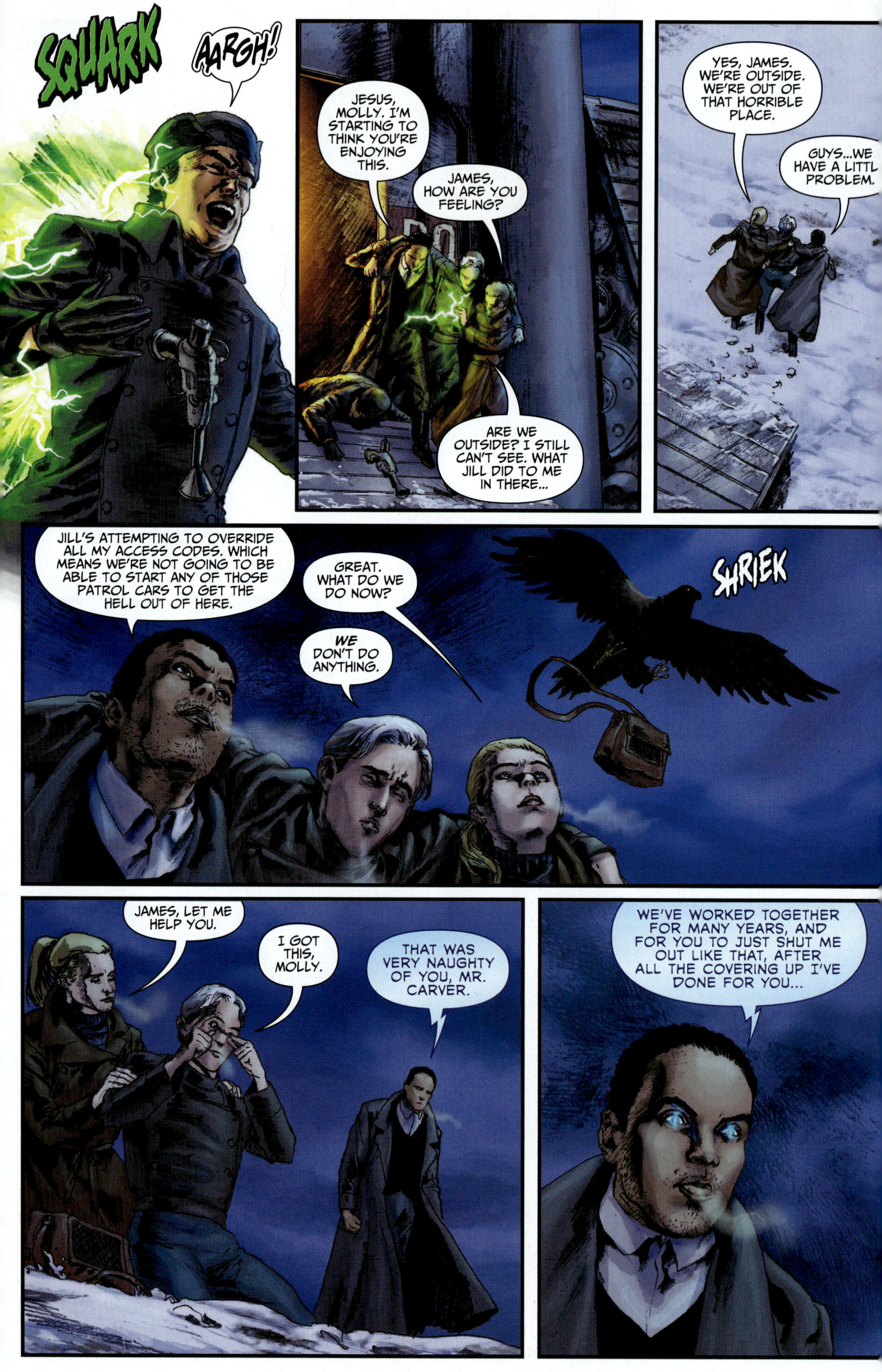
SQUARK
AARGH!
JESUS, MOLLY. I'M STARTING TO THINK YOU'RE ENJOYING THIS.
JAMES, HOW ARE YOU FEELING?
ARE WE OUTSIDE? I STILL CAN'T SEE. WHAT JILL DID TO ME IN THERE...
YES, JAMES. WE'RE OUTSIDE. WE'RE OUT OF THAT HORRIBLE PLACE.
GUYS...WE HAVE A LITTL PROBLEM.
JILL'S ATTEMPTING TO OVERRIDE ALL MY ACCESS CODES. WHICH MEANS WE'RE NOT GOING TO BE ABLE TO START ANY OF THOSE PATROL CARS TO GET THE HELL OUT OF HERE.
GREAT. WHAT DO WE DO NOW?
WE DON'T DO ANYTHING.
SHRIEK
JAMES, LET ME HELP YOU.
I GOT THIS, MOLLY.
THAT WAS VERY NAUGHTY OF YOU, MR. CARVER.
WE'VE WORKED TOGETHER FOR MANY YEARS, AND FOR YOU TO JUST SHUT ME OUT LIKE THAT, AFTER ALL THE COVERING UP I'VE DONE FOR YOU...

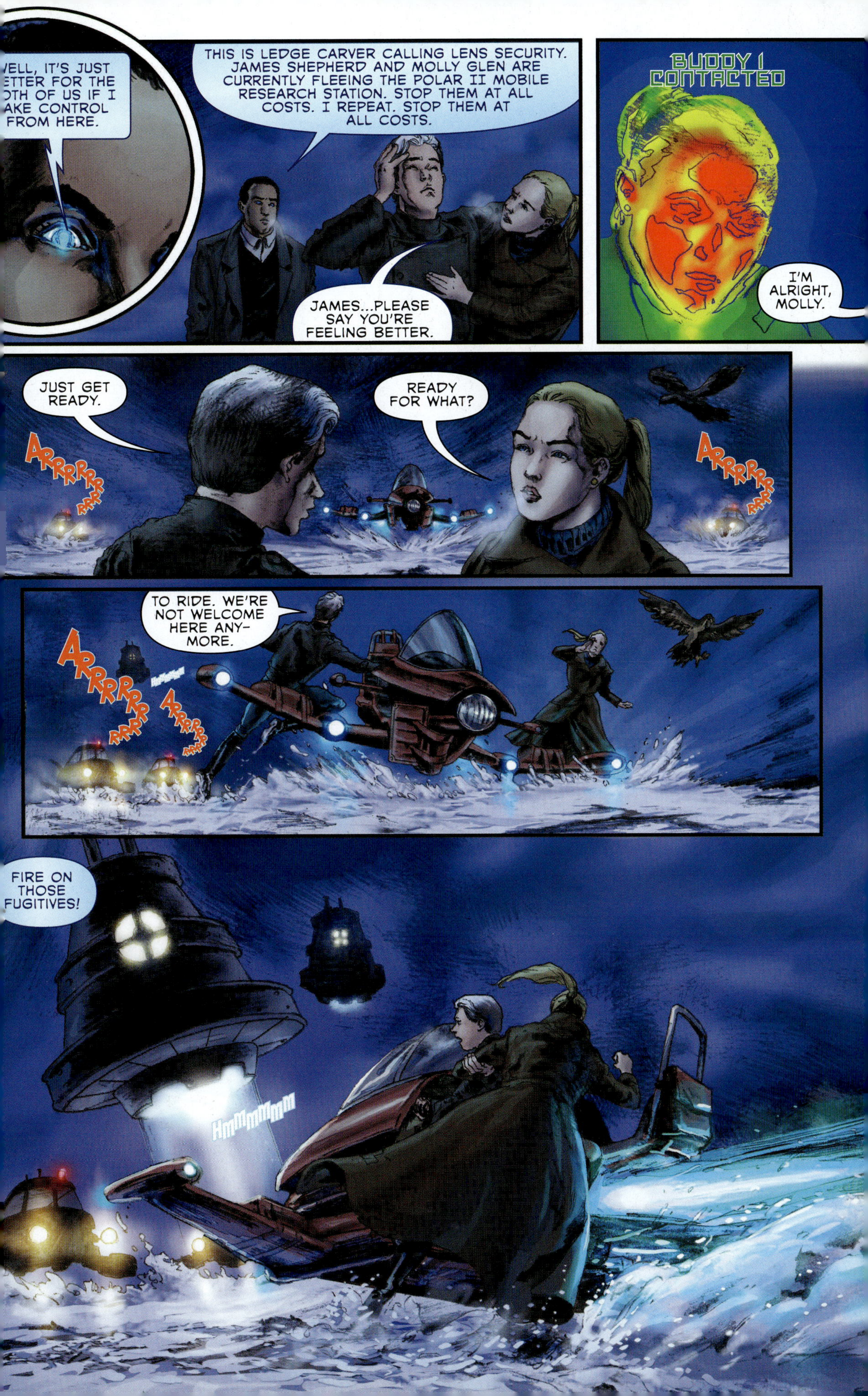
ELL, IT'S JUST ETTER FOR THE OTH OF US IF I AKE CONTROL FROM HERE.
THIS IS LEDGE CARVER CALLING LENS SECURITY. JAMES SHEPHERD AND MOLLY GLEN ARE CURRENTLY FLEEING THE POLAR II MOBILE RESEARCH STATION. STOP THEM AT ALL COSTS. I REPEAT. STOP THEM AT ALL COSTS.
JAMES...PLEASE SAY YOU'RE FEELING BETTER.
BUDDY I CONTACTED
I'M ALRIGHT, MOLLY.
JUST GET READY.
READY FOR WHAT?
ARRRRRRRRR
ARRRRRRRRR
TO RIDE. WE'RE NOT WELCOME HERE ANY-MORE.
ARRRRRRRRR
ARRRRRRRR
FIRE ON THOSE FUGITIVES!
HMMMMMM

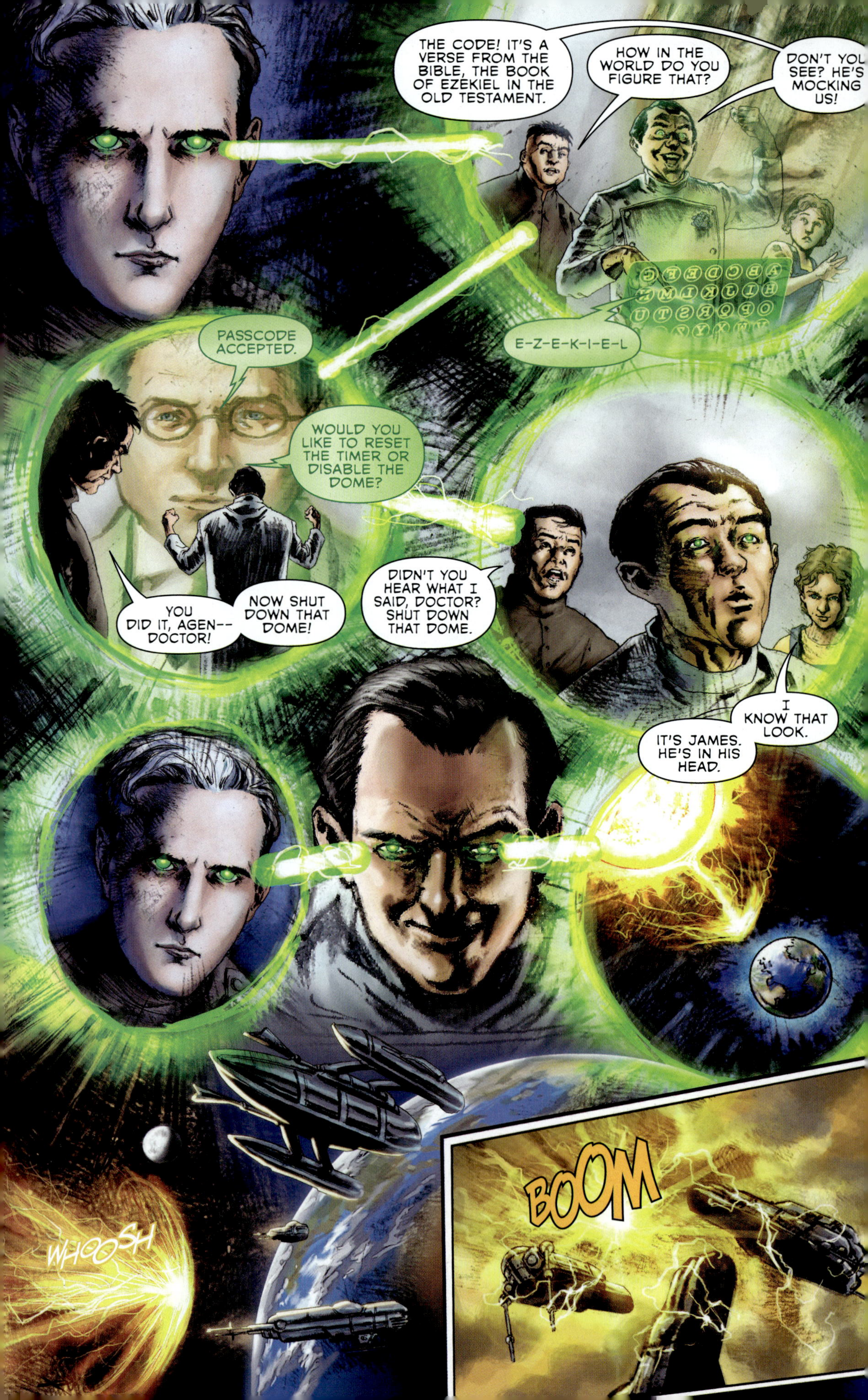

THE CODE! IT'S A VERSE FROM THE BIBLE, THE BOOK OF EZEKIEL IN THE OLD TESTAMENT.
HOW IN THE WORLD DO YOU FIGURE THAT?
DON'T YOU SEE? HE'S MOCKING US!
E-Z-E-K-I-E-L
PASSCODE ACCEPTED.
WOULD YOU LIKE TO RESET THE TIMER OR DISABLE THE DOME?
YOU DID IT, AGEN-- DOCTOR!
NOW SHUT DOWN THAT DOME!
DIDN'T YOU HEAR WHAT I SAID, DOCTOR? SHUT DOWN THAT DOME.
I KNOW THAT LOOK.
IT'S JAMES. HE'S IN HIS HEAD.
WHOOSH
BOOM

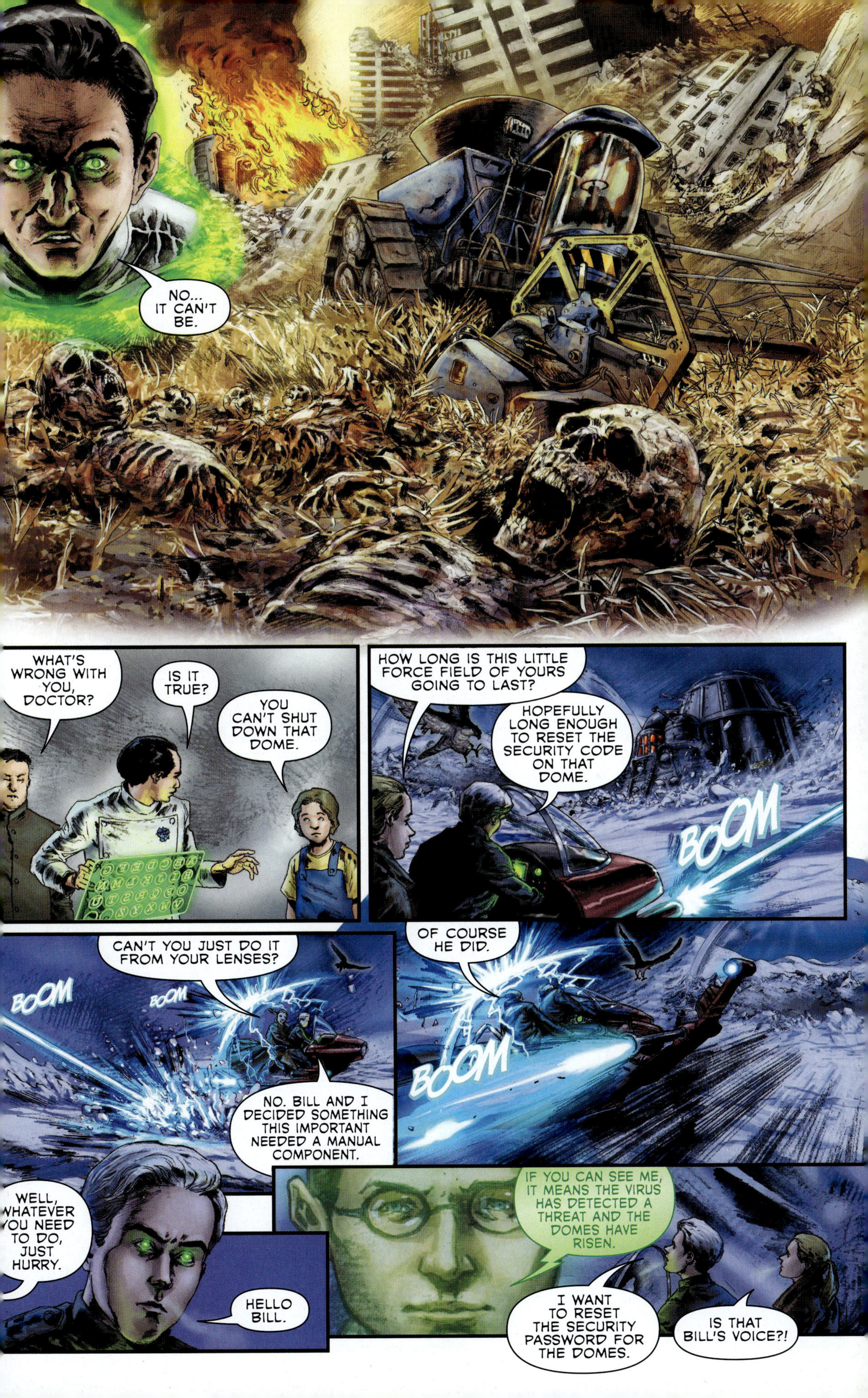
NO... IT CAN'T BE.
WHAT'S WRONG WITH YOU, DOCTOR?
IS IT TRUE?
YOU CAN'T SHUT DOWN THAT DOME.
HOW LONG IS THIS LITTLE FORCE FIELD OF YOURS GOING TO LAST?
HOPEFULLY LONG ENOUGH TO RESET THE SECURITY CODE ON THAT DOME.
BOOM
BOOM
BOOM
CAN'T YOU JUST DO IT FROM YOUR LENSES?
NO. BILL AND I DECIDED SOMETHING THIS IMPORTANT NEEDED A MANUAL COMPONENT.
OF COURSE HE DID.
BOOM
WELL, WHATEVER YOU NEED TO DO, JUST HURRY.
HELLO BILL.
IF YOU CAN SEE ME, IT MEANS THE VIRUS HAS DETECTED A THREAT AND THE DOMES HAVE RISEN.
I WANT TO RESET THE SECURITY PASSWORD FOR THE DOMES.
IS THAT BILL'S VOICE?!

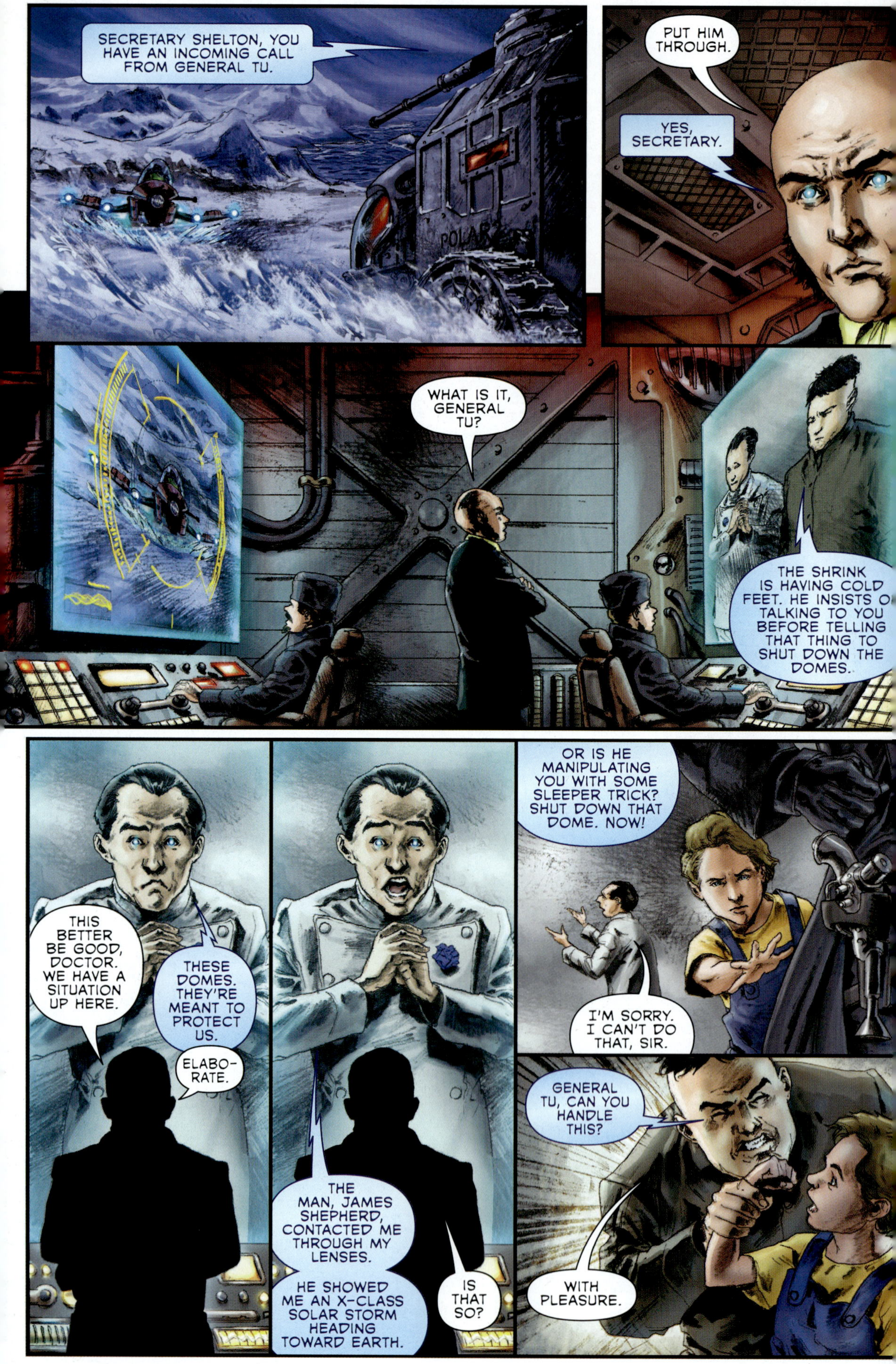
SECRETARY SHELTON, YOU HAVE AN INCOMING CALL FROM GENERAL TU.
POLAR
PUT HIM THROUGH.
YES, SECRETARY.
WHAT IS IT, GENERAL TU?
THE SHRINK IS HAVING COLD FEET. HE INSISTS O TALKING TO YOU BEFORE TELLING THAT THING TO SHUT DOWN THE DOMES.
THIS BETTER BE GOOD, DOCTOR. WE HAVE A SITUATION UP HERE.
THESE DOMES. THEY'RE MEANT TO PROTECT US.
ELABO-RATE.
THE MAN, JAMES SHEPHERD, CONTACTED ME THROUGH MY LENSES.
HE SHOWED ME AN X-CLASS SOLAR STORM HEADING TOWARD EARTH.
IS THAT SO?
OR IS HE MANIPULATING YOU WITH SOME SLEEPER TRICK? SHUT DOWN THAT DOME. NOW!
I'M SORRY. I CAN'T DO THAT, SIR.
GENERAL TU, CAN YOU HANDLE THIS?
WITH PLEASURE.

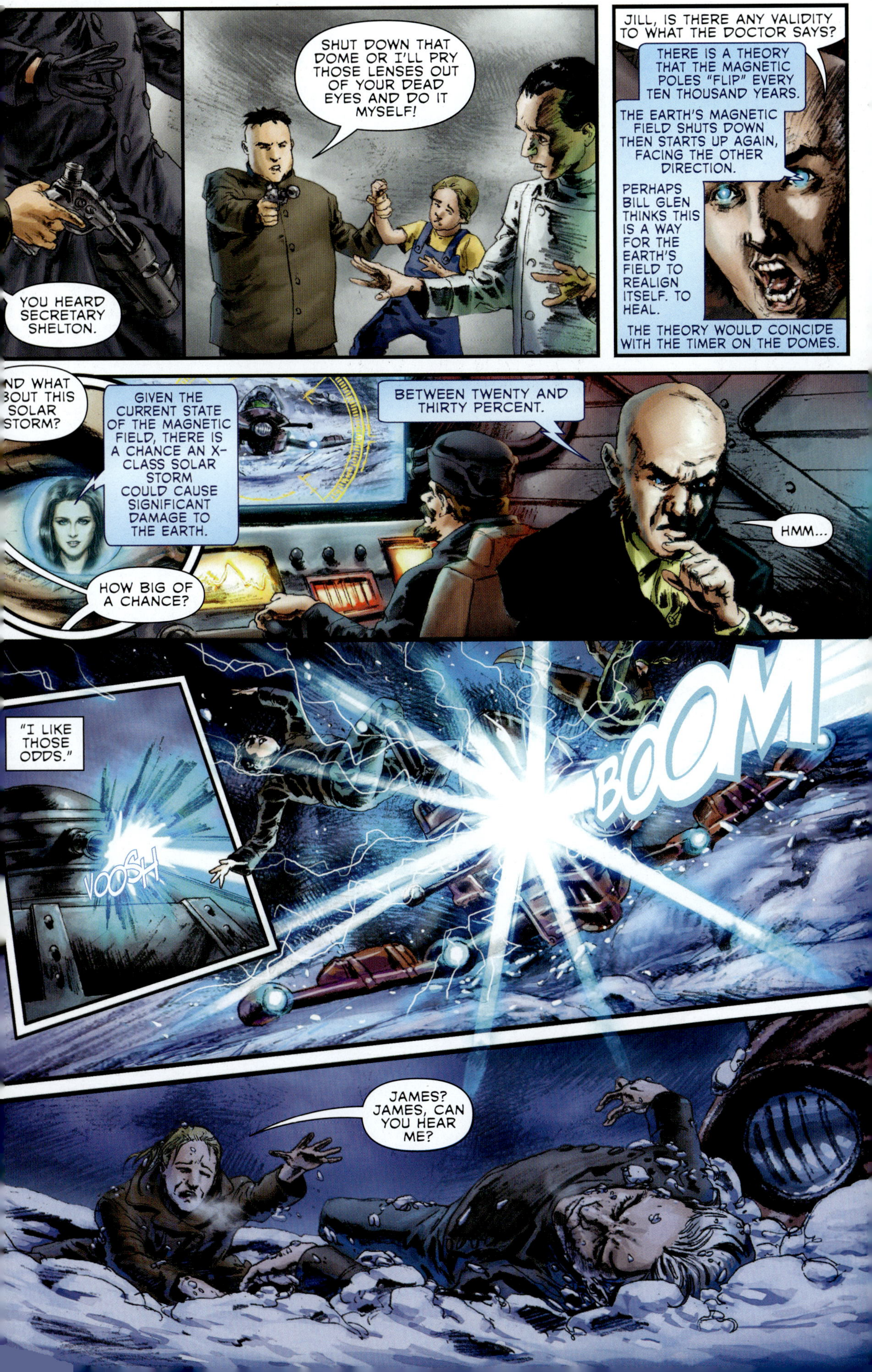
YOU HEARD SECRETARY SHELTON.
SHUT DOWN THAT DOME OR I'LL PRY THOSE LENSES OUT OF YOUR DEAD EYES AND DO IT MYSELF!
JILL, IS THERE ANY VALIDITY TO WHAT THE DOCTOR SAYS?
THERE IS A THEORY THAT THE MAGNETIC POLES "FLIP" EVERY TEN THOUSAND YEARS.
THE EARTH'S MAGNETIC FIELD SHUTS DOWN THEN STARTS UP AGAIN, FACING THE OTHER DIRECTION.
PERHAPS BILL GLEN THINKS THIS IS A WAY FOR THE EARTH'S FIELD TO REALIGN ITSELF. TO HEAL.
THE THEORY WOULD COINCIDE WITH THE TIMER ON THE DOMES.
ND WHAT BOUT THIS SOLAR STORM?
GIVEN THE CURRENT STATE OF THE MAGNETIC FIELD, THERE IS A CHANCE AN X-CLASS SOLAR STORM COULD CAUSE SIGNIFICANT DAMAGE TO THE EARTH.
HOW BIG OF A CHANCE?
BETWEEN TWENTY AND THIRTY PERCENT.
HMM...
"I LIKE THOSE ODDS."
VOOSH
BOOM
JAMES? JAMES, CAN YOU HEAR ME?

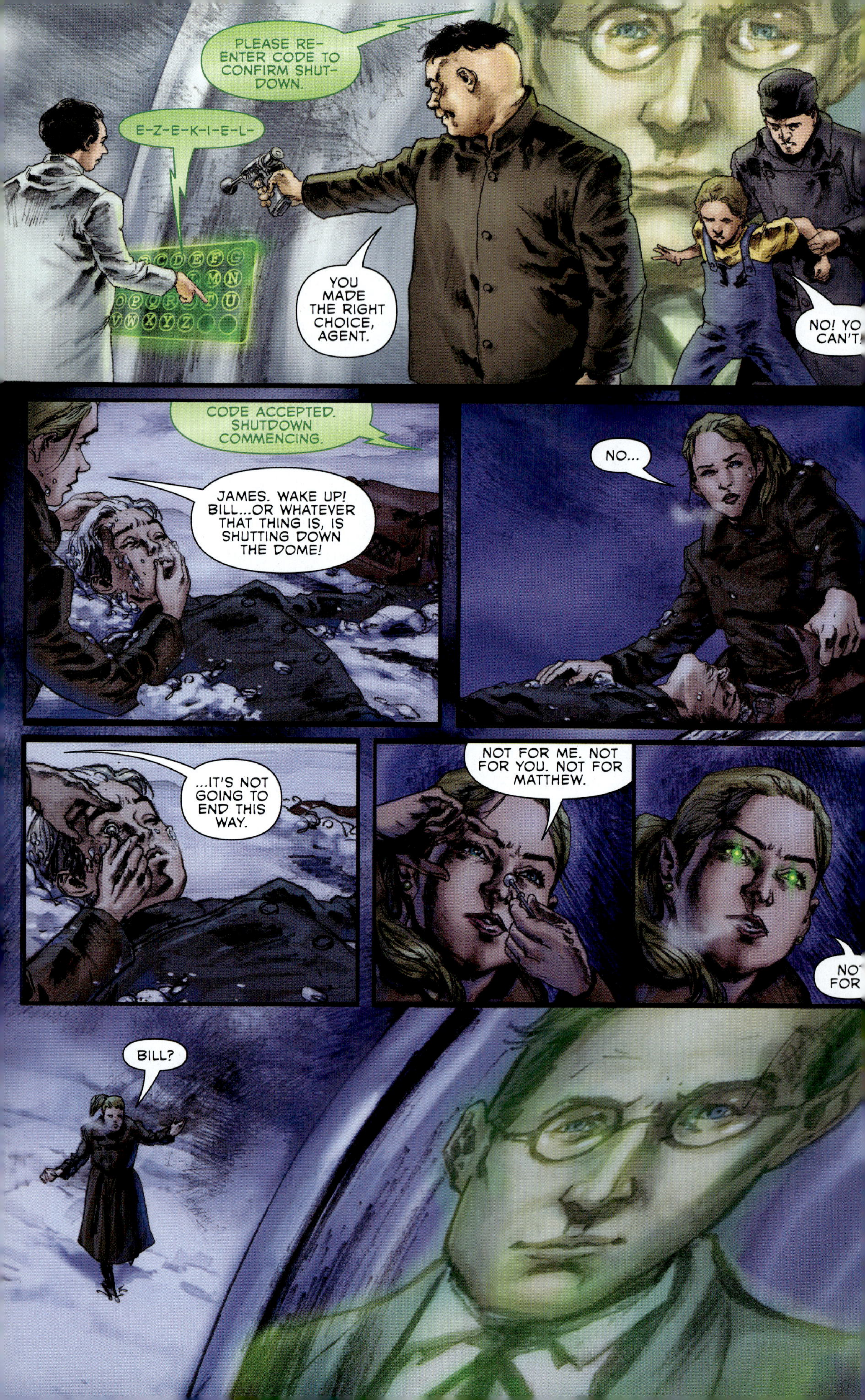
PLEASE RE-ENTER CODE TO CONFIRM SHUT-DOWN.
E-Z-E-K-I-E-L-
YOU MADE THE RIGHT CHOICE, AGENT.
NO! YO CAN'T
CODE ACCEPTED. SHUTDOWN COMMENCING.
JAMES. WAKE UP! BILL...OR WHATEVER THAT THING IS, IS SHUTTING DOWN THE DOME!
NO...
...IT'S NOT GOING TO END THIS WAY.
NOT FOR ME. NOT FOR YOU. NOT FOR MATTHEW.
NO FOR
BILL?

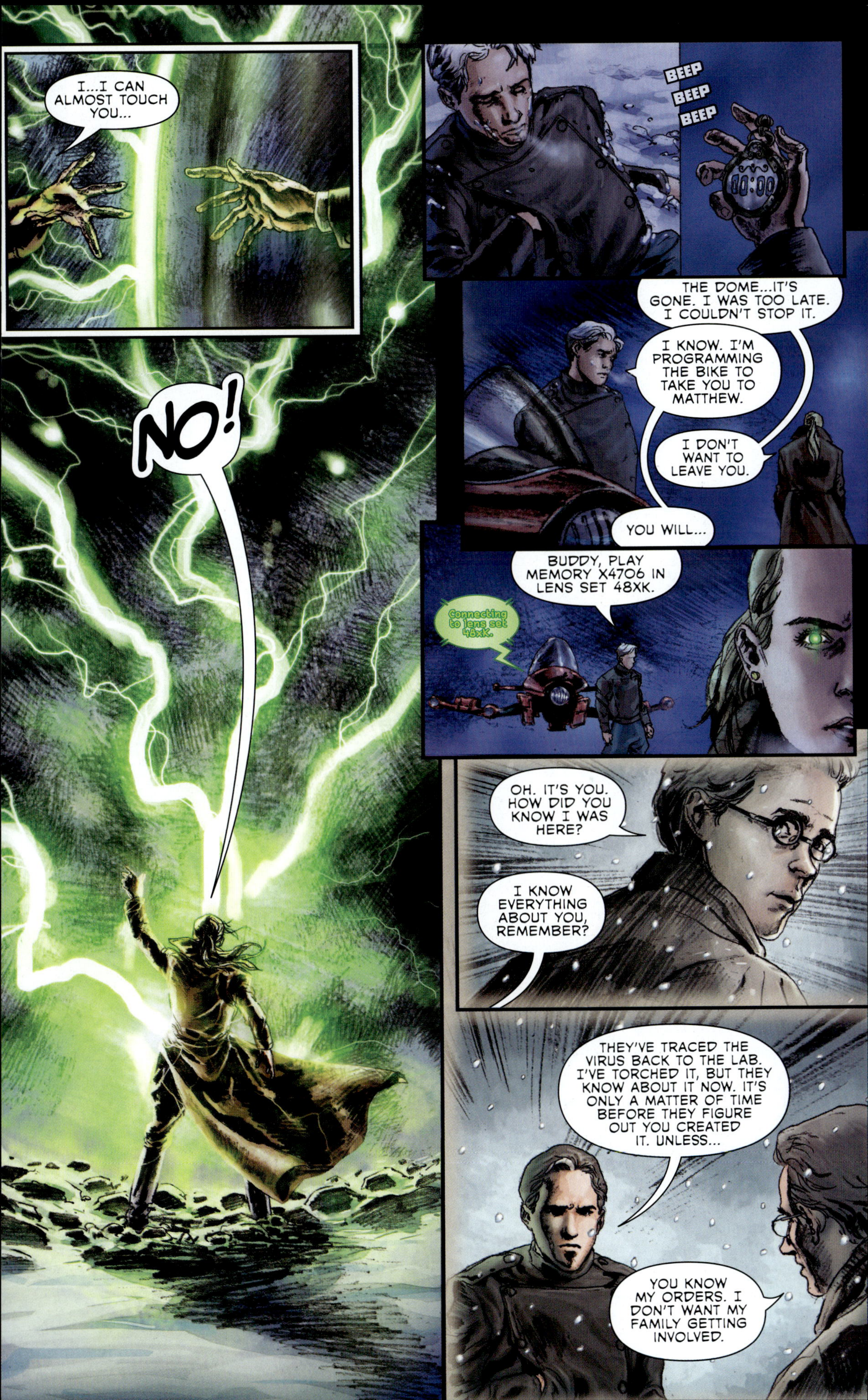
I...I CAN ALMOST TOUCH YOU...
NO!
BEEP
BEEP
BEEP
00:00
THE DOME...IT'S GONE. I WAS TOO LATE. I COULDN'T STOP IT.
I KNOW. I'M PROGRAMMING THE BIKE TO TAKE YOU TO MATTHEW.
I DON'T WANT TO LEAVE YOU.
YOU WILL...
BUDDY, PLAY MEMORY X4706 IN LENS SET 48XK.
Connecting to lens set 48xK.
OH. IT'S YOU. HOW DID YOU KNOW I WAS HERE?
I KNOW EVERYTHING ABOUT YOU, REMEMBER?
THEY'VE TRACED THE VIRUS BACK TO THE LAB. I'VE TORCHED IT, BUT THEY KNOW ABOUT IT NOW. IT'S ONLY A MATTER OF TIME BEFORE THEY FIGURE OUT YOU CREATED IT. UNLESS...
YOU KNOW MY ORDERS. I DON'T WANT MY FAMILY GETTING INVOLVED.

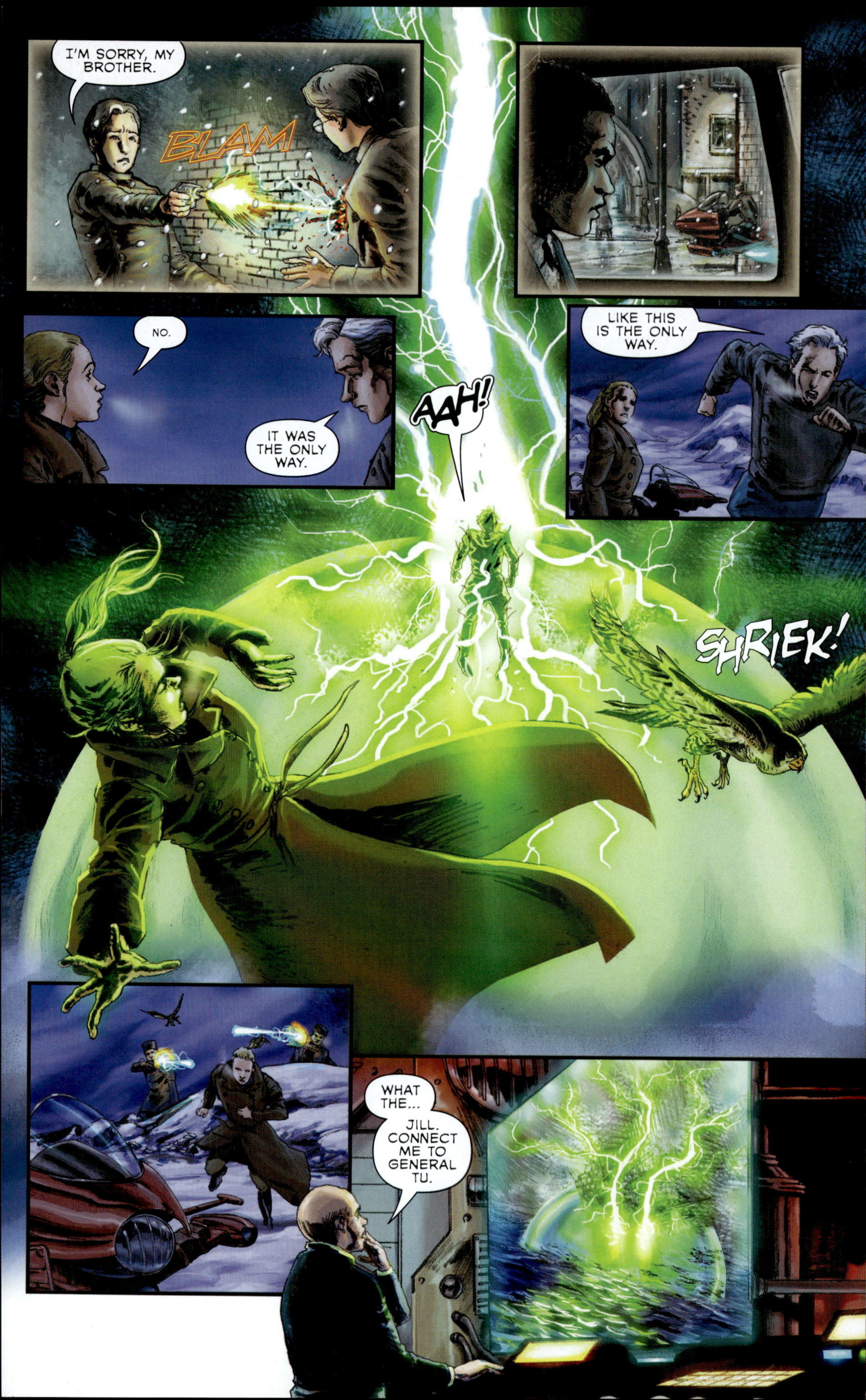
I'M SORRY, MY BROTHER.
BLAM
NO.
IT WAS THE ONLY WAY.
LIKE THIS IS THE ONLY WAY.
AAH!
SHRIEK!
WHAT THE...
JILL. CONNECT ME TO GENERAL TU.

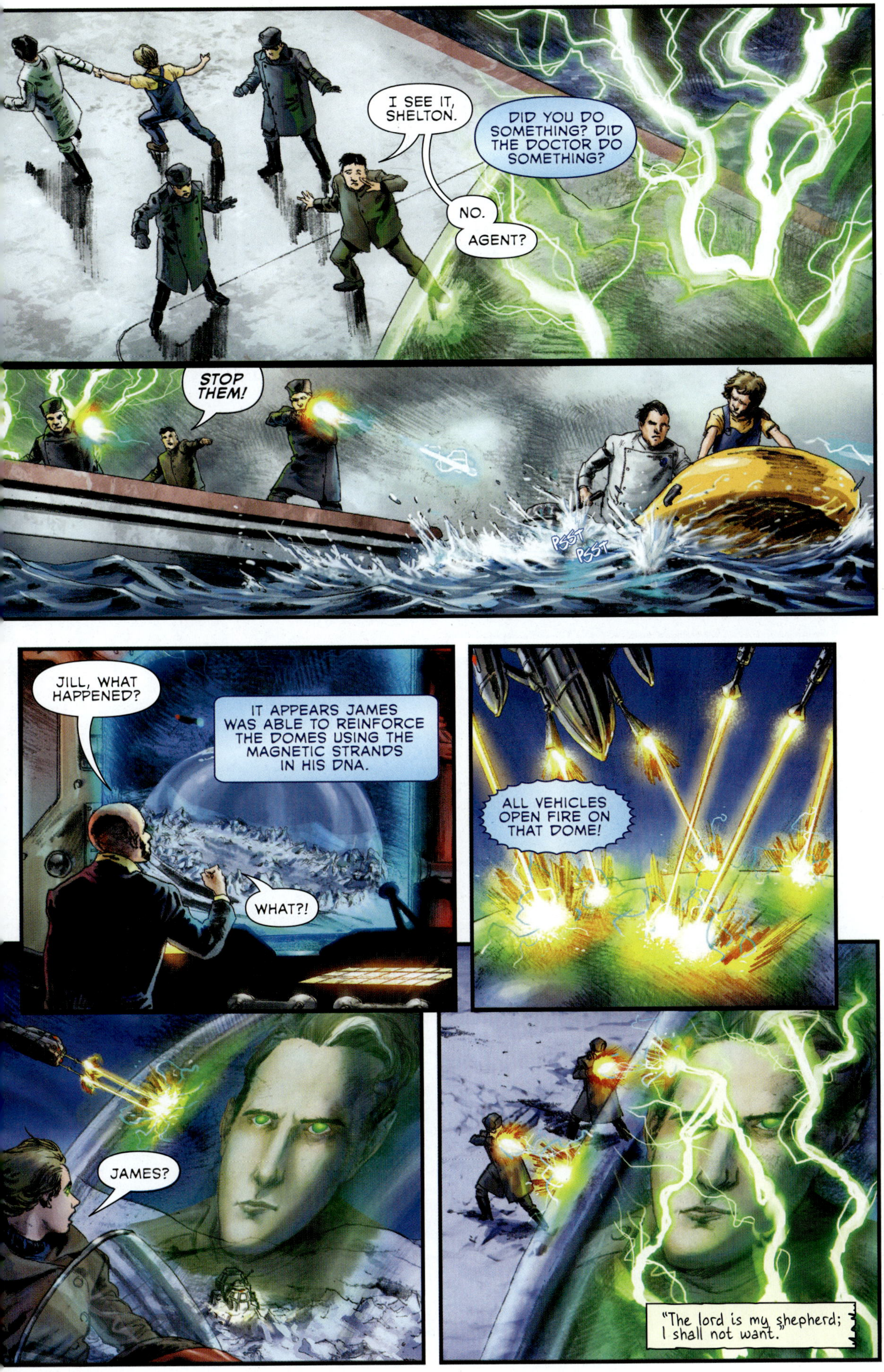
I SEE IT, SHELTON.
DID YOU DO SOMETHING? DID THE DOCTOR DO SOMETHING?
NO.
AGENT?
STOP THEM!
PSST PSST
JILL, WHAT HAPPENED?
IT APPEARS JAMES WAS ABLE TO REINFORCE THE DOMES USING THE MAGNETIC STRANDS IN HIS DNA.
WHAT?!
ALL VEHICLES OPEN FIRE ON THAT DOME!
JAMES?
"The lord is my shepherd; I shall not want."

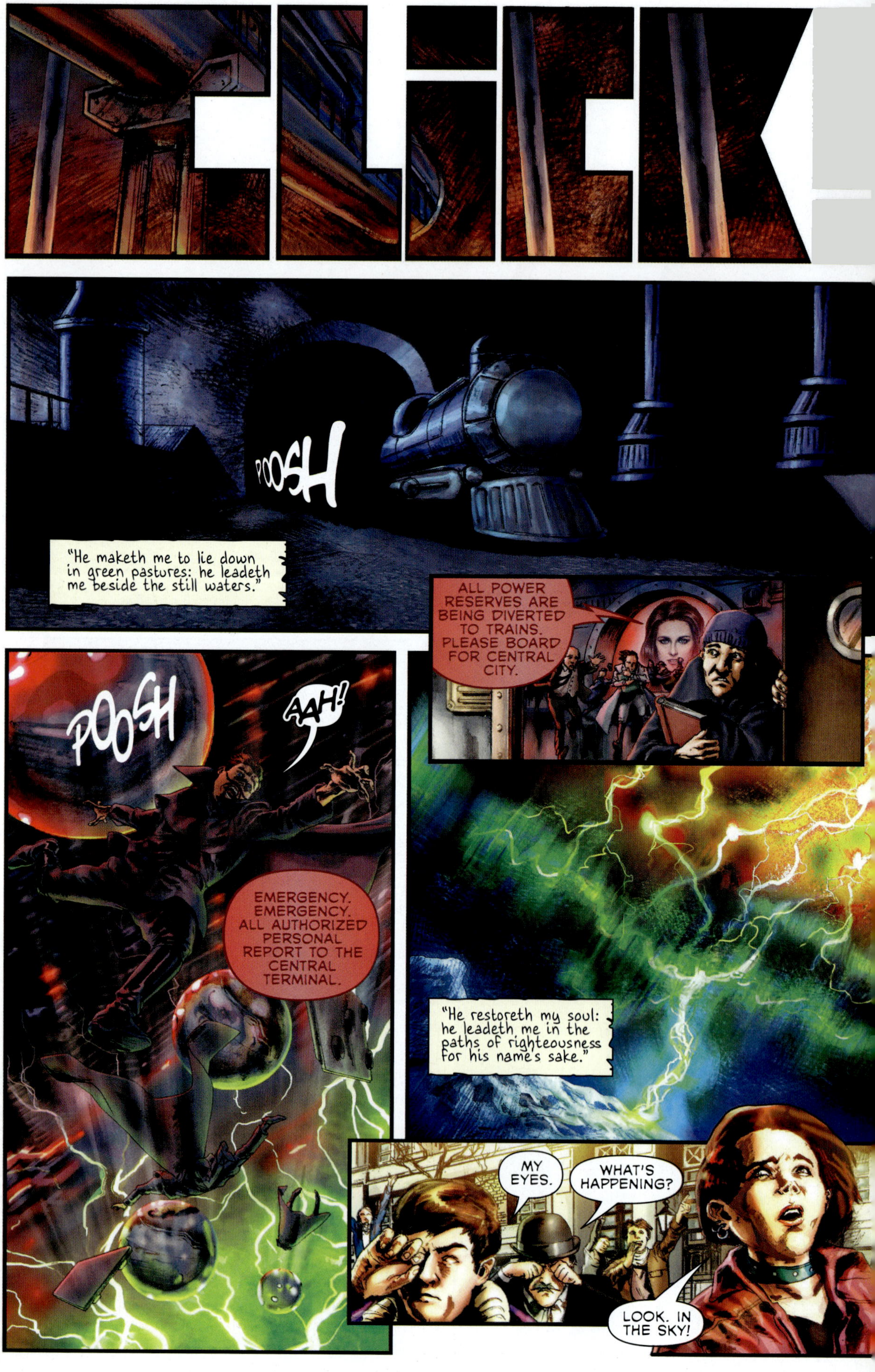
CLICK
POOSH
"He maketh me to lie down in green pastures: he leadeth me beside the still waters."
ALL POWER RESERVES ARE BEING DIVERTED TO TRAINS. PLEASE BOARD FOR CENTRAL CITY.
POOSH
AAH!
EMERGENCY. EMERGENCY. ALL AUTHORIZED PERSONAL REPORT TO THE CENTRAL TERMINAL.
"He restoreth my soul: he leadeth me in the paths of righteousness for his name's sake."
MY EYES.
WHAT'S HAPPENING?
LOOK. IN THE SKY!

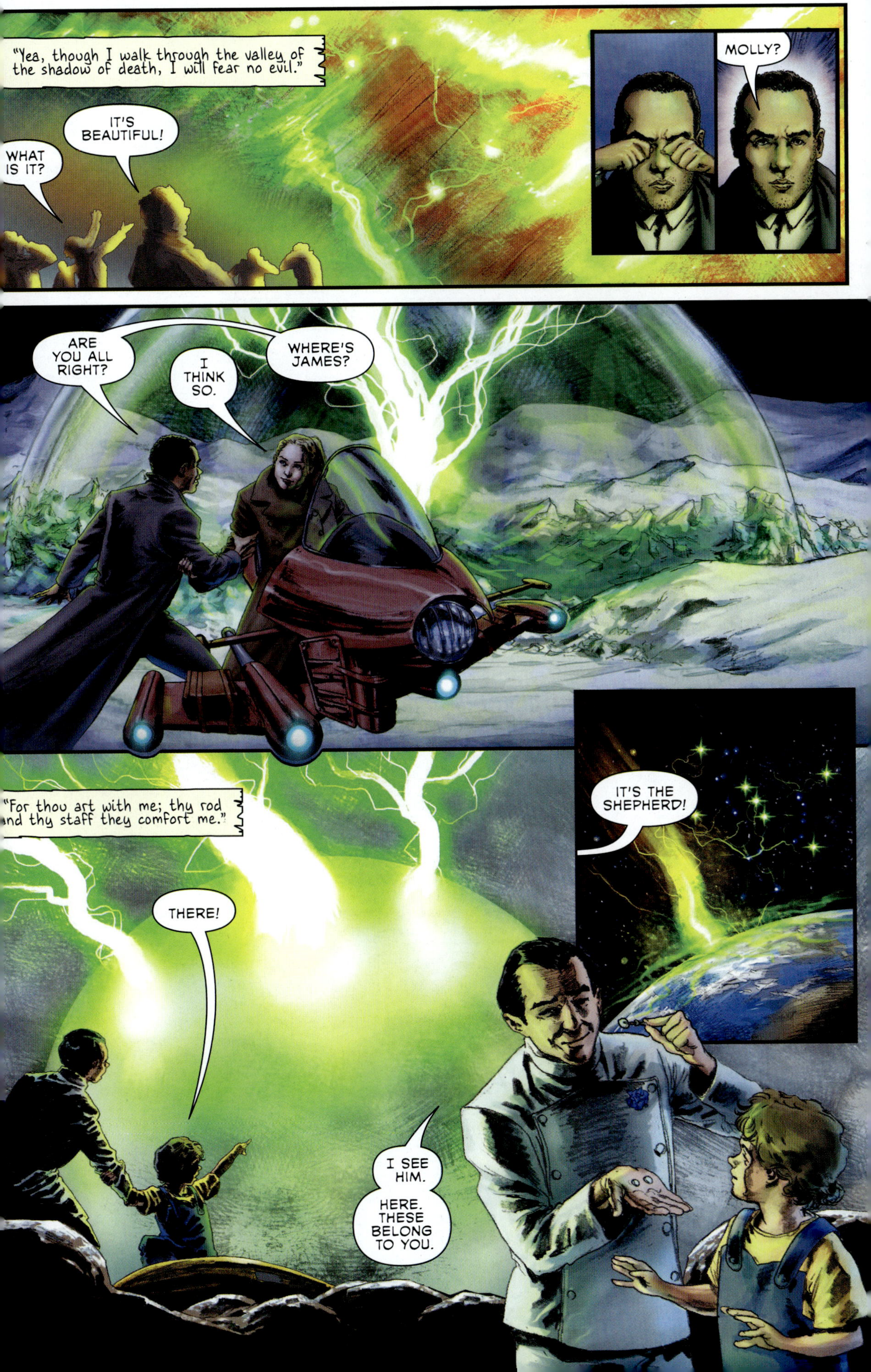
"Yea, though I walk through the valley of the shadow of death, I will fear no evil."
IT'S BEAUTIFUL!
WHAT IS IT?
MOLLY?
ARE YOU ALL RIGHT?
WHERE'S JAMES?
I THINK SO.
"For thou art with me; thy rod and thy staff they comfort me."
IT'S THE SHEPHERD!
THERE!
I SEE HIM.
HERE. THESE BELONG TO YOU.

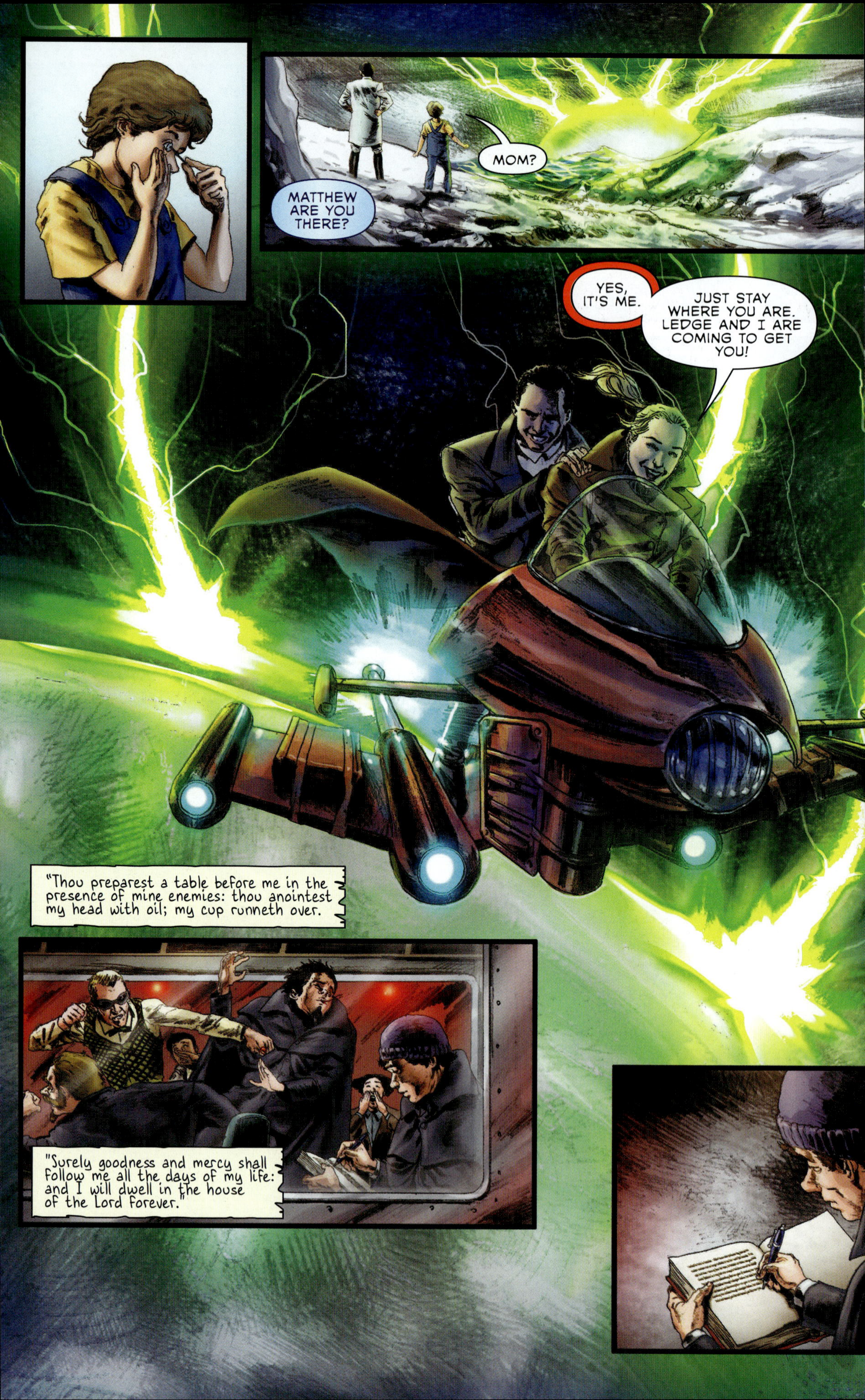
MOM?
MATTHEW ARE YOU THERE?
YES, IT'S ME.
JUST STAY WHERE YOU ARE. LEDGE AND I ARE COMING TO GET YOU!
"Thou preparest a table before me in the presence of mine enemies: thou anointest my head with oil; my cup runneth over.
"Surely goodness and mercy shall follow me all the days of my life: and I will dwell in the house of the Lord forever."

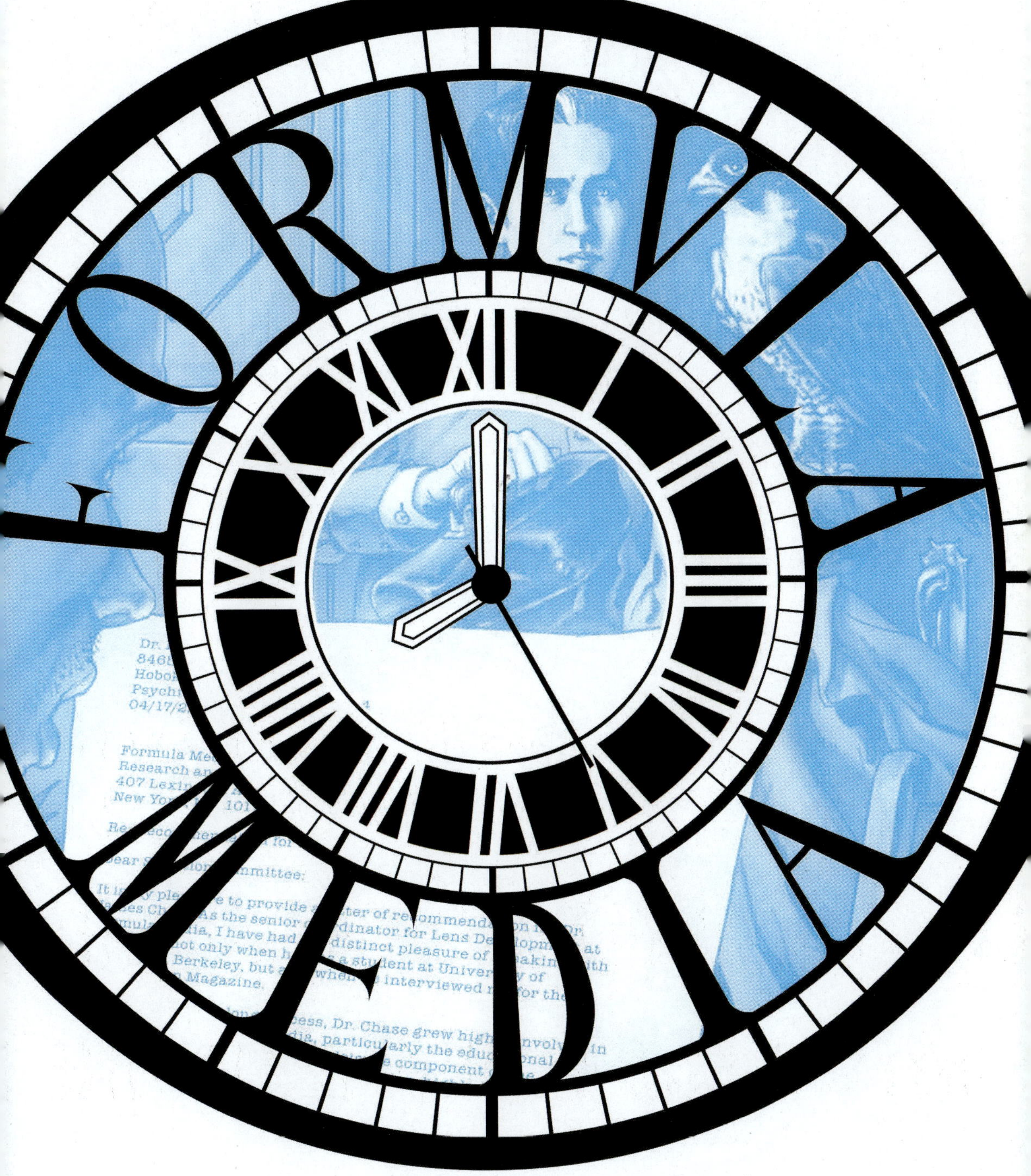
FORMULA
MEDIA

EPILOGUE 08

Originally publshed as a short story on www.drunkenboat.com.

ART BY | RONILSON FREIRE

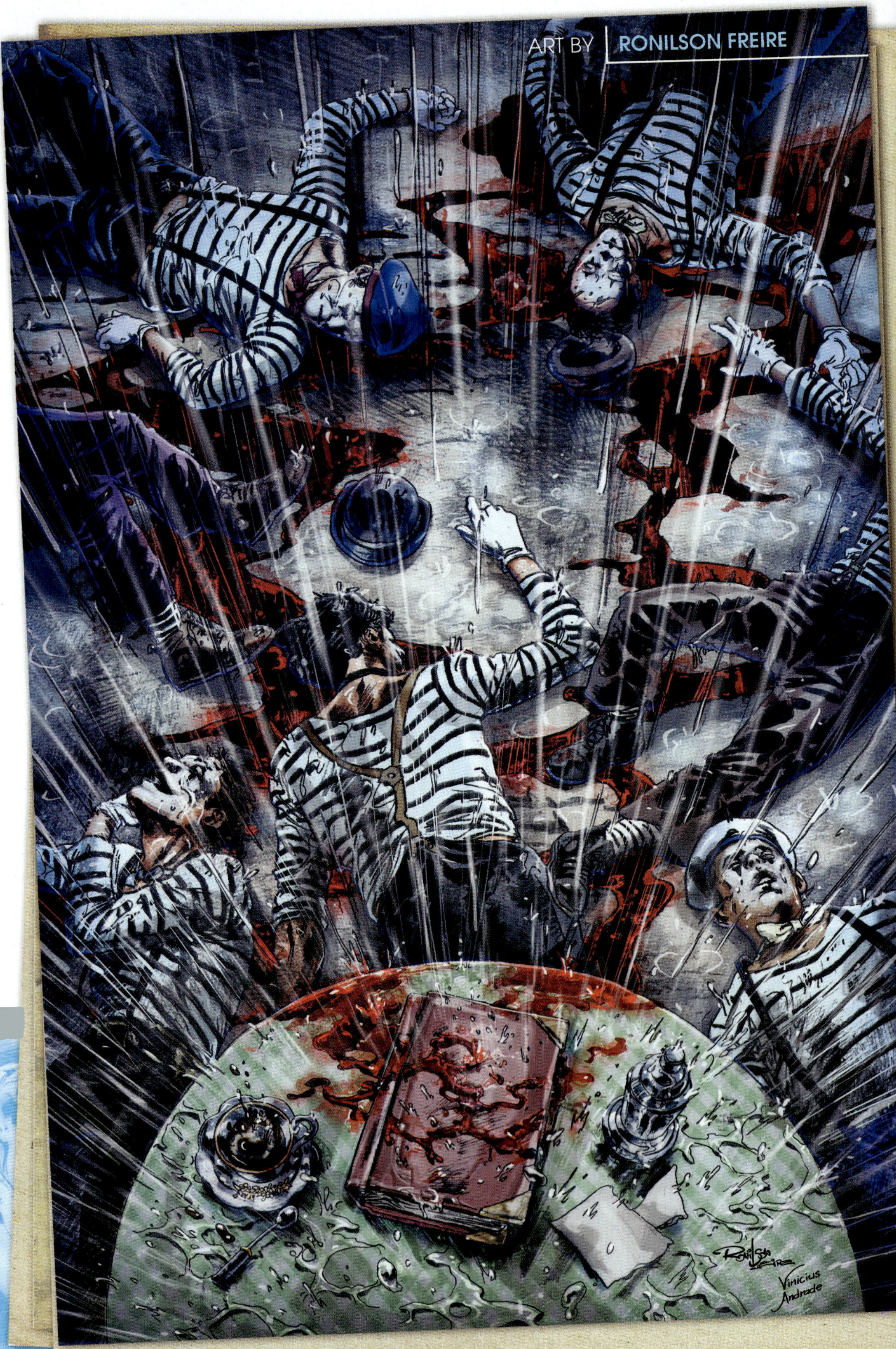

Ronilson Freire
Vinicius Andrade

UNTANGLING FROM THE LENSES:
A CONCLUSION TO A PHILOSOPHY THESIS

One night, after a particularly grueling shift, Patrick showed me the lens tool he carried around his neck in a purple velvet pouch. He had taken it from his father, a surgeon in London, before the power grid collapsed, and it allowed him to take off his lenses whenever he wanted. I too had a similar tool that I swiped from re-lensing during the blackout in Central Lens, but all it did was disable the Formula Media Assistants long enough that I was able to navigate the continent without being told where I could and couldn't go. Patrick and I talked about this, our unique lives on the other side of the lenses, usually until dawn spread over the Mediterranean, sunny-side up. Then one day he confided that he knew of a town in Greece where the water was just as beautiful as Argeles and people walked around lens free. Renegades? I thought.

"Don't worry," he replied as if he were reading my mind. "There isn't any danger in Nafplio."

I didn't go to work that night. Patrick paid a fisherman a large sum of money to rent a boat, and by morning we were coming into the harbor of Nafplio. The sun rose over a maze of pastel-colored houses under the protection of Palamidi, an ancient castle looming atop on one of the mountains that surrounds the city. Patrick knew a lot about the history of the castle, as well as the woman who rented us a room in a small hotel that had a view of Bourtzi, the fortress just offshore, in the center of the harbor. We fell asleep under its magnificence. It was a long and tiring journey, and when I woke, Patrick was gone. I didn't immediately panic. The Hydrofoils jumping around Bourtzi transfixed me.(8) Their silver bodies glinted under the sunlight, and when I finally came down into the mezzanine, the woman who ran the hotel told me that Patrick had paid for two weeks stay and said that I should enjoy the town until his return. I reflected on this as I walked through the narrow streets of Nafplio, how despite being free of the C.L.N., the woman who ran the hotel--as well as almost everyone I met in town--still did not look me directly in the eyes when speaking.

"Sleepers," Patrick clarified when he returned several days later. He was filled with energy as he explained more about Nafplio, how he had stumbled upon the town during his travels, and how the woman who ran the hotel was also the town's oldest Sleeper. The last time he had visited she had started teaching Patrick the art of fortune-telling. He was a natural at the craft, he said she said; in fact, it was during one of their tarot lessons he saw me and left for Argeles. He said the cards had told him that my research was part of a larger purpose and gave him a "plan" that would help complete my work. When I asked him what the plan was, he explained that's where he had been for the past several days, getting the word out about two young men in

Nafplio who could read futures. His hope was that once people were able to think without the assistance of the Central Lens Network, it would push them to break free from the remainder of its hold. The idea of finally untangling from the lenses filled me with excitement, but it was tempered by my skepticism of such supposed gifts that the Sleeper woman and Patrick claimed they had. I was alone in this skepticism, it turned out. The following day we woke to a line of people in the mezzanine wanting to know answers that could no longer be found in the Formula Media Lens, and Patrick was more than happy to oblige.

    Love, success, death--Patrick answered the concerns of our patrons the way most fortune-tellers did. On a positive note: very rich, very long, and very much in love; meanwhile, I noted the duration in which they paused after Patrick gave them their answers. I then correlated these durations with the topics that were discussed, and noted which human emotions were more commonly handled with or without the guidance of a Formula Media Assistant. Patrick seemed to love the show more than the research. When it was time to read someone's fortune, he'd step through the wall of beads hanging behind the front desk and walk solemnly up to the table, wearing the most ridiculous bandana around his head. After he dealt the usual seven-card spread, he would let his fingers hover over it. His expression that followed was based on whichever suit was prominent. An airy look of optimism accompanied the suit of cups; frowns were for too many swords; and the rubbing of fingers came with a majority of pentacles.

    "The real challenge..." he explained one night on the balcony, while I expanded upon the day's observations in my journal "...are the arcana cards. They don't have a uniform meaning like the suit cards, so you have to remember what each card means, then connect that meaning to all the other cards and roll it all up into one expression." He swore he saw things inside their lenses. Assistants, agents, government officials, all in a panic, and he used this to persuade the fortune seekers to let him remove their lenses with the lens tool he took from his father. Many said no, but as the lenses became more unreliable, the glass jar he kept of discarded lenses began to fill. I looked at it every day, and when it had finally reached the top, I took the final step in my liberation, and asked Patrick to take off my lenses as well.

    To see real eyes, no longer outlined in the blue dim of the Formula Media Lens, was more breathtaking than the parrotfish that circled in the harbor of Nafplio. A sense of certainty came over me, validating what I really thought about the fortune seekers after weeks of observation: it wasn't the failing lenses that pushed them to seek our help; they simply choose to be led rather than lead. I said this to Patrick one night after our last patron left, and it sent him into what seemed like an unjustified rage. He called me a judgmental intellect, then flicked the deck of tarot cards in his hands across the lobby and stormed out of the hotel. The Sleeper woman came to see what the commotion was. She looked at the cards then at me and shook her head sadly. "You still cannot see the future no matter how much it is shown to you. Very well…"

She produced a deck of tarot cards of her own and splayed them on the table: The Lovers, The Hanged Man, The II of Pentacles and the IX of Wands. She said The Lover's card suggested that a person I love would be influencing a future journey. The Hanged Man was asking me to rise above the way things have always been. The II of Pentacles told me that I needed to let go in order to prepare for new opportunities. The IX of Wands asked that I should fight for what I believe in, that my projects are near completion. I asked the Sleeper woman if the cards knew when Patrick was coming back, and she fished the purple pouch he wore around his neck from the cards that Patrick had strewn over the floor. She turned it upside down and when nothing slid out of the loose neck, I knew what he had done, what had happened to his parents. They had been taken, and he hoped by looking into the lenses of as many people as he could, that he might be able to find them.

I spent all night looking for him. The longer he had those lenses on, the more I feared something terrible would happen, that he might be caught. Or worse, reactivate something, somehow bring the C.L.N. back to its full force. I lingered in all our favorite spots before deciding it was best to wait for him back at the hotel. When I arrived, the Sleeper woman had my bags packed. She said there wasn't much time, that she had a vision and I needed to go to Paris and find a way to publish my "amazing story" about the man who had rescued me from Central Lens. I wondered if Patrick told her about the man, then recalled I had made a point to keep him a secret, even from Patrick, in fear he might search for the man himself. I suddenly believed in the Sleeper's powers, but before I could ask any more questions, she told me to leave from the back door, and while crossing to the opposite block, I saw several men in black suits walking up to the hotel. I could see her eyes not meeting theirs, and into the night, as I traveled into the dense woods of Solovia, I wondered about the agents, if the government was already trying to restart the network and reestablish their hold. (9)

"I sometimes imagine that others deceive themselves in the things which they think they know best, how do I know that I am not deceived every time that I add two and three, or count the sides of a square, or judge of things yet simpler, if anything simpler can be imagined?" (10)

Descartes understood that once "one" gave up the practice of methodical doubt, truth would be lost. In a moment of weakness--no doubt from the guilt of implicating his parents in a C.L.N. investigation by using his father's medical tool to remove his lenses--Patrick had fallen victim to his own belief that he could somehow rectify what he had done by reattaching his lenses. I spent many nights criticizing myself for not recognizing the depth of his guilt. For not pressing him more about the pouch around his neck. In turn my own guilt grew, crowding out the Sleeper woman's vision about my research, until my only motivation of going to Paris was to escape the countryside which reminded me of Patrick and our short life together.

It worked. Paris was nothing like the boarded up wasteland I remembered before the collapse of the network. The theaters and museums were open; the streets filled with tourists; people laid down in parks and enjoyed each other's company while basking in the sun. At first this gush of humanity appeared to be the doorway into the human psyche I needed to conclude this thesis, but just like in London (where I had finally resurfaced from the core) these human aspects never played out to their rightful ends. Any feeling or thought considered too controversial summoned a Formula Media Assistant, and though the assistants had become a flickering shadow of what they once were--their icons stalled, their search results incomplete--nobody knew what to do about it. During these awkward moments, when the individuals appeared to be speaking to themselves or staring off into space, trying to make sense of what had happened to the world they once knew, I began to wonder if the Central Lens Network might recover, or if, over time, the technology would fail completely, and the general population would finally take off their lenses for good.

The answer to this question came partially to me one day while I was strolling along the Canal Saint-Martin. At least a dozen mimes were being arrested and nobody even looked up from their fancy coffees to notice. Not far from the incident was the baker who had previously let me sleep in the doorway of his shop, back when I was living in Paris, posing as a mime myself. He told me that not long after I left for New York, a crackdown had occurred on street performers. Hundreds of mimes were killed. I had heard rumors of The Great Mime Massacre of Paris while wondering the streets of Nafplio, but I never dreamed that my capture in New York (and the subsequent scanning of my memories in Central Lens) may have been the catalyst for it. Whatever joy I felt seeing Paris return to a semi-normal state was gone. I began to think of the Sleeper woman's warning, but mostly about Patrick. I wondered if he was in the woods of Solovia, or if he had come to his senses and returned to Nafplio to take out his lenses. I decided to follow the patrol cars; they didn't drive far, just up to the Metro station, at Chatelet Les Halles, where I had first arrived in Paris by accident all those months ago.

The agents marched the mimes down the grand steps at gunpoint. Inside, a government train awaited them, though it was much different than the one I remembered. Where before each window was vibrant with the face of a Formula Media Assistant, all of them working together to scan the traveling tubes for its metallic integrity, now there was just one assistant on the door, flickering like a flame gasping for air. She spoke the name of each prisoner as they boarded the train, and when Patrick's full name was called out, I opened my mouth to say something but fell silent at the sight of him.

He looked dirty and bruised, but the worst part was his eyes. A faint, blue glow. They strapped him into one of the seats, and when the train sped forward toward the core, I knew that he had planned this. He knew mimes were a target after hearing about my travels and understood that an arrest was the best way to Central Lens, where he hoped his parents might still be alive.

I became aware of more arrests after that. More civilians being marched into government trains at gunpoint. I wondered if there was a method in regaining order, or if this was a hysterical reaction to a dying bureaucratic system. There was the city underground. The one I passed on my journey to re-lensing. Maybe the government was regrouping there. Either way it confirmed the Sleeper woman's vision. France was getting too dangerous. I needed to head back to New York; there I knew people--professors, agents, scholars--who would help publish my work, and later that night, I jumped a failing turnstile and hopped on the next subway traveling under the Atlantic towards North America.

Perhaps these last-minute observations are the best way to conclude this thesis. The Sleeper woman had been right; our own unwillingness to see beyond the limitations of the human eye is what will doom us to repeat the past. Despite everything the C.L.N. wants to control, they still cannot stop a man without lenses from writing on paper. I offer this to you. A parchment. A reminder. A gift.

---

1. The Central Lens Network, commonly known as the C.L.N., is a data transfer network servicing the Formula Media Lens.

2. Cool Plastic is a superalloy plastic able to withstand thousands of degrees in temperature; however, it is lined with lodestone, magnetite and gadolinuim in order to help attract the train to the nickel and iron ore lined subway tubes.

3. Super Farms is the nickname for government-funded incubation areas where genetic breeding is performed.

4. Wolvertons are genetically engineered dogs meant to protect the perimeters of the Super Farms.

5. Columba Livia are what was once known as the common pigeon back in the early 20th century. They have a magnette between the eyes that converts magnetic waves and light into nerve impulses.

7. Contacts were used in the pre-lens era to correct vision. I had used contacts on a few occasions to confuse agents in Lexington Station who tried to get into my head about why I choose to be homeless.

8. Hydrofoils are flying dolphins that are not known to be products of genetic engineering or natural evolution.

9. Solovia is the unrecognized government of the Sleepers over a landmass that had once been considered Eastern Europe.

10. From Rene Descartes' essay "Knowledge Is Not Ultimately Sense Knowledge." Publisher illegible.

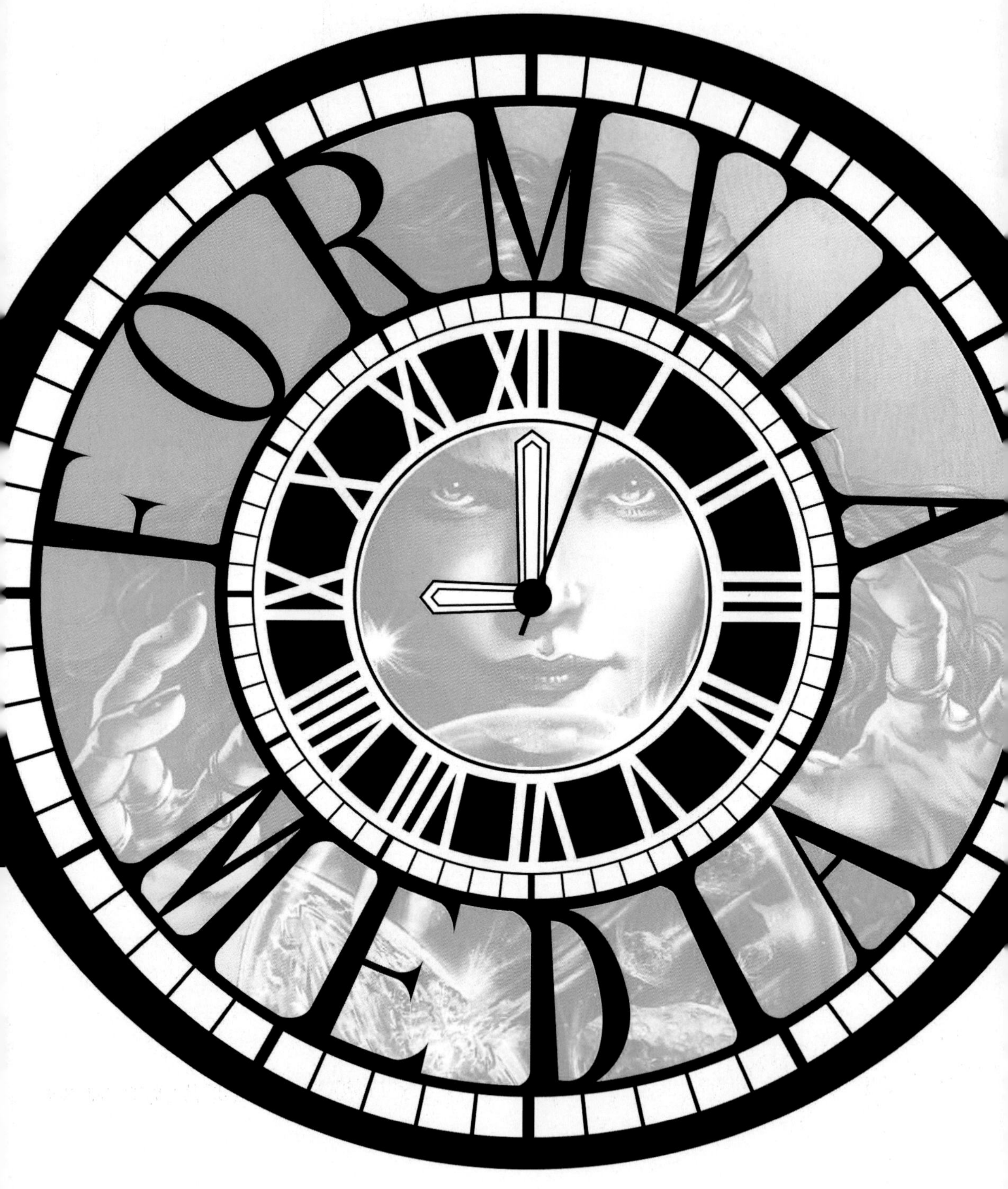

09 ARTIST ALLEY

SKETCHBOOK BY **PATRICK BERKENKOTTER**

Clamshell rear doors, back of car can accomodate up to 8 perps.

PATROL 1

All-black body with chrome front grill, head lights, window trim, rear bumpers, etc. Rood siren has a chrome frame.

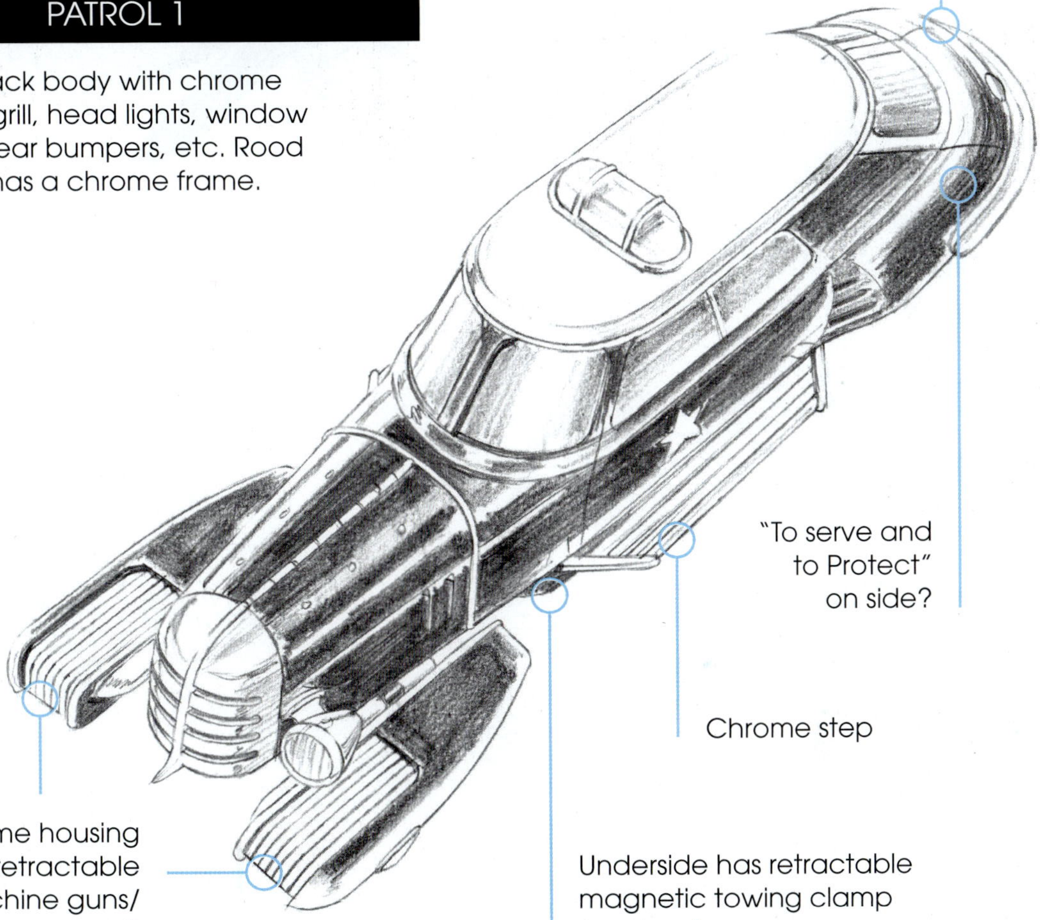

"To serve and to Protect" on side?

Chrome step

Chrome housing for retractable machine guns/ cannons?

Underside has retractable magnetic towing clamp (or claws)

POLAR BEAR

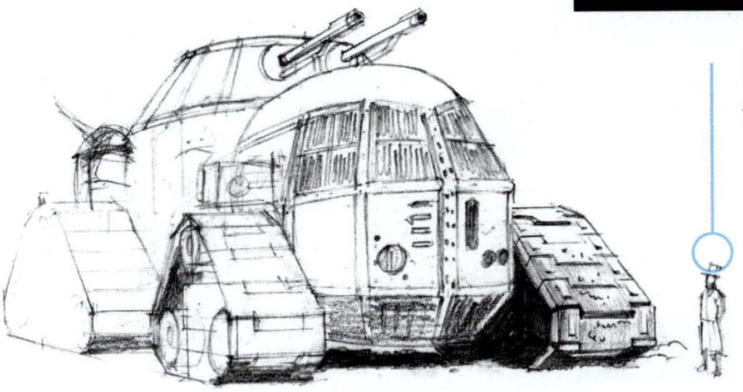

In scale figure

HUDSON STONE

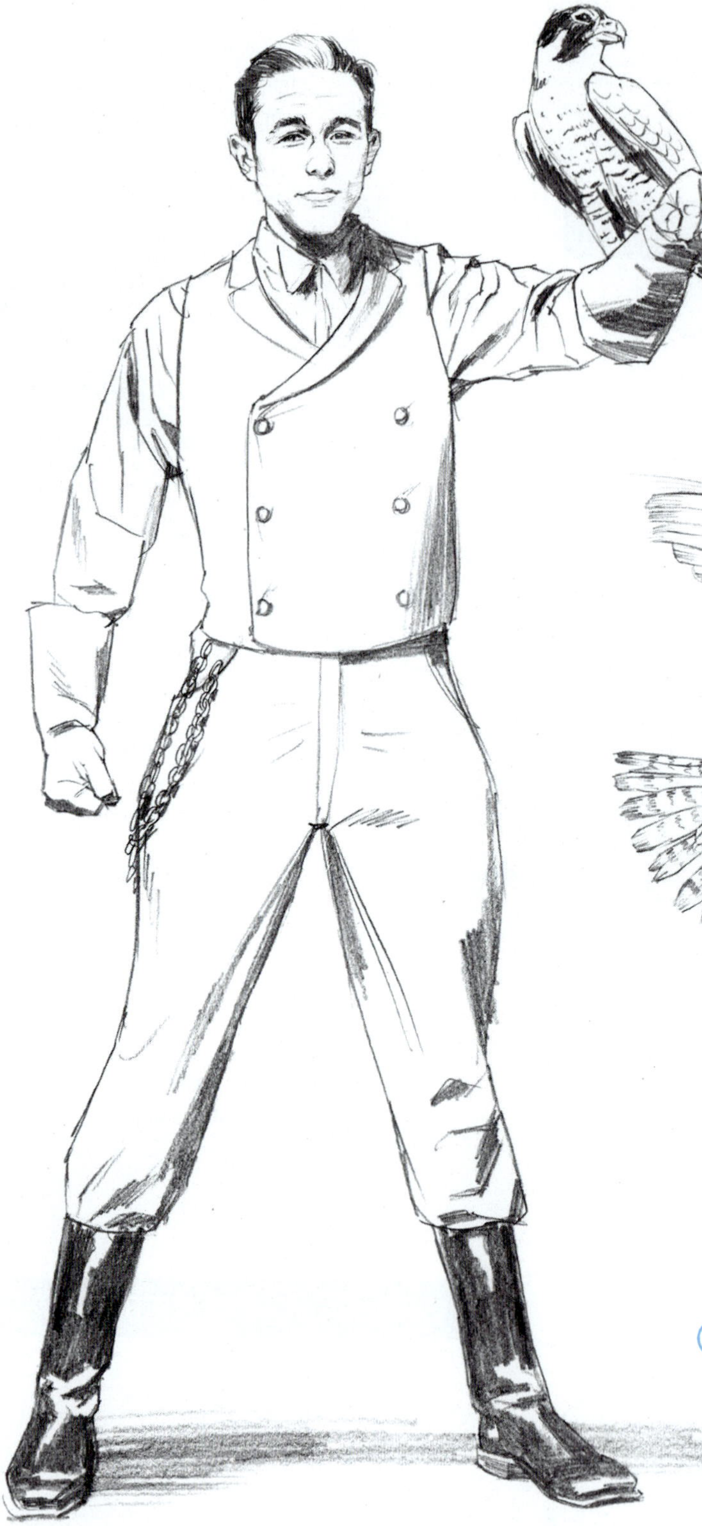

Hudson
in flight

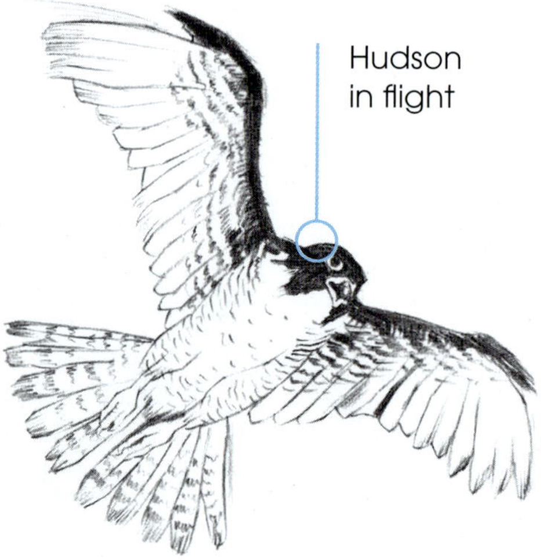

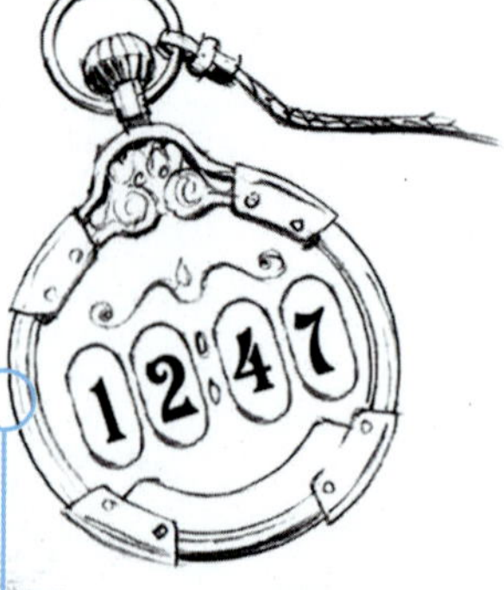

Pocket watch
suggestions:
- tarnished brass casing
- "digital" display
- Victorian era numbers/ fonts

JAMES CHASE

FORMULA MEDIA

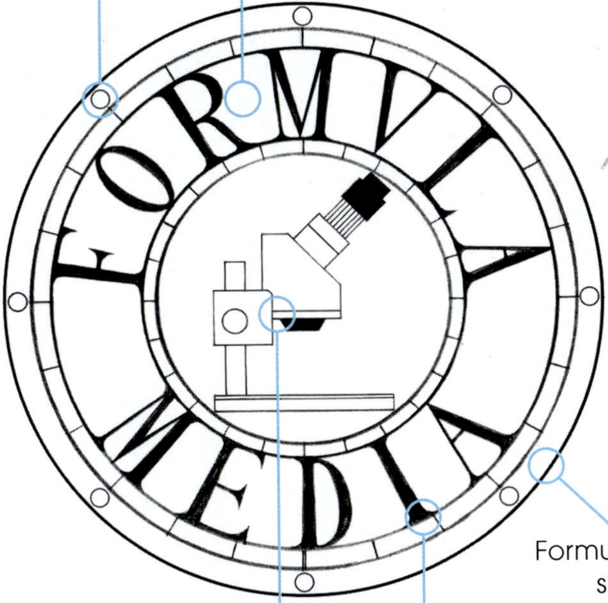
Actual rivets,
should look 3D
The FMC shield is
all polished bronze
FORMVLA
MEDIA
Center microscope
can be embossed/
slightly bas-relief.
Letters and lines
can be recessed

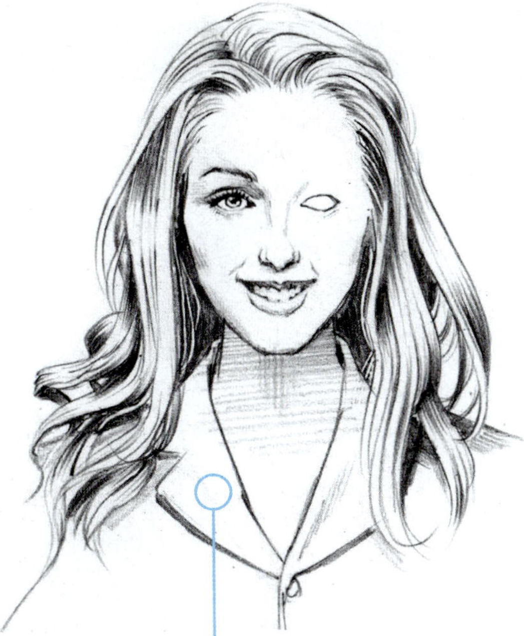
Formula assistant

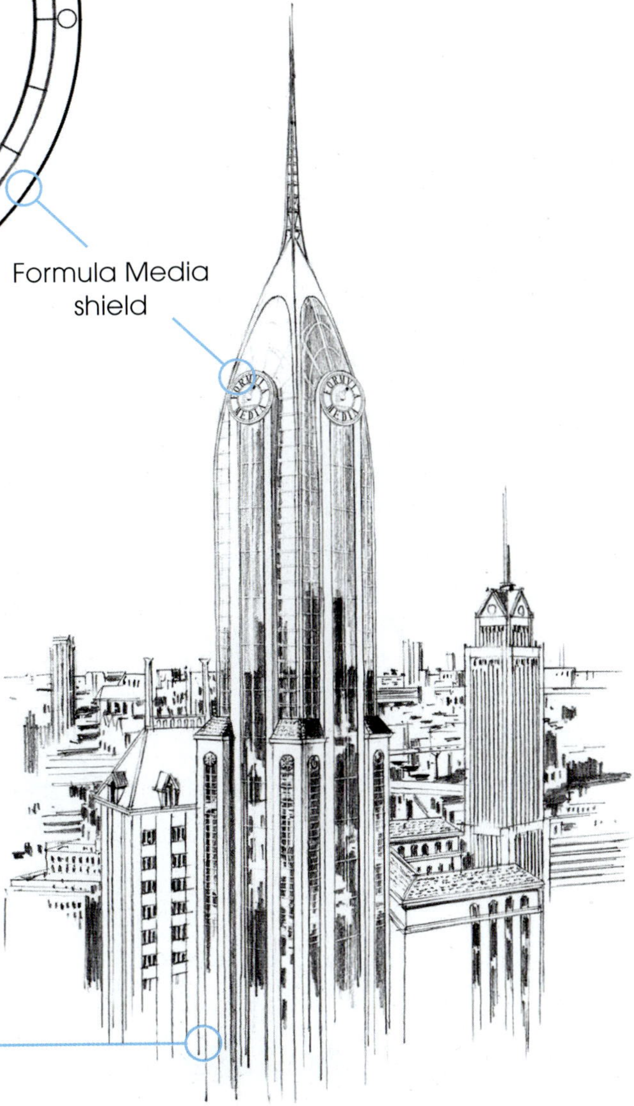
Formula Media
shield
Formula Media building

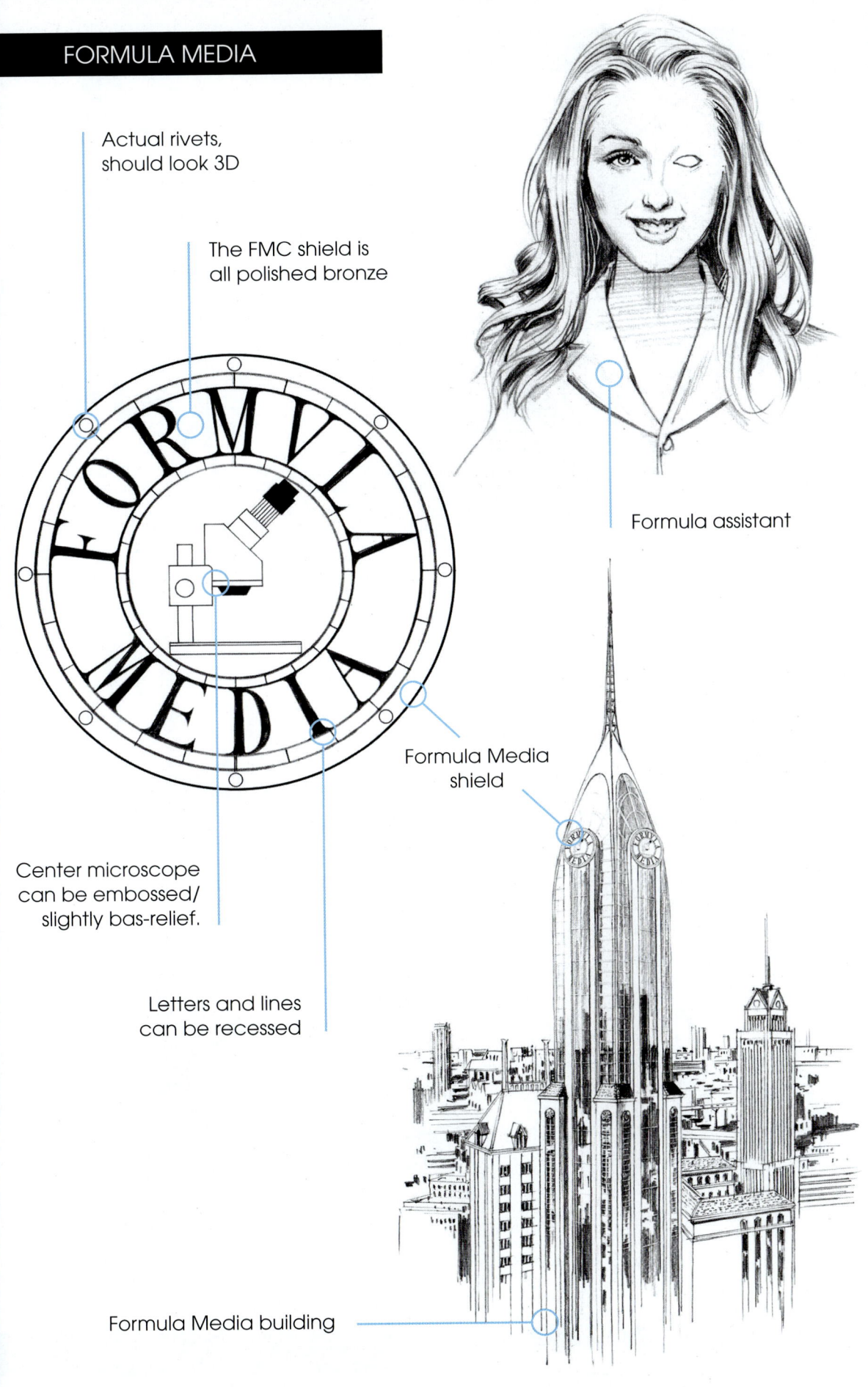

LEDGE CARVER

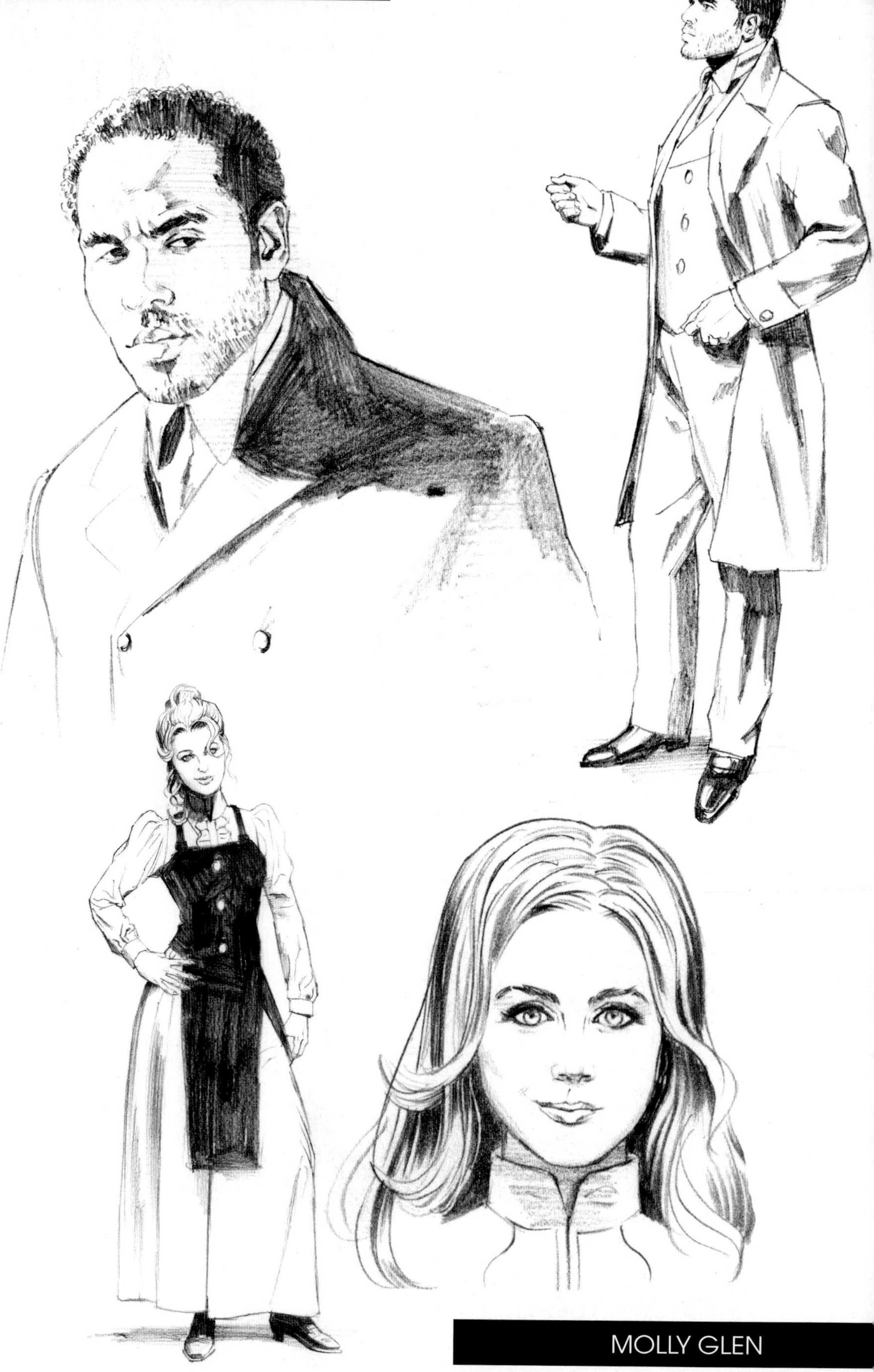

MOLLY GLEN

AGENTS

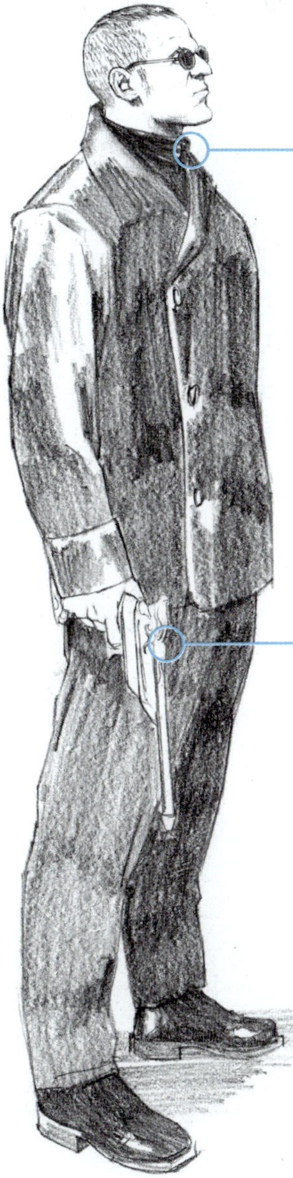
Turtleneck shirt under 6-button leather suit.
Chrome or gold slim pistol

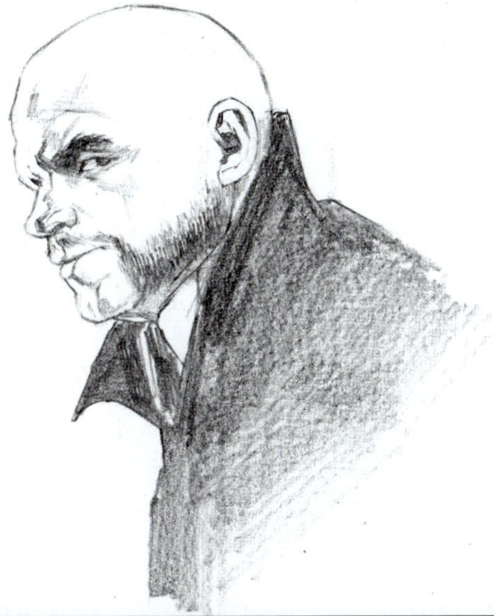

AGENT SHELTON

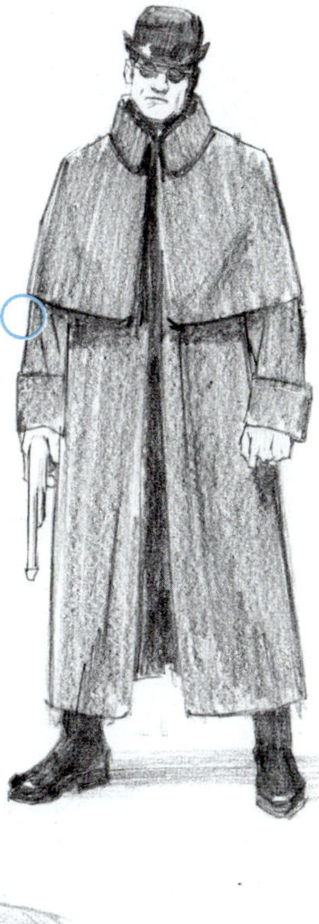
Outdoor hat & coat

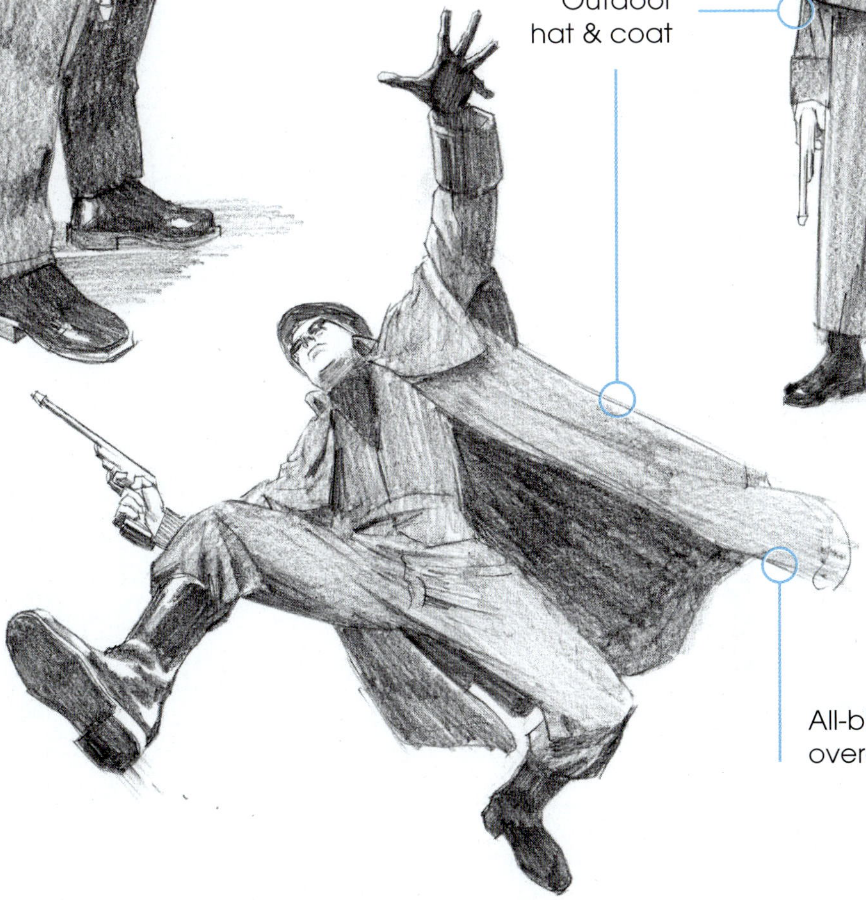
All-black overcoat

MISCELLANEA

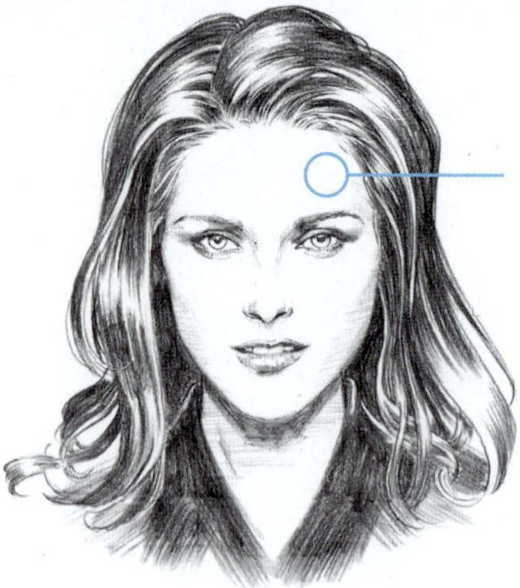

Jill

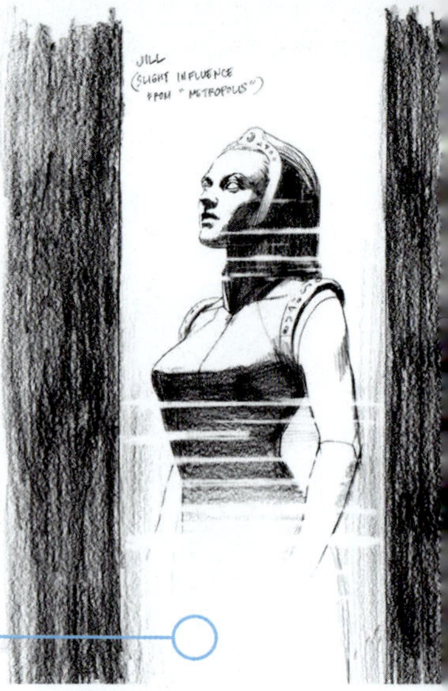
JILL
(SLIGHT INFLUENCE
FROM "METROPOLIS")

Jill (slight influence from "Metropolis")

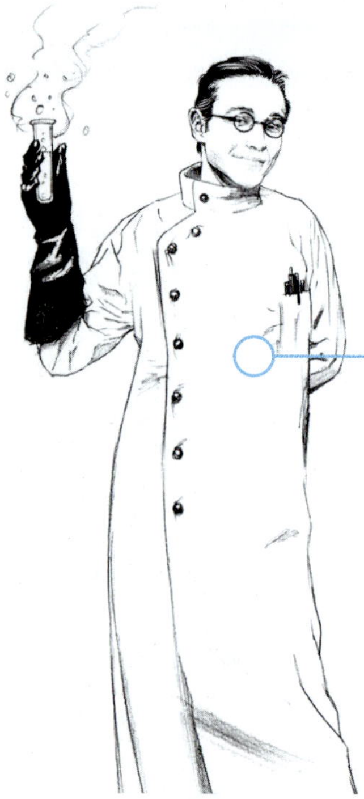

Bill Glen

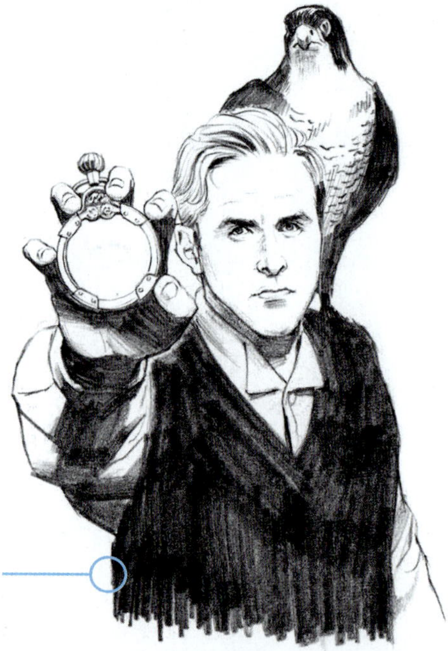

James with watch

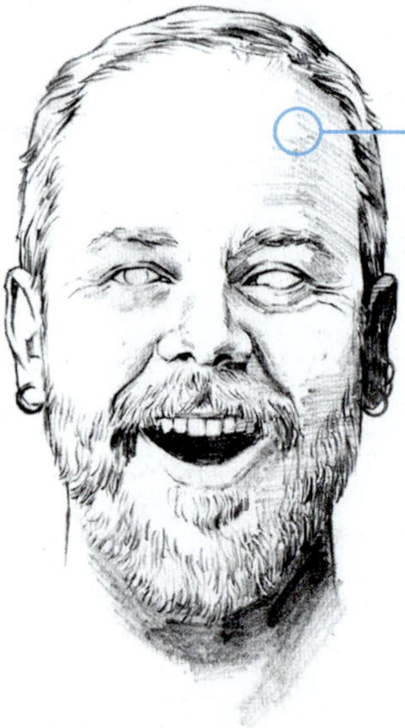

Jeff Wilson

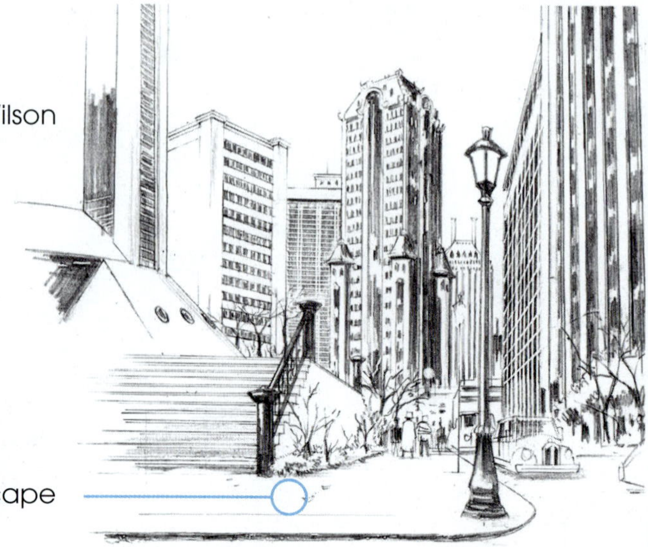

Cityscape

ART BY | RONILSON FREIRE

Line art for chapter 1 cover

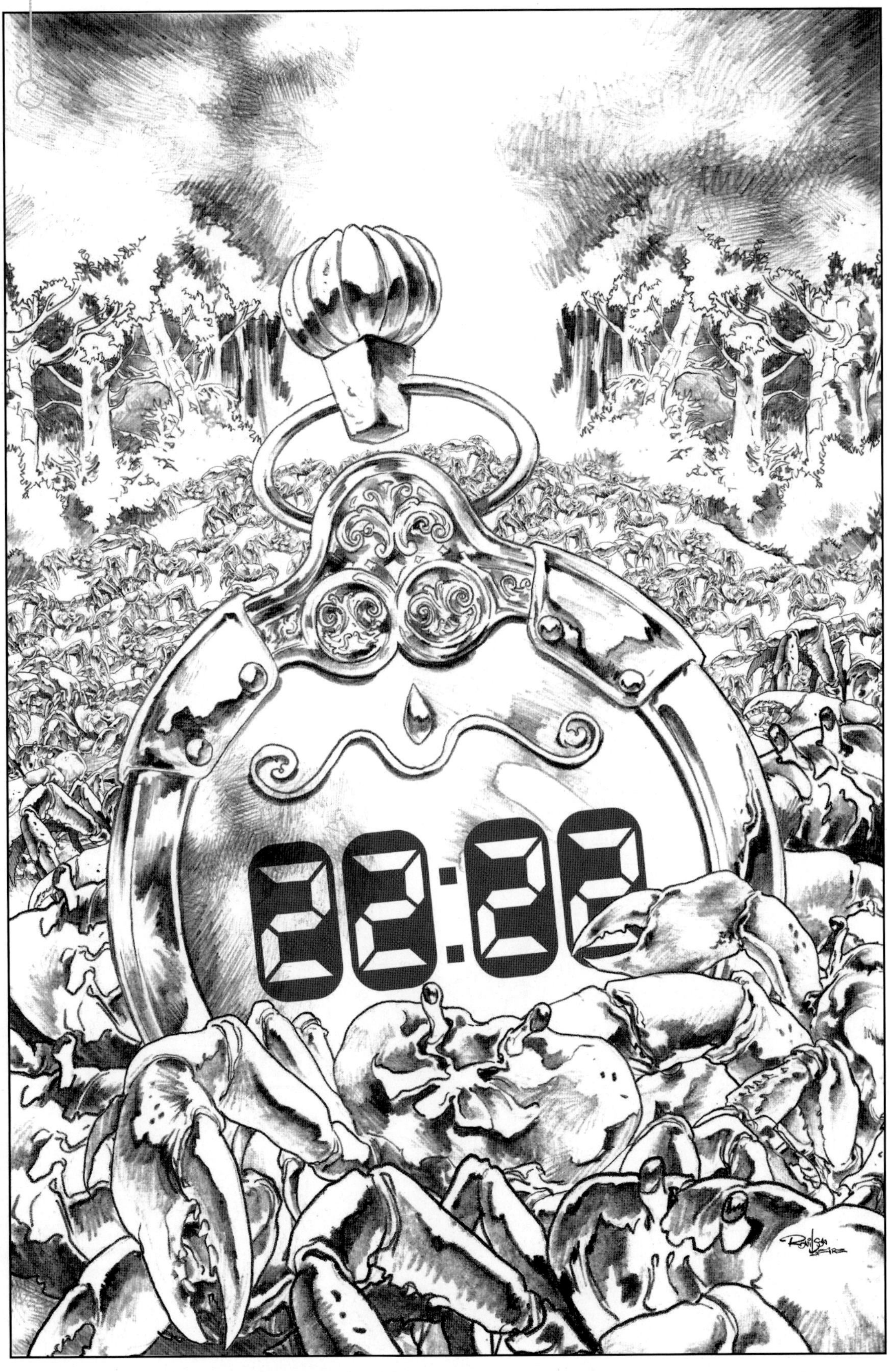
22:22

Line art for chapter 3 cover

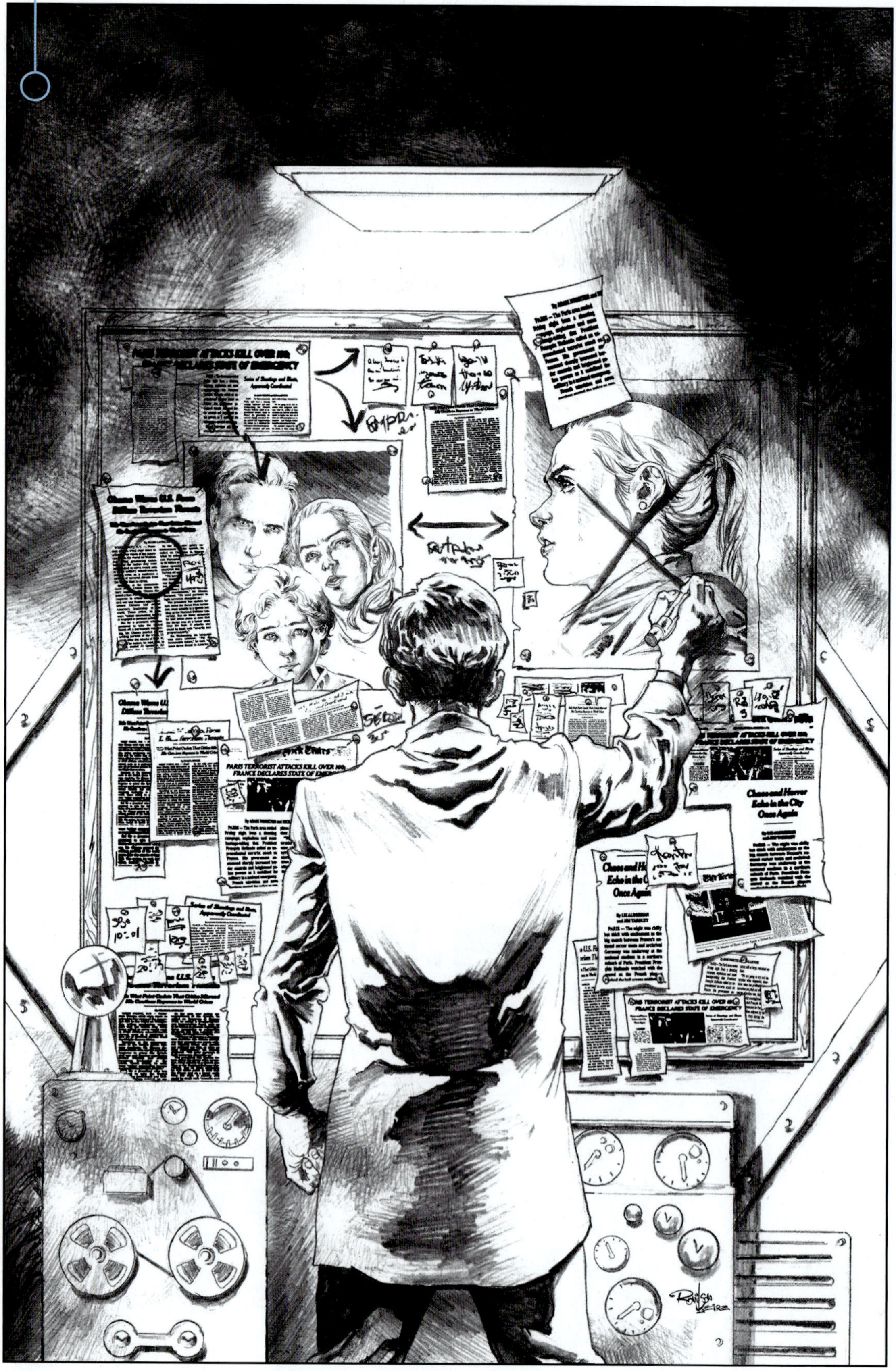
PARIS TERRORIST ATTACKS KILL OVER 100;
FRANCE DECLARES STATE OF EMERGENCY
Series of Shootings and Blasts Apparently Coordinated
Chaos and Horror Echo in the City Once Again

Line art for chapter 6 cover

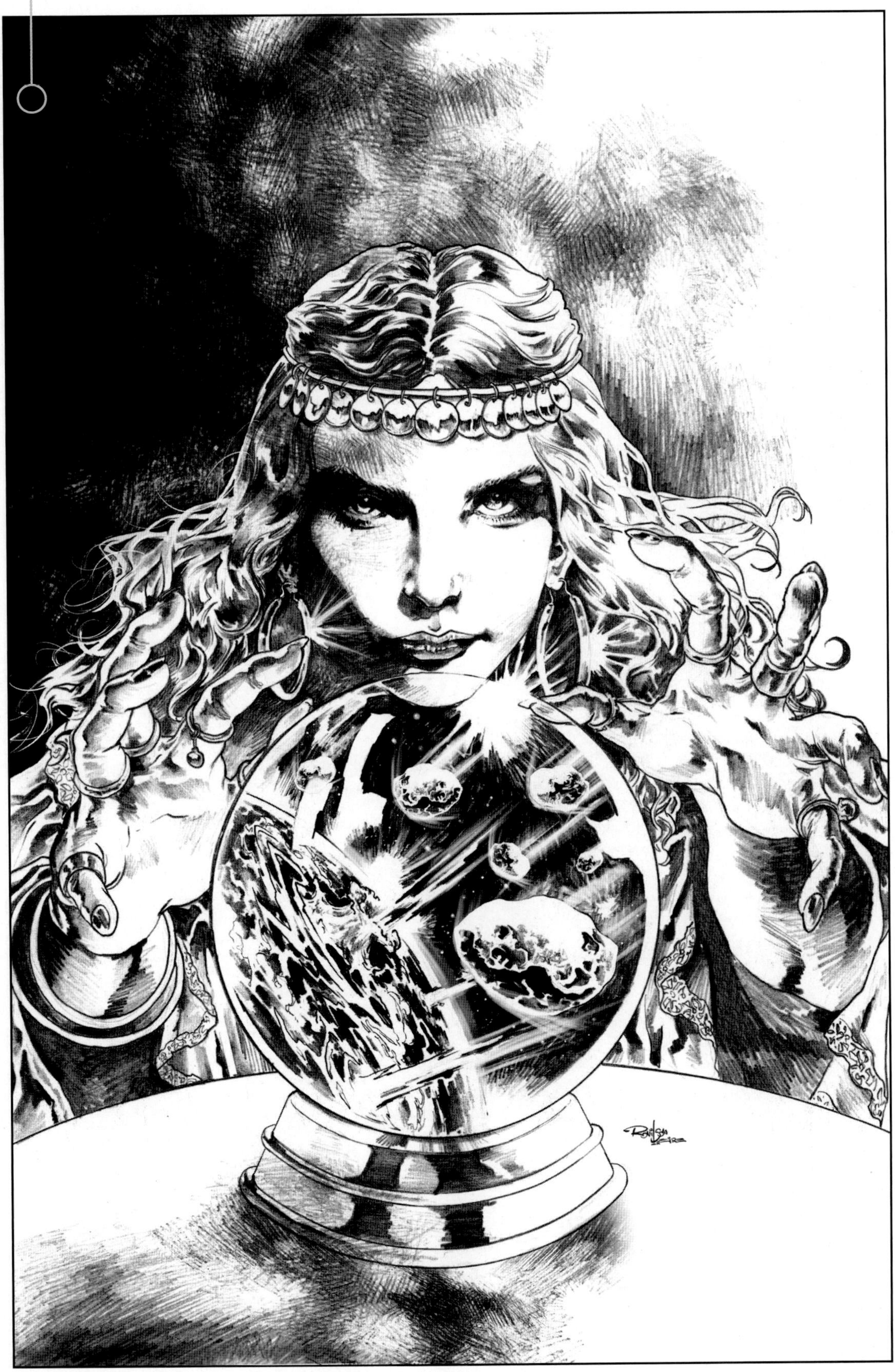

Line art for epilogue cover

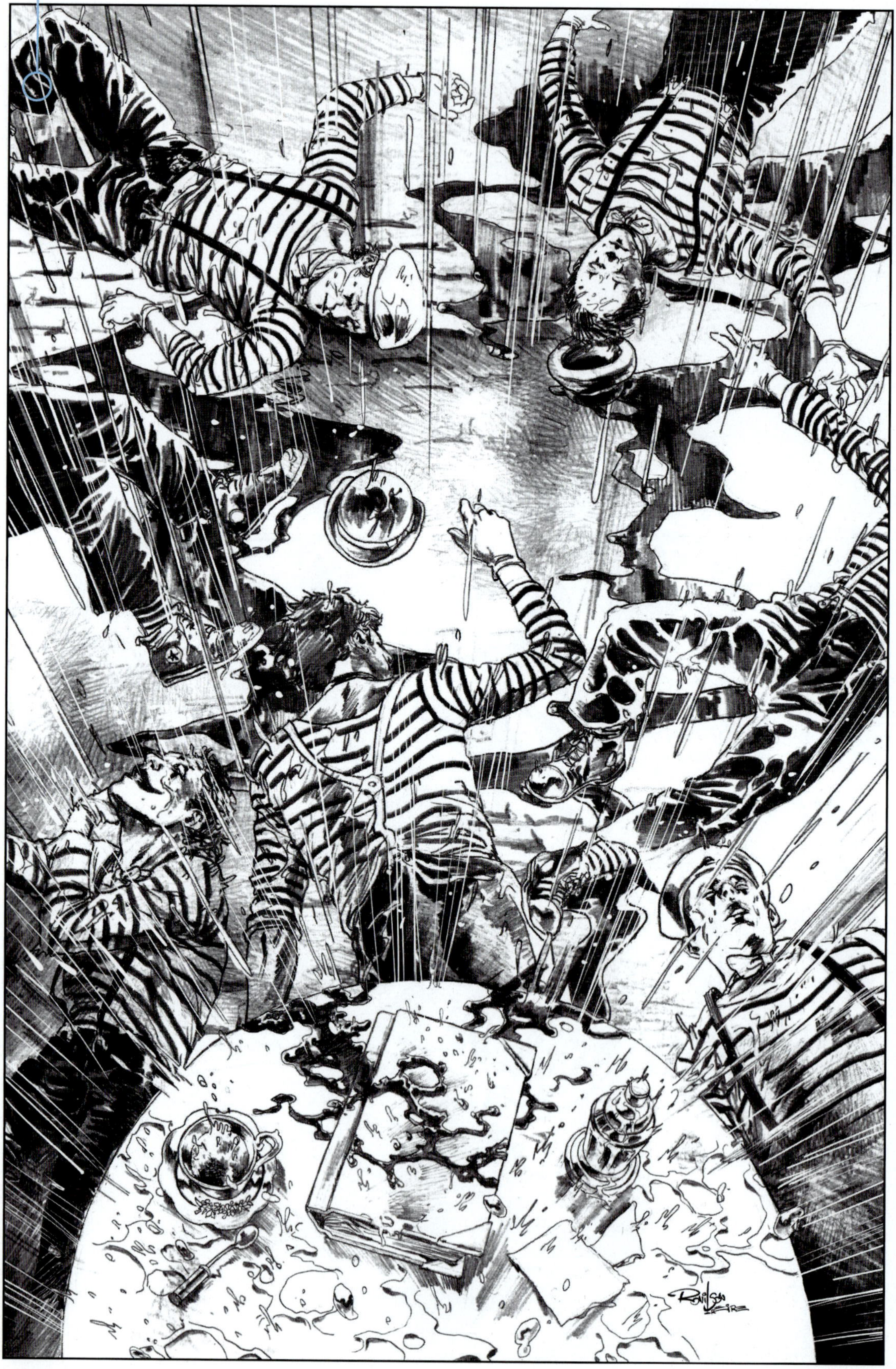

MEET THE MYOPIA CREATORS

Richard Dent:
In addition to writing comics, the Ringo-nominated writer has won accolades for his screenwriting from The Austin Film Festival, Francis Ford Coppola, and Nichols screenwriting competitions. He received an MFA in Poetry from the University of Arizona, and his poetry and fiction have been published in many literary magazines such as *Crazyhorse* and *The Drunken Boat*. He lives in Los Angeles and teaches Creative Writing at Cal State Los Angeles, and in the National University MFA program.

Ronilson Freire:
Born on the island of São Luís in the Northeast of Brazil and with more than ten years of experience in the international comics market, Ronilson has worked for several publishers in the U.S., Canada, England, France and Asia. His most significant works include *Green Hornet*, *Vampirella*, and *The Avenger* for Dynamite. He has also worked on the series *Ninjack* (Valiant), *Call of Dutty* (Activision), *Doctor Who*, and *Wolfenstein* (Titan). Ronilson has illustrated scripts by writers including Mark Waid, Grant Morrison, Nancy A. Collins, Stephen Bissette, Peter Milligan, Cristophe Bec, and Dan Watters. He is currently the designer of the steampunk series PROMÉTHÉE ALFA (Delcourt Soleil).

Patrick Berkenkotter:
Patrick has been a comic book penciller for Marvel Comics' *Avengers/Invaders*, *The Torch*, and Dynamite Entertainment's *Project Superpowers: Christmas Special 2010*, *Red Sonja* (covers and interiors) and *Vampirella*. He has also provided covers for Dynamite's *Athena*, *Warlord of Mars*, and *Dejah Thores*.

Vinicius Andrade:
Vinicius is a comic book colorist who has worked on hundreds of best-selling comic books, including, *Red Sonja*, *Witchblade*, *Invaders Now*, *Project Superpowers*, *Army of Darkness*, and *Battlestar Galactica*.

Mohan:
Mohan is a comic book colorist who has worked on hundreds of best-selling comic books including, *Jim Butcher's Dresden Files*, *Elvira*, *Patricia Brigg's Alpha Omega*, *Dean Koontz's Frankenstein*, *Grumpy Cat*, *Kiss*, and *Patricia Brigg's Mercy Thompson*.

Taylor Esposito:
Taylor Esposito is a comic book lettering professional, owner of Ghost Glyph Studios and teacher at the legendary Kubert School. A former staff letterer at DC and production artist at Marvel, he has lettered titles such as *Red Hood and The Outlaws* and *Constantine* (DC), *Interceptor*, *Heavy*, *Finger Guns* (Vault Comics), *Exorsisters*, *Jook Joint* (Image), *Babyteeth*, *Hot Lunch Special*, *Knock 'em Dead* (Aftershock), and *No One Left to Fight* (Dark Horse). Other publishers he has worked with include Line Webtoon (*Caster*, *Backchannel*) Dynamite (*Elvira*, *Red Sonja and Vampirella meet Betty and Veronica*, *Green Hornet*), and IDW (*Scarlett's Strike Force*).

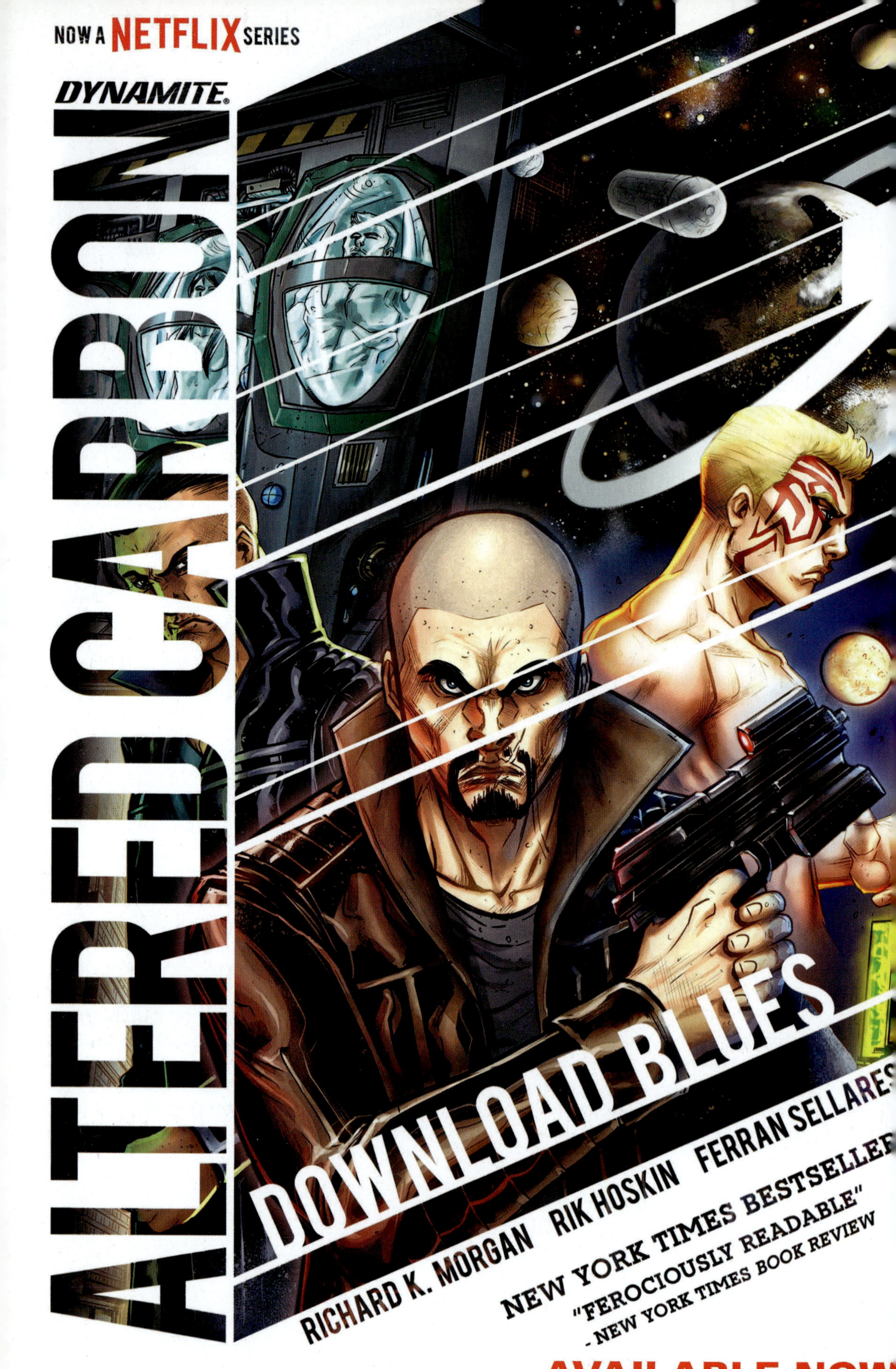
NOW A NETFLIX SERIES
DYNAMITE
ALTERED CARBON
DOWNLOAD BLUES
RICHARD K. MORGAN RIK HOSKIN FERRAN SELLARES
NEW YORK TIMES BESTSELLER
"FEROCIOUSLY READABLE"
- NEW YORK TIMES BOOK REVIEW
AVAILABLE NOW